Darklands

M.L. Spencer

Stoneguard Publications

DARKLANDS

STONEGUARD PUBLICATIONS

Cover by Damonza
Edited by Morgan Smith

ISBN: 978-0-9971779-9-2

Printed in the United States of America

The Southern Continent

Praise for Darklands

"Exemplifies the raw talent of an author, which
Spencer exudes from page-to-page, and book-to-book."
San Diego Book Review

"Ms. Spencer is a fresh new voice to the scene."
Fantasy Book Review

"An extraordinary fantasy with exceptional characters."
Readers' Favorite

"A powerful saga of confrontation and survival."
Midwest Book Review

"A complete, dark, anything-goes fantasy."
West Coast Book Reviews

DARKLANDS

M.L. Spencer

THE RHENWARS SAGA

Chapter One
Infernal Commission

Aerysius, The Rhen

The old man wandered the dark corridor toward his death, the girl trailing after him.

The girl's right hand clutched a thin-bladed knife, the sort of knife once used by hunters of the clans to scrape the flesh of beasts away from bone. But the girl had encountered no such beasts in her nineteen years of existence. The knife in her hand wasn't meant for the flesh of animals. It thirsted for the blood of the old man.

Azár glared ahead at her master's life-weary gait with a scowl of derision on her face. Zamir was selfish, and his selfishness had imperiled all the clans. He should have made this last journey months ago, back when his death might have actually counted for something. Now, too late, Zamir's belated gesture of sacrifice was just as wretched and irrelevant as the old man himself.

"Here." Zamir grimaced, bringing a trembling, rheumatic hand up to trail down the weeping surface of the stone passage. In the darkness, his damp and gnarled fingers resembled the tangled roots of trees. Azár's gaze lingered on them, apathetic, her hand compressing the hilt of the knife in her palm.

She waited, staring dully, and said nothing.

Azár watched in silence as her master shambled forward through the nebulous tendrils of magelight that churned at his feet. Her eyes remained fixed on the scraps of colorless fabric that clung to his emaciated back. She made no move to follow him into the shadowy chamber beyond, not until his voice called out from the darkness to rebuke her. Azár forced herself to move forward through the doorway.

She stopped, mouth agape. Her hand on the blade fell limply to her side as she gazed at the bleak images that confronted her. To one side of the chamber was a dark stone altar set with four ancient, rusted chains. To the other side of the room stood an ominous ring of man-carved stone.

Azár watched with morbid curiosity as Zamir sat himself down upon the worn surface of the altar that rose from stagnant pools of water collected on the floor. He lay himself back, adjusting his position, folding his arms across his chest. His age-leathered face gazed upward into the shadows, eyes fiercely introspective.

"Recite the forward sequence," he instructed her in a gravelly voice.

Azár's gaze swept across the room in the direction of the well.

The Well of Tears appeared exactly as she'd expected, exactly as she'd feared. It was made of staggered granite blocks stacked as high as her waist. Carved all around the rim were runes at once both sinister and familiar, sad vestiges of a lost heritage one thousand years dead. The runes themselves seemed to beckon, compelling her to approach.

Azár scowled at the markings, resenting them. It was because of the runes that they were here, such a far and dangerous distance away from anywhere they were supposed to be. The runes were a key that unlocked a door, a door between worlds. Azár had spent the past two years preparing for this journey. Even so, she felt horrendously anxious. This was a path she had never desired for herself, would never wish upon anyone.

"*Sistru, qurzi, calebra, ghein, vimru...*" Her voice faltered. Azár cleared her throat, edging cautiously forward as she continued reciting from memory the order of the ancient cypher. "*Ranu, benthos, metha, zhein, noctua...ledros. Dacros.*"

She dropped to a crouch beside the Well of Tears as her voice trailed off into a festering silence. She lifted a finger to trace over the first of the sacred markings to confront her: *dacros*. The final rune of the sequence. Ancient symbol of Xerys, God of Chaos and Lord of the Netherworld.

"You make me proud," uttered the old man from behind her. "What will be is better than what is gone."

Azár didn't turn back around to look at him. Instead, she remained squatting in a tarry pool of stagnant water with her hand raised before her face. Her eyes considered the rune that seemed to glare out at her like a brand seared into the Well's stony hide. Azár slowly lowered her hand and cast a wordless glance back over her shoulder.

Zamir yet lay on his back on the stone altar, arms folded across his chest. His tired eyes stared upward at the ceiling or perhaps straight ahead into eternity. He made no further effort to instruct her. There was no need.

Azár rose to her feet and stalked back across the chamber. From the woven belt at her waist, she produced a small pewter cup, which she set down on the rough surface of the altar rock at her master's side.

Face utterly impassive, Azár took Zamir's arm into her hand. Wielding the thin-bladed knife, she drew a deep slit into his skin all the way from his elbow to his wrist. Azár stared down at the blood that welled from the gaping incision. As she watched, the dark fluid coursed over her fingers and ran, dribbling, over her hand. Gradually, she became aware of the sound of the old man's voice muttering the phrases of the *dhumma*, the prayer that is spoken with the last breath before dying.

Azár studied Zamir's face, gazing with curiosity into the old man's dimming eyes. She set the knife down and centered the pewter cup beneath the running trickle of blood to better collect the spilt offering. The vessel filled quickly to the brim. Azár gazed down into his face as his lifeblood drained out of him.

The girl said nothing. She stood there, holding her master's hand, watching as the last light faded quietly from his eyes. As it did, Azár felt the warm stirring of power that grew within her fingertips. Her eyes went wide, her breath catching in her lungs.

The swelling warmth of the Transference swept up her hand into her arm, spreading outward through her chest, raging like a firestorm through her veins. The power coursed through her, filling her, penetrating every fiber of her being.

Then, abruptly, Azár felt the conduit slam closed.

She cried out, cringing back away from the emptied husk of the old man. Her eyes bright with alarm, she took a staggering step away, her breath coming in sharp and panicked gasps. Her gaze darted wildly around the dark chamber, her brain struggling to make sense of the confused perceptions that assaulted it. Tears wrung from her eyes by the violence of the Transference streaked her face, dribbling from her chin. Her whole body was shaking, weakened from the deluge of powerful energies.

Panting, Azár summoned a faint glow of magelight. A shimmering mist was inspired into being, roiling tendrils exploring the wet floor around her feet. The magelight pierced the shadows of the chamber, driving them back against the recesses of the walls. By the light of her own newfound power, Azár's eyes were drawn once again toward the Well of Tears. She glared at the portal, despising it utterly.

Steeling herself, Azár reached for the life-warm pewter cup at her side. Taking it into her hand, she made her way across the chamber. She knelt beside the Well, holding the cup of her master's blood with trembling hands. She dipped a shaking finger into the cup and then raised it up before her face. Turning her finger slowly, she observed the wet sheen of blood in the soft tendrils of magelight. Azár leaned forward and applied Zamir's spent lifeblood to the first rune of the sequence. The blood absorbed quickly into the porous stone as if sucked inside.

Before her eyes, the ancient rune *sistru* awakened from sleep and began to glow with a green, ethereal light. Azár moved around to the far side of the Well, to the next marking of the sequence. She brought that rune, too, to life. Then she moved on to the next. Calm and deliberate, Azár took her time, working meticulously all around the rim until, at last, all of the ancient markings glowed with their own inner light.

When Azár was finished, she stood up and backed away. She regarded her work, satisfied. The gateway was unlocked in this world. But someone else would have to open it from the other side.

Azár rose and used her nascent powers to slide the cover off the Well of Tears. The thick granite slab lifted of its own volition and glided smoothly aside. It hovered for a moment in the air, as if suspended from invisible strings, before lowering the rest of the way to the floor.

Azár turned back toward her master. Zamir had one last journey to make. The Well of Tears demanded a sacrifice, and the old man's soul would be the final gesture that would unseal the gateway.

Zamir had been frail, but the dead weight of his corpse was still too much for Azár's slight build to manage. So she closed her eyes, aligning her thoughts with the rhythmic pulse of the magic field, allowing the power of her mind to supplement the strength of her flesh. Azár lifted Zamir's body up over the Well's rim, giving him a shove.

With the slightest scraping noise, the corpse slipped into the gaping shaft and tumbled downward into darkness.

Azár turned away. It would take some time for Zamir's spirit to complete the final task he had set for himself. There was still yet time to ascend the long flights of steps to the level of the surface. She would have to hurry; her part was still far from complete.

Azár sent her magelight roaming forward, her feet following its glowing trail out of the chamber and into the dark passage beyond. She knew exactly which direction to turn; her master had made certain she would not falter in her task. The corridor she traversed was part of a larger warren of passageways that infested the mountainside below what had once been proud Aerysius, city of the mages. Now just a sad and desolate foundation that stood forlorn three thousand feet above the Vale of Amberlie.

Following the map she had committed to memory, Azár let her feet carry her up a narrow stair, moving through a glowing trail of magelight that spilled ahead of her. Her eyes rejoiced in the texture of the light, awed by the magelight's warm, summery glow. It was her own creation, her very first. A lifegiving thing of wonder and graceful beauty.

Azár sent her mind out, sampling the pulse and rhythm of the magic field in this place. It was soothing and vibrant. It was hers, now, to command as she pleased. She could feel Zamir's power stirring within her, a wondrous and potent legacy.

She emerged at last from the depths of the mountain into a cool, clear night. She gazed out upon the terrace that stretched before her, captivated by the stark austerity of Aerysius' bare foundations. Azár gazed upward into the sky, tilting her head back as an abrupt gust of wind seized her long, dark braid.

Before her, violent energies shot toward the sky, penetrating the dome of the heavens with a violence that was alarming. Lightning licked down to assault that awful spire, raining trails of sparks across the sky.

Confronted with such a daunting vision, Azár felt her courage falter. She lowered her gaze, biting her lip. She concentrated on the sound of her breath, willing her mind to focus. When she opened her eyes again, she regarded the gateway with newfound resolve.

Azár's breath caught in her throat.

From out of the dazzling brilliance of the column, dark figures were emerging. Stirred by the sight of them, Azár's heart quickened its pace. She stood her ground with fists balled against her sides, feet apart, back rigid. Shivering with excitement, Azár looked on as the first man-shaped silhouettes drew forth from the glaring wash of light to converge on her position.

The man who approached first was easily identified by the spiked weapon he bore: Byron Connel, ancient Warden of Battlemages, wielder of the legendary talisman Thar'gon. To his right strode an elegant woman in a flowing white gown, dark of hair as well as skin. A demon-hound with menacing green eyes stalked at her side. Azár had heard enough tales of the Eight to recognize Myria Anassis, ancient Querer of the Lyceum.

Another woman with loose chestnut hair approached Azár. She strolled alongside a man just as handsomely sinister as the woman was deceptively beautiful: Sareen Qadir and Nashir Arman. The pair approached gracefully. The woman's eyes seemed to glisten, a smile of excitement growing on her lips.

So distracted was she by the pair that Azár almost didn't notice the two men approaching from the opposite direction. She turned, startled to find herself confronted by the imposing forms of Zavier Renquist and Cyrus Krane. The two ancient Prime Wardens drew up together before her, the white cloaks of their office billowing behind them, stirred by gusts of wind displaced by the gateway. Cyrus Krane regarded Azár with a sneer rendered all the more cruel by the jagged red scar that bisected his face. His dark eyes were murky pools of unveiled threat.

Zavier Renquist paused before her, arms behind his back, gazing down upon Azár with an expression of somber esteem. His dark hair was pulled back from his face, gathered into a thick braid at the top of his head. He gazed at her expectantly, as if calmly waiting for her to speak first. Had he been any other man in the world, Azár might have considered it.

Appearing satisfied, Zavier Renquist lifted his chin and addressed Azár in a deep and resonant voice: "Our Master extends to you His gratitude. In you, Xerys is well-pleased. He commits to you the services of the Eight and His army of the night until the initial purpose of our summoning is fulfilled. So, my child, it is time to speak your desires. What shall be your command?"

Azár swallowed, unable to look away from the mesmerizing shadows that simmered in Zavier Renquist's eyes. She held his gaze with her own as she summoned a fragile voice, praying her words would not falter and betray her fear.

"I command you to save my people." Azár channeled every scrap of assertiveness she could muster into her tone. She squared her shoulders, lifting her chin. Her fists were still clenched tightly at her sides. "Deliver us from the darkness. Raise us up from the ashes. Return to us our birthright—this is my command!"

Zavier Renquist stood there regarding her for a prolonged, searching minute. It was impossible to read his expression; the ancient demon's face was altogether blank, without any hint or trace of emotion. He stared deeply into Azár's eyes as if scrutinizing her worth, contemplating the fabric of her soul, weighing the mettle of her character. At last, apparently satisfied, he gave a terse nod.

"Then it shall be as you command," he said, shifting his weight over his feet. His indigo robes swayed with his motion. He turned to cast a predatory stare across at Cyrus Krane then turned again toward Azár. Very formally, he spread his hands and assured her:

"Malikar's deliverance is long overdue. And this time, there will be nothing in this world that can deter us from our goal. Allow me to introduce to you the man whose responsibility it shall be to reclaim the light and heritage that was lost so long ago when Caladorn fell into darkness."

He gestured with his hand, indicating a man who had drawn up silently behind the others and now stood with hands clasped in front of him, head bowed against his chest. As Azár's attention focused on him, the man glanced up through matted strands of long, black hair that had fallen forward over his face. His yellow-green eyes locked on hers with an intensity that was frightening.

Azár felt herself taken sharply aback; she had no idea who this man was. He fit none of the descriptions she had ever heard spoken of the Eight. The look in his eyes chilled her very soul.

She frowned in consternation, her brow nettling. "I don't understand," Azár whispered. "What has become of our mistress? Who is this man? How is it that he alone is expected to accomplish what all Eight of you could not achieve before?"

Zavier Renquist clasped his fingers together in front of him: a gesture of patience. "Your mistress failed. Her soul has been consigned to Oblivion." He fixed Azár with a flat, significant stare. He extended his hand, indicating to Azár the stranger across from her with the haunted eyes. "This is the man who bested your mistress in combat and has replaced her at my side. He has assumed all of Arden Hannah's rights, privileges, and obligations."

Azár fixed this newcomer with an incredulous stare, shaking her head in confounded dismay. "Who *is* he?"

Zavier Renquist explained, "Darien Lauchlin is the lone Sentinel who laid waste to Malikar's legions at the base of Xerys' Pedestal."

Azár's mouth dropped open. She had not been present at the massacre, but she had heard of the atrocities committed by Aerysius' Last Sentinel, his final act of desperation. Thousands of brave warriors had not returned from that campaign, their bodies reduced to charred ash scattered on the wind. Azár shivered as she regarded the disquieting man before her, coming to the slow conclusion that Zavier Renquist had to be telling the truth about him. It was the only explanation for the depths of torment in those harrowing eyes.

"This is impossible!" Azár managed at last. "The man you speak of is dead!"

"As am I," the Prime Warden reminded her with a shrug and a smile. Spreading his hands, he went on to explain, "Darien Lauchlin committed his soul to the service of Xerys. He is now one with us in purpose. He has assumed all rights, responsibilities, and covenants of the Servant he replaces. So Darien is, in every respect, the overlord your people have been so long awaiting. Your request is his singular purpose to fulfill."

Azár turned her head and spat upon the ground. Whirling away, she exclaimed in anger, "I will not suffer the company of this man! He is not even a man—he is a demon, a monster!"

"Perhaps." The ancient Prime Warden raised his eyebrows. He did not appear affronted in the least by Azár's accusation. "But I would strongly advise you to reconsider and think very carefully before declining Darien's assistance. Because, considering the nature of your demands, it sounds like a monster is exactly what you need."

Azár gazed at him with dread in her eyes, knowing deep down in her gut that Renquist's assessment was probably accurate. She sighed, giving in, heart heavy with dismay.

"Go with her," Zavier Renquist commanded his newest Servant in a voice suffused with arrogance and ice. "You heard her demands. Go forth and fulfill them."

The dark-haired demon nodded slightly. "I will do my best, Prime Warden." His voice sounded terse, strained. He strode forward.

"Stop."

Renquist's sharp command halted him in his tracks. As Azár looked on in fascination, Darien Lauchlin turned back around with weary patience in his eyes.

Zavier Renquist promised him, "Your best isn't going to be good enough. Instead of your best, *I demand your worst.* You must let go of your past and embrace your destiny. Unchain your inner demons. Conquer your own ghosts just as you once conquered my armies. Transcend the constraints you have used to shackle your conscience and experience firsthand what true freedom feels like."

Darien Lauchlin nodded, dark strands of hair swaying forward into his face. "It shall be as you ask, Prime Warden."

"It had better be. For your sake. And for hers."

Azár stared long and hard at the two men, her brow furrowed in consternation. Renquist's threat had not been directed toward herself. She let her gaze linger on the man trudging toward her, a demon-hound jogging behind in his wake. Frowning, she wondered which woman's life Zavier Renquist had just threatened. And why that woman's life mattered so much to this tormented monster of a man.

Chapter Two
Message from the Past

Rothscard, The Rhen

Kyel Archer gazed up at the corrugated towers of Emmery Palace with a growing feeling of trepidation gnawing at his already soured stomach. He'd never liked Rothscard, and today's visit was certainly no exception. Kyel's every experience of the city had been riddled with misfortune in some significant way. The first time he'd passed through Rothscard, Kyel had found himself falsely accused of murder, chained, and swept away to the Front as a conscript to fight in the war. His second visit to the city had ended with him in chains of a very different nature, though the experience had been no less demeaning. Kyel couldn't help but wonder if this visit would prove just as treacherous. This time, the matching pair of chains he wore on his wrists were of his own creation, forged by his own convictions. But that did little to ease the burden of their weight, or to render their harsh constraints less difficult to bear.

Kyel gazed up at the ramparts of the palace with a whimsical expression, one thumb stroking the new growth of beard he wore on his face. As the coach drew up before an elegant fountain in the courtyard, Kyel cast a quick glance at Naia, seated across from him on a leather bench. The smile of reassurance she gifted him helped a little. It gave Kyel enough strength to conjure up a fleeting smile of his own.

Naia appeared exceptionally in her element, he realized, completely at ease. The former priestess seemed more radiant than usual, her dark auburn hair gathered in a bun. Her face, once kept concealed by the white veil of Death, was almost shocking in its beauty. In the past two years, Kyel had grown more accustomed to the sight of Naia's naked face, though he had never been able to take it entirely for granted. The absence of the veil remained conspicuous.

Their coach drew to a halt with a sudden jolt. Kyel swallowed against a hard lump in his throat, surveying the tall towers of the palace through the window.

He could hear Meiran's voice beside him, muttering in her usual, no-nonsense alto, "Breathe, Kyel. You look like you're going to be ill."

"I'm still not sure that I won't be."

There was a sharp clank as someone outside threw open the door of the coach. Kyel stared for a moment at the door's leather skin, then let his gaze drop to the boots of the footman awaiting them.

Kyel took his time about climbing down out of the coach; it had been hours since he'd last had a chance to stretch his legs. Fortunately, the footman had positioned a small stool just under the carriage, making the drop down to the ground far less of an undertaking. Kyel took a few unsteady steps, gazing around as his hands went to straighten the thick black cloak that hung from his shoulders.

Naia alighted gently at his side, followed immediately by Meiran, who strode forward between the two of them. The white cloak of her office flowed gracefully down her back, swaying with each movement of her body, the embroidered Silver Star glistening in the sunlight.

Kyel fell in behind her, Naia at his side, the uniformed guards of Emmery Palace forming ranks behind their small entourage. Kyel had to rush to keep up with Meiran's long strides; she hadn't bothered to wait for an escort. Instead, she set her own course up the white marble steps as dignitaries rushed forward to intercept her.

"Thank you, Prime Warden, for your swift response to our invitation." The first breathless minister fell in beside Meiran, matching her stride for stride. He wore an opulent ensemble, sporting a plumed hat and a cape.

"Of course." Meiran didn't favor the man with so much as a glance. She kept her gaze fixed straight ahead as she strode swiftly into the depths of the palace, forcing the man to take hurried strides to keep up. "It's never a problem. Without the support of Emmery's Crown, our time in exile would be much less comfortable. Queen Romana has been a most generous benefactor."

The minister smiled with an accommodating nod. He brought a folded kerchief up to dab at his brow as he continued to keep pace with Meiran's long strides. "My Lady Queen thanks you for making such haste. Her Majesty is anxious to hear your opinion on a certain, most urgent matter, and is wondering—"

Meiran cut him off in mid-sentence, snapping, "If your Lady Queen is so anxious for my opinion, then why isn't she here to greet us personally?" Meiran raised her eyebrows in speculation as she finally turned to regard the man laboring beside her. Kyel allowed himself an amused grin as he watched the interaction. He could hardly imagine anyone more suited for the office of Prime Warden than Meiran Withersby.

Blotting at the sheen of perspiration on his brow, the minister looked troubled. "My apologies, Prime Warden, but Queen Romana requests that you convene with her in the Blue Room."

"So, I've been relegated to the Blue Room, now, have I?" Meiran sounded irritated. Following behind her, Kyel couldn't get a good look at her face. But he had no trouble imagining the characteristic scowl she must be wearing. "Has Romana become skittish of magefolk again, or is this 'urgent matter' really that desperate?"

The minister led her around a corner and into a long corridor lined with painted wood panels. "I'm afraid I couldn't begin to speculate, Prime Warden," he murmured in placating tones.

Meiran harrumphed. "No, I don't suppose you're capable. Ah. Here we are."

She drew up before a wide set of double doors as Kyel almost stumbled into her back. He shot a small, knowing grin in Naia's direction, who returned the expression in kind. They waited, Kyel glancing around as liveried servants threw open the paneled doors, exposing the bright interior of the chamber.

Meiran swept forward into the room, quickly crossing the patterned rugs. There, in the center of the room, she drew herself up formally and simply waited. Her cloak swung from her thin frame, which was covered by a sumptuous gown of pristine white. Her rich brown hair was gathered behind her head in an elegant twist. Her gaze moved over the interior of the chamber in critical assessment. She drew herself up, shoulders squared and head held regally. Her very presence was suffused with authority.

"The Prime Warden of Aerysius, Meiran Withersby," the voice of the minister announced belatedly.

Kyel's eyes shot in the direction of the man, catching just a glimpse of him as the doors swung closed, shuddering as they latched. A long, tense silence followed. With a wrench of nausea, Kyel forced himself to look Romana Norengail in the eye.

Emmery's Queen had matured in the two years since he'd last seen her. Romana was no longer the disarming young girl he'd first met in her solarium. She seemed even more regal now, as though years and experience had somehow consecrated her right to her throne. She wore the Sapphire Crown of Emmery on her head, her shoulders draped in winter ermine. Her lovely face was both patient and serene.

At her side, seated in a chair not quite as tall or elaborately carved, was Nigel Swain, Romana's husband. Kyel's stomach physically squirmed at the sight of the prince consort. Even after all this time, Kyel was still not sure how he felt about the man. Swain had conspired to murder Darien Lauchlin and had manipulated Kyel into helping him. The underhanded way he'd gone about it still galled. Swain was a harsh man, uncompromising in his character. But his loyalty to Romana was flawless.

Confronted with the presence of the Prime Warden, both Romana and Swain stood and, taking a step forward in unison, dropped to their knees upon the rugs spread before them on the floor.

"Arise," Meiran directed them with a curt wave of her hand.

Without any further attempt at ceremony, she seated herself in one of the chairs arranged before them, Kyel taking the seat to her right as Naia claimed the one beside him.

"Tea?" a butler inquired, indicating a wheeled cart that held an elegant silver service.

"Yes, that would be lovely." Meiran's hands moved to smooth the fabric of her gown.

The butler thrust an elegant cup and saucer into Kyel's hands. Yes, he wanted cream. No, he didn't care for any honey. No wafers, thank you very much. He brought the teacup to his lips, holding the saucer in his left hand as he managed a sip. The tea was fragrant with chamomile and very hot. He lowered the cup back down, resting it against his leg.

Queen Romana made a majestic but half-hearted attempt at a smile. "Prime Warden, let me first begin by saying—"

"Please." Meiran cut her off, lowering her own teacup from her lips. "Let us dispense with formalities. We're all very tired from the journey. So, just tell me: what has happened?"

The smile vanished from the lips of Emmery's Queen. Her gaze wandered toward her husband. Kyel studied the two of them, trying to find meaning in the silent conversation that passed between them in the span of a single heartbeat. Turning back to Meiran, Queen Romana said in a troubled voice:

"A green spire of light has been reported in the skies above Aerysius."

Kyel sputtered as he choked on a swallow of tea. Coughing, he leaned forward over his legs and set the cup and saucer down on the floor beside his chair.

"Has this report been confirmed?" Meiran sat as if frozen, her cup paused halfway to her lips.

Nigel Swain nodded. His grey-streaked hair swayed forward into his face. "The gateway is very visible, especially at night. It can be seen for miles in all directions."

"It's been only two years," Naia whispered at Kyel's side. The despair in her voice was painful to hear. "How could this be happening already? Who could have opened it? Who *would* have?"

Meiran cast a withering glance in Naia's direction. She took a deep breath, appearing to be collecting herself, then uttered with a scowl, "It doesn't matter. What's done is done. No matter how it was accomplished, we now must deal with the consequences."

Kyel squirmed in his chair, his thoughts pulled in a hundred separate directions at once. He found himself transported back in time, back to a dark room in a damp cavern in the heart of an ancient mountain. Where a granite well encircled with glowing, sinister markings awaited him. It had been his job to seal those runes, to burn them clean of the blood that fed them life.

Apparently, his work had been undone.

"Have there been…other types of reports?" he said to no one in particular.

Queen Romana answered his question. "Not yet. But we must assume that the Eight walk the earth again. We need to consider the possibility that war might soon be upon us."

"They are no longer Eight," Naia corrected her. "Darien destroyed Arden Hannah. Their number has been reduced to seven."

The Prime Warden shrugged dismissively. "One less darkmage won't make a bit of difference. There's only three of us, each fettered by the Oath of Harmony. Kyel is the closest thing we have to a Sentinel."

Swain leaned forward, elbows resting on his knees. "Which order did Naia take?"

Meiran responded, "I've been training Naia as a Querer."

Swain leaned back in his chair, eyes narrowing. "So. We've got one half-trained Sentinel and one half-trained Querer. And a Prime Warden we can't risk letting anywhere near a field of battle. Those are our assets. Against seven Unbound demons. Including Byron Connel, one of the greatest military minds the world has ever known."

Naia's gaze lifted to confront him. In a voice thick with the lilt of Chamsbrey, she asked Swain, "Perhaps now you can appreciate Darien's quandary?" The resentment in her tone was scathing.

Nigel Swain shook his head. "No. I don't. Because here we are again two years later, in the same situation as before. All Darien did was buy us time. Nothing more."

Naia glared at him, her lips compressed with bitterness. "No," she growled in a voice low and defiant. "Darien's sacrifice was not in vain. I will not believe that. I cannot believe that."

Swain leaned forward, capturing her eyes with a cold, unfeeling stare. "It doesn't matter what you believe; the portal's open again. They'll be coming. And this time, Darien's not here to save or damn us."

Kyel found himself gazing down absently at the chain on his right wrist, rotating his arm so that the markings shimmered in the light. "We must reseal the Well of Tears," he said. "That will cut them off from their source of power." He didn't dare voice his next thought: that one of their own number would have to volunteer to be the next sacrifice demanded by the gateway. It had to be a Grand Master. Naia was only third tier; she ranked too low to be an option. That left only Meiran and himself.

Meiran was fingering the necklace she always wore around her neck. It was a habit she had, something she tended to do whenever something troubled her. The necklace had a silver pendant that looked to be made of one sinuous, intertwined strand that wove around about itself without beginning or end. The symbol was called an eternity knot. Darien had given her that necklace the day he'd left Aerysius for Greystone Keep. The same day Meiran had presented him with the sword he could never bring himself to part with.

"No," Meiran sighed at last, still fingering the fragile pendant on its chain. "They'll be expecting us to move against the Well. This time, they'll be guarding it much more carefully. The Well of Tears will have to remain open, at least for now."

Romana leaned forward, her hands squeezing the arms of her chair. "What, then?"

Meiran dropped her hand, looking up into the face of Emmery's Queen. "I've spent the past two years rallying the southern kingdoms in support of our cause. It's time for those monarchies to do more than just offer lip service. On the morrow, I will pronounce a formal declaration of war. Let's see how many battalions the South will be willing to muster."

Looking at Swain, she asked, "What's the status of Greystone Keep and Ironguard Pass?"

Nigel Swain shrugged. "Fortifications are well underway, though neither keep is combat-ready."

Kyel frowned. "Has Force Commander Craig been notified of this?"

"I sent a bird to him before I sent for you."

A liveried servant entered the room, swiftly circling the small ring of chairs and leaning over to whisper in Swain's ear. The man's voice was much too low for Kyel to hear. But he could see Swain's reaction. The prince's eyes widened reflexively, his body stiffening in his chair.

"Wait here," he growled as he rose to his feet. He crossed the room in three cat-like strides and was already out the door before Kyel could wonder what had happened. He kept his gaze focused on the doorway, frowning after the man.

Naia was still talking, going on as though she hadn't noticed Swain's abrupt disappearance. "We should talk about making use of the temples. I could travel to the Valley of the Gods and speak with my father. It's not far."

"That's not a bad idea," Meiran muttered, looking at the doorway rather than at Naia. "Do me a favor and bring it up again later."

A loud noise echoed from outside. The sound of many running footsteps rang clearly from the hallway. Kyel started, surging to his feet just as a cluster of blue-cloaked guardsmen spilled into the room, sweeping forward around the chairs to converge on their Queen.

Romana was on her feet in an instant, eyes wide with alarm, as the guardsmen encircled her, forming a protective ring. Meiran and Naia were forced to back away to make room for the swarm of armored bodies. Kyel found himself reaching for the magic field, holding it ready.

"Naia, retire with the Queen."

Kyel whirled at the sound of Swain's voice calling out from the doorway. He clutched the scabbard of a longsword. He was flanked by two more guards with bars of rank upon their sleeves. Kyel stepped forward, inserting himself between Meiran and Swain, shielding the Prime Warden with his own body. He had no idea what was happening, had no clear evidence whether the guards were security or threat. He only knew that Meiran's life had to be protected at all cost. And he was the only thing close to a Sentinel they had.

Turning to the prince, Kyel demanded, "What happened? What's going on?"

Eyes only for his Queen, Swain responded, "Two of Renquist's demons just showed up on our doorstep." To his guardsmen he instructed, "Escort the Queen and Master Naia to the Residence."

Naia opened her mouth as if to argue as guards moved in close, pressing her backward with their bodies. She turned to Meiran with a questioning look in her eyes. The Prime Warden nodded, bestowing her assent, eyes glazed with worry.

"Protect the Queen," she said.

Naia dropped a formal curtsy before turning away. The guards immediately surrounded her, directing her along with Romana toward a door on the opposite wall. Within seconds, both women were gone. The room was swiftly emptied. Kyel turned back to Swain.

"Now what, exactly, is going on?"

Swain explained as he donned his sword, "My men detained two darkmages at the palace gates. They carry a badge of truce. They say they desire parley with the Prime Warden."

Face aghast, Meiran strode toward him. "Who are they? Did they give their names?"

The prince only shrugged, adjusting the strap of the baldric that crossed his chest. "I have no idea who they are. I didn't care to ask. I had them escorted across the grounds to the citadel. I didn't want them under the same roof as the Queen."

The Prime Warden stopped, lifting a pair of perfectly arched eyebrows. "You had them detained? Under a badge of *truce?*"

Swain grimaced. "Give me a little credit, Meiran. It wasn't that kind of escort."

Kyel frowned, not liking the situation one bit. He stared down at the markings of the chain on his wrist, gazing at it as cold prickles of dread needled his skin. There was little he could do against two darkmages. Strong as he was, there was only so much he could manage within the confines of his Oath of Harmony.

Never to harm.

The words he had spoken to Darien beneath Orien's Finger echoed in his memory, chilling him just as thoroughly as they had the moment he'd uttered them. He had never doubted his decision to take that Oath, had never questioned it, not even once.

Never, until now.

Meiran was already moving toward the door. "Very well. Kyel, you're with me."

Kyel had to move quickly to catch up. Swain swept ahead of them with a glare, two guards bringing up the rear. He moved with the casual grace of a blademaster, a stride that reminded Kyel of the way a cat stalks a bird. There was no attempt at conversation as they continued down the long, paneled corridors of the palace. It became apparent that every door was warded, guards stationed at intervals all up and down the length of the hallways. There were many more than he remembered.

They followed their escort out of the palace and across the grounds. Kyel kept pace at Meiran's side, his black cloak rippling behind him as he moved, the Silver Star of Aerysius glistening at his back. They moved through a maze of garden walkways bordered by boxwood hedges. At the far side of the inner ward was the citadel, a sprawling building surrounded with what looked like an entire company of Bluecloaks. Kyel had been inside the citadel once before. It had been there, in that prison, that Kyel had received the Transference through the Soulstone.

They paused at the entrance to a circular chamber ringed by guards. There, Swain bid them halt as he strode toward an officer, pausing to confer quietly with the man. Kyel gazed around, taking in the martial look of the place, the combined scents of oiled metal and aged leather.

Swain nodded and took a step back. The officer barked an

order. The guards that ringed the chamber turned and strode together toward the door, clearing the room. The door was shut, the bar thrown.

The three of them were alone.

Meiran turned to Swain, expectantly cocking an eyebrow. The prince motioned with his head in the direction of a door, at the same time reaching up to remove the sword from his back, leaning both sword and scabbard up against the wall. Meiran nodded, eyes narrowing as she considered the doorway. Then she started toward it.

Kyel fell in behind her, drawing in more of the magic field until the song of it swelled inside his head and the energy bled from his body in a visible, golden nimbus that surrounded him. Whatever happened, he wanted to be ready.

At the door, Meiran hesitated. She reached out and clenched the handle and, closing her eyes as if uttering a prayer, pulled the door open.

As they moved through the doorway, Kyel's eyes immediately widened in dismay. He pulled harder on the magic field, sending a spill of magelight forward into the shadowy corridor ahead.

He hadn't known what to expect. Certainly, not this.

He halted in mid-stride, confronted by the most beautiful woman he'd ever seen. She stood waiting in the center of the dark hallway, poised, a congenial smile on her face, chestnut hair spilling down her back. She wore an indigo robe with the image of the Silver Star embroidered on the breast. Kyel frowned at the sight of it, his eyes roving over the woman with blatant curiosity. She didn't look evil; there was no amount of malevolence in her eyes. In her upraised hand, she held a white drape of torn fabric: the badge of truce Swain had spoken of.

Beside the woman stood a man with dark, unkempt hair that curled about his collar. He appeared very thin, even gaunt. He was wearing a long black coat that covered a knee-length tunic. He held a black felt hat in front of his chest. There was a quiet sadness about his eyes that Kyel found intriguing. He couldn't help but wonder the reason for it.

Meiran raised her hand, stopping a short distance away from

their visitors. She stood there, considering the man and woman before her. She merely regarded them, her eyes narrowed and pensive. Kyel realized that Meiran had produced a glowing shield around her own body, a blue nimbus barely visible against the shadows.

She demanded in a firm voice, "What are your names?"

The woman brought a hand up to her chest. "I am Sareen Qadir." She spoke in a voice thick with a rich and melodic accent. "This is my partner, Quinlan Reis. You must be Prime Warden Meiran Withersby."

Meiran nodded, her face devoid of all emotion. "I am," she responded flatly. "But help me clarify something. You both claim to be Servants of Xerys. So why is it that history has no record of your names?"

A good question, Kyel thought. He gazed expectantly at the two darkmages before him, realizing for the first time that he was staring at two people one thousand years dead.

The chestnut-haired woman offered Meiran an indulgent smile. "Trust me when I say that many things have become lost since our time in this world came to an end. Our names, unfortunately, were not the greatest casualties of Bryn Calazar's fall."

At her side, the man replaced his hat back on his head, adjusting the brim low over his eyes. Gazing at Meiran, he told her, "I once heard that Prime Warden Sephana Clemley had my name expunged from the record books. It's my guess she didn't want my reputation to tarnish my brother's good name."

Meiran frowned at his words, gazing at the man with kindled interest in her eyes. "And who was your brother?"

"Braden Reis," the darkmage responded without hesitation.

Kyel's mouth dropped open.

"Your brother was the *First Sentinel?*" Meiran gasped, obviously just as shocked as Kyel. She made a searching gesture with her hands. "And yet…you're a Servant of Xerys. Explain."

The darkmage sucked in a cheek, issuing a slight shrug. "It seemed like the right decision at the time I made it. Of course, in retrospect, I often find myself wondering why I didn't do things rather differently."

Kyel couldn't help but stare at the man. He was fascinated by the two of them. He found himself far more intrigued than afraid, even though he knew that defied common sense.

"Why are you here?" Meiran asked.

The woman spread her hands. "We are here to deliver a message to you from Prime Warden Zavier Renquist."

Kyel shivered at the very mention of that terrible name. He needed no further reminders that these two mages were very dangerous, indeed. He had been wrong to lower his guard. Kyel chanced a glance over his shoulder at Swain, finding the prince looking none too pleased and very much on edge. His sword arm twitched at his side, seeming to hunger for the hilt of his blade.

Meiran bowed her head for a moment. When she brought her eyes up again, her gaze was rigid. "Very well. Deliver your message and then be gone from this place."

The woman named Sareen nodded formally, giving no indication that she had taken any offense to Meiran's terse command. She said, "Prime Warden Renquist has no desire for a war between our two nations at this time. Instead, what he proposes is an alliance. I have been sent to guide you north with me to Bryn Calazar, where Zavier Renquist desires to meet with you to negotiate the terms of a treaty that will be forged between our two peoples. I am to accompany you, Prime Warden, as your protector and guardian through the Black Lands. I have been instructed to leave Quin behind as assurance for your safe return."

Kyel realized that he had stopped breathing long before the woman had stopped talking. Meiran couldn't accept such an offer. It was much too dangerous.

"And what if I refuse to come with you?" Meiran wondered. Kyel stared at Sareen, very interested in hearing what her response would be.

"I would advise against it," the chestnut-haired beauty shrugged, casting her eyes downward and to the side. "That would leave our Prime Warden with little recourse but to act."

Meiran stared at her unblinking. At last she said, "I will think on it. Is there anything else?"

"Yes."

It was Quinlan Reis who stepped forward, offering out a scroll of parchment toward Meiran in his hand. "I bear another message for you. This one is from Darien Lauchlin."

Kyel stiffened at the mention of that name.

He took a step back away from the offered scroll. Meiran remained where she was. She stared down at the parchment as if it were a venomous snake, the color draining slowly from her face. Her blue eyes were wide with revulsion. Long moments ticked by. She stood staring at the scroll in the darkmage's hand, refusing to accept it.

"I don't understand," she whispered at last. "Darien Lauchlin is dead."

"As am I," Quinlan Reis reminded her, gazing deeply into her eyes. "Like myself, Darien is now a Servant of Xerys."

Kyel gaped at the darkmage, paralyzed by revulsion and dismay. His eyes darted to Meiran. He wanted to go to her, but he couldn't bring himself to move. He remained rooted where he was, heart frozen in dread.

"Darien is one of the Eight?" Meiran gasped in a voice full of despair. She shook her head, gazing down at the scroll as her face collapsed into grief. But then she clenched her jaw, brittle strength returning to her eyes. She shook her head firmly. "No. I don't believe you. Darien would never do such a thing. *You are lying.*"

Quinlan Reis just shrugged, hand still extended toward her in the air. "He wasn't left with much of a choice, I'm afraid. It was the only way he could secure the release of your own soul from the Netherworld."

Kyel closed his eyes, bowing his head. There was little doubt left in his mind; he knew the demon before him was telling the truth. He had to be.

Meiran's whisper was barely audible. "My soul...? *That was the price?*"

Quinlan Reis nodded. "I'm sorry if these tidings bring you grief. I know how much you meant to him. Here. Take it."

He pressed the scroll into Meiran's hand, squeezing her fingers closed around it. Then he stepped back. His eyes seemed even more saddened than they had before.

"Excuse me," Meiran gasped.

She turned and fled the room, leaving Kyel and Swain alone with the two unlikely emissaries. Kyel turned back to regard the darkmages who stood before him, waiting.

He felt completely at a loss.

He had no idea what to do.

Chapter Three
Demon

Aerysius, The Rhen

Darien awoke to the lambent orange glow of flickering torchlight distorting the shadows on the stone walls. The fact that he was even awake and alert in this world at all was strange enough, a sensation that was half-remembered, like a dream. The ruddy hue of the crackling flames seemed surreal, saturated with a bright intensity of color. A vibrant contrast to the monochromatic palette of the Netherworld. The flames of the torches seemed animated, intense, *alive*. They writhed in a vivacious dance, fueled by a breeze that stirred from the depths of the warrens.

He was awake and alert in this world, the same world that, somewhere, Meiran also occupied. Darien's first thought was that he wanted to go to her. He wanted that very badly. He wanted to tell her how grateful he was that she had been there with him at the end.

Meiran's presence at his side had kept the fear of death at bay. Her soothing touch had been the last thing Darien felt as death rose to claim him, catching him up and bearing him away, downward into darkness.

But the darkness had not been eternal.

On the other side, there *had* been light. An unholy light. A sickening pallor, the color of pestilence, of corruption, of decay. Within that cold and brittle light, Darien's soul had been received with delight by his new Master.

He'd had much to atone for.

Darien sat up, shivering, filled with a terrible sense of dread. He drew his knees up against his chest and leaned back against the rough stone wall. He sat there for a long time, letting the chill horror of the memories slowly recede. All across the underground chamber, the other members of their party were beginning to stir. It would be morning soon. Almost time to depart.

He glanced down at the clothes he was wearing, the same tattered outfit he had worn to his death. He was dressed all in black: black breeches, a frayed linen shirt, the same black cloak he'd taken from an abandoned tent in the Chamsbrey encampment below Orien's Finger. There was no Silver Star embroidered on the back; as far as Darien was concerned, he'd lost the right to wear that emblem. He wore only a simple, plain wool cloak, something an officer might sport. Not a mage's cloak. He was a Sentinel of Aerysius no longer.

On the ground beside him lay the sword that Meiran had given him. It rested in its worn leather scabbard, the rubies set into the hilt glimmering like crystalline droplets of blood. His hand went to the sword, sliding it possessively nearer. It was the only thing he had left of her, the only thing he was likely to ever have.

Darien figured the letter he'd written should be enough to destroy any lingering feelings Meiran might still have for him.

He turned toward the sound of approaching footsteps. His hand closed reflexively around the hilt of his sword. But when Darien saw the face of the man who approached, he released his grip. Common steel could not defend him against such a monster.

Nashir Arman dropped into a crouch at Darien's side. His face was angular and chiseled, his stare intense and penetrating. Darien froze under the severe inspection of those eyes, dropping his own stare to the ground. In the Netherworld, Nashir had been assigned the role of Darien's tormentor. The demon took great pleasure in delivering pain. And he was very good at it.

Nashir stared at Darien with an ice-dead gaze. "You took the life of my woman," he said in a low and threatening tone, soft enough so that the others couldn't hear. "I promise you this:

before you leave this world again, I'll see to it that you pay."

Darien kept his eyes lowered, focusing his own gaze on the floor. He knew by now not to try to look Nashir in the eye. The pain simply wasn't worth it.

The darkmage leaned forward, staring him in the face. "Perhaps I'll take the life of your woman. Flesh for flesh. Blood for blood. Pain for pain."

Darien glared his hatred at Nashir. It was the only thing he could do, the only defense he had against the sinister demon. He couldn't even sense the magic field, thanks to Cyrus Krane. The man had severed his connection with the field, and that damper was still in place.

"Stop provoking him, Nashir."

Byron Connel drew up behind Nashir, Myria Anassis at his side. Connel wore the indigo robes of the Lyceum of Bryn Calazar, the talisman Thar'gon swaying from a leather strap affixed to his belt. Darien was relieved the two of them had come to his defense, but not surprised. Connel seemed a man of character, patient and even-tempered. Myria was a stalwart intellectual, kind and sincere.

Nashir acknowledged Connel with a stiff nod of his chin. He rose to his feet, his eyes still intently focused on Darien. He turned and stalked away, but not without casting a significant glare back over his shoulder. Darien kept his eyes trained on Nashir, not trusting him at all.

Byron Connel knelt at Darien's side. "Never lower your guard around Nashir Arman," the Battlemage cautioned. "He can be...unprincipled. And unpredictable."

"I know." Darien's attention was still focused on Nashir's retreating back.

"Do you?" inquired Myria, hovering over them with arms crossed in front of her. "I don't know if you appreciate how dangerous he can be."

Darien allowed his gaze to wander upward. Gazing into Myria's face, he assured her, "I can be dangerous, too."

Myria Anassis shook her head, her long, dark hair swaying like a curtain to her waist. "No. Not like him. You have a conscience.

A creature like Nashir does not."

Byron Connel adjusted his posture, draping an arm over one knee. "Compared to Nashir, you're like a child, Darien. He was trained as a weapon from birth. He's well-schooled in both offensive magic and tactics, and he's had a thousand years to hone those skills. Your training as a Sentinel was grossly deficient. You wouldn't last a minute against him."

"Then teach me," Darien challenged.

Connel grinned, shaking his head. He cast an amused glance up at Myria. "Sorry, but I can't do that. My duties lie elsewhere, unfortunately. Just remember to watch your back." He reached out, clapping Darien on the shoulder as he rose to take his leave.

Myria regarded Darien with a look of sympathy. "I'm sorry. I wish I could be of more help to you."

Darien found himself intrigued. "Why?"

She paused in the action of turning away. She gave a slight shrug. "Because you remind me of someone I once knew."

"Who?"

The look on Myria's face made it obvious she had not expected either question. "Just a man," she responded after a moment's hesitation. "A man who's been dead for a thousand years."

Darien considered her answer carefully. "Did you love him?"

Myria blinked. Then she frowned. "No. But I did admire him." Still frowning, she turned and strolled away.

Darien allowed his gaze to follow the pale texture of her gown that seemed to flare like fire in the torchlight. Like Byron Connel, Myria defied the concept of darkmage he had nurtured so carefully for so very long. He had thought they would prove to be all just like Nashir Arman and Arden Hannah. Sadistic and power-hungry. Potently cruel, like Cyrus Krane. But there seemed to be more than one type of demon. Apparently, there were many shades and gradations of evil. He wondered where on that continuum his own soul would rank.

At his side, the thanacryst made a noise that sounded almost like purring. Darien moved his hand to its neck, ruffling the course and matted fur. He had been surprised to find out that the demon-hound had once belonged to Nashir. He had offered to return it, but Nashir had wanted nothing to do with his former pet. Darien was grateful; in all the world, the thanacryst was the only friend he seemed to have left.

He gazed across the chamber at the others going about the business of breaking down their small encampment. His eyes found Azár, the Enemy mage whose action of unsealing the Well of Tears had undone everything Darien had given his life for. Azár was awake and rummaging through her pack. She'd made her bed on the far side of the chamber, as far away from him as she could possibly manage. It was very obvious to Darien that he wasn't the savior Azár had been anticipating.

She glanced up and, for the briefest instant, their gaze met. Her eyes narrowed in anger before darting quickly away. Azár was ferocious despite her small size. She was thin and delicate, with ink-black hair that hung in a thick braid all the way down her back. She had a proud and slender nose, smooth bronze skin, and wide, almond-shaped eyes that liked to gleam at him with hatred.

Darien pushed himself up off the ground and strode away from her toward the doorway. As he walked, he shrugged the baldric of his sword on over his shoulder, letting the scabbard fall down across his back. They were still within the warrens beneath Aerysius, in a chamber somewhere in the levels beneath the Well of Tears. The Servants had used these rooms as a kind of headquarters during their last campaign. There were still plenty of supplies left over from that time: dried food stores, blankets, even weapons. They had lingered there for the past two days: provisioning, formulating plans.

Darien followed the damp passage ahead toward a narrow rise of stairs, the demon-hound padding along at his side. He wanted to go up that long flight of steps. He desired one last view of the mountainside before he had to leave, just one last glimpse of the foundations of dead Aerysius.

But it was not meant to be.

The sound of his name stopped him short. Darien turned, glancing behind down the passageway in the direction he had come from. Zavier Renquist was standing there, lingering in the doorway, face stern and expectant. Darien moved immediately to retrace his steps. Of one thing he was completely certain: Zavier Renquist was a hundred times more dangerous than Nashir could ever be.

As Darien drew up before him, he ducked his head in silent deference. The ancient Prime Warden reached out and draped an arm over Darien's shoulders, pulling him in familiarly close. "Let us take our leave," he uttered in a deep baritone voice. With gentle pressure, he steered Darien back toward the deep bowels of the warrens. Glowing tendrils of magelight appeared at their feet, swirling to illuminate the path ahead. Darien's shoulders tensed at the feel of Renquist's hand on his back directing him forward.

"I thought you'd be interested to know that Quin and Sareen arrived safely in Rothscard," the Prime Warden said. "Hopefully, all will go well with their embassy. The letter you prepared should help. In the meantime, the hour has come for us to depart and be about our separate responsibilities."

His stomach clenched at the thought of the letter Renquist had compelled him to write. Darien had spilled his soul out in ink onto that parchment, knowing how imperative it was that Meiran believed him. If she didn't, the consequences were too terrible to consider.

Renquist continued, "Myria told me about Nashir. Be at ease. I've spoken with him."

Darien nodded his gratitude, his thoughts still on Meiran. He wondered what she must be thinking of him now, after reading that letter. The very thought of her reaction to his news made him feel physically ill with shame.

It didn't really matter what Meiran thought of him. In the scheme of things, that was of little consequence. All that mattered was that she believed him. Meiran could despise him for all eternity, so long as her anger kept her and the others alive.

"I want you to know that I have the highest expectations of you, Darien," Renquist said as they strode side by side down the dark corridor, glowing mist swirling beneath their feet. "Of all my chosen Servants, you are by far the most powerful and also the most decisive. You don't shy away from the hard decisions, the kind that keep most men awake at night. You are intelligent, resourceful, and uninhibited. Once you have been properly trained, you will be the greatest Battlemage our world has ever known."

Darien muttered, "If you say so, Prime Warden."

Zavier Renquist stopped, taking Darien by the shoulders and turning him to face him. Darien forced himself to look the Prime Warden directly in the eye. It took every scrap of nerve he possessed to confront Renquist's indomitable stare.

"I realize this is not easy for you," the ancient darkmage confided in a gentler tone. "You made the right decision, Darien. You made the choice that was in the best interest of both our peoples. I think, finally, you're beginning to understand just how imperative our work is here. I have every faith and confidence in your ability to succeed where others have failed."

Darien couldn't help it. He dropped his gaze to the floor under the weight of Renquist's expectations. "Thank you, Prime Warden."

Renquist patted him on the arm. "You'll do just fine. Now. I'm going to remove your field damper. When I do, you'll have a choice to make."

Darien nodded, still staring at the floor. He understood. Renquist was going to give him back the magic field. When he did, there would be nothing preventing him from lashing out with his ability. But Renquist knew he presented little danger; Darien already had a deep appreciation for the consequences of such a betrayal.

Nashir had taught him that lesson very well.

The Prime Warden's eyes narrowed slightly, his face going rigid in concentration. Then the magic field came flooding headlong into Darien's mind like a river overwhelming a dam. He closed his eyes and reeled with the thrill of it, savoring the sweet ecstasy he had gone so long without. Darien took a deep breath, cherishing the feeling of comfort and sentiment the magic field inspired in his mind. Then he opened his eyes, conjuring a mist of his own.

Wondrously, his own magelight appeared at their feet, a shimmering blue glow that mingled with the turbulent vapor Renquist had already summoned.

"I don't understand," he whispered, reveling in the splendor of the cobalt mist, the signature color of the legacy he had surrendered at death. "The Soulstone took my gift. It drained everything from me."

Renquist informed him flatly, "You don't need the gift anymore. You're not alive."

Darien glanced up from the ground, confused and suddenly uncertain. "If I'm not alive, then what am I?"

Renquist allowed him a sad and fleeting smile, the kind of smile a father might bestow upon a young, wayward son. "You have been remade and brought back into being for a time," explained the ancient darkmage. "You are clothed in your own flesh only by the will of Xerys. Through the Onslaught, you have access to the magic field. But only for a time."

Darien shook his head, spreading his hands out before him. "I don't understand. I breathe. I hunger. *I feel.*"

The Prime Warden dismissed his arguments with a shrug. "You are not alive, Darien, and you would do well to never forget that. You are a Servant of Xerys. A demon. Your soul has given up any chance or hope of salvation. When this brief flirtation with life is over, the best you can hope for is a return to our Master's dominion. But, should Xerys ever become displeased with the quality of your service, He will exile your spirit into Oblivion. Your soul will be unmade, and you will simply cease to exist. It will be as though you had never been born. There's no coming back from such a banishment."

Darien considered this information, mulling it over, at last nodding his acceptance. He speculated, "Is that what happened to Arden?"

Renquist nodded. "Yes. That is exactly what happened to Arden." He started down the passage, compelling Darien forward with a hand on his shoulder.

"What did Arden do to earn such displeasure from our Master?"

"She failed," Renquist responded simply.

Darien understood. Failure was something their Master had little tolerance for. He was quiet for a long time as he contemplated the idea. He arrived at the conclusion that such a harsh penalty for failure was not as frightening as it first seemed; at least there was another option besides an eternity spent in hell. It was some small comfort knowing that. Darien pondered the notion as he followed Renquist down a flight of long, twisting steps that seemed to descend forever into blackness.

"Release the magic field," Renquist commanded. "From here, we walk together in darkness."

Darien understood the request. They were descending the long staircase buried deep within the heart of the mountain, the same one he had travelled with Kyel, Swain, and Naia two years before. Somewhere along that stair they would run into the vortex that surrounded Aerysius. He would need to shield his mind from it; the magic field would be inaccessible for a time.

He was reluctant to release the field's soothing energies. But he did, allowing them to ebb and drain away. Complete darkness stole in around them. Darien could see nothing, not even the stairs beneath his feet. The pressure of Renquist's hand on his arm compelled him forward. Together, side by side, they descended the stairs in consummate blackness.

"What other duties shall you have for me?" Darien wondered into the darkness. He could hear the sound of the thanacryst's paws padding after them, keeping pace at a distance.

"Nothing for now," Renquist's voice responded. "You have enough on your plate. Attend to Azár and her people. That's sufficient, for now. We'll be using the transfer portal beneath Orien's Finger. It will take us to Bryn Calazar. From there, Azár will lead you westward to the ancestral lands of her people."

A cold breeze stirred up from the depths, playing with Darien's cloak. He shivered. The air wasn't fresh; the scent was stale, as if it had remained pooled within the mountain for a very long time.

They traveled together in silence down long flights of stairs broken every so often by the occasional landing. The journey took hours. The stairs led them ever downward, deeper into the mountain's cold and clammy heart. They paused occasionally to rest in the thick blackness amidst the shadows. Neither man spoke; the descent was taxing, demanding a good deal of concentration. Eventually, they reached the bottom of the steps. The stairs leveled off, arriving at a rock wall that marked the entrance to the warrens.

"*Qurfin,*" Renquist whispered. A door appeared like a growing crack in the rock wall ahead, yawning open with a silvery glow.

They stepped out of the mountainside into a pale gray morning. Darien was surprised to find that the other members of their party had already arrived ahead of them. Then he remembered: the stair within the mountain was like the Catacombs, a place where time and distance had little consistency. The other members of their party could have started out much later in the day and yet still arrived at the bottom of the mountain ahead of them.

He looked to the east, where dawn warmed the horizon beyond the dark frame of the valley walls. The tall pedestal of Orien's Finger loomed ominously in the center of a horseshoe-shaped canyon. The ground at their feet was blackened, as well as the surrounding cliffs. There was no trace of green, not even a single blade of grass. The entire canyon was charred and scorched. Darien bowed his head, knowing this was his own doing. His intention had been to protect this land. Instead, he had defiled it.

As if sensing the direction of his thoughts, Azár turned to gaze at him with accusation in her eyes. Just looking at her rattled Darien's nerves. She hated him, with good reason. The damage he'd inflicted upon the rocks of this canyon was trivial compared to the horrors he'd wrought against Azár's own people. Thousands of lives torn instantly asunder. Charred remains, blackened to ash. Scattered about the ground and tossed by the wind.

"Azár," Renquist called out. "Take Darien ahead to the transfer portal. Meet up with us in Bryn Calazar."

The girl nodded, still glaring at Darien with hostile contempt in her eyes. Then, shouldering her cloth pack, she turned and stalked away, crossing the black canyon floor toward the jutting tower of rock.

Flustered, Darien watched her go.

"What are you waiting for?" Byron Connel chided mildly, drawing up at Darien's side. He nodded his head in the direction of Azár. "Better go after her before she leaves you behind."

Darien grimaced. He hooked his hand around the leather baldric that crossed his chest and trudged after Azár. He trailed her around the wide base of the rock pillar until, mercifully, she drew to a halt on the far side. There, she stopped with her back to him and moved no further.

Darien approached her cautiously. She was standing stock-still, facing the orange disk of the rising sun. Darien paused, gazing at her with a questioning look.

Azár was staring straight ahead, her mouth slack, eyes wide with startled amazement. Her lips quivered. She was trembling all over, he realized, her whole body shaking. Darien took a hesitant step toward her, then another.

"You've never seen the sun before," he surmised in wonder.

Azár tensed, her mouth snapping shut at the sound of his voice. She shot a smoldering glare his way. Then she shook her head, looking ashamed.

Darien chanced another step in her direction. "It can't hurt you," he assured her, trying to guess the cause of her reaction.

She glared at him with searing hatred in her eyes. He could almost visualize the anger bleeding off her skin to saturate the air between them. But then, suddenly, Azár's expression faltered.

"What if it falls?" she whispered.

Darien was mildly shocked by the question. "What makes you think it will fall?"

"They say that is what happened to my homeland," Azár explained without looking at him. "They say that the sun fell from the sky and charred the ground."

Darien frowned, knowing for a fact that was not what happened. He'd met the man responsible for Caladorn's demise. The sun was innocent of any such wrongdoing. A gust of wind seized his hair, whipping it forward into his face. Darien reached up, pushing it back out of his eyes.

"I don't think that's going to happen here," he said.

Azár fixed him with a cold, lingering stare. "Why not?"

"Because I won't let it happen."

Her gaze trailed slowly up the length of his body. Her lips curled in distaste, as if she despised everything she saw. "You are a very arrogant man," she said at last. "And you are also a hypocrite."

"Why am I a hypocrite?" Darien demanded, baiting her intentionally. This was the most he'd ever heard her speak. He was intrigued. He wanted to know more about this woman, this mage of the Enemy.

Azár gestured around them with a wave of her hand, eyes wide and incredulous. "Look around. The ground is charred, just as black as the soil of my own country. You did this. You desecrated your own homeland. You murdered a *hundred thousand* of my people!"

Darien nodded, knowing this had to be the source of her hatred. "There was a hundred thousand of them and only one of me. I did what I had to do."

Azár seemed repulsed by his response. "You immolated an entire generation of warriors!"

Darien could only shrug, accepting full responsibility. "I swore an oath to defend my land and my people."

Now it was Azár's turn to take a step forward, her presence looming with hostility despite her size. Arms crossed in front of her chest, she sneered at him, "And now you've sworn another oath to defend *my* land and *my* people!"

Darien closed his mouth, having no idea how to respond to that. He dropped his gaze to the demon-hound, sitting on its haunches against the dark and ruined earth.

"You *are* a hypocrite," Azár accused. "What are you going to do if you have to protect my homeland at the expense of your own?"

Darien could only glare at her in sullen silence. He had no answer to that. She had very quickly isolated and exposed his greatest weakness, his gravest fear. His naked vulnerability. She stood there before him, arms crossed, eyebrows raised expectantly. Awaiting his response.

"So much talk," she mocked him, "and now you have absolutely nothing to say! Why am I burdened with you? You are not a man to be trusted!"

Darien seethed at her in anger, his eyes scalding pools of resentment. He took a last step forward, closing the gap between them, and raised a finger before her face.

"I'm not a man," he reminded her in a voice hoarse with caustic fury. "And you'd do very well not to trust me. I've broken every promise I ever made."

With that, he turned and trudged away, back toward Orien's pedestal. The thanacryst remained behind, growling at Azár, teeth barred and hackles raised.

"*Theanoch*," Darien called back at it. With a yelp, the demon-dog sprang after him, bounding to catch up.

Chapter Four
Deal with a Devil

Rothscard, The Rhen

K yel raised his hand to knock on the door. He clenched his fist instead, lowering it back down again to his side. He scowled, staring down at his hand as he contemplated the wisdom behind his intended act. He was having second thoughts, maybe even third or fourth thoughts. He took a deep breath, holding the air in his lungs for a long moment before letting it back out again. Then he raised his fist with firmer resolve.

He knocked twice upon the wood. Then he waited. He could hear the soft sound of footsteps approaching from the other side. A sharp, metallic click as the bolt inside was thrown. The sound of the door creaking open.

Meiran's pale and grief-weathered face confronted him in the doorway. Just one look in her eyes told Kyel that all his fears had been justified. He grimaced, shaking his head. He hated being right.

"I'm so sorry, Meiran," was all he could bring himself to say.

She collapsed against him, her whole body quaking. Kyel wrapped his arms around her as she hugged him back, clinging to him fiercely. He felt the warm moisture of her tears against his neck. Her back shook as she cried against his shoulder, shedding her sorrow into the black wool of his cloak.

Eventually, the tears subsided. Meiran withdrew, pulling away and swiping angrily at her eyes with a sleeve. She wandered back into the depths of the dimly-lit quarters. Kyel lingered behind a moment before following, pushing the door closed behind him.

He glanced around, taking in the dark features of the guest room.

Meiran stood beside a painted writing desk, composing herself. Her hand was on her necklace again, fingering the interlaced pendant on its silver chain, her eyes gazing off into nothing. She was wearing a white wide-sleeved gown, her dark hair falling in loose waves down her back. She looked vulnerable, like a lost and frightened child.

"Are you all right?" Kyel asked softly.

She shook her head, eyes haunted by misery. "No, Kyel. I'm not all right."

She gestured helplessly at a curled page on the writing desk: Darien's letter, given to her by the darkmage Quinlan Reis. Kyel recognized the bold, flowing script from across the room. Meiran scooped the parchment up into her hand, rolling it back up before offering it out toward him.

"Go ahead. Read it."

Kyel swallowed as he accepted the letter. He stared down at the scroll in trepidation, loath to unfurl it and view the message it contained. As if denial could make the whole situation somehow evaporate. Kyel had many reasons for not wanting to read that letter, but they all really boiled down to one simple thing: Darien Lauchlin had been his friend. That was the way Kyel wished to remember him.

As he unrolled the scroll, Kyel's fingers were already shaking.

My Dearest Meiran,

I have no idea how to tell you this, so I suppose I'll just come right out and say it: before I died, I committed my soul to Chaos. I have taken Arden Hannah's place at Zavier Renquist's side. I am a Servant of Xerys.

Kyel had to stop, squeezing his eyes shut against a pang of horror. He glanced up at Meiran with sorrow in his eyes, a look that mirrored her own. He forced himself to continue reading, a terrible feeling of dread gnawing at his heart.

I know how atrocious this must sound to you, the most grievous of all betrayals. I understand. I don't expect your forgiveness. But, I beg you, please hear me out. I am still myself; nothing inside me has changed except for my perspective. I have gained a depth of understanding that was unavailable to me before.

Please believe me, Meiran, when I say there is another side to this story. There are many facts we were ignorant of, things omitted from the histories. Maybe our ancestors didn't know the whole story. Or perhaps they suppressed the knowledge on purpose. I don't wish to speculate; I'm not here to judge. I am only here to bear witness.

By now, you must have heard that Zavier Renquist desires to negotiate the terms of a treaty. I urge you to consider his offer carefully. You can trust Quin. Please accept whatever proposal he brings you.

I do love you, Meiran. I know that you will probably no longer bear any love for me, especially after reading these words. I am sorry for that. I want you to know that what I did—the decisions I made—none of that was your fault. I did what I felt I had to do. If I made one mistake, it was not realizing that the Well of Tears could be reopened again so quickly. I never imagined that we would end up in the same war but on two different sides. Had I known that, I still don't think it would have changed anything. I can honestly say that I have no regrets.

All My Love,

Darien

Kyel lowered the letter, letting the scroll roll itself back up in his hand. He stood there silent for a minute, frozen in place, unable to do anything but gaze woodenly down at the floor in front of his feet. The tiles were cold and polished, reflecting the wavering light of the tapers ensconced around the room. Kyel gazed at their shimmering gold reflection as his mind scrambled for clarity in a roiling cauldron of conflicting emotions.

"I was afraid of something like this," he whispered at last. He moved forward, setting the scroll back down on the writing desk.

Meiran made no comment. She stood with her hands clasped in front of her, dark waves of hair falling about her shoulders. She looked very young, completely bereft of her characteristic fortitude.

"Do you believe him?" Kyel asked, his eyes searching her face.

Meiran blinked, bringing her arms up to hug herself.

"It doesn't matter what I believe," she muttered. "This letter can bear no weight on my decision."

Kyel nodded. "What are you going to do?" he asked. "Have you decided?"

Meiran flashed him a look of resentment. "I'm certainly not going to give Renquist what he wants." Color bloomed on her cheeks as Meiran quickly recovered herself. Kyel understood why Darien had so loved this woman. Though no older than himself, Meiran had more grit and tenacity than anyone Kyel had ever met.

"What does Renquist want?"

"It's obvious what he wants," Meiran snapped, pacing away. "He wants *me*. What I don't understand is why."

"He wanted Darien, too," Kyel reminded her ominously. He ran his hand along the surface of the writing desk, eyes lingering on the scroll.

"And he got Darien, didn't he?"

Kyel swallowed. "Aye. Apparently, he did."

That settled it, then. Kyel rounded on her, eyes full of galvanized resolve. "You can't treat with him, Meiran. It's too dangerous. I saw Darien after his parley with Renquist. It destroyed him. He couldn't live with himself after that."

"Because that's how Zavier Renquist operates," declared a voice from behind them.

Kyel whirled, reaching immediately for the magic field. He had a shield thrown up in front of them before he could think.

Hands clasped behind his back, Quinlan Reis strolled forward into the sitting room, nodding his approval toward Kyel. He paused, shutting the door quietly behind him. Then he continued talking as if nothing at all was out of sorts:

"He discovers what matters to you most. That's what he uses as leverage against you. He takes something you love and twists it into a knife to slide between your ribs."

He reached up and scooped his black felt hat off his head. Holding it against his chest, the darkmage remarked to Kyel, "You have absolutely no idea what you're doing, do you?"

Eyes ablaze with ire, Meiran advanced on him, waving a finger. "You don't have permission to be here! *Get out now.*"

Eyes only for Kyel, Quinlan Reis smiled and assured her with calm disregard, "I'm not here in an official capacity."

Meiran pointed at the door. "You have three seconds to get out."

"Or what? You'll frown at me? I'm sorry, but those chains on your wrists aren't very intimidating."

Meiran drew herself up, hands going to her sides. Very formally, she addressed him, "You disregard a badge of truce. Have you abandoned all honor?"

The hat-wielding darkmage scowled. "I never had any honor when I was alive, so why would I suddenly come into it after death? I don't think inheritance works in that direction." He turned back to Kyel with a derisive glare. "You can drop that shield now. If I came here to kill you, you'd already be dead."

Kyel ignored him, maintaining the glowing shield that was their only protection from the demon. Quinlan Reis waited, scrutinizing him derisively. When it became obvious that Kyel had no intention of doing as he bid, the man simply shrugged, replacing his hat back on his head.

"I came to make you an offer." He glanced at Meiran out of the corner of his eye.

"I don't make deals with demons," she promised, indignant.

Quinlan Reis glowered at her. "Wait until you've heard my offer, Prime Warden. You may rethink your policy."

Meiran stared at him for a long, searching moment. A soft and fleeting expression passed across her face, unreadable. She appeared to be groping with her feelings. At last, she calmly turned to Kyel. "Leave us, please."

Kyel's throat went dry. He glanced up at Meiran in alarm. "Prime Warden?"

Meiran nodded, her face full of conviction. She raised her hand, pointing toward the door.

"Go."

Kyel blinked, staring back and forth between Meiran and the darkmage. She was serious, he realized. With a pang of dread, he released his hold on his golden shield, letting its pale glow dissipate into the surrounding air. Kyel glared hard and long at Quinlan Reis. Then, against his better judgement, Kyel did the only thing he could do.

He followed his Prime Warden's command, exiting the guest room and leaving Meiran alone with a Servant of Xerys.

Kyel's head was spinning in a daze of confusion by the time he reached the ground floor of the palace. His body had broken out into a cold sweat, his emotions on the cusp of panic. He had no idea why Meiran had dismissed him from the room. In the face of grave danger, she had sent him away. Just as Darien had done before Black Solstice.

Kyel ran down the long corridor, shouting at the first stationed guardsman he could find. "The Prime Warden's in danger! Summon the captain! Summon the prince! *Now!*" He bellowed the last word, prompting the man into action.

The guard dashed off with a look of mortified panic on his face. Kyel remained behind, battling the urgent compulsion to run back up the stairs. He settled on pacing back and forth across the long hall, addled by fear and nervous energy. He kept glancing back up the stairs, resisting the impulse to storm up there and invite the demon to a duel.

But he knew better. He was no match for Quinlan Reis. Or Meiran's ire.

More than that; his Oath of Harmony wouldn't allow it.

It was long minutes before Nigel Swain finally arrived, flanked by a small contingent of guardsmen. The prince consort was carrying a longsword in his hand, his face tense with focused aggression.

"What the hell's all the ruckus?" Swain demanded, drawing up in front of Kyel. The guards behind him had their weapons drawn, shields at ready.

"The Prime Warden's in danger!" Kyel said. "One of the darkmages slipped in past the guards! He has her cornered up there!" He pointed up the stairs in the direction of the guest rooms.

Swain's gaze followed Kyel's motion. "So, there's only one up there? *Where's the other one?*"

"I don't know!"

Swain turned to his men. "Fall back to the Residence and protect the Queen! *You,*" he growled at the man nearest him, "gather reinforcements and meet me upstairs!"

Kyel turned and started toward the steps.

"Where do you think you're going?"

He stopped and turned back around. "I'm coming with you."

Swain shook his head, strands of chin-length hair swinging forward into his face. "You're going to stay the hell away from there. You're not trained for this."

Kyel glared at him. "Neither are you."

The two men stared at each other across the empty hallway. Kyel waited, eyebrows raised, hands spread wide in question. Nigel Swain at last issued a stiff nod. He strode forward, passing up Kyel in three large strides.

Kyel reached within for the magic field, holding it at ready in the back of his mind. When they arrived at the second-floor hallway, he was surprised to see the door to Meiran's room already ajar. He remembered closing it when he'd left. Swain brought a hand up. He pointed at the door and made a quick series of gestures. Kyel just stared at him, unable to fathom what the man was trying to communicate.

"You call yourself a Sentinel?" Swain growled under his breath.

"*What?*" Kyel mouthed silently.

"Just get behind me. *And try not to hurt yourself.*"

A group of guardsmen spilled past them over the top of the stairs in a rush of armored bodies. They fanned out across the hallway, weapons drawn.

Swain held up his fist. He extended a finger, pointing forward. The guards swept past him on both sides, storming into the guest room. Kyel moved behind them, cloaking them all in a glowing shield of light.

"*Meiran!*" Kyel shouted, gaze darting frantically around the room. Except for the milling clot of blue-cloaked guards, the sitting room was empty.

Heart thundering, Kyel charged toward the bedchamber. That room, too, was unoccupied. He swung back around, dropping the magic field like a hot brick.

"They're not here," he gasped in confusion. He wandered forward, eyes fumbling over the room as he groped through a barrage of desperate feelings he simply didn't understand. He glanced at the painted writing desk. Darien's letter was gone.

"Which one was it?" Swain demanded.

"Which one what?"

"*The man or the woman—which one was in here?*"

Kyel wrenched his gaze up off the surface of the writing desk. "The man."

Swain was already moving toward the door. "*Come on.*"

"Where are we going?" Kyel called after him.

"To find the woman!"

Kyel's eyes widened in alarm. He followed Swain and his men back down the stairs and out into the night. The palace grounds were abuzz with frantic guards and liveried servants running every which direction. They crossed the inner ward to the citadel, where they joined a throng of men already gathered at the tower's entrance.

A shout from the guard captain opened up a path before them. Sheathing his sword, Nigel Swain strode between his men into the tower's base. There, under the vaulted roof, he drew up sharply with a whispered oath. Kyel stopped behind him, staring down in shock at the body sprawled across the stone floor in front of them.

Sareen Qadir lay face-down, chestnut hair fanned out like a gilded halo around her head. Blood was leaking from a wound somewhere underneath her, running along the crevices between the floor tiles like irrigation through a field.

"It's her," Kyel gasped, kneeling down at her side. He placed his hand on the woman's back, closing his eyes in concentration. The image that came to him was definitive: there was nothing left to heal.

"She's dead," Kyel pronounced, staring down at a woman who, by his reckoning, had cheated death at least twice already. He didn't trust it.

The look on Swain's face could have curdled milk. The prince leaned forward and ran his hands over the corpse, searching through the garments. He combed through the pockets, pried open Sareen's clenched fingers. He dug beneath her fingernails. He rolled her over, expertly probing even the lining of her robes.

"Nothing," Swain grumbled, standing up. He swiped a hand back through his hair, eyes roving upward toward the ceiling.

"Handle that," he ordered the guard captain, pointing down at the corpse.

The man gazed down at the carcass, face skewed with uncertainty. "How…do you want it handled, Your Grace?"

Swain worked his lips against clenched teeth. "Burn it."

Hearing that, Kyel anxiously shook his head. "No. We need Naia."

Swain nodded thoughtfully, running his tongue over his lips. "Then go get her."

Chapter Five
City of the Damned

Orien's Finger, The Rhen

Darien swung around, glaring back over his shoulder at Azár. At his side, the demon-dog yipped at him, cocking its head. He ran his hand through its coarse fur as he stared back at Azár in annoyance. She was still standing in the same place, arms crossed over her chest, the orange sun rising at her back.

She chortled a derisive laugh in his direction. "You have no idea where you're going, do you?"

Darien closed his eyes, groping within to find the peace and patience he would need to weather this woman's scorn. He drew in a deep breath, letting it back out again slowly. When he opened his eyes, he saw that Azár was strutting toward him across the blackened ground. She brought a hand up to fend off wisps of dark hair that had escaped her braid.

He waited, stroking the thanacryst as she approached. Azár drew up in front of him, dark eyes mocking him in silence as she stared up into his face. She was a tiny thing; the top of her head reached no more than the center of his chest. She narrowed her eyes. Then she turned her head and spat upon the ground.

Darien glanced down to consider the wet stain of her spittle upon the blackened rocks. He wondered if Azár was even aware that her action had just desecrated what amounted to the mass gravesite of her countrymen. He doubted that she had even considered it.

"Would you show me where the transfer portal is, please?" Darien asked in as kindly a tone as he could muster.

He waited as she continued to glare up at him, hands on her hips. His gaze fell to the dagger she wore at her belt. The ebony hilt reminded him of the knife once carried by Garret Proctor, yet another man whose grave Azár's action had just defiled. For the first time, Darien took notice of the garments she was wearing. Azár's clothing was of ash-dark cotton, thickly layered for warmth. There was absolutely no leather or hide anywhere on her body; even her sandals and belt were woven from what looked like coarse fibers of reed. She wore a thick shawl tied around her shoulders. There were many holes and tears in the fabric. Darien took note of these subtle inconsistencies. She was of the mage class of her society. Yet, Azár dressed as an indigent.

She was still staring up at him, unblinking.

"I know I'm not what you expected," Darien said. "I'm sorry. What do you want me to do? Do you want me to leave?"

"I want you to die." She was gazing steadily upwards into his face.

"I did that already," he said flatly.

"A thousand deaths are not enough for you. The transfer portal is this way."

She moved away from him, feet crunching over the rocks and molten glass scattered everywhere across the ground. Darien tracked her motion with his eyes, watching her as she approached the charred rock wall of Orien's Finger. There, she muttered something under her breath. A Word of Command, he surmised. The fractured basalt rock of the pedestal seemed to shimmer, wavering for a moment. Then it disappeared altogether, revealing a gaping entrance cut into the side of the cliff itself.

Fascinated, Darien moved to follow her as she disappeared within. He conjured up a mist of magelight as he entered the dark chamber at the base of the pedestal, sending its glow spreading forward into the room.

He allowed his eyes to roam upward as he stood in the threshold of the doorway. The dark walls and tall ceiling glimmered with the sheen of thousands of tiny crystals that sparkled in the magelight. He watched as Azár moved forward into the center of the chamber, toward a tall, cross-vaulted arch. The arch was made of ruddy-colored marble that looked particularly out of place.

"I'd no idea this was here," Darien muttered.

"That's because you are ignorant."

Darien shook his head, bringing a hand up to rub his eyes. "I'm still in hell," he whispered under his breath.

Azár glanced back over her shoulder with a smirk. "Come. Take my hand."

Darien raised his eyebrows in surprise as he crossed the chamber toward her. He contemplated her offered hand for a long moment before accepting it. Her olive skin was smooth and silken, like none other he had ever felt before. He couldn't help himself; he ran his thumb across the back of her hand, noting the complete absence of lines. It was the softest hand he'd ever held.

"How old are you, Azár?" he wondered in awe.

She glared up at him, looking ready to snatch her hand back out of his grasp. "Empty your mind," she said, anger roiling under her tone.

Darien closed his eyes and did as she commanded. She pulled him forward with her under the arch. He followed, letting go of the magelight and allowing the chamber's natural darkness to settle in around them. He felt the transition as his feet stepped onto the marble foundation of the arch.

Then the whole chamber jolted and seemed suddenly to shift.

Bryn Calazar, The Black Lands

Darien staggered and almost fell, catching himself on the marble pillar of the portal itself. He turned in a confused circle, taking in the new surroundings that confronted them.

He was in a different room, somewhere completely dissimilar to the one he had just been standing in only moments before. This room was large and brightly lit by braziers and flaming torches. They were not alone. Darien's hand reached reflexively for his blade.

The cold prick of steel at his throat stopped his motion. Darien lowered his hand slowly, spreading his arms out at his sides. He could hear the thanacryst growl.

Azár stepped in front of him with a satisfied smirk.

"Peace," she said at last. "He's no threat."

The sword retracted. Darien reached up to rub at the spot where the blade had scored his neck. His thumb came away with a slight stain of blood. Azár frowned, studying the cut with cold and critical eyes.

"So, a demon can bleed," she commented.

Darien wiped the blood off onto his shirtsleeve, turning around to confront the man who had assailed him. He found himself staring up into the black-helmed face of an Enemy soldier wearing full battle plate. And the man was not alone. The room was ringed with them, at least a dozen plate-mailed guards. Darien felt a shiver of chill creep over him at the sight. The last time he had been surrounded by such men had been at his ill-fated parley with Zavier Renquist.

Azár motioned him forward away from the transfer portal. As he walked, Darien let his gaze rove over the room. Startled, he noticed that there were many of the cross-vaulted arches arranged in concentric rings. A few of the columns had collapsed, now only heaps of spilled rubble. He stared in wonder at the sight, understanding immediately the significance of what he was looking at. Each of the archways must be a portal to somewhere else, a transit system the ancients had once used. There had been nothing like it in Aerysius; such industry had been lost long ago.

There was a blinding flash of light. Blinking against the glare, Darien saw that Byron Connel and Nashir Arman had joined them in the chamber. With two more brilliant flashes, the rest of their party emerged. Zavier Renquist appeared last in a glimmering pool of light, striding behind the white-cloaked form of Cyrus Krane. He moved forward toward the center of the room as, all around him, plate-mailed bodies lowered to abase themselves upon the ground at the Prime Warden's feet.

"You may rise," Renquist commanded. "I must speak with the

grand vizier. Bring him to me at once."

There was a stir as two sentries ran out of the room to comply. Darien stood still, bringing a hand up to dab at his neck. The guards that ringed the room yet lingered at their stations with weapons drawn, blades held at ready across their chests, shields at their backs.

After minutes, the sound of marching feet echoed from above. A large retinue spilled down a flight of curving stairs: more plate-mailed bodies followed by men dressed in fine cloth. At the rear of the procession strode a bearded man dressed in embroidered robes and a tanned leather vest, a tall hat upon his head. The newcomers knelt before Renquist immediately upon their arrival in the chamber. Even the man in silk and leather dropped to his knees, pressing his forehead against the floor.

"Arise," the ancient Prime Warden greeted his servant.

The large man regained his feet, sweeping forward to embrace Renquist warmly, as one brother to another.

"Thank the gods you have returned! Honor and glory to you, Prime Warden." His voice was deep and throaty, with a thick accent that sounded nothing like Renquist's own. Darien realized the difference must be the result of the centuries that separated the two men.

Zavier Renquist smiled, returning the vizier's embrace. "Peace and blessings, Vizier Sarik. It is only through the sacrifice of the Asyaadi Lightweaver that our return to Malikar has been achieved. It is to him the honor and glory is owed."

The nobleman turned to regard Azár. "Peace to you, Lightweaver. I am Sarik Uthmar, Grand Vizier of the city-state of Bryn Calazar. I offer congratulations upon your ascendance."

To Darien's amazement, Azár looked down, lowering her gaze before the vizier. The young woman seemed humble, a state altogether out of character.

"Very kind of you, Vizier," she whispered, her voice full of humility.

Zavier Renquist stepped forward, draping his hand over the nobleman's broad shoulders as he pulled the man close. "Vizier Sarik. Perhaps you can help us with a difficult situation." He motioned to Darien, urging him forward.

Darien complied with a wary glance at the nearest guard. He strode across the room toward the two men, drawing to a halt before the Prime Warden.

Renquist indicated him with his hand. "Vizier Sarik, I present to you Darien Lauchlin of Amberlie, Aerysius' Last Sentinel. He is the newest of our Master's faithful Servants."

The bearded man's eyes narrowed at first, then widened slowly. "Prime Warden...are you saying this man is the self-same abomination who rained fiery death upon Malikar's legions?"

"The same."

Darien found it almost impossible to maintain eye contact with the man as the vizier leaned forward to peer directly into his face. The intensity of his stare was alarming, burning with the righteous fire of a zealot. Darien couldn't manage it. He dropped his gaze to his feet.

"*Ash'zeri!*" the man exclaimed under his breath. "Prime Warden, you have vanquished Malikar's greatest enemy and delivered him to our cause! There are no words to adequately express the greatness of your works!"

To Darien's dismay, the man's hands were suddenly upon him, taking him roughly by the shoulders. To his men, the vizier cried, "Light the braziers of the ziggurat and call forth the citizens of Bryn Calazar! This is a wonder that must be witnessed by all!"

The vizier turned to Renquist, lowering his voice to explain, "We must take great care in how we handle this, Prime Warden. The legend of Aerysius' Last Sentinel is steeped in horrors and atrocity. The people will demand his lifeblood to fuel our fires. We must bring him before the citizens of Bryn Calazar as a captured slave is brought before the master of the house. Even then, we risk revolt if we do not compensate blood for blood."

Darien stared hard at Renquist, his brow furrowed in concern. He mistrusted this bearded zealot. He was gravely troubled by the man's words.

"Very well." Zavier Renquist turned to face Darien, his face devoid of all expression. "I command you to bear what comes with shame and humility."

Darien understood. He lowered his eyes, a sinking feeling settling deeply into his gut. He swallowed against the sudden dryness in his throat.

"Aye, Prime Warden."

The vizier stepped forward, pointing down. "Kneel," he commanded.

Darien obeyed, dropping to his knees on the floor. He glanced at the demon-hound that suddenly stood growling with hackles raised, eyes glowing a menacing green.

"*Theanoch!*" he commanded it. The hound fell down on its belly with a whine, head between its paws.

Vizier Sarik gazed down at Darien from under his tall red hat. He was fat; his bearded cheeks were ripe, his lips puffy and puckered like a fish. Nevertheless, he was strong. He brought his arm back, forming his hand into a fist. With a grunt, he struck Darien across the face with all the strength and weight of his body.

Darien's head whiplashed around as blood sprayed from the force of the blow. Reeling, he almost fell over. He was caught and held upright by Azár's firm grasp on his shoulders. The vizier hit him again, this time from the other side. Darien leaned forward, spitting blood onto the ground in a thick stream that dribbled from his chin.

The vizier leaned forward, hovering close over Darien's head. In a deathly calm voice, he explained, "That is for the blood of Malikar's sons and daughters you spilled upon the ground. Strip to your waist."

Darien had no choice but to comply. He shrugged out of the baldric, laying his longsword down on the floor at his side. With trembling hands, he removed his black cloak and stripped his shirt off over his head. Those, he let fall to the ground around him.

"Bind him," the vizier ordered his men.

Darien did not resist as two mailed bodies swept forward, one holding him securely as the other tied his wrists together in front of him with a woven cord.

"Let his blood flow," the vizier whispered.

Darien closed his eyes and cringed as the blows began to fall. One man beat him with a coiled rope, the other with a gauntleted fist. Another man joined in, kicking him several times in the ribs. Darien fell to the floor, drawing his knees up to his chest.

"Enough!"

The soldiers withdrew. Darien rolled onto his back, chest heaving, his whole body shaking and wet, glistening with a slick sheen of blood and sweat. A sharp pain stabbed at his side with every drawn breath.

"Stand, Darien Lauchlin, last of the fallen Sentinels," the vizier commanded.

He could do nothing but obey. Trembling, Darien rose unsteadily to his knees and then, staggering, to his feet. Blood ran from wounds on his back, arms, and head. His lip was split, his left eye throbbing. He caught a glimpse of Nashir's satisfied smirk. Darien glared at the darkmage with smoldering hatred in his eyes.

The vizier stood in front of Darien, placing his enormous hands on Darien's shoulders. Then, leaning forward, he pressed a kiss against first Darien's right cheek and then his left.

"That is for the grace and mercy Xerys has shown you," he said, drawing back. To the guards, he commanded, "Collar him as a slave is collared."

An armored man came forward and wrapped a supple cord around his neck, tying it with a slipknot attached to a length of rope. This he offered to the vizier.

Sarik shook his head. With a finger, he indicated Azár. The black-helmed guardsman strode over to the girl and placed Darien's lead into her hand. Azár accepted the rope gravely, allowing her gaze to travel up its length toward the collar, her eyes progressing upward to Darien's face. He expected her to sneer at him again as she had before. To Azár's credit, she did not.

Darien lowered his head. His eye was already beginning to swell. He could have healed it in a heartbeat. He dared not.

Vizier Sarik informed him, "You will be presented to the citizens of Bryn Calazar as one who is utterly vanquished, defeated in body as well as spirit. You must submit yourself before the populace in shame. This is necessary. You can show no amount of pride or resistance. Do you understand what is expected of you?"

Darien could only nod, still staring at the ground. His mouth was once again filling with blood. This time he swallowed it, gritting his teeth against the taste. He noticed Azár studying him closely. He felt discomfited by her cold, unfeeling eyes.

"Whenever you are ready, Prime Warden," the vizier announced.

"By all means. Lead the way."

Renquist's words were spoken with dispassionate authority. He stooped to retrieve Darien's sword from off the ground. He held the scabbard up in his hands, clutching the weapon in front of him. He turned it slightly, allowing the rubies to catch the fire of the torchlight. Then, followed by the others, the ancient Prime Warden strode out of the chamber.

Darien was made to follow at the rear of their small procession, Azár leading him by the rope. She did not tug at his collar. Instead, she commanded him forward with the cold authority of her eyes. Darien followed her lead; he had no choice. The thanacryst trailed behind, nose to the ground, tail tucked between its legs.

Black-armored guards fell in behind. He was led out of the chamber of portals into a rock-encrusted hallway that seemed to stretch a very long distance ahead. Darien limped forward, favoring his right leg. His side pained him with each breath. He despised what they were doing, even as he understood the necessity. This was still part of his atonement, just like the other tortures he'd already been forced to endure. He would bear this one, as well.

After minutes of walking, they emerged from a cliff side into the thick darkness of night. There, they paused on a high terrace overlooking the city of Bryn Calazar. The smell of the night air assaulted Darien's nostrils. It had a hideous odor, thick and acrid, like black smoke from a forge. Darien tried to catch a glimpse of the city below through the press of bodies that surrounded him.

He could see nothing. He moved forward, pulling the leash taught as he leaned over the edge of a crumbling balustrade.

The view below was chilling.

Darkness encased the city, but it was not the natural darkness of night. It was like the blackness that consumed the Shadowspears and the Pass of Lor-Gamorth. The ancient curse that had blackened the skies above Caladorn so long ago. Overhead, a cold and angry wind propelled a thick bank of cloudcover across the sky, tumbling and churning like the foaming froth of an ocean. Sheet lightning flickered from deep within that roiling mass. With a shiver of dismay, Darien realized he was gazing out across the corrupted heart of the Black Lands. And it was more thoroughly despoiled than he had ever imagined.

Sprawling outward to the distant horizon, the city of Bryn Calazar was revealed before him in all its tortured desecration. Thick plumes of smoke billowed over the city, fed by fires that seemed to burn everywhere. The smoke had a foul and oily taste to it, thick and bitter. The structures resembled distorted honeycombs, built of successive layers, one atop the other, dark walls haphazardly thrown up at odd angles. The roads were paved with tar and lined by great, snakelike clusters of pipes that twined and coiled about the twisted heart of the city. The heavens wept hot tears of ash that drifted softly to the ground, wafting from the skies like despoiled snow.

Darien stared open-mouthed at the sight, struggling to come to terms with the terrible *wrongness* of it. There was nothing left; all trace of nature had been either corrupted or consumed. This was not civilization, he realized.

This was hell.

A tug on his leash pulled Darien away from the edge of the terrace. Still, he couldn't tear his eyes away from the vision of the repulsive city below. He stared down the side of the cliff, out across the dark waters of an ocean that seemed to bleed thick streaks of oil from its tides. In the harbor, iron-clad ships rode at their moors.

Eyes wide, he turned in horror to Azár.

"Maybe, now, you understand," she snarled, twisting the length of his leash once about her hand. With a sharp tug, she jerked him forward after her as the others started moving.

Darien struggled to keep up with her brisk strides, gasping at the pain that flared in his side with every step. The road they traveled led down and off the hillside, out into the tar-paved streets of the city. There, the citizens of Bryn Calazar had gathered to line the boulevard ahead.

At the sight of their approaching party, a tremendous cry was raised from the assembled masses. People came running, flooding in from the side-streets, jostling and vying for a better view of their Prime Warden's entourage. For the first time in his life, Darien had an unobstructed view of the inhabitants of the Black Lands. A people who, before, he had only known collectively as the Enemy.

They were people, just as he had always known they'd be. He had seen their dead, questioned their prisoners. Azár was the first Enemy that Darien had actually ever spoken with except under condition of duress.

Before him, bobbing and shoving like a roiling mass that bristled with thin arms and bulbous knees, was a population of starving, indigent, and yet jubilant people. They were clothed in filthy rags darkened by years of soil and ash. Most wore scarves tied over their mouths and noses, exposing only their eyes. Eyes that peered out through skin obscured by soot and grime. They were screaming, bellowing, waving weapons or brandishing oil-soaked torches in the air.

On the left, a fight broke out over a coveted viewing spot. The instigator was quickly put down with a sword through his chest. Two other men surged forward, ostensibly to avenge the loser, but ended up suffering the same fate. Their bodies were left lying in the street, trampled over by the crowds that just kept gushing in from outlying districts.

Black-armored bodies with weapons drawn and shields raised rushed forward to contain the surging masses. The throng was pushed back, clearing a path for the Prime Warden's party to pass. The crowds cheered, the sound an explosive thunder as their entourage gained the level of the street.

Darien tripped, almost falling as he struggled to keep up with Azár's ruthless pace. The pain in his side was worsening, and his wounds ached from the salty sweat that streaked his body. His left eye was now thoroughly swollen shut. He staggered, Azár jerking him forward with a tug on his lead.

Something grazed the back of his head. Another object hit him hard between the shoulder blades. Darien whirled, sweat spraying from his forehead, to find that a group of men were picking apart the street to gather rocks to assault him with.

Their party turned, mounting a long flight of stairs that rose above the level of the city. The steps led up a tall, terraced structure to what looked like a temple far above. The ramp of stairs was lined with copper braziers that lit their path, spewing choking, caustic smoke and sparks into the air. Darien ducked as a rock streaked by, nearly hitting him in the head.

They rose ever upward above the city, the stairs a relentless, unbroken rise to the top of the terraced structure. Upon gaining the summit, their party came to a halt beneath the portico of a marble temple. There, Zavier Renquist and his Servants assembled together in a single line. The two Prime Wardens, Renquist and Cyrus Krane, stood at the center. Byron Connel and Nashir Arman stood together to Renquist's right. Myria Anassis took her place to the left of Cyrus Krane. Before them lingered Azár, still holding tight to Darien's leash, and Vizier Sarik, standing before them all with arms raised over his head.

Gradually, the crowds quieted. Silence descended upon the city as the grand vizier stepped forward to announce:

"People of Bryn Calazar, by the grace of Xerys, His Chosen Servants have been restored to us once again! *Ishil'zeri!*"

To Darien's amazement, the entire gathered population dropped to the ground as one, abasing themselves before the ancient darkmages. They remained on their knees for seconds. Then, together as one, the masses rose collectively again to their feet.

Darien stared with a mixture of awe and dismay at the sight, having no reference at all in which to frame it.

"Citizens of Bryn Calazar, Prime Warden Zavier Renquist presents to you his prisoner, his man-slave, his spoil of war." The vizier raised his hand, indicating Darien. "Before you stands the defiled Last Sentinel of Aerysius, Darien Lauchlin of Amberlie, vanquished by Prime Warden Renquist's own hand!"

There was a tremendous outcry from the crowd below as the mob surged against the restraint of the guards. People brandished torches and weapons. Spears were hurled into the sky, landing far below on the long rise of steps. Darien could almost feel the scalding hatred of the populace that was directed toward him. He stepped back, face slack with dismay.

The vizier told him, "Turn and abase yourself before the people."

Darien didn't hesitate. He went instantly to his knees, bending over until his forehead touched the ground. He could hear the timbre of the crowd instantly change as the result of his action. Once again, the voice of the masses rose in exuberant jubilation. People blew horns, beat weapons against shields, stomped at the ground with their feet. The thunder of their outcry was deafening.

The vizier had to shout to be heard over the cacophony:

"Now abase yourself before your Prime Warden!"

Darien obeyed. He rose first to his knees and then to his feet, staring down with trepidation at the raucous crowd. Then he turned and faced Zavier Renquist. Once again, he dropped to his knees and bent forward until his long hair was spread out on the ground beside his face.

The sound of the crowd climaxed, the furor terrifying.

Darien remained in that position, trembling, sweat mingled with blood dribbling off his chin.

"Rise," the Prime Warden commanded.

Darien obeyed, heaving his weight up off the ground despite the stabbing pain in his ribs. He gazed into Zavier Renquist's face with his one good eye. He was surprised to find that there was no trace of malice in the Prime Warden's expression.

Darien saw that Zavier Renquist was still holding his own sword. His hand moved to close around the hilt, drawing the blade forth from its scabbard. The ancient darkmage held Darien's sword aloft over his head, rotating it slightly, allowing the steel to catch the light of the braziers' flames.

Then he lowered it until the blade was level with Darien's heart. Face expressionless, he drew a slice across his chest.

Renquist turned the sword in his hand, bathing the flat of the blade in the blood that welled from the cut. He turned the sword around, liberally wetting the other side. Then he brought the weapon up next to his face, caressing the melded folds of steel with his hand, using his palm to ritually wash the blade with the blood of its master.

Accepting the scabbard back from Connel, Zavier Renquist resheathed the purified steel. To the vizier, he gave a slight nod.

Vizier Sarik stepped forward and stoically removed the rope and collar from around Darien's neck, unbinding his hands. There was a quiet rustle behind him. Suddenly, a mass of fabric was being lowered over his shoulders, pulled down over his body. Someone drew the cloth over his breeches, arranging it about his feet. Darien spread his hands, gazing down at his new garments with an acute feeling of trepidation.

They had vested him in the formal indigo robes of the Lyceum of Bryn Calazar, the Silver Star emblazoned over his heart.

The taste of bile rose in his throat. Darien choked, swallowing against it.

Zavier Renquist offered out his hand. The expression on his face was merciful. "Please. Take your place at my side."

He gestured to his right.

Darien looked down once again at his chest, at the emblem of the Silver Star, at the small stain of his own blood that was quickly spreading across the fabric. Then he glanced up into the Prime Warden's expectant face. He looked to Nashir, at the malevolent sneer on the man's lips.

In a dim haze of confusion and pain, Darien Lauchlin moved forward and fell into line beside Nashir, assuming his place in the line of Servants. Below, in the streets, the crowd erupted into a thunderous din.

Vizier Sarik strode forward, hands in the air, waving the

pandemonium into silence. It took a moment. But, slowly, an ominous quiet stole over the city of Bryn Calazar. Into that gaping space the vizier proclaimed:

"Let it be known throughout the lands that Darien Lauchlin of Amberlie, the Last Sentinel of Aerysius, has sworn allegiance to Xerys, God of Chaos and Lord of the Netherworld! His service has been accepted by Prime Warden Renquist and the Citizens of Bryn Calazar! Let the people of the Rhen tremble and despair, for their savior has returned to become their subjugator!"

Chapter Six
Enemy or Ally

Rothscard, The Rhen

Kyel stared down into the reposed face of Sareen Qadir. Her flesh had not yet taken on the cold pallor of death. Instead, her face was still a warm bronze, an alluring combination taken together with the dark sheen of her hair. The only woman Kyel had ever seen who might be capable of rivaling her in beauty had been Arden Hannah, the seductive darkmage Darien had slain at Orien's Finger. But while Arden's allure had been diminished by her cruelty, any evil kept locked within Sareen's heart had never had a chance to reveal itself. Her beauty remained untainted by the corruption within.

Kyel didn't trust it.

Naia had lain her out upon a table, composing Sareen's limbs and arranging her robes about her body. The fatal wound to her chest had been tended and wrapped to prevent seepage. Naia was still lingering over the corpse, making small adjustments here and there, like an artist obsessing over the perfection of her craft. Naia had once been in the business of ministering to the dead, and it seemed that she had forgotten little of her art. She tended to Sareen with all the care she would have shown a sister.

"Has there been any word?" Naia asked.

Kyel shook his head, still gazing warily at the corpse. "Nothing." He wished he had better news to report. "There's no trace of either of them."

Naia muttered, "I pray to the gods that she's safe."

Kyel gestured down at the body. "What of her?"

"Oh, she's very much dead," Naia assured him, plucking a fiber of lint off Sareen's indigo robe. "I suspect it's probably not the first time."

She reached down and took a folded sheet of linen into her hands. Carefully unfurling the cloth over the body, she drew it up to cover the whole of the corpse. The shroud was thin and did a rather poor job of concealing what lay beneath. Sareen's outline was still very visible in silhouette.

It was strange how such evil could be concealed behind such a pleasing façade. It was a shame, really. The woman hadn't *seemed* all that bad. Not like the man who had accompanied her. Quinlan Reis had projected an inherent aura of cunning and threat that had chilled Kyel's blood. He had sensed no such menace coming from Sareen.

"What do we do with her?" he wondered.

Naia responded, "Prince Nigel is correct. We need to burn this corpse."

"Why burn it?"

Naia glanced up at him, her hand going to correct the drape of the shroud over Sareen's face. "Do you know why the Enemy always executed our mages by ritual immolation?"

Kyel frowned, disturbed by Naia's mention of the practice. He had been witness to one such gruesome act. When Arden Hannah had tried to burn Darien alive. "I suppose I really hadn't thought about it."

"Well, there are two reasons. First, so that the mage's gift could not be Transferred upon death to another. But there was more to it than just that. It was also to make certain their soul could never be reunited with their body."

"So, there's some chance that this woman could actually come back to life?"

"She is a Servant of Xerys," Naia reminded him. "That dark god wields enough power to part the veil of death. I'd rather not take the chance."

Kyel nodded, reaching up to scratch the growth of beard on his face.

"Unless..." Naia whispered.

Kyel glanced up at her. "Unless what?"

She turned toward him, eyes suddenly bright with intensity. "If Quinlan Reis is responsible for Meiran's disappearance, then this woman is likely dead because she tried to stop him. Sareen was sent to bring Meiran to meet with Renquist. What if Reis abducted Meiran to foil that plan?"

Kyel raised his hands. "Why would he do that?"

"I don't know. But Sareen is dead, and Meiran is missing. I doubt that's coincidence."

Kyel warily considered the draped body. "That still doesn't make Sareen our ally."

"Perhaps not. But there's a good chance she knows what happened to Meiran. And she may be willing to help us get her back."

"For all we know, Meiran could have left of her own accord," Kyel argued.

"Without getting word to us? What is the chance of that?"

Kyel turned to confront her. "My point is this: we know *nothing*. All we have is conjecture. The one thing we *do* know for certain is that this woman is extremely dangerous. If she comes back to life and decides to murder us, there's precious little we could do to stop her." He swallowed, his throat suddenly tight with sorrow. "And besides. There's a good chance Meiran's not coming back. Quinlan Reis probably killed her, too."

"But we don't *know.*" Glancing at the corpse, Naia whispered, "What if we could bring her back?"

"Bring her back?" he echoed, incredulous. "And what happens if we do manage to 'bring her back?' How could we guarantee our safety? She's Unbound, Naia! And we are not."

"We could take her to the Catacombs," Naia pressed. "Her body will not decay, and there are plenty of spots where the magic field is highly unstable. We would have to obtain permission, of course. I'd have to ask my father…"

Kyel shot her a questioning glare. "I thought you weren't on speaking terms. Has he ever forgiven you?"

Naia's father was the High Priest of Death. Naia had once been a priestess, her father's own chosen successor. But that was before she'd abandoned her duties for Darien…before she'd inherited his legacy of power.

"I never gave my father the *opportunity* to forgive me," Naia admitted, her gaze cast downward at the floor. Kyel nodded, understanding. He had been confronted once by Luther Penthos himself. The man could be quite intimidating.

"All right, then," he decided. "What do we do?"

"You stay with her," Naia said, starting toward the doorway. "I'll head to the Temple of Death and inform them there's a cadaver in need of attention."

She brought her hands up, drawing the cowl of her cloak over her head.

Kyel stared after Naia even after she was gone from the doorway.

Then he pulled up a chair, spinning it around and straddling the seat with his arms draped over the back, cradling his chin. He sat there, gazing down at the contours of the body beneath the drape.

He still didn't trust it.

It seemed to take Naia an awful long time to return. Kyel wasn't certain how many hours it was since she'd left. He had dozed off over the back of the chair, losing all track of time. He hadn't gotten any sleep the night before, and the exhaustion had caught up with him. He startled awake at the sound of the door opening, blearily rubbing his eyes.

Naia entered the room, drawing back her cowl. Behind her followed a man dressed all in white robes with a stole draped over his shoulders. His fine, pale hair hung in limp strands to the middle of his back. He drew behind him a long cart with a curved wooden handle. The man leaned the handle up against the doorframe, leaving the cart behind in the hall.

Naia gestured with her hand. "Brother Carol, please allow me to introduce Kyel Archer of the Order of Sentinels. Grand Master Kyel, this is Brother Carol Desmond of the Temple of Death."

The pale priest of Death strode forward with a loathsome

smile, clasping Kyel's offered hand. "Such an honor, Great Master." The touch of his eyes seemed tentative, as if not wishing to linger on Kyel's face. Instead, his attention was drawn rapidly downward to the corpse. He studied the outline of Sareen's body under the shroud with professional detachment.

"Thank you for coming, Brother Carol," Kyel responded, releasing the man's clammy hand.

"My condolences on your loss," the priest muttered. He reached down and drew the shroud back to reveal Sareen's face. He stood over her, his face devoid of expression. After a moment, he replaced the shroud, reverently smoothing the fabric's drape.

Naia said, "Condolences are unnecessary, Brother. This woman was no friend of ours."

The man seemed taken aback. "Pardon, but where is the deceased's next of kin?"

Naia shook her head. "She doesn't have any next of kin. Look, Brother. This is not your typical corpse. I apologize, but I am really not at liberty to explain. I need to beg a favor of you on a highly delicate matter. I need these remains transported to the High Temple in Glen Farquist. The Grand Master and I will be accompanying you through the Catacombs. We must seek the advice of my father."

The priest of Death appeared exceptionally concerned by this revelation. He gazed at Naia with a look of confusion, slender fingers cupping his chin. "I'm sorry, Great Lady, but what you ask is…irregular, to say the least."

Naia clasped her hands, squaring her shoulders formally. "Believe me, Brother Carol. This corpse merits such irregularities. Now, pray, don't push me further. As representatives of the Hall, I demand our right of passage through the Catacombs."

Hearing her words, the young priest's face hardened. "Such a demand can only be issued by the Prime Warden herself."

Naia's stare wandered as if internally grasping at straws. Somehow, her eyes ended up on Kyel. "The Prime Warden would ask you herself, were she here. Unfortunately, she's taken a leave of absence. Grand Master Kyel is acting in her stead."

Kyel shot Naia a look of alarm. "Now, hold on just one moment! We haven't discussed this!"

The pale priest blurted out, "Has something happened to the Prime Warden?"

Naia raised her hand, drawing in a long-suffering breath. "Brother Carol. Please. Help us get this corpse to Glen Farquist. As you can probably tell, our need is quite dire."

Brother Carol looked even paler now than he had upon arrival. His face was grimly set, thin lips pressed together in consternation. "Yes. Yes, of course. Please, if you will excuse me, I must make a few ministrations before the body can be transported."

But Naia shook her head. "Hold off on any ministrations, Brother. This corpse must be left pristine."

The man's frown deepened considerably. "That is...inadvisable. But it will be as you say, Great Lady."

He moved toward the door and grasped the handle of the cart he had left there, pulling it forward into the room. Kyel realized immediately what the contraption was: a wheeled bier, crafted of wood with the purpose of transporting the dead to the temple.

Brother Carol cautioned, "We'll have to handle her carefully. She must be kept as level as possible. I'll need your help."

Kyel felt a pang of queasiness in his gut. The sudden thought of body fluids made his stomach twist into knots. He stepped forward, regardless.

"Thank you, Great Master," the priest muttered. "I'll take the head if you take the legs."

Kyel swallowed, feeling suddenly rather ill.

Chapter Seven
Daffodils in Winter

Emmery, The Rhen

Meiran Withersby glanced over at the silent darkmage who rode at her side and felt suddenly very afraid. She wasn't afraid for herself. She had given up long ago on the delusion that her life would ever be peaceful or fulfilling. Everything important to her had already been cut away, severed and cast down the Well of Tears. The man riding next to her on his shaggy horse was just another reminder of how desolate her life had actually become.

The sun was at their backs, filtering down through a dense, white blanket of haze. Meiran loosened the coarsely woven shawl she wore over her shoulders. She had purchased the shawl from a peddler on their way out of the city. Her white cloak of office she'd left in the guest room back at the palace. In the thick winter garments of a peasant, Meiran knew that few would be able to recognize her. Only the chains on her wrists might identify her, and only then to a very observant eye.

"So where, exactly, are you taking me?" she asked of her silent companion. Quinlan Reis hadn't spoken so much as a word since they'd left the city gates. Meiran reached down and patted the neck of the brown mare she was riding. The horse snorted and twitched its hide beneath her touch as if shaking off flies.

"I'm taking you to Malikar. What you know as the Black Lands," the somber darkmage answered without looking at her.

Meiran peered over at him skeptically. "Then aren't we heading in the wrong direction?"

"We're not riding all the way to the Khazahar, Prime Warden.

Especially not in this intolerable contraption." The man gestured down, indicating the leather saddle beneath him with a grimace of distaste. "Believe me, I've endured enough torments already. I'd rather not have to suffer any more."

Meiran raised her eyebrows. So, either the man wasn't familiar with horses or was more practiced at riding bareback. She suspected the former. Although, in the case of Quinlan Reis, anything was possible.

She gazed openly into his chiseled, almost skeletal face. Meiran couldn't help herself; she found the darkmage fascinating. For one thing, Quinlan Reis was from a time and place that no longer existed in the world. His skin was olive, darker in pigment than any person Meiran had ever met. His features were distinctly different, foreign, and yet somehow vaguely familiar. He might have been rather handsome if he weren't so terribly gaunt.

"Then, where *are* we riding?" she demanded.

The man shrugged. "We're riding to the nearest transfer portal. From there we'll transfer north to the Black Lands. After that, we'll have to walk a fair distance to get to where we're going. I'm afraid we can't take the horses."

Meiran was intrigued. "What is a transfer portal?"

The man's eyes snapped wide open, clearly astounded by her question. "Why, Prime Warden, how is it possible that you're so thoroughly unenlightened?" Shaking his head, he flashed her a scornful grin. "Upon second thought, perhaps I shouldn't be all that surprised. I'm likely the reason you're so grossly ill-informed."

Meiran opened her mouth to respond but closed it again quickly. His reaction shocked her. On the surface, Quinlan Reis seemed nothing more than a sardonic, self-absorbed ass. But there was far more to it than that, Meiran was starting to realize. She was beginning to wonder just how far Quin's egotism went. And what flaws it had been cultivated to mask.

"Was that supposed to be some kind of answer? Or are you trying to be purposely evasive?"

The darkmage managed to smile through a sneer. "In my time, there was an entire transit portal system. Unfortunately, I destroyed the Portal Chamber beneath Aerysius, which, actually, does explain your ignorance. Without that hub, most of the Rhen's satellite portals would have stopped working."

Meiran raised her eyebrows, absorbing this new information in silence. She was uncertain which she found more intriguing: the existence of a lost technology that surpassed any wonder she'd ever heard of, or the knowledge that her newfound companion was the person responsible for its loss.

She demanded, "Where is this portal?"

Quinlan nodded ahead of them, gazing down the empty path. "A few hours' ride to the west of here."

Meiran stared at him hard, speculating on the scale of destruction this man had wrought in his lifetime. "Tell me," she pressed. "What made you choose to become a Servant of Xerys?"

Quinlan Reis frowned, twin lines etching themselves deeply across the bridge of his nose. He lifted his hat and stroked his hand back through his hair. "My brother and I sought to defy Renquist," he answered, replacing his hat and adjusting the brim. "We were captured. Things didn't go so very well, as you can probably imagine. Renquist can be…persuasive…when he wants to be. My brother refused him and was put to death. Suffice it to say that I lacked that kind of courage."

"I'm very sorry," Meiran said. "About your brother, I mean."

The darkmage scowled. "There's nothing for you to feel sorry about. Braden died a thousand years ago. As much as it pains me to admit it, I can't remember what he even looked like." His scowl deepened, the shadows sculpting his gaunt face.

"What was he like?"

He drew in a slow breath, his mouth screwed into a grimace. "Braden was a man of integrity. Not like me." He shook his head sadly. "I've never had one scrap of honor."

She gazed at him for a long moment, waiting to see if there was any more insight forthcoming. But Quinlan Reis bowed his head, slouching in the saddle as his gaze drifted downward to the ground.

Meiran's mind wandered back to the events of the previous

evening. When she had stood in her guest room in Emmery Palace, attempting to gauge this same man's character.

As soon as the door had closed, Meiran spun back around to confront the darkmage.

"You've got one minute. Start talking."

Quinlan Reis responded with a gushing torrent of words. "Darien sent me. Well, Renquist sent me—but I'm really here for Darien. He needs you to—"

"You have fifty seconds. Start making sense."

"I'm trying! It's complicated." He was starting to look angry. Frustrated.

"Forty-five seconds."

He threw up his hands. "My people—you know them as the Enemy—they're all going to die unless you can help us escape the Black Lands."

"Why is that?" Meiran demanded.

"Because the magic field is going to reverse in polarity. We tried to stop it before, but all we really did was put it off for a thousand years. When the Reversal finally does happen, every person living north of the Shadowspears is going to die."

Meiran scowled. "Thirty seconds. Why?"

"The light is going to go out," he growled. "Without light, there will be no crops. Without crops, there will be no food. Everyone in Malikar is going to starve to death if we can't escape the darkness."

Meiran contemplated his words. "What does Renquist want?"

"He wants to deliver his people, Meiran. That's all. Renquist is leading a nation of refugees who, for a thousand years, have wanted nothing more than to simply escape the Black Lands."

But that wasn't true. Quinlan Reis was lying, at least about this.

"They've never come to us as refugees," Meiran argued. "Always, they have come as invaders. As conquerors. Never once have your people ever laid down their arms and thrown themselves on our mercy."

He sighed. "Well...there's a catch."

"What's the catch?"

"Xerys is the catch. If we come, the Dark God comes with us. It's part of the covenant we made a thousand years ago. If we use the Hellpower to stabilize the magic field, then we must remain His servants. We can be subject to no laws but His own."

"I see," Meiran muttered. "Thank you, Quinlan, for your honesty. What does Darien have to say about all this?"

"Darien has a lot to say, actually. But he wants to say it to you himself. In person. Not through me. Will you come with me and hear him out?"

Meiran shook her head, not trusting this man at all. "I'll think on it."

"Unfortunately, you don't have time to think on it. We have to go. Now. Without telling anyone where we're going. You can trust me, Meiran. I'll take you to Darien."

"Why?" she demanded. "Why do we have to leave here with such urgency? Why can't this wait till the morrow?"

"Because I just killed Sareen."

Meiran gasped, her eyes growing wide.

Relentless, Quinlan Reis continued, "Renquist wanted to use you to guarantee Darien's allegiance. Sareen was part of that plan. But when Renquist finds out what I've done, he's going to come looking for us. We can't tell anyone where we're going. If they know, they'll be made to talk. It'll go worse for them. And worse for us."

Meiran was reeling. If he spoke the truth, then they were all in terrible danger.

"I don't trust you," she whispered.

"You don't have to trust me," he asserted. "Trust Darien. You read his note. If you don't come with me then you'll all be executed. They'll show you no mercy, Meiran. Renquist's legions will march over the Rhen, conquering and subjugating everyone in their path. Darien and I won't be able to do a damned thing to stop any of it."

Meiran didn't trust Quinlan Reis at all. But she did trust Darien. She couldn't help it, even though he had given her every reason in the world not to. Meiran existed in a state of flux, caught

73

somewhere between abhorrence and guilt. Hating him while blaming herself. It was a horrendous place to be.

"I can't just leave!" she exclaimed. "I have to tell Kyel and Naia. I have to warn them. If what you say is true, then their lives are in grave danger!"

"They can know nothing!" he insisted with a feverish heat in his eyes.

Trembling, Meiran scooped up Darien's letter into her hand. She bent to retrieve her pack off the floor, shoving the scroll inside. She moved to the wardrobe, stuffing her white cloak deep within.

"Gods damn you both!" she swore at Quinlan Reis as she stalked toward the door.

The darkmage glared at her with a wounded expression. "Well, isn't that just original."

They rode in silence for a very long time. Meiran occupied herself by keeping track of the vegetation that grew on either side of the rutted roadway. The valley was aglow with an unseasonal supply of yellow daffodils. Meiran frowned at the sight of the cheerful blossoms dancing on the breeze, hundreds of them. The sight brought back a half-remembered saying from her youth: 'Daffodils in winter herald misery in spring.' Considering their present set of circumstances, Meiran found the sight of the joyful flowers full of ominous portent.

She turned and inquired of her companion, "So, tell me, Quinlan. If you've never had any honor, then why does Darien trust you?"

The acerbic darkmage took the reins of his horse together in his left hand. With his other hand, he reached down and brought a water skin up to his lips, taking a long, thirsty sip. He wiped his mouth on his sleeve before answering her.

"There's an old proverb," he explained. "I suppose it's now an ancient proverb. Translated, it would go something like this: 'I and my brother against my cousin. My cousin and I against the world.'"

Meiran contemplated his words carefully, trying to get a sense of their meaning.

Noticing her struggle, Quinlan elaborated, "I grew up in a tribal society. In Caladorn, loyalty was always kinship-based. Immediate family comes first, then extended family. Then clan." Meiran nodded slowly. "I think I understand. But what does that have to do with Darien's trust in you?"

Quin shot a sad smile in her direction. "Because Darien's mother was born Emelda Clemley, daughter of Lester Clemley. She descends in a direct line from Prime Warden Sephana Clemley and my own brother, Braden Reis. So that makes Darien and I very distant kin. In truth, he's the closest thing to family I have left in the entire world."

Meiran gaped at Quinlan Reis in shock. "You're serious, aren't you?" she whispered, not sure whether she should be feeling more awed or appalled.

"I'm afraid so," he muttered. "I am sworn to the service of Xerys. But, after that, my loyalty is to Darien. Even ahead of Renquist."

Meiran stared back down at the worn road, her eyes wandering to the nearest clump of daffodils. The bright yellow flowers bobbed their heads in the breeze. Meiran considered them joylessly. The sight filled her only with melancholy.

They travelled in silence for the remainder of the day. At sunset, they arrived at a place where the road curved around a sharp rock spur that ambled up into the high country toward the Craghorns. There, they turned their horses off the road. It was already getting dark, the sun shedding its last light over the ridge in front of them. Quinlan nodded ahead with his chin.

"The transfer portal is up this way."

With that, he climbed down off his mount. He staggered as his shoe caught in the stirrup. While he struggled to free it, Quinlan's gelding continued walking forward. He reached out and took the horse by the bridle, forcing its head around and pulling the animal firmly to a halt against his chest. The gelding stamped its hoof in protest as Quin managed to reclaim his foot.

"Whoever invented such a contraption obviously knew

nothing of horsemanship," he muttered testily, claiming his pack and sword from the saddle. He turned back to Meiran, face expectant. "Are you coming, Prime Warden? It's starting to get dark. Better say your farewells to the sun while you still can. You won't be seeing it again for a long time."

He loosened the horse's girth strap and lifted the saddle off its back. He removed the blanket, stroking the beast's damp fur with the palm of his hand. Then he slipped the bridle over the horse's ears and off its head. With a slap on the rump, he set the animal free. The shaggy horse sprinted forward, head and tail carried high.

Meiran reached the ground with much more grace and set immediately about the task of liberating her own mount. She glanced back at Quinlan as she uncinched the saddle's girth.

"What do we do if this transfer portal doesn't work?" she asked.

"It will work," he assured her, adjusting his hat. "It's one of the portals tied in with the Bryn Calazar hub." He shouldered his pack and fixed his sword's scabbard to his belt.

Meiran turned her horse loose and watched the mare trot away. Standing there with her pack, she glanced sideways at Quinlan Reis. For the first time, she noticed the intricate artistry of the belt he wore at his waist. It had a large golden buckle that was worked into the image of a horse bent over backwards. It was a beautiful piece that had the look of something from antiquity.

"Your belt," she stated, nodding toward it. "What type of craftsmanship is it?"

Quinlan glanced down at the buckle, running his hand across the body of the golden stallion. "Omeyan," he answered. "My family's clan. This was my brother's warbelt."

Meiran admired the belt, noticing the small collection of implements and sacks that hung from the worked leather. "It's beautiful," she told him sincerely. Her eyes went to the weapon that hung at his side.

"Your sword. Show me?"

Quinlan shrugged, drawing the curved blade from its scabbard and offering it up to Meiran with both hands. She didn't accept it. Instead, she examined the blade as he held it up in front of her. Reaching out, she touched the thin scimitar with her hand, letting her fingers trace the carved elegance of the sword's ivory hilt.

"It's a masterwork," she commented. "I've never seen anything like it before."

"Nor shall you ever again," Quinlan Reis smiled. "Zanikar is the only one of its kind."

Meiran nodded in appreciation. "Where did you come by such a weapon?"

"I forged it."

Meiran blinked. She crossed her arms over her chest. "*You* forged it? Quinlan Reis, are you an Arcanist?"

"I was," Quinlan responded as he slid Zanikar back into its scabbard. "A long time ago. Not anymore."

"What are you now?" Meiran whispered, almost afraid to hear his response.

"Now?" Quinlan shrugged, looking down at the ground at his feet. "Now I'm just a demon. The only thing I create anymore is pain."

Chapter Eight
Ignoble Protector

Bryn Calazar, The Black Lands

Darien sat on the edge of the bed and gazed blearily around at the stark confines of the guest room they had provided him. The walls were made of baked mud bricks, as black as the scorched earth they had been molded from. There were no wood furnishings anywhere, not even a door. The bed itself was little more than a straw-stuffed sack covered by a thin blanket with a pillow thrown on top. A granite stand set against one of the walls supported a beaten copper washbowl and ewer. There were no rugs or carpets, no tapestries of any kind. A clay oil lamp rested on the floor in a corner. It produced a softly glowing flame, the only source of light in the room. The indigo robes they had given him lay in a wad on the floor where he'd thrown them down.

Darien stood, pushing himself up slowly with a grimace of pain, and wandered over to the washstand. There, he leaned over, gripping the edge of the cold stone surface with his hands, stretching out the aching muscles of his back. His hands and arms were caked with dried layers of blood.

At least there was water in the ewer. Darien poured it into the copper bowl and dipped his hands in, scrubbing them together vigorously. He continued the motion up his scarred wrists, cupping his hand to scoop the water onto the backs of his arms. He worked the crusted blood into a lather, smearing it around more than actually washing it off.

"May I come in?"

Darien started, flinching at the sound of the voice. Since there was no door, the bedchamber was defined only by a curtain made of strands of beads that hung across the room's entrance. Through that thin drape, he could make out the serene features of Myria Anassis.

Darien glanced down at himself. He stood clothed only in blood and bruises from the waist up. His arms were dripping fouled water onto the dark bricks of the floor. He was in no shape to receive company.

There was a soft tinkle as Myria's hand parted the drape of beads enough to peer inside. From the corner of the room, the thanacryst growled.

"*Theanoch,*" Darien commanded it, wiping his hands on the wool of his breeches. The beast went immediately silent, resting its jowls on its paws.

"I hope it's not a bad time?" Myria asked, pushing toward him through the veil of beads. She had changed clothes, he noticed. She was now wearing a simple but elegant shift woven of raw linen. Her raven hair hung in lustrous waves down her back, all the way to her slender waist.

Myria drew toward him, a look of concern in her eyes. "I wasn't sure whether you had knowledge of mending." She reached her hand toward the side of his face.

Darien winced at the feel of her touch. "I know how to heal. I just didn't know if it was permitted." He reached up to where her fingers had so lightly brushed his swollen cheek.

Myria scowled. "Of course it's permitted. That business down there was all for show. The populace wanted blood. You gave them a taste of it. Now, sit down." Her tone was suddenly all business-like. She gestured briskly toward the bed.

Darien obeyed even though he was very capable of tending to himself. He sat down on the edge of the stuffed mattress, gazing up into her wide, dark eyes. Myria moved toward him and, bending over, cupped his face with her soft hands. She closed her eyes in concentration.

He could feel the probe she sent through him to ascertain the nature of his injuries. The feel of her power was warm and comforting. Darien closed his eyes, steadying himself for what he knew was about to come next. He gasped when the violent surge of energies hit. At first he fought against it, his mind on the edge of panic from the sudden force of raw power she applied. The healing washed over him like a wave breaking on a shoreline. The pain was erased completely, swept clean away, replaced by a soothing flush of contentment.

He couldn't fight it any longer. Darien fell back against the mattress, his mind drifting away, born on peaceful tides of slumber.

When he awoke, Myria was still there, still keeping watch over him. She sat on the side of the bed, her face tranquil in the wavering lantern light. Darien reached up and rubbed his eyes. Disoriented, he glanced down. His body was still unclothed, but remarkably whole and clean. The only marks left were old white scars, along with the gruesome markings the Oath had left behind on his wrists. Those would never be healed. They would remain with him always, a constant reminder of the betrayal he had committed.

"You slept a long time," Myria remarked, peering down at him with a smile. "I didn't realize you were that injured. Those men were brutes. Here. I brought you some food."

She stood up from the bed and knelt down, lifting a round serving platter up off the floor. On it were arranged three metal bowls and a copper cup. She slid the platter onto the mattress beside him.

Darien glanced up as the smell of hot food immediately captivated his interest. He squirmed into a reclining position on the bed, gazing down at the platter. All of the small bowls were only partially filled, one with rice, another with a thin red broth. The largest bowl contained a small amount of what looked like vegetable stew.

"My thanks," he muttered. The healing sleep had left him ravenous. He picked up the bowl of rice first, holding it in his left hand as he spooned the grains into his mouth with his fingers.

"I apologize there is no meat," Myria informed him as he dined, settling back down on her knees. "In Malikar, it is forbidden to eat the flesh of animals."

Darien didn't mind. The spices in the broth consumed his senses. He drank it down thirstily, throwing his head back and draining the small bowl. When he lifted the stew to his lips, he opened his eyes and realized that Myria was still gazing at him.

Suddenly self-conscious, Darien lowered the bowl, replacing it on the serving platter. He wiped his mouth with the back of his hand. Her eyes still lingered on him, a quiet smile on her lips. He didn't understand why she was even still there.

Darien shifted uncomfortably. "Is there...something more you need from me?"

Myria's face brightened at his question. Her eyes sought his. "There is," she admitted with a shrug. "I think you know why I'm here. You're a desirable man, Darien. We have some time before dinner."

He blinked, taken completely aback by her candor. Never in his life had he ever heard a woman speak so forwardly. He didn't know what to say. Discomfited, he dropped his gaze to the bed.

"I'm sorry." He shook his head in confused wonder. "I can't help you with that."

Myria reached up, stroking the side of his face with her hand. Her fingers found a stray lock of hair and brushed it aside. She gazed deeply into his eyes with a wistful expression. "Why not? Do you not find me pleasing?"

Darien couldn't help the half-smile that slipped to his lips as he mused where women like Myria might have been when he was younger. Her dark brown skin was smooth and flawless, her lips plump and perfectly shaped. She was an attractive, elegant woman. And intelligent, perhaps her most compelling feature.

"You're pleasing enough," he admitted in all honesty. "But my heart belongs to another. I'm afraid it wouldn't be fair to either of you. Or to me, for that matter."

Myria sat back, retracting her hand. She canted her head slightly to the side, her eyes dark and penetrating. "Have you given any consideration to her heart?"

Darien frowned, not taking her meaning. "What are you saying?"

"Meiran isn't going to want you any more, Darien."

Her words were just as brutal as they were honest. They hurt more than the wounds she had healed on him. With a grunt, he shoved himself up off the bed. *"You can't know that."*

Hands on his hips, Darien stalked away across the room toward the wash basin. The thanacryst tracked him with its eyes, a low growl lingering in its throat as it sensed the tension in the air.

Behind him, Myria rose to her feet. To his back, she stated, "Then let me ask you something. Doesn't Meiran deserve a man she can spend eternity with? Or, at the very least, a lifetime?"

Her words halted Darien in his tracks. He clenched his hands into fists until his nails bit into the flesh of his palms. He closed his eyes as the cruelty of her remark sank home, thrusting like a knifepoint into his chest.

"Get out."

He didn't look at her again, but he could feel her leaving. The tinkling sound of the beads told him that she had paused in the doorway. Her voice, sad and calm, filtered back toward him.

"Someone had to point that out to you, Darien. I'm just sorry it had to be me." The strings of painted beads made fragile music as she withdrew. "I'll be here if you change your mind. Don't forget to come down for dinner."

When she was gone, he set the platter on the floor and threw himself back down on the mattress, staring miserably up at the ceiling. Gradually, the rate of his breathing finally slowed. His pulse was still a loud drumming in his ears. Try as he might, he couldn't get her cold logic out of his brain.

She was right.

That's why it hurt so much.

The demon-hound stood up and yawned expansively, thrusting its hindquarters up in the air and stretching out its front legs. Then it turned and jumped up onto the mattress behind him. With a desolate whine, the beast nudged its great head between Darien's shoulder blades as it curled up against his back.

Darien lay there on his side, staring off into nothing. Eventually, he fell back to sleep.

The sound of clinking beads awoke him. Darien sat up, hand going behind him to steady the growling hound. He was almost relieved when he looked up into Byron Connel's face. In all the Black Lands, the red-bearded darkmage was the closest thing he had to an ally.

The man stood over him, arms crossed over his chest. "Renquist is looking for you. You were supposed to come down for dinner. I told him you were probably still sitting up here sulking."

Darien raised his eyebrows. "Oh, is that what I've been doing?"

Connel smirked. "That's what it looks like to me. Anyway, collect your things. You're leaving."

Darien pushed himself up off the bed. The demon-hound jumped down onto the floor beside him. "Leaving for where?"

"The Khazahar," Connel informed him.

Darien frowned as he bent over to retrieve his blue robes from off the ground. "Where is Azár?"

"She's with the Prime Warden. I suggest you join them."

Darien pulled the indigo robes on over his head. He spread his hands out, shaking the sleeves down over his arms. The garments felt foreign and altogether unfamiliar. Heavy. He still wasn't sure exactly what emotion wearing them evoked.

He reached for his longsword, drawing the baldric on over his head. Seeing it, Connel took a step toward him, reaching up to admire the hilt.

"That's one hell of a weapon," he remarked.

Darien glanced down at the silver morning star that hung from a leather strap at Connel's waist. "So is that," he said appreciatively. "May I hold it?"

Byron Connel chortled, his eyes glistening with mirth. "Only over my dead body."

Darien glanced at him sideways. "I didn't mean to offend."

The ancient Battlemage shrugged. "No offense taken." He reached down to his waist, untying the weapon and offering it haft-first to Darien. "Here. Take it."

Darien frowned, sensing that something wasn't right. He reached out, his fingers closing around the weapon's leather-wrapped haft as Connel released his hold.

The morning star fell through his grip with the weight of ten iron anvils. It impacted with the floor with a loud *thump.*

Darien glanced up at Connel with startled eyes. The Battlemage chuckled. "Go ahead. Pick it up."

Darien already knew that he couldn't. But he bent over and tried, anyway. Just as he suspected, the weapon refused to be shifted by his hand. It held fast to the floor, unyielding even as he exerted all his strength against it.

"Thar'gon is an artifact," Byron Connel explained. "It can be wielded only by the hand of the Warden of Battlemages."

Darien righted himself, gazing down at the silver morning star on the floor. "But the Lyceum doesn't exist anymore."

"Nevertheless." Connel scooped the talisman up easily into his big hand. He held it up before him, wielding it like a club. "If I should ever fall, Thar'gon will pass to Nashir. After that," he shrugged. "Then I suppose it would pass to you. If we can ever get you properly trained, you'll be the only other Battlemage amongst our number."

He reached out, clapping Darien on the back. Then he tied the weapon to his belt. "Let's go. You already missed dinner. It's never a good idea to keep the Prime Warden waiting."

Darien followed him through narrow corridors lined with dark bricks that seemed erratically placed. The floor was coarse and uneven. It was hard to walk without tripping. Wall-mounted oil lamps supplied enough dim light to see by.

Connel led him deep into to the dark bowels of the ziggurat. It was cool but not cold within; the mud bricks did an excellent job of regulating the temperature of the air. They passed through a drape of beads into a long room lined with many-colored tapestries and colorful drapes of cloth that hung down the walls from the ceiling.

Darien stopped, gazing around as his eyes adjusted to the brightness of the chamber. The entire room was richly aglow with the light of hundreds of lanterns, each of a different shape, size, and workmanship. The wash of color was almost jarring after the dim austerity his senses had become accustomed to.

It was obvious that a banquet had been served. Bowls of every size were arranged on wide platters scattered across the rugs, surrounded by brightly embroidered cushions and tall pitchers of drink. Very little was left, Darien realized. Servants moved silently on the fringes of the room, clearing away the remnants of the feast. Of their own party, only Myria, Renquist and Azár remained. The others had already departed.

Upon seeing his arrival, Myria stood and approached. Darien's stomach tightened as she drew near. She leaned forward, her lips softly brushing first his right cheek then his left.

"Go in peace," she whispered softly in his ear. Her hand caressed his. Then she turned and left.

When she was gone, Darien continued to stare into the space she had just occupied, vexed by conflicting emotions. He had nothing against Myria; the more he thought about it, the more he realized she was absolutely correct. But neither was he attracted to her. Her cruel words had quenched any spark of desire he otherwise might have felt.

"Nur a'nach," the Prime Warden uttered in greeting. "Please. Come join us." With a sweep of his hand, he indicated a spread of embroidered cushions in front of him. Azár yet remained seated at his side.

Darien frowned, puzzled by his master's greeting. "Dark's grace?" he said, his mind groping through his knowledge of the language for the correct interpretation.

"Evening's grace," Zavier Renquist corrected him. "That would be the literal translation. It simply means, 'good evening.'"

"Peace," Byron Connel whispered as he turned to go. He squeezed Darien's arm in warm reassurance before departing.

Darien gestured with his hand, stationing the demon-dog at the chamber's entrance. Then he approached the Prime Warden and sat down upon a cushion on the floor across from him. He gazed down at the nearest platter of food, eyes wandering over the wide assortment of dishes that remained. One in particular attracted his attention. It was a plate of grilled meat served with herbs over a bed of grain.

"I thought flesh was forbidden," he said.

Renquist cast him a stare weighted with ominous significance. "Nothing is forbidden me."

Darien nodded, silently absorbing the import of the man's assertion. He gazed straight ahead at the plate of meat.

"Go ahead," Renquist offered. "Have some. I will arrange for more if you find it to your taste."

Darien shook his head. "Thank you, no, Prime Warden. I ate earlier."

Zavier Renquist leaned forward, eyes raking over Darien's face and down the robes that covered his body. His dark eyes narrowed. At last, he nodded slightly, seeming satisfied.

"Myria tended you well," he said. "Do you resent me, Darien, for consenting to have you beaten?"

Resent him? No. Darien did not resent him. It had not been Renquist's intent to do him lasting harm. It had been his own actions that had brought about the necessity. Darien understood that, now, and accepted it. It had taken him a long time spent in contemplation and suffering to achieve that level of acceptance. The demons that haunted the Netherworld dealt harsh but practical lessons. They had little patience with justification or intent.

"I don't resent you," Darien assured him quietly. "I understand why it was necessary."

Zavier Renquist nodded. "I was very proud of you today. You displayed the appropriate amount of restraint and humility. Even the vizier commented on how naturally you complete our Circle of Eight. He sees in you the same thing I do."

"What is that, Prime Warden?"

"A man capable of making even the hardest decisions. I can trust you to always make the right choice, no matter what it costs you."

Feeling a flush of humility, Darien glanced downward at the

floor. Instantly, the Prime Warden's hand shot out across the platter between them and caught his chin. Renquist's eyes were suddenly wide as if enraged, his jaw set in anger. With the pressure of his fingers, he forced Darien's head back up, capturing his stare with the shadowed intensity of his gaze.

"Never lower your eyes, Darien." His voice was soft but full of fire. "Never. Not even to me. It is considered a sign of weakness."

His fingers tightened, becoming painful. Darien said nothing, holding the Prime Warden's stare with his own unwavering gaze. Renquist released him, sitting back and returning his attention to his plate.

He plucked a date up into his hand, plunging it into his mouth and sucking the flesh off the pit.

"Do you know what your name means in Venthic?"

Darien swallowed, unnerved by the man's unpredictable temperament. "I'm told it means 'Protector.'"

"That's right. You are a protector of *my* people, now. Apparently, that's what you were born to be."

Darien considered Renquist's words. He knew why his mother and father had chosen his name; it was because of his birth order. His elder brother, Aidan, had been slated to follow their mother's path toward political gains. Darien, being the second-born son, had been intended to follow their father's example and become a Sentinel. Hence the name: Darien. Protector. He swallowed, awash in the miserable knowledge that, even though he had lived up to the name his parents had given him, he had also thoroughly disgraced his family's legacy of honor.

"I don't believe fate is predetermined," he said at last.

Zavier Renquist shrugged. "Fate is simply the result of our actions. There are always consequences to the choices we make. Those consequences define our destiny."

He set the pit of the date he was chewing down on the side of his plate. "So. Darien. Your chance has come. Are you willing to embrace the destiny you have created for yourself?"

Darien nodded. "Aye, Prime Warden."

Renquist turned to the slight woman beside him, who had so

far been listening in silence to their conversation. "Lightweaver Azár, you speak for all of the Khazahar. Will you accept this man's offer of protection? Will you allow Darien Lauchlin of Amberlie to assume domination over the hinterlands?"

Azár's eyes shot toward Darien, considering him with a contemptuous scowl. "If there is no other choice, Prime Warden."

Renquist worked his lips, sucking them together. "There is not. Not for the purposes you have defined. Darien is by far the strongest mage at our disposal. And, because of his unique training, he is also the most versatile. There is not one amongst our number more suited to your needs."

Azár looked as though she would rather throw her support behind anyone else in the world. Her eyes full of disdain, she said, "The Khazahar will have to decide for itself if it is to accept this man's protection, Prime Warden. I will lead him westward to my village. From there, he can work to gain the support of the Tanisars."

"Very well," Renquist allowed, at last seeming satisfied. He looked at Darien, then, standing up.

Following the Prime Warden's lead, Darien rose and moved to stand before him. Renquist took his hands into his own, considering him quietly with a long and searching gaze.

"Darien Lauchlin, I proclaim you Overlord of the Khazahar. Go in peace. Live up to the name your parents saw fit to bestow upon you. Become the protector our people have so long awaited and so rightfully deserve."

He turned to the woman beside him, taking both of her hands together into one of his own, joining the three of them together in bond. "Lightweaver Azár, you must strive to forgive the past and put aside your preconceptions. What is gone is dead. Your new overlord knows nothing of his people nor of the challenges he will face. Take him by the hand. He will be in dire need of your support."

Azár's eyes did not falter as she looked at him. "I understand, Prime Warden. On my head and my eyes, this man will have my support."

"Call him by his name."

The woman blinked, her face suddenly uncertain. She frowned, shifting her weight over her feet. "His name, Prime Warden?"

"His name. I have yet to hear you actually speak it."

Azár blinked. Her lips parted slightly. "You will have my support, Darien Lauchlin of Amberlie."

Darien stood appraising her, distrusting the sudden change. She continued staring at the ground, showing him only the top of her head and the long strands of dark hair that escaped her thick braid.

"Call me Darien," he said. It was not a request.

"Darien," Azár repeated. "You will have my support."

Darien nodded, satisfied. "Then you shall have mine."

Renquist released both their hands. "Go in peace with the grace and blessings of the gods."

He turned toward Azár and kissed her on the cheek. Then he took Darien and drew him into a rigid embrace, locking his arms around him and resting his nose against his face. "Go in peace."

Darien closed his eyes, made anxious by Renquist's close proximity. When the Prime Warden withdrew, he had to fight to keep his gaze off the floor. He turned and strode out of the room, Azár following behind him. He pushed the tinkling drape of beads aside, moving out into the corridor. At his whistle, the demon-dog sprinted after him.

"Darien."

He stopped, shocked that Azár had actually used his name again, and so soon. He turned toward her.

"You murdered my sister in your fire," she informed him coldly. "You took her soul. That is why I hate you. I thought you should know."

Chapter Nine
Ties that Bind

Glen Farquist, The Rhen

Naia gazed up into the carved face of the Goddess of the Eternal Requiem, seeking for solace but finding none. The statue's stone eyes appeared harsh and judgmental. As well they should be; Naia had betrayed the goddess she'd once served. She had sacrificed her vows and veil in favor of the chains she now wore on her wrists and the mage's power that burned in her veins. All for a man who had betrayed his own purpose and had striven at every step to push her further away.

"Are you all right?" she heard Kyel ask.

Naia blinked, unable to tear her eyes from the critical visage of the goddess above her. "I'm not," she admitted, her voice breaking with emotion. "What if all this is really my own fault? I helped Darien vow his Bloodquest, right here in this very shrine. I struck the chains from his wrists with my own hands. I set his feet down this path and I held him up when he couldn't walk it alone."

"None of this is your fault," Kyel said, putting a comforting hand on her shoulder. "Naia. It's not."

She managed to wrench her gaze away from the statue, compelled by the insistence in his voice. She turned toward him. Kyel's face was careworn, his eyes full of concern.

"You didn't make Darien's choices for him," Kyel said. "All you did was follow him down that road."

"I didn't see where his path was leading him," she said. "I should have tried harder to stop him."

"He wouldn't have listened to you. You did all you could do.

You did your best."

She looked up again into the face of the statue, silently imploring her goddess for forgiveness. Maybe if she hadn't betrayed her vows, none of this would have happened. Maybe this was all some sort of punishment for her own transgressions.

"I need to speak with my father," she whispered.

Kyel nodded, looking as though he understood. "I'm going to go across the valley. I'll be back later tonight, or perhaps tomorrow."

Naia reached out and caught his arm. "Good luck," she said, pressing a kiss against his cheek.

Kyel nodded, pulling back. She listened to the sound of his footsteps as he strode away, leaving her alone at the feet of the marble statue.

Naia placed her hand on the rough oaken door, feeling the coarse grain of the wood through her fingers. Curling her hand into a fist, she knocked twice. From the other side, she could hear the sound of approaching footsteps. Then the door swung open, revealing the form of an old man she almost didn't recognize.

"Father?"

Naia gasped, bringing her hand up to cover her mouth. Tears filled her eyes. She did nothing to wipe them away. She stood there in the doorway, silently willing the old man in front of her to show some sign of recognition. At last, he did. Luther Penthos' lips parted as he sucked in a sharp gasp of air. He took his daughter into his arms, hugging her against his chest.

Naia couldn't believe how fragile her father had become. She could feel his sharp bones through the rich fabric of his vestments. He quivered in her arms, his bony fingers rubbing her back. Her father's frailty made Naia cry even harder. She kissed his forehead, clinging to him as her shoulders shook with shame and grief.

"Stand back and let me look at you," he whispered, cupping her face with his hands.

Naia obeyed, wiping her eyes. She backed away from his embrace, doing her best to smile at him through her tears.

When his eyes had finally had their fill of her, he nodded slightly. "I've missed you. Why didn't you come sooner?"

Naia shrugged, spreading her hands to reveal the matching set of chains on both wrists. "I didn't know how to tell you," she admitted. "I was so afraid I'd broken your heart."

"No, my child. You could never break my heart," he assured her, stepping back and inviting her within.

Naia moved inside, brushing past him as she walked across the small room to his desk. There, she took a seat in one of the chairs. She brought out a kerchief to dab at her eyes. Her father moved behind her, setting his hands on her shoulders and squeezing her gently before edging past. He sat himself down in his own chair across the desk from her, leaning back and folding his hands in his lap.

"You are just as beautiful a mage as you ever were a priestess," Luther Penthos commented.

Naia smiled her gratitude, clutching her kerchief in her hands as she brought it down from her face.

"Thank you."

Her father looked very different. Older. Thinner. Careworn by years and grief. But he was still very much in command of his faculties, she could tell. He was, every inch, a High Priest.

"So, tell me. Which order did you take? What tier are you?"

"I am a Querer, Father. But only third tier."

His smile was warm and proud. "That is nothing to be ashamed of. My daughter has become a powerful mage."

Naia blotted away tears of joy that clouded her eyes at the sound of his acceptance. "To be honest, the Prime Warden hasn't had much time to devote to my training."

Her father looked down at the surface of his desk, his smile retreating. "That's unfortunate." There was a long gap of silence. At last he spoke, his voice sad and serious. "Why did you abandon me, Naia? Why did you leave me for *him?*"

"Because I believed in him, Father."

That was the simple truth. She could have elaborated. She

could have told him all the things that had gone through her mind on the day she'd left Glen Farquist with Darien. She could have talked about how much she had come to admire the man in the short amount of time she had spent with him. She could have spoken of how lost and alone he had seemed, how defiant and courageous. Darien's plight had tugged at her heartstrings. She had not been able to stand aside and watch him destroy himself.

"Did you love him?"

Naia's throat clenched in grief. "Yes," she admitted with a grimace. "I did...and I still do."

"I don't understand." Luther Penthos frowned, leaning forward. "Naia, what are you trying to tell me?"

She drew in a deep breath, dreading to confess the depth of her anguish. "Before he died, Darien swore his soul to Xerys. He's become a demon, Father, just like Renquist. And the Well of Tears is open once again. I'm scared, Father. I'm scared because..." Her voice trailed off. Naia swallowed, summoning enough courage to continue. "I'm scared because I'm still in love with him. *I'm in love with a demon.*"

There. It was out. She looked up into her father's pale face and saw his expression.

He'd been wrong.

She still had the power to break his heart.

Kyel followed the brown-robed cleric through the maze of underground passages that made up the Temple of Wisdom beneath the Valley of the Gods. Scores of clerics moved about them; the broad corridor was a busy thoroughfare that cut right through the center of the temple. No one paid Kyel any mind; they had become used to his frequent visits. He had been using Om's temple as a retreat, a place where he could meditate in quiet and practice the countless exercises Meiran was always giving him. He found the temple quiet and soothing, very much to his liking. Within the last year, Kyel had frequented the temple so often that he'd almost started thinking of his quarters there as home.

The cleric before him drew up, gesturing at a door in front of them. He then turned and walked away, leaving Kyel on his own. With only the slightest moment of hesitation, Kyel reached out and turned the knob. The door swung inward, revealing the room beyond.

"Papa!"

Kyel was almost knocked over backwards by the force of the small body that collided with his own. He scooped his son up into his arms, clutching him tight against his chest. He attacked the plump cheeks with the wiry growth of his new beard.

"No, Papa, no!"

Gil kicked and giggled in his arms as Kyel laughed, overwhelmed with joy at the feel of him. At last he relented, letting the child squirm away. But it was only seconds before Gil was back, begging for his attention.

"More, Papa, *more!*"

Kyel laughed, grabbing him up and tickling him under the arms as Gil squealed and bucked to get away. Kyel set him down, motioning for him to stay.

"I've got something for you," Kyel said, squatting down and reaching his hand into the deep pocket of his cloak. He pulled out a small sack, offering it out to the boy. Gil gasped at the sight of it, his blue eyes going wide and round.

"What is it, Papa?"

"It's a birthday surprise," Kyel told him. "You didn't think I'd forget your birthday, did you? Go ahead. Open it."

Gil undid the cord that held the sack closed, his four-year-old fingers working clumsily at the knot. He shook the sack, letting the contents spill out into his hand. He gasped, staring down wondrously at the painted object in his palm.

"A toy!" he exclaimed, turning the red piece of wood over in his hands. He unwound the string that was looped around it.

"It's a top," said Kyel, ruffling Gil's hair with his hand. "Give it here. I'll show you how it works."

He wound the string around the top's axis and, setting the wooden toy down on the floor, gave the string a solid tug. The red top flew suddenly into motion, scooting away from them toward the center of the floor. Gil squealed, clapping his hands in delight as the top danced around in slowly compressing spirals until it finally came to a rest on its side.

The boy ran forward, catching it up in his hands.

"Don't forget to wind the string!"

Kyel tossed the wadded string over to him. It fell to the floor as Gil laughed, his reactions not quite fast enough to catch it. Kyel smiled as his son ducked out into the corridor to play with his new toy.

The smile fell from his lips at the sight of Cadmus. The layman stood up from his chair, ambling toward him with his hands clasped in front of him. He wore the simple clothes of a commoner, a tan vest over a stained wool shirt.

"How's he been?" Kyel asked, his voice full of concern.

Cadmus shrugged. His thinning brown hair was parted too far over on the side, giving him an almost comical appearance. "He's been missing his father. And he's been missing his mum."

Kyel's gaze dropped to the floor at the mention of Amelia.

His stomach soured as he remembered the day of his homecoming. He had knocked at the door of his own home and waited for his wife to answer. He wasn't sure why he'd even bothered to knock; it was his own door, after all.

But he'd wanted to surprise her.

Only, the face that confronted him through the cracked doorway had not belonged to Amelia.

"Kyel...?"

His father swept Kyel into a long, crushing embrace. When he finally let go, his father took him inside and broke the news to his son.

Kyel had been gone from home for an awfully long time. While he was away, his family had received word from Rothscard of his fate. They were told that Kyel had been found guilty of murder. That he and Traver had been tried, convicted and condemned.

Kyel's wife had mourned him for dead.

And then Amelia had done the only sensible thing she could

do: she married another man.

Kyel blamed himself, not her. He'd never been able to forgive himself for not being there, not being at her side. For putting her through that. By the time he'd arrived home, Amelia and her new husband were already expecting a child of their own. There was very little Kyel could do at that point.

He'd shaken the man's hand and bid Amelia goodbye. He'd collected up his son. And then he'd left Covendrey forever.

"His Eminence requires a word with you."

Kyel blinked at the sound of Cadmus' voice. He glanced up bleakly at the man, roused from his dark reverie. His Eminence was always requiring a word with him. Every time Kyel visited the temple, the High Priest of Om was always eager for a chat.

"I figured." Kyel sighed.

Cadmus' stare went blank for a long moment, his eyes wandering up and to the side. At last his focus solidified. "His Eminence wishes to know if you have come here to discuss the unsealing of the Well of Tears?"

Kyel was used to this form of communication; it didn't surprise him any longer. What shocked him was that Om's clerics had already guessed the nature of his visit. He still didn't know how they came by much of their information.

"We don't know who did it," he admitted. "All we know is that it's been opened. Renquist and his darkmages are loose upon the world again. And Darien Lauchlin is with them."

Cadmus' stare drifted away. He was gone a long time, his mind focused elsewhere. Then:

"This is very ill tidings, indeed. His Eminence extends to you his sympathy. Your master was a courageous man with noble intentions. It's a tragedy that he did not show better restraint."

Kyel couldn't agree more. "Already, Renquist has moved against us. Quinlan Reis and Sareen Qadir came to Rothscard to treat with the Prime Warden. We found Sareen murdered. The other one—Reis—disappeared along with Meiran. We fear she's been taken. Or worse."

Cadmus showed no visible reaction to the news. Instead, his eyes glassed over. This time, he was gone for a very long while. When he finally came back, his face was grimly set.

"It is lamentable that you are even aware of those names, Grand Master Kyel," Cadmus said at last. "That the Prime Warden might be at the mercy of a monster such as Quinlan Reis is truly harrowing."

"You know of him?" Kyel was surprised.

Cadmus nodded. "We know only what has been recorded, which is very little. But what we do know is enough cause for grave concern. Quinlan Reis is perhaps the most dangerous man in all of history."

Kyel frowned. "If Reis is so dangerous, then how is it that no one's ever heard of him?"

It took a long moment for Cadmus to answer. "His name was purposefully expunged from the annals of Aerysius. It was not, however, excluded from the texts of Om's temple."

Kyel nodded, remembering the darkmage mentioning something about that. "What can you tell me about him?"

Cadmus closed his eyes, appearing to concentrate. He stood there for minutes, face slack, arms dangling at his sides. When he opened his eyes again, his expression was very bleak. "Quinlan Reis was the brother of Braden Reis, the First Sentinel. From what our historians have managed to reconstruct, it was Quinlan's betrayal that resulted in his own brother's execution. He was also personally responsible for the Desecration of Caladorn. The man was noted in his lifetime to have few moral scruples. According to one text, he was actually a trained assassin. A mage-hunter. If Quinlan Reis truly has kidnapped the Prime Warden, then her life is in grave danger."

"That's what we're afraid of," Kyel said, feeling dismal. "We've taken the body of Sareen Qadir to the Temple of Death. We're hoping that there might be some way she can be brought back to life, so we can glean some information from her."

Hearing that, Cadmus winced. He closed his eyes for a time. "That is a very reckless endeavor," he said at last. "His Eminence would strongly advise you against such action. The corpse of

Sareen Qadir must be speedily put to the torch." There was a pause. "I hope you understand…the same holds true for your former master, should the opportunity arise."

Kyel blinked. "Darien…he was more than just my master. He was also my friend. I don't think I could do that."

A delighted squeal from outside in the corridor assured Kyel that his son was still enjoying his new toy. He turned toward the doorway, suddenly very grateful he had found such a distracting gift.

"Some time spent in our vaults would do you great benefit, Grand Master Kyel," Cadmus offered stiffly.

Kyel shook his head. "Thank you, but I've got to be going."

"You really ought to consider making the time, if you deem it reasonable to try negotiating with a darkmage. Even a dead one."

"Then what would you suggest?" Kyel demanded. "How do we go about finding the Prime Warden?"

"You are advised to abandon that effort," Cadmus said, reaching out and patting him on the shoulder. "Let Meiran find you. Or count her name among the lost. If she is truly in thrall to Quinlan Reis, then there are only two possible outcomes. Neither one is very hopeful."

Kyel sighed wearily. Casting a beleaguered glance around the small room, he discovered an empty chair and wandered over to it, plopping his weight down dismally.

"Does His Eminence think Renquist will invade again?"

It took only a moment for the man to answer. "His Eminence would rather not venture to guess. Of course, if Zavier Renquist does have your master as an ally, that puts us at a distinct disadvantage."

"Why?"

"Because, in life, Darien Lauchlin had intimate knowledge of the Rhen's defenses. As a Sentinel, he was very well-versed in all of our military assets as well as the limitations of those assets. He fought alongside many of our greatest commanders. He knows how they think."

"That's true," Kyel agreed reluctantly. "Do we even stand a chance?"

Cadmus' eyes drifted to the side. "His Eminence says we must focus our efforts on neutralizing their darkmages."

"How do we go about doing that?"

"That will take a great deal of planning and careful coordination." Cadmus walked forward, pulling up a chair of his own. He sat down on it next to Kyel. "But it's possible. It can be done. His Eminence thinks we should begin with your former master. He will be the easiest to target, as he still has ties that bind his heart."

Kyel frowned, not liking the sound of that. From the corridor, he could hear Gil clapping in delight.

He was suddenly reminded of Darien's own son, who had died before his father had ever had a chance to come to know him. The thought made his heart sink.

Naia gazed over the desk at her father, whose face looked no better to her than stretched leather mounted over a thin scaffold of bone.

"We will need the help of the temples, Father," she said. "It's the only way we'll have the strength to make a stand."

Her father shook his head. "The temples are forbidden from interfering in this conflict."

But she dismissed his argument with a wave of her hand. "This isn't a border dispute between two rival nations. This is something far more insidious. The temples themselves are directly threatened by Xerys' legions."

"It doesn't matter," Luther Penthos insisted. "Still, we must respect and honor our covenants."

"Those covenants were made with two Assemblies that no longer exist. The Lyceum was destroyed a thousand years ago. And now Aerysius itself has fallen."

"And yet the temples still remain."

"That will not be the case if the Enemy is allowed to run roughshod over us. The temples will not be spared. Just as they weren't spared when Caladorn fell."

"No." Her father shook his head. "We cannot actively

participate in this dispute."

Naia was beginning to feel exasperated. "Father, without the might of the temples behind us, all is lost. There aren't enough mages to bolster our military. Kyel is our only Sentinel. I'm strong, Father. But I'm untrained. I'm begging you. Kyel and I can't do it alone."

Her father sat back in his chair. For a long while, he didn't speak. He appeared to be ruminating on her words. At length, he said, "I will convene a Conclave so that you may present your case before the Great Temples of Glen Farquist. That is the best I can do."

Hearing his words, Naia surged out of her seat with a sudden rush of joy. She rounded his desk, throwing her arms around him. "Thank you, Father!"

He brought his hand up to pat her back. She pressed her cheek against his head, holding him tight before releasing him.

"Thank you," Naia said again as she returned to settle back into her seat. "You know I wouldn't be asking this if it wasn't absolutely imperative."

"What you ask has never been considered since the Great Schism," her father reminded her sternly. He leaned forward, folding his hands atop his desk. "I need to warn you: you are a Master, now. But before that, you were a priestess. And not just any priestess; you were the First Daughter, my own chosen successor. You have much more knowledge of temple secrets than any mage has any right to know. The amalgamation of those two knowledge bases can be a very dangerous combination. You would do well to forget everything you ever learned during your time here."

Naia knew exactly what he was saying and why he was saying it. She understood completely. Nevertheless, she knew it would be impossible to follow his advice. "I can't, Father. The Temple of Death is just as much a part of me as the gift I inherited from Darien. I can't simply forget everything I learned."

Her father closed his eyes, bowing his head.

"So, the gift that moves within you did, in fact, come from *him.*"

"Yes," Naia admitted.

Her father sighed, shaking his head. "It yet astounds me that one man could have possibly wrought so much damage in such a short period of time. It pains me that you had to inherit such a corrupted legacy."

His words, though well-intentioned, provoked Naia's ire. She responded defensively, "Darien was a very courageous and passionate man, unmatched in his commitment to duty. The Rhen has never known a greater champion."

Luther Penthos sat back in his chair, gazing at his daughter with sadness in his eyes. Ominously, he uttered, "And now the Rhen has never faced a fiercer adversary."

Naia threw back her head, knowing he was right. Fresh tears filled her eyes. In a small voice, she whispered, "That's why we need the help of the temples, Father."

The High Priest of Death nodded his understanding.

"I'll see what I can do."

Chapter Ten
The Caravansary

Bryn Calazar, The Black Lands

Darien gazed out across the writhing horde of citizens gathered at the base of the ziggurat, the sight making his stomach sour. The throng was tumultuous, surging against the efforts of guardsmen in full battle plate who labored to hold back the churning masses. He'd hoped the crowd would have dispersed since that morning, when the rabid hatred of the entire populace had been directed against him.

But there was an entirely different tenor in the air this evening, as if the atmosphere of the city had inverted with the change of tide. The crowd seemed impelled by a fanatical zeal. At the sight of Darien and Azár emerging from the temple at the top of the ziggurat, there was a loud outcry from the roiling masses below. Bodies surged wildly, clamoring toward the long ramp of steps. The armed guards managed to contain the multitudes, but only just barely. The mob seemed fomented to a rage.

A harsh gust of wind kicked up, bitingly cold and scented with the salt of the ocean. It rippled Darien's blue robes and whipped his hair into his face. He started down the long ramp of steps, Azár stalking silently at his side. The demon-hound followed behind them both, unholy eyes gleaming like twin green embers in the shadows. Braziers lined the stairway, defying the darkness with wavering orange glows. The din of the crowd swelled as the two of them neared the level of the street. People surged against the line of guards, shouting and brandishing torches, even weapons, in the air.

Guards spilled forward, forming a shield wall around them

while pressing the crowd back away from their path. Darien and Azár moved forward in the midst of the ring of guards out into the crowded street. The throng opened up to receive them, reluctantly giving way before their passage. Darien tried to see past the wall of armored bodies that surrounded him, but it was impossible to glimpse much of anything. His efforts frustrated, he instead focused his attention on Azár. He was still more than a little numbed by the confession she had made about her sister.

At least he understood, now, why she hated him. He knew very well how it felt to lose someone you loved.

Their party finally managed to break out of the throng. The guards fanned out, sweeping back to flank them on either side. The streets ahead were dark and sparsely populated. Only shadows moved against the walls that lined the roadside.

Thick smoke billowed across the avenue, drifting like noxious plumes of miasma. Darien inhaled a burning chestful of harsh fumes that made his eyes water. "How do you breathe this air?" he complained to Azár. "It's thick enough to scald the lungs!"

Azár's eyes ticked toward him. "The smoke is from hearth fires. There is nothing to be done about it."

Darien scowled at the taste of the oily film that coated the inside of his throat. He had never breathed anything so noxious in his life. "What sort of fuel are you using?"

"Coal cakes are used for cooking and heating," Azár said with a shrug. "The coal does not burn cleanly."

Darien gaped at her, incredulous. *"Coal?* Why not use wood?"

"Wood is very precious in Malikar," Azár explained. Her words were terse; there was very little patience left in her voice. "Wood cannot be wasted or used for burning."

Darien's eyes widened in understanding as he followed her line of reasoning to its logical end. "I take it there aren't many forests in the Black Lands."

Azár nodded, squinting her contempt at him. "It takes much light and time to grow a tree. Look up at the sky. What do you see?"

Darien glanced up at the swirling mass of cloudcover that choked the heavens above. He realized that he really had no idea if it was even day or night; there was absolutely no distinction between the two in this hellish land. It was just like the Pass of Lor-Gamorth, just like the skies above Greystone Keep. The glowing luminescence in the clouds was the only source of light in a vast wasteland of shadow. Beneath those dark skies, no plant could ever grow.

Azar cast a smug grin. "I think, perhaps, you begin to understand."

Darien nodded, still gazing upward at the clouds in mute consternation. He *was* beginning to understand. His mind was just starting to grapple with the logistics of providing for an entire population clutched in the grip of yearlong darkness. Softly, he asked, "How do you feed your people, Azár?"

She looked at him with an arrogant sneer on her face. "Wait until we are outside of the vortex that surrounds Bryn Calazar. There, I will show you."

At last, they reached their destination: a wide portal cut out of a mud-brick wall on the side of the boulevard. The opening was broad and encased by a tall horseshoe arch set in stone. Azár walked through the entrance, her dark braid writhing like a snake in the wind. Darien followed, shooting one last glance up at the hostile cloudscape. The demon-dog came along behind, stalking with its nose to the ground.

On the other side of the portal, Darien paused. They were in some type of dim courtyard bordered on all sides by a honeycomb of niche-like openings. The courtyard was not empty; it teemed with people and flickering torches. Darien followed in Azár's wake as she wound through the press of bodies. The buzz of conversation was an incessant drone. A few people shot curious glances their way, eyes widening when they took in the sight of the thanacryst. A few stepped away to let them pass. One man, noticing the emblem of the Silver Star on Darien's chest, bowed and backed quickly out of their path.

Azár led him toward a circle of men gathered before a fountain in the center of the yard. The men were laughing and carrying on; no one paid them any mind as they drew up in their midst. Darien stood patiently beside Azár, watching in curiosity as the men bantered playfully back and forth in their native tongue. He couldn't make out much of what was being said. It was Venthic, but of a dialect that he was utterly unfamiliar with.

Azár strutted forward, angling toward a tall, bearded man who stood slouching against a wall. The man had a subtle air of authority about him. It was something intangible, but immediately apparent. Maybe it was in the way the other men deferred to him, giving him extra space and grinning at his every comment. Or perhaps it was the careless grace of his posture.

Azár walked right up to the slouching man and launched into what appeared to be a fluid bout of negotiation. Darien hung back, watching as her body language conveyed her intentions just as much as her words, which were beyond his level of comprehension. He waited, one hand clutching the leather strap of the baldric that crossed his chest. His gaze roamed from face to face around the group of surrounding men.

Azár at last turned away, glancing back at Darien with concern in her eyes. "This man—his name is Haleem—he is the caravan master. He asks that you remove his wife's consumption. In exchange, he is willing to offer us a place in his caravan and on his barge, as well as food and water for the journey. You do have knowledge of healing?"

Darien glanced at the man, considering the offer. Haleem was grinning broadly in his own direction as the other men around him continued their bantering. Darien wasn't sure he liked the look of him. The man's smile did not come close to touching his eyes.

Grudgingly, he nodded. "Tell him I'd be honored to look in on his wife."

Azár translated his words to the grinning Haleem, whose thin smile only broadened. He took Azár's hand in his own and, bending forward at the waist, pressed a kiss against her fingers. He then pushed his weight off the wall and strode forward until he was standing before Darien, offering his hand. Haleem's handshake was firm, and he did not release it immediately. Instead, he stood holding Darien's hand as the smile crept back to his face.

"Ranu kadreesh, nach'tier," he uttered in a deep and melodic voice.

The salutation was one that Darien understood. *May you know peace, darkmage.* The man's use of his Venthic title made Darien's skin crawl.

"Akadreesh iranu," he responded stiffly, gazing stone-faced at the caravan master.

The man finally released his hand, taking him instead by the arm. Darien allowed himself to be guided back through the throng of men. Haleem led him through the opening of a dark niche built into the opposite wall. There, on the floor all around, were stacked man-high piles of provisions. Haleem led him toward the back of the niche, to a narrow doorway at the far end. At the opening, Haleem paused, shaking the shoes from his feet.

"You will need to remove your shoes," Azár's voice commanded from behind.

Darien obeyed, bending over to slide the worn leather boots from his feet. Haleem took him once again by the arm, urging him forward through the narrow entrance into the interior of the building.

Darien ducked through a woven curtain, finding himself in a narrow room with walls that squeezed oppressively close. He could scarcely see; the dim glow of a single oil lamp did a poor job of dispelling the shadows. He could make out the forms of bodies huddled together on the floor against the opposite wall. There was a rustle of fabric. Someone coughed, the sound wet and rasping.

Darien conjured a mist of blue magelight at his feet. One of the women gave a piercing shriek, the whole cluster of bodies writhing back away from him toward the wall.

Haleem raised his hands, a rapid string of words spilling from his mouth. Darien waited, cautiously assessing the faces of the women huddled before him. He thought he could tell which one was Haleem's wife. She was young but sickly, her skin moist with perspiration.

Raising his hands, Darien took a step toward her. "Tell her I'll have to touch her," he cautioned Azár. He waited for his words to be translated. The sick woman before him gave a slight nod.

Darien lowered himself to the ground before her, crouching as he took the woman's hand into his own. He brought her fingers up to his mouth, kissing them the same way he had seen Haleem kiss Azár's hand. The woman seemed shocked by his gesture, her eyes shooting up to find her husband.

"It is not appropriate to kiss the hand of a woman," Azár corrected him sternly. "It is she who must kiss your hand."

Darien frowned. "But Haleem—"

"I am a Lightweaver," Azár snapped. "My status is much greater than that of a caravan master."

Darien understood. He turned back to Haleem's wife. "What is your name?" he asked, seeking to put her more at ease. *"Ismir'och?"*

"Esvir."

"Esvir," Darien repeated, testing the feel of the name on his tongue. He looked deeply into the young woman's eyes, surprised by what he found there. "I'll need to see inside you, Esvir." He glanced up at Azár, pausing for her to translate. "You'll sense something…a stirring. It won't hurt."

He took Esvir's hand and rubbed her soft skin in reassurance as he waited for Azár to finish communicating his intentions. The young woman nodded, inviting him to proceed. Darien leaned forward, cupping her pale face in his hands and closing his eyes. It didn't take a moment to probe her condition, to sense the extent of the corruption in her damaged tissues.

Dairen inhaled a deep breath. Then he sent a gush of healing energies flooding through Esvir's body, repairing the injury that had been done to her airways and burning the corruption from her blood. The woman stiffened, her eyes rolling back in their sockets. She swooned, falling forward against his chest.

"Ishil'zeri!" Haleem cried out, catching his unconscious wife in his arms.

Darien kept his hands on Esvir until he was certain that the poisons had been driven completely from her frail body. He kept a measure of the beat of her pulse, the steady rhythm of her chest. Through his fingertips, he could sense her vitality renewing. At last, Darien opened his eyes and removed his hands.

"She'll sleep," he informed Azár. "When she awakens, she'll be hungry. Tell Haleem she must have all the food she can eat."

"Sukrien," Haleem muttered, cradling his sleeping wife against his chest.

Darien nodded, standing up. Without another word, he left the dark room, brushing the curtain aside as he passed through the doorway. He replaced his boots and strode back outside to the courtyard. There, he glanced up at the sky, feeling the weariness of the healing sink deeply into his bones. He heard the sound of Azár's soft footsteps dashing up behind him.

"That woman," Darien said softly without looking at her. "Esvir. She has the potential. Do you need an apprentice, Azár?"

"No. I will not take an apprentice. I will be the last of my kind."

Darien scowled, not understanding what she meant. "Why? Why would you be the last, Azár?"

"Because, one way or another, Malikar will not be needing another generation of Lightweavers."

Darien spread his hands, turning to face her. His eyes sought her own. "Perhaps. Perhaps not. But surely another use could be found for the gift that lives inside you. There aren't many mages left in all the world."

Azár glared at him for a long, silent moment, hating him with her eyes. "Find a place to sleep," she said at last. She turned and stalked away. His words halted her.

"I'm sorry about your sister, Azár. I'd take it back if I could."

She whirled back around, her thick braid undulating like a whip. She snarled as she promised him, "Someday you, too, will lose someone you love. On that day, I will smile as you weep."

She grinned then, a joyous expression that brightened her entire face. It touched her eyes, plumped out her cheeks. The delight that filled her eyes chilled Darien's heart. He had seen such a look once before in a woman's eyes. A woman he had been forced to murder.

"There's no joy in hatred, Azár," he cautioned her. "Find something else to do with your anger. You don't want to end up like me."

Azár's mouth opened as if she had a retort ready to let fly. But then she turned away, instead. She stalked back toward the fountain, braid swaying with her gait.

Darien spent the night huddled up in a niche-like compartment off the central courtyard of the caravansary with the thanacryst curled up against his side. The wind howled most of the night, making sleep all but impossible. By morning, he was stiff and exhausted, his joints aching from the cold.

The morning brought no dawn, only more of the same dark expanse of cloudcover. Perhaps the sky was a little brighter than it had been at night; it was hard to say. The wind was still up, bitingly cold and brutally fierce. Darien left the shelter of the niche and sought the comfort of a fire. The smell of burning coal was dreadful, but the warmth was necessary. He stood, huddling in the indigo robes they had given him, warming his hands as the acrid smoke wrung tears from his eyes.

"My wife is well this morning."

Darien turned, startled to find Haleem standing beside him.

"You are welcome to my food, my fire, and my protection," the caravan master told him solemnly. This time, the warmth of his smile touched his eyes.

Darien considered him. "I didn't think you spoke Rhenic."

"He doesn't."

Darien turned to find that Azár had come up silently behind them.

"He asked me for the words," she clarified. "He wanted to tell you himself how thankful he is. Here. This is for you from Haleem and his wife."

She offered a woven satchel out to him. Darien accepted it, opening the flap and taking a look inside. It was filled with gear. He realized he would have to sit down and take his time if he wanted to go through all of it.

"This bag is called a *sufan,*" Azár said.

Darien nodded in gratitude and sat down on the ground. He

upended the *sufan*, spilling its contents into the lap of his robe. He ran his hand through it all, stirring the assortment of items around. He picked up the first thing that caught his eyes: a curving knife, about as long as his hand. There was also a ceramic pipe. Darien turned the pipe over in his hands, wondering at it. Such an object was hardly a necessity. There was also a flint and striker, a charcloth, a pair of tweezers and a small blade. A patterned scarf was folded neatly into a small square, along with various assorted objects.

"You have my thanks," he muttered, replacing the items back into the *sufan*.

"There is also this." Azár handed him a waterskin that hung from a long hemp cord. "The Khazahar can be a thirsty place."

"Again, thank you," Darien said, glancing up gratefully at Haleem. *"Sukrien."*

The man bowed, bringing a hand up to his chest, and backed away.

"Haleem says it is not a good day to travel," Azár informed him, watching his movements out of the corner of her eye as she stared at the brazier's dancing flames. "We will stay here today and head out tomorrow, instead."

Darien didn't like the sound of that. "Why's today not a good day to travel?"

Azár shrugged. "It is the fourth day of the month. The fourth day is never a good day to travel."

Darien looked up at her, carefully studying her face. The young woman appeared quite serious. He stood up, dusting off his long blue robes. "So, is the fifth day of the month any better for travelling?"

"It is better," Azár confirmed.

Darien broke into a grin. "Then, I suppose we ought to wait till the morrow."

The next morning, Haleem at last gave his consent to move out. Darien was impressed at the speed with which his group of laborers assembled in the courtyard, swiftly filing into lines that stretched all the way down the middle of the yard and out of the gate into the open street. Many men had equipped themselves with travois loaded with bags of provisions. Others pulled two-wheeled carts constructed of woven rattan and reinforced by metal bars. There were no animals; manpower alone would be exerted to transport Haleem's supplies to the river.

Darien had changed out of the robes they had given him in favor of the far more practical black shirt and breeches he was used to. He folded the robes of the Lyceum carefully and stored them in the bottom of a large pack Azár had purchased for him. Over his shirt, he donned a set of black metal spaulders, another gift from the Lightweaver. She had supplied herself with a similar pack, just the same as every other member of the caravan. The large packs were filled with all of the personal provisions each person would need for their own sustenance along the journey.

"Why are there no beasts of burden?" Darien wondered aloud. "Just one pair of oxen would make all the difference in the world."

Azár motioned upward at the sky. "Do you have any idea how much light it takes to feed just one ox? Haleem is a prosperous merchant, but even one such as he has never seen the amount of wealth it would require to sustain such a beast."

Darien shook his head, unable to comprehend how such a society could have possibly managed to continue for so long without collapse. They had no animals, no wood. No leather, no meat. And yet, in some respects, the Enemy's civilization seemed more advanced than the Rhen. What they had learned to accomplish with coal and oil was unsurpassed by any technology he had ever seen.

There was a shout from the rear of the yard, and then the long line of men began to move out. Darien and Azár fell in behind a throng of women. The wives were laboring just as hard as their men, pulling behind them wheeled carts filled with coal bricks and cooking supplies. They wore long, dark dresses covered by coarsely woven shawls. Darien noticed that Haleem's wife was there, walking in their midst. Esvir seemed completely hale, casting a thankful smile in his direction before turning to mind the cart she pulled behind her.

The smoke that blanketed the city was thick, made worse by the dust kicked up by so many wheels and feet. As they started out, Darien quickly found himself reduced to fits of coughing. He glanced beside him at Azár, wondering how the woman could stand it. He saw that she was in the process of wrapping a scarf around her head, tying it in place to cover her mouth and nose.

"You have one in your sufan," Azár reminded him. Her voice sounded almost as if she were smiling, but it was impossible to tell. Darien reached down and fished his own scarf out of the satchel Haleem had given him, shaking out the folds. He tried to wrap it around his head, first one way and then the other. Despite his efforts, he couldn't manage to make it stay in place.

"That is completely wrong," Azár scolded, observing his struggle. "Fold it first into a triangle, then wrap it over your head. Leave one side longer than the other," she instructed. "You bring it around your face and then up behind your head."

The whole while she was speaking, she was wrapping the fabric around him, finally securing it with a harsh tug. Darien could see only her eyes, the rest of her face hidden beneath the patterned cloth. The look emphasized the shine of the gift in her eyes.

They followed the long line of people down the street. Their group passed through the city gates and out into the vast expanse of black nothingness beyond. Darien paused to consider the sprawling wastes that lay ahead of them, league upon league of black, frozen terrain that stretched in every direction to the cloud-choked horizons. Above them, the heavens churned and flickered with the light of electrical storms that teemed deep within the cloudbank. Far to the west, a diffuse white glow could be seen. A breeze kicked up, flinging smoke toward them from Bryn Calazar.

Azár said, "We will follow this road until we reach the village of Ibri. There, the river is deep enough for boats. In Ibri, there will be a barge waiting to take us up the river. We will be entering the vortex that surrounds Bryn Calazar. Shut your mind away from it."

Darien frowned, immediately throwing up a shield to protect himself. A vortex was like a cyclone of power, a place where the lines of the magic field converged. The fury of a vortex was overwhelming, lethal to any mage. Darien had no idea how far out the Bryn Calazar vortex extended. He only knew that while they were within the grasp of those energies, he would be forced to keep his mind shielded from it. He would be vulnerable, a state he detested.

The absence of the magic field reminded him of when Arden Hannah had cornered him in a node, a place where the field lines cancelled out. Arden had tied him to a stake, hanging him out to roast over a searing fire. He would have died on that stake had it not been for Devlin Craig. Cut off from the magic field, all he could do was writhe and scream as his flesh was broiled off his bones. He'd been utterly powerless, completely at Arden's sick mercy.

That's why he so despised the shield he was forced to throw up to protect his mind from Bryn Calazar's vortex. It cut him off from the comfort of the field. The knowledge made his skin crawl, sending shivers of dread down his spine. He could almost feel the heat of Arden's flames licking at his flesh.

"What is it?" Azár pressed, staring intently into his eyes.

Darien shook his head, adjusting the scarf over his face.

"Something is bothering you. What is it?"

"It's nothing." He clenched his hands into fists, squeezing his fingers until his knuckles went white. He could feel the raging torrent of power already clawing at his skin.

"How big is this vortex?" he grumbled. "How long till we're out of it?"

"Two days."

A surge of panic seized Darien's throat, choking him. He winced, recoiling with dread. He gasped for air, but still couldn't get enough breath to fill his lungs. Reaching up, he ripped the scarf away from his face. He bent forward, hands on his knees, panting as his vision swam with sudden vertigo.

"Something happened to you in a vortex," Azár guessed, dark eyes widening. "Take hold of your nerves!"

Two days.

"What happened in the vortex, Darien?"

Two.

Days.

"Tell me what happened!"

Darien closed his eyes, bringing his hands up to cover his ears as he struggled to conquer his panic.

"It wasn't a vortex," he admitted. "It was a node."

"What happened?" Azár's eyes were bright with excitement.

"Arden Hannah," he gasped, squeezing his eyes shut against the pain of the memory. "She tried to immolate me."

Azár glared at him. "Good," she said at last. "I hope you screamed until your lungs blistered."

Darien opened his eyes, gaping up at her in revulsion. He'd forgotten all about Azár's sister. The satisfaction in her eyes was appalling to witness.

"Why do you hate me so much?" he gasped, jerking back away from her. *"You're sick."*

"And you're a murderous demon. What is there not to hate?"

All Darien could do was stare at her, unable to think of a suitable retort. Azár stood before him with arms crossed, eyebrows raised. There was a low growl from behind him. Darien realized that the demon-dog had become alerted to his mood. He spread his fingers wide, motioning for the beast to desist.

"Keep your distance," he warned Azár, striding away from her. He didn't trust the woman in a vortex.

"Darien!" she called after him. "The moment you died—what was the last thing you were thinking?"

He turned and glared back at her over his shoulder, incredulous that she would dare ask such a thing. *That's none of your gods-damned business.*

As he stalked away, he caught a brief glimpse of the smile in her eyes.

Chapter Eleven
Ishara

Ishara, The Black Lands

M eiran spilled forward, her body slapping hard against stone. She glanced around fearfully, startled by the absolute darkness that encased her. There was no light at all. She could see nothing, not even the outline of Quin's body at her side. And it was freezing. The ground beneath her legs felt like ice, sucking the warmth right out of her body through her skin.

Quin's features resolved beside her in a wash of wine-colored magelight. Its churning glow spread outward across the ground away from his feet. Meiran gasped, her eyes scanning quickly over the walls of the small cavern. The room they were in was like a grotto carved out of black volcanic rock of a rough and porous texture. The ceiling was high, tapering to a point far above the portal's cross-vaulted arch.

"Welcome to Malikar, Prime Warden."

Meiran turned to Quinlan Reis. "Malikar. Where did that name come from?"

"Well, they couldn't very well call it Caladorn anymore, now, could they? Not after the Onslaught wiped it off the map. Malikar literally means 'Cursed Lands.' That's where you are, my dear. Everything around you is cursed. The sky. The air. The rocks, the people. Even the gods here are cursed."

Meiran stared at him. Cautiously, she opened her mind and formed a tentative link between herself and the unsuspecting darkmage. Through that thin sliver of connection, she could sense Quinlan Reis' mood. A profound sadness filled him as he spoke, the same sorrow that lent a life-weary texture to his voice. And there was something else there, as well. Something she hadn't expected to find at all.

Guilt.

Guilt infested this man like maggots in an old, rotten corpse.

Meiran raised her eyebrows in surprise. There was little doubt in her mind that Quinlan Reis had a lot to do with Caladorn's transformation into Malikar. It was obvious that he felt responsible for the curse that had befallen his homeland. Which made sense, she supposed; the man was a Servant of Xerys. Meiran wondered just how direct a part he had played in that tragedy.

"Why is it all cursed, Quin?" Meiran pressed, abandoning formality. "Tell me."

His eyes narrowed as she stared at him, but he said nothing. Instead, Quin Reis walked toward the volcanic rock that formed the cavern's thick wall. With a phrase muttered beneath his breath and a casual flip of his hand, the rock before him seemed to dissipate, dissolving into gaping space. In place of the wall, there was now a doorway into cold, black emptiness.

Into that dim and murky space Quinlan Reis strode ahead, reaching up to secure his hat against a fierce gale of wind.

Meiran stole after him, the wall of rock solidifying behind her as she exited the chamber. The moment she stepped foot out of the protection of the hillside, the wind seized her hair, whipping it forward into her eyes and tossing it about her face. She brought her hands up, trying to constrain it as she called out to Quin. But either the darkmage didn't hear or didn't care. He walked on ahead into the wind, holding his hat against his head, black longcoat billowing.

Meiran turned, glancing behind. Beyond the small volcanic hill that housed the portal chamber arose an exceptionally tall peak, its crown frosted white with snow. The ice blazed as a strobe of lightning zigzagged down from a thick cloudbank overhead. Below and slightly to the right was another mountain, swaybacked, its ridgelines distinctive and familiar. Meiran knew the names of those two peaks, even if she had only seen them in sketches and read their descriptions in text: Orguleth and Maidenclaw. Infamous landmarks that marked the gateway to the Black Lands. As far as she was aware, no person from the Rhen had ever managed to view those two peaks from this angle. No one who'd lived to tell about it, anyway.

Meiran was shocked to discover just how black the Black Lands really were. From one horizon to the other stretched a flat plain of barren darkness. The sky was draped with sinister stormclouds, just as dark as the earth they eclipsed. Meiran's eyes went wide, her jaw going slack at the sight of forked streaks of lightning jabbing down in every direction from the sky.

"Mother of the gods," she whispered.

Ahead, Quin Reis stopped to smirk. "What did you expect, Prime Warden? It's called the Black Lands for a reason."

Meiran blinked at him, still groping with the magnitude of devastation that surrounded her. She whispered, "Where are we going?"

Quin gestured ahead with a finger. "To the north."

"How far to the north?"

"Far enough to get to know each other a little better." He made a sweeping gesture with his hand. "After you, darling."

A harsh gust of wind whipped at her dress as Meiran strode past him into the night. The air was chill and miserable, reeking of sulphur and ash. Ahead of them, glowing magma spilled down the steep sides of a cinder cone in slow-creeping rivulets.

"Where are we?" she asked, staring around at the frozen, sterile wastes that stretched expansively to the far horizons.

"Skara," Quin responded. "Well, it used to be called Skara. Now they call it Ishara, but it's the same damn place. The town's up ahead. We can hold up there for the night before moving on in the morning."

"There are actually towns here? With people?" Meiran was surprised.

Quin fixed her with a stunned expression. He shook his head slowly in amazement. "Yes, Prime Warden. There are towns here. With people, even. What were you expecting? A race of savage hordes wandering the open wastes, feeding off the remains of their own dead?"

Meiran sighed. "I'm sorry, Quinlan. A thousand years of warfare does tend to breed a seed or two of resentment."

The darkmage cracked a loathsome grin. "A seed or two, I could understand. But you act as though we're not too far removed from animals. I can assure you, we're far beyond that. A thousand years of darkness is a brutal penance, but it does make for a resilient population. Anyone unworthy of survival has no chance to endure. In the Black Lands, only the strongest and most resourceful survive. The weak and ill-equipped have long since perished. You know, Prime Warden, I do think the people of Malikar may surprise you more than you think."

There was very little talking after that; the ice-chill gale sapped Meiran's strength, leeching it right out of her. They trudged on against the wind into the endless shadows of the hostile wastes. To the left, the cinder cone belched a thick spew of bright orange magma. A glowing river of lava meandered toward their path, spanned by a narrow arch of volcanic rock. Meiran followed Quin up and over that treacherous bridge.

After perhaps an hour of walking, a diffuse white glow appeared on the northern horizon. Quin angled toward it, holding his hat with his hand. The wind still labored against their progress, struggling to impede their every step. Meiran walked leaning forward, her arms hugging her chest. Her fingers were numb, her body shivering violently.

"What is that?" she called to Quin, indicating the bright horizon with a nod.

"The lightfields of Ishara," Quin informed her.

Meiran did not press him to elaborate. He didn't look as though he cared to and, besides, she didn't have the energy. Up ahead a creaking vertical windmill spun violently around its axis in the gusting wind. It was missing more than a few steel blades, like a smile that lacked enough teeth to sustain it.

"Ah. We must be getting close to civilization," her darkmage companion muttered.

Meiran's gaze lingered on the windmill as they passed, wondering where the people were who tended the mechanism.

She didn't have long to wonder. Within minutes, a tall wall appeared ahead of their path, built of massive stones. At the sight of it, Quin pulled up, turning back to her with a worried expression on his face.

"That's Ishara. In just a few minutes, we'll be walking through the town gate. From this point on, I want you to keep your mouth shut and let me do all the talking. Some people still speak Rhenic here, or, rather, a version of it. But your accent would take a fair amount of explaining. Especially if someone gets a glimpse of those chains on your wrists. If anyone sees those, you'll be lucky if you don't end up skewered in a bonfire. Do you understand, Prime Warden? From here on out, you're mute."

Meiran nodded. She had no desire to be identified. She pulled the long sleeves of her gown down lower over her hands, making certain the marks of the chains on her wrists were well and truly covered.

"What is my name going to be?"

Quinlan Reis glanced at her sideways. "What?"

"My name," she insisted. "You can't call me Meiran Withersby."

He shrugged. "You can still be Meiran. It's a common enough name, even here."

"Meiran what?"

"There's no family names here. We use different conventions." He frowned. But then he smiled, amusement glimmering in his eyes. "We'll tell everyone you're my wife. It's the best way to avoid uncomfortable questions."

Meiran's mouth fell open as shocked anger kindled in her eyes. But Quin held up his hand, halting her protest.

"Listen, darling. Try not to get too excited; you're really not my type. I prefer my women more...affable." He supplied a wry grin. "It's just the best way to keep attention off of you and onto me. As my wife, you'll be all but invisible. But if I bring an available young woman into a border town like Ishara, I'll be fighting every man to the death. I very much doubt you'd want that kind of attention. Am I correct, Prime Warden?"

"No," Meiran was forced to admit. "I don't."

Quin shot her a sardonic grin. "Good. Then we're in agreement. Let's go, *my dear.*"

To her horror, Quin caught her by the hand, pulling her in familiarly close. He kept his eyes off her, at least. Arm in arm, they strolled toward Ishara's fortified outer wall, toward a wide opening that appeared to serve as the town gate.

There, Meiran found herself confronted by the first man of the Enemy she had ever seen.

A stationed guardsman stood to the side of the entrance, surveying their approach. Like Quin, his skin was olive, his dark hair thick and lustrous. A long nose, thin and proudly arched, lent dignity to his face. The guard was dressed in a thick gray tunic over a lean and muscular frame. He wore an iron breastplate and carried a spear in one hand, a round shield at his back. The guard glared at them as they approached, the expression on his face openly hostile.

Quin walked right up to the man, holding his hat against the wind. *"Ranu kadreesh,"* he shouted loud enough to be heard over the gale. As the guard glowered at him in silence, Quin launched into a harsh-sounding string of words that Meiran had no hope of comprehending.

By the time Quin was finished speaking, the guardsman was on his belly on the ground in front of Quin, folded over his knees in the dirt. The darkmage waved his hand in the air over the man's head in a gesture that looked something like a benediction or blessing.

He turned back with a smile, inquiring of Meiran, "Well, then. Shall we, my dear?"

He took her again by the arm, guiding Meiran through the gate and leaving the guardsman lowered in the dirt.

Meiran started to speak but was instantly halted by a shake of Quin's head. Turning, she caught sight of scattered villagers scurrying through the dark and narrow streets. The town stank of coal smoke, mud, and human waste. Some people carried baskets that dangled from yokes worn over their shoulders or pushed carts loaded with goods. There was smoke everywhere. No one looked as though they'd had much to eat in a very long time.

Meiran glanced down and saw that Quin was walking in a pool of magelight that swirled about the ground at his feet. Those who were moving toward them stopped, often mid-stride, when they saw that glowing mist. Men and women bowed forward before backing deferentially away, clearing a path for them. It was obvious they had a good understanding of Quin's nature and were certain of his status in their society. Taking Meiran's hand in his, the darkmage led her toward the center of town. Quin's glowing mist roamed ahead of them like vaporous wisps of dark-red flame.

"The magelight marks me as a Servant of Xerys," he explained under his breath. "Their Lightweavers don't have the energy to waste on such indulgence. Nor can they produce anything close to this saturation of color."

Meiran frowned, not fully understanding what Quin was trying to say. Up ahead, she noticed a large group of people gathered at the base of a terraced structure. Meiran glanced at Quin with a questioning look.

"The Temple of Xerys," he informed her.

Meiran's eyes widened. They walked toward the temple, striding through the glow of Quin's magelight. The people in the back of the crowd took notice of them first, drawing back out of their way. The crowd seemed to ripple as it opened up before them, folding back to clear a path ahead of them to the temple steps.

Meiran glanced over at Quin, noticing that the darkmage did not seem surprised by the crowd's reaction. Instead, he seemed indifferent to it. She opened a thin link between them, gauging his emotions. To her surprise, she found that Quinlan Reis was a compressed bundle of nerves. She never would have guessed that just by looking at his face. His hand guided her firmly forward at his side as he mounted the temple steps.

Meiran allowed her gaze to wander toward the gray-columned portico at the top of the highest terrace. There, at the summit of the steps, knelt a trembling and shirtless youth. Tears streaked the boy's cheeks. Above him a dark-robed man was wielding a long, reed-shaped cane. Meiran gasped, glancing sharply at Quin.

"Don't speak," he growled under his breath.

Meiran glared at him, eyes full of ire. By the vexed expression on his face, Quin took her meaning. He worked his lips in frustration as they drew up before the cowering boy.

"Who is responsible for this child?" Quin demanded, glancing around. He repeated the statement in his own language. A dark-robed man stepped forward, hefting a long cane in his hand.

Meiran knelt down and reached out her hand, resting it gently on the boy's quivering shoulder as she examined the raised welts on his back. Above her, Quin erupted into a furious dialogue with the boy's tormentor. Meiran closed her eyes, establishing a link between herself and the child. What she sensed filled her with fury.

"No!" Quin shouted at her, too late.

The boy's wounds were already healed. His eyes rolled back in his head and he fell forward against Meiran's chest, soundly asleep. She caught him up, enfolding him protectively in her arms as the shouting above her turned abruptly hostile. The next thing she knew, Quin was tugging at her arm, trying to get her to follow after him. She fought back, wrestling with him for control of her own hand.

"We need to go, *wife,*" he rebuked her acidly.

Meiran couldn't bring herself to leave the child behind. She refused to budge, clutching the boy fiercely against her chest.

"He's a criminal," Quin insisted. "He stole coin from the temple coffers!"

The boy's protruding ribs and sunken cheeks were explanation enough for Meiran. She glared at Quin, refusing him with her eyes.

Realizing his quandary, Quinlan Reis licked his lips, scowling in frustration. Behind him, two priests of Xerys were approaching. They turned and barked at their companions in their guttural language. All of the men gathered on the temple steps withdrew to the side, appearing to confer. Quin remained, standing protectively over Meiran, feet spread apart in the semblance of a fighting stance.

At last, the small node of men seemed to reach some kind of agreement. They broke apart, the oldest priest striding toward Quin, head bowed in deference. Staring at the ground, he mumbled something to the darkmage. A short conversation ensued. Meiran listened hard, trying her best to pick out as many words as she could.

At last, Quin Reis seemed satisfied. "We've reached an accord," he told her softly. "You can relax, now."

She glared up at him, skeptical.

"The temple priests are displeased," he explained. "Although the boy's punishment was delivered, your healing interfered with the impact of the lesson. I have managed to convince them to accept compensation in lieu of punishing the child further for his crime."

Meiran stared up at him, eyes questioning.

He elaborated, "The priests initially wanted you to bear the penalty for the boy's crime of theft. I explained to them that, as my wife, there was no chance in hell that I'd be allowing that. So they have asked me to bear the child's punishment in your stead."

Meiran gaped up at him, jaw dropping.

"I have decided to accept their offer. It is a matter of *sharaq*, what we call honor. All I ask is that you stay here, keep your mouth shut, and *don't intervene.*"

Stunned, Meiran watched as Quin promptly removed his hat, thrusting it into her keeping. Then he reached up and wriggled out of his black longcoat and cotton tunic. He folded both garments primly and set them aside on the ground. Startled, Meiran gazed up at the man's naked torso, appalled by the sight. Quinlan Reis was emaciated, his angular bones jutting against his tight and sallow skin.

"You don't have to stare," he admonished her, turning away. "Even here, amongst us uncivilized barbarians, it's considered quite rude."

He lowered himself to his knees in the place the boy had occupied at the top of the temple steps. To Meiran's horror, the eldest priest stepped forward, wielding a thin rattan cane that was longer than his arm. He lifted the cane up high in the air, bringing it down forcefully across the darkmage's back with a shocking *crack.*

Quin winced, jaw clenching in pain.

Meiran brought her hand up, covering her mouth in revulsion as she reflexively squeezed the unconscious boy tighter against her chest.

The cane was brought down again, scoring another mark. And another. The cane rose and fell several more times, cracking sharply each time it scored another welt across Quin's bare flesh. He suffered in silence, eyes squeezed shut, fists clenched against his sides. Meiran counted: ten lashes were delivered in all. The last one left Quin bowed forward over his knees. The robed priest handed the cane off to a man behind him, at last nodding in satisfaction before stepping away.

Meiran was shaking by the time it was done, horrified by the shocking brutality she had just been forced to witness. She remained where she was, cradling the unconscious boy against her, as the crowd at the base of the steps slowly began to disperse. Minutes crept by. At last, she realized that the priests had retreated. They were finally alone on the temple steps.

"Are you all right?" she whispered to Quin.

He nodded, eyes squeezed closed. He hadn't moved from the spot where they'd left him. His back was crisscrossed with raised welts. A couple of the stripes had parted his skin, penetrating into the deep tissue beneath. The priests had not gone easy on him, despite his status. Perhaps they had been even harsher on him because of it.

"Can you walk?" she asked.

Again, Quin just nodded. He opened his damp eyes, pushing himself up off the ground slowly with both hands, grimacing as he straightened his back. He squared his shoulders. Then he indicated his hat in Meiran's hands.

Meiran lay the boy down gently and rose, offering the darkmage back his hat. She concentrated, opening a link to him. Probing Quin, she sensed his condition. He was in a good deal of pain, but there was surprisingly no resentment within him.

"Does Darien know you're a sensitive?"

Meiran blinked, gazing in shock into Quin's eyes. "How did you know?" she whispered.

The darkmage scowled. Or perhaps it was a grin. With Quin, it was often hard to tell the difference. "I was in love with a sensitive, once. A long time ago. There's a certain look she used to get on her face whenever she read me. You get the same look. Does Darien know?"

"He knows," Meiran admitted, keeping her voice low.

"And he doesn't mind? My, but that's rare. Most people would have a big problem with it."

Meiran gazed at him levelly. "Did you ever mind?"

Quin shook his head. "With Amani? Never. I was always glad that she could tell what I was feeling; I had nothing to hide from her. I always enjoyed having her in my head, all the way up to the day she died. But that day...no. It was no good." His voice trailed off as he shook his head.

"What happened?" Meiran prodded softly.

Quin lowered his chin until his eyes were lost under the shadows of his hat. "The day Amani died was the first day I ever drank. I drank until I pissed myself, hoping that would stop her from reading me. I didn't want her feeling my emotions. She had enough to deal with already."

He turned away. With his hat in his hand, he gestured at the sleeping boy. "Somewhere that child has parents. Maybe we can talk them into giving us a meal and a place to sleep."

"Wait. Let me heal you," Meiran insisted.

"No, darling. I'll be wearing these stripes for another day or two. At least until we're out of this gods-forsaken town." His face became stern. "But just so we're clear on this: next time, Prime Warden, you can pay the price for your own decisions. I've already got enough on my tab."

They remained at the temple entrance until the boy's father finally arrived, sprinting up the steps, confused and belligerent. Meiran couldn't understand anything the man was shouting at

Quin, only that he was fierce and hostile, the brunt of his anger directed at the darkmage. He scooped his son up in his arms, tossing the boy over his shoulder like a sack and, still shouting curses behind him, carried the flailing body of his child down and off the temple steps.

"Well, that's gratitude if I ever saw it," the darkmage seethed, watching the pair disappear into the streets. "Rub *my* nose in the sand, will you?" He turned his head to the side and spat.

Meiran could only shake her head. "These people are awful," she muttered quietly. "They're barbarians."

"No, Prime Warden. They're not barbarians. They're just desperate," Quin corrected her, staring off into the shadowed distance. "A brutal country makes for brutal people. They've endured so much for so very long." He sighed, adjusting his hat. "Come on, let's get going."

"Going where?"

Quin gritted his teeth as he bent over to retrieve his clothing from off the ground. Then he turned and trudged away from her, his gait stiff as he wandered toward the entrance to the temple. "The priests offered us a place to stay for the night. Since that child's father wasn't inclined to shelter us, I figure we should take the clerics up on their offer of hospitality."

Meiran tensed at the idea, not liking it one bit. She had no desire to spend an evening in a house of Quin's dark god. "Is there another option?"

Quin shook his head. "Not if you want to eat."

He strode back toward the temple, carrying his coat and tunic wadded against his side. A thin line of blood leaked from one of the welts raised on his back. Meiran followed him, a gust of wind fanning the strands of her long brown hair.

Within was a narrow corridor lit by blazing torches ensconced upon the walls. The passage angled sharply downward, curving. It was chill within, but not nearly as cold as the ground outside. The air was moist, thick with smoke and the stench of oil and decay. Meiran walked with her eyes on Quin's wounds, silently counting his protruding ribs. In life, Quinlan Reis had not been a healthy man. In death, he hadn't fared much better.

That last thought made her stop. For a moment, Meiran stood frozen between strides, her weight balanced over her feet. For some reason, it hit her. Just then. Quinlan Reis was not alive. Even though he stood there bleeding before her, he was not a living human being.

"Everything all right, darling?"

He had paused to turn back and stare at her, eyebrows raised expectantly.

Meiran gaped at him, appalled. "Are you truly dead, Quin?"

His face turned into a troubled mask of confusion. Slowly, understanding grew in his dark eyes. "Oh, I am very dead, I assure you." he told her gently. "Reunited with my body, but only just temporarily. I'm afraid it's not a permanent condition. But then again, life is never a permanent condition, now, is it?"

"No. It's not," Meiran whispered. She swallowed. "So, tell me, Quin. What is the difference?"

He stared at her flatly. "Are you asking me what it means to be a demon?"

Meiran nodded.

Quinlan reached up and scratched his chin. He moved toward her until he was gazing down into her face. His expression was very solemn and very tired. "It means that this is all there is," he said softly. "This is all that's left for me. No more."

Meiran frowned up at him. "I don't understand."

"Well, let's take you, for example. You've got your life to live, Prime Warden. Maybe you'll make a difference and maybe you won't. Maybe you'll be happy. Maybe you won't. It really doesn't matter. Because when you die, no matter what, you get to move on to a better place. A place where you can be with the people you love and who love you. You will know happiness and peace.

"But for me, this is it. This is as good as it gets." He spread his arms, turning slowly around, displaying the angry stripes that crossed his back. "I have nothing to look forward to. This is my moment of glory. My chance to prove myself. Either I make a difference now or my entire existence has been for absolutely nothing. Because if the Well of Tears is ever sealed again, I won't be coming back. I'll be trapped in hell forever—and hell is not a happy place to be. In truth, I wouldn't wish it on anyone."

Meiran found herself staring at the ground by the time he had finished speaking. She had drawn a link with him and had been reading his emotions the entire time. She knew that Quin Reis was telling the truth. She could feel the weight of his weary despair.

At last, she finally understood the price Darien had paid to bring her back. He had given up far more than just his life; he had sacrificed his every last hope of peace.

"There must be something you can do," she protested, feeling a hot stab of grief tightening her chest. "There must be some way you can redeem yourself."

Quin quirked his mouth, shrugging slightly. "There is. But I would have to accomplish something profound enough to tip the balance of my soul."

Meiran considered his words. "You don't seem so very evil," she argued. "Such an act might be possible."

"Oh, I'm evil enough, have no doubt," the darkmage assured her.

Through her link with him, Meiran could sense the truth of his words. As unbelievable as it seemed, Quinlan Reis spoke nothing but fact.

"How can that be?" she asked. "I don't sense that kind of evil in you."

"There is nothing *but* evil left in me, darling. Don't you understand?" He leaned forward until his face was only scant inches from her own. An angry desperation seethed in his eyes. "I betrayed the woman I loved. I betrayed my own brother. I betrayed the Lyceum, my clansmen, my entire nation. I even betrayed my own gods! There is literally no one alive in this world today whose life hasn't been impacted by my choices. Don't you get it? *I* caused the Desecration. *Me!* No one else. All of this horror that you see all around you: the darkness, the starvation, the suffering, the wars, the death — *it's all my own damn fault!*"

Meiran stared up at him, too horrified to speak. For long seconds, all she could do was gape. "How can that be?" she demanded, face twisted in disgust. "You didn't create the Well of Tears."

Quin Reis pulled back from her and spun away. He reached up, settling the brim of his hat lower on his head, adjusting it down until his eyes were lost in shadow.

"You're right," he agreed. "I didn't create the Well of Tears. But I swear by all the gods, I'm going to be the one who destroys it."

Chapter Twelve
The Black Lands

The Ghost Waste, The Black Lands

Darien stared out across the bow of the vessel that carried them, smoking and sputtering, against the river's swift current. The terrain on both sides of the watercourse was dark and undulating, blacker than the pit of hell and twice as deadly. It was as if they were adrift in a tempestuous sea of shadowy dunes that rolled like the swells of an ocean, broken only by the occasional rock that seemed to bob like flotsam in the rolling darkscape.

The boat they had boarded in Ibri was contrary to anything in Darien's personal experience. Instead of sails, the barge was powered by steam. River water was heated in an iron boiler and then condensed, its energy directed through long, corkscrewing shafts that drove two paddle wheels on opposite sides of the vessel. The barge was flat and long, big enough to hold every person in Haleem's caravan, along with the assortment of goods they carried. The craft was fitted with two large stacks that belched forth dense plumes of smoke into the air. The going was tedious, painfully slow.

"They call this the Ghost Waste."

Darien nodded in silent acknowledgement. He hadn't been able to bring himself to speak to Azár in two days. The anxiety provoked by the absence of the magic field taxed his patience; he didn't trust himself to speak. Funny; ever since he had made a purposeful decision to ignore the woman, Azár seemed hell-bent on conversation.

"They call it the Ghost Waste because the Spirits of the Wild roam this desert," Azár elaborated. She was leaning on her elbows over the rail beside him.

Darien didn't reply. Instead, he focused his attention on the deck just under his feet and did his best to ignore her. The loss of the magic field made his skin crawl. Even after two days, he hadn't been able to rid himself of the feeling of infestation, like a host of parasites burrowing just beneath the surface of his skin. For the twentieth time that hour, he scratched at the same red spot on the back of his arm. It didn't help. No matter what he did, he couldn't be rid of the feeling that there were insects crawling over him.

"It is said that the Spirits of the Wild are the shades of all the animals that once roamed these wastes," Azár went on. "I cannot tell you if that is accurate. All I know is that they wander endlessly and hunger endlessly. They are very dangerous and must be avoided at all cost."

Again, Darien could only bring himself to nod. She was speaking in answer to a question he'd never asked. He raked his nails over the back of his hand then brought his arm up to scrub the acrid sting of smoke out of his eyes.

The desert was cold and clear. Despite the darkness, it was just as parched as any desert he'd ever looked upon. Azár insisted that the Ghost Waste had once been a rich and fertile grassland. But that was before the Desecration. Now, with no plants to hold down the topsoil, wind had eroded the steppe into a denuded expanse of black sand drifts. The thin line of the River Nym followed a meandering course along the bases of the dunes, progressing ever westward.

Darien glanced up and blinked, frowning intensely.

"Is that *magelight?*"

Ahead, in the distance, the horizon was bathed in a diffuse warm glow, like a blanketing, ethereal haze.

"Those are the lightfields of Bryn Calazar," Azár said, drawing herself up straight. "When we reach the lightfields, we will then be outside of the power vortex. There, you can feel safe again."

Darien glared at her. His foul mood had as much to do with this woman's contempt for him as it had with the vortex. He grimaced, regretting ever speaking to Azár at all. He lowered his hand back to his side, taking comfort in the thanacryst's presence. He scratched the demon-hound on the back of the neck, running his hand up and over an ear. The beast leaned its head back, nuzzling Darien's thigh in gratitude for the attention.

The boat glided onward, following the course of the river as it snaked its way around the gravelly base of an eroded drumlin. A breeze came up, pungent with the smell of coal-soot. The glow on the horizon grew ever-brighter as they neared, like a golden aurora washing the sky in sparkling tides of light.

And then he saw the impossible: vibrant, living fields of green.

The black plains ahead miraculously yielded to sprawling acres of verdant farmland, extending outward away from them as far as the eye could see.

Darien moved forward, his hand fiercely gripping the steel rail of the barge. His mouth gaped in disbelief. Under the sinuous ribbons of magelight grew enough food to sustain all of Bryn Calazar. Perhaps all of Malikar.

"Lightfields," he whispered. "You use magelight to grow your crops. How can that be? Plants require such a broad range of colors. How can you produce enough magelight to cover enough of the sun's spectrum?"

Azár smiled with pride. "Many legacies were brought together long ago to produce the most effective blend of light."

Darien regarded her in wonder. That explained the golden brilliance of the magelight that mirrored the light of the Rhen's living sun. It was a mixture, the combination of many magical lineages. Because that's how sunlight worked; it wasn't like paint, where blending all of the colors together on a palette would only yield black. Sunlight was the result of mixing together every color of the rainbow at once.

Such an undertaking, though...such a tragedy. Blending enough magical legacies to produce this character of light must have required rivers of mage-blood.

"Gods' mercy," Darien whispered, voice gruff with horror. "How many deaths did that take?"

"Not as many as you would think," Azár assured him, looking

both proud and dreadful at the same time. "There were not many mages left after the Desecration; all those trapped within the Lyceum were killed. So, it took a lot of time. Many generations. Many years of starvation, until we could begin to approach the quality of light that was necessary."

"You're a Lightweaver," Darien spat almost accusingly. "How many combined lineages are inside you? What tier do you rank?"

Azár shrugged. "The number of lineages doesn't matter. There is no record of that. But I can tell you that I am second tier."

"Second tier?"

"Yes. Second tier."

Darien spread his hands, indicating the wide swath of magelight that rippled across the sky above them. "How can you come close to managing something as vast as all this if you are only second tier?"

Azár lifted her chin, her eyes hostile and seething. "Because this is what we are trained to do. It is *all* that we do. When we arrive back at my village, I will weave the light. That is *all* I will do, every day of my life, until my death. Then someone else will weave the light after me."

At last, Darien finally understood. He understood completely.

He lowered his eyes, too appalled to gaze any longer at the verdant fields that lined the riverway. He understood the tremendous sacrifice it took to grow those fields, of the lives of the mages who sustained them.

He walked back toward the stern of the boat, leaving both Lightweaver and thanacryst behind. Soft golden rays streamed down from the sky, dappling his shoulders and warming the skin of his face. Even the cool breeze moving across the bow couldn't suppress that glowing warmth. Darien closed his eyes. He spread his hands beneath the coruscating ribbons, savoring the warm texture of the magelight. For just a moment, he felt almost content.

The Khazahar Desert, The Black Lands

They were a week out from Bryn Calazar's lightfields. The sky had grown dark once again, the clouds stretching high overhead, hostile and angry, ever-brooding. A queer green light emanated from deep within their depths, fluttering spastically like a failing heartbeat.

Darien hadn't spoken to Azár again. He stood now at the bow of the steam vessel, feet apart, cloak drawn out behind him on the wind. He gazed out across the still, black waters and dark expanse of terrain. The hardpan of the desert bristled with a forest of vertical pipes that were shoved hither and thither like great spikes driven fast into the ground. Every so often one would give a great, fat belch of flames. More pipes sprawled across the soil, twisting like iron snakes.

He didn't know what manner of hell the pipes brought forth from the ground. He only knew that the sight and stench of such industry caused a thick lump of dread to catch in his throat like a ball of half-chewed food. He swallowed against that lump, forcing it down into his stomach. There, it sat like a brick, eating at his middle.

The sound of shouts came from behind them. Darien turned. Men were running toward the side of the craft, carrying thick coils of rope over their shoulders that they cast out over the railing of the steamer.

They were putting into shore.

"This is as far as the river will take us. After this, the water becomes too shallow. Get your pack. We walk from here."

Darien flinched at the sound of Azár's voice. It was the first time she had spoken since the lightfields. He complied without a word, striding over to where he had left his pack, picking it up and shrugging it on over his shoulders. He straightened his back under the weight of it, then looked expectantly at Azár.

Haleem's people disembarked first, dragging their possessions along after them in a drawn-out, single-file train. Darien and Azár fell in toward the end of the line, the demon-hound trotting dutifully after.

A paved road led away from the way station, cutting through the black center of the desert. It was lined with rocks and human bones and all manner of debris. On either side of the road, the barren waste appeared exceptionally sinister and foreboding. The blackened sand shifted and shimmered with tiny flecks of mica that sparkled like stars in the brief flashes of cloud light.

Azár smiled and asked, "How long are you going to remain sulking?"

Darien ignored the woman. He concentrated on the path under his feet, on the clank of items that shifted in his pack at every stride. On the crunch of gravel just under his boots.

"There is much you need to learn. Like this. Do you even know what this means?"

She was gesturing at a formation of long, flat stones stacked purposefully one atop the other, arranged into a knee-high projection along the side of the path.

Darien shrugged. He didn't know or care about the purpose of the rocks.

"It is a marker." Azár fumed at him with turbulent eyes. "It says, 'Water is this way.' Another could say, 'A village lies this way.' Things like that."

Darien stopped. He wandered over to the column of arranged stones and considered it for a moment. He thought about knocking the damn thing over with his boot. The notion was tempting. Instead, he scowled at Azár, glaring at her through a dark lock of hair that had fallen forward into his face.

"You need to decide how you feel about me," he said flatly.

Azár narrowed her eyes, lifting her chin in defiance. "What do you mean?"

"You can't keep doing this. Either you forgive me or you don't. Either you despise me or you don't. You can't have it both ways. So, which will it be?"

Azár's lips compressed together into a thin line. Resentment smoldered in her dark eyes. She didn't answer him.

He waited, staring at her as members of Haleem's caravan ambled by, considering the pair of them with kindly smiles and warm curiosity. Behind him, the thanacryst growled softly.

At last, Darien nodded.

"All right, then. You've made your choice."

He turned and started walking away. Her voice stopped him.

"I chose nothing!"

He didn't turn around. "Aye, you did."

"I did not!"

"You *did,*" he insisted, casting a weary glance back over his shoulder. "You've made your decision, Azár. Now, leave me be."

A gust of wind came up, raking at his cloak. He turned his face in the direction of the wind, gazing out into the darkness that encased the sky.

The expression on his face collapsed.

"What is that?"

Azár whirled, startled eyes lurching in the direction of his gaze. Her mouth fell open.

"That is death!" she shrieked over the sudden howl of the wind. "We must find shelter! *Run!*"

She scrambled forward and caught Darien by the arm, yanking him after her as she careened off the road. People were panicking, fleeing, dropping their burdens in the dirt and dodging off the path in every direction. Darien glanced back at the surging mass that loomed like a thick black curtain across the center of the desert, obscuring all evidence of the horizon.

The day grew suddenly, impossibly, darker.

A tidal wave of sand was hurling toward them, a churning wall that reached high into the sky and loomed ominously, threatening to consume everything in its path. Ahead of the storm, forked tongues of lightning stabbed downward at the ground, strobing across the desert.

Darien gripped the straps of his pack, fighting against the wind to keep up with Azár as she dragged him forward off the road toward a crumbling, eroded embankment. He had to fight at every step against the brutality of the wind.

The wall of sand was right behind them, spanning the desert's broad length, reaching the way station and the river. The wind scooped the steam barge right up out of the water and tossed it high into the air like a child's toy. It landed bow-first, speared like a skewer into the desert.

Darien yanked his arm out of Azár's hold, turning back to face the violent assault of the storm.

"What are you doing?" Azár screamed at him, jerking frantically at his arm. "This is *sakeem!* A man-killer! We must find shelter!"

Darien gazed at the scattered provisions left haphazardly where they lay. Far down the trail, two women struggled toward them, one tugging with both hands on an iron cart handle while the other pushed from behind. One wheel of the cart had become mired in a rut.

Darien took a step forward, closing his eyes, and sampled the currents of the magic field. He sent his mind out across tides of air, testing his will against the fury of the storm. It was far worse than he'd thought, a severe disturbance in the air that encompassed much more of the atmosphere than he'd thought. Against such a force, he found his own strength seriously wanting.

Darien opened his eyes, feeling numb.

"I can't do this alone," he admitted.

Azár gazed at him with wide, terrified eyes. She brought her hand up to draw her scarf across her face, fixing it in place against the fine grains of sand that pebbled them with scouring fury.

"This thing cannot be done," she insisted. "Please! It is *sakeem!* It will eat your flesh and throw away your bones!"

Darien shook his head, offering his hand. "Feel through me. I'll show you what to do."

Azár backed away as if repulsed. "What you ask..."

Darien waited silently, palm extended. After a moment's hesitation, Azár finally swallowed and took his hand. He closed his fingers around hers, locking his grip firmly around her own. He closed his eyes. He could hear the howl of the storm, feel the sting of the sand biting his face. He could sense the torrent of charged energies carried toward them by the gale. The wall of needling death was almost on top of them.

Darien filled his mind with a startling, amber calm.

Once again, he sent his thoughts out across the air, groping at the violent reaches of the sky. He grappled mentally with the force of the wind, struggling to quell its sinister fury. Overhead, lightning flared and thunder exploded as the clouds retaliated with violence against his meddling.

Balls of hail rained down from the sky, pelting the ground all around them.

Darien clutched Azár's hand, imploring her silently. Her fingers trembled in his grasp.

All that he had was not enough. Nowhere close to enough.

But then Darien realized: without knowing it, he'd been holding back. The magic field was not the only resource he was capable of tapping. Despite his reservations, Darien realized that he could no longer afford the luxury of denying the darker aspects of his nature.

He had died and been remade.

He was no longer a man. He was a demon.

A demon with a confused but sinister purpose.

For the very first time, Darien Lauchlin opened his mind to the power of hell and drew on the cold fury of the Onslaught, letting it ravage his brain with velvet claws.

He gasped, falling to his knees, tormented by rapturous waves of bliss unlike anything he'd ever experienced.

Compared to the seductive violence of the Onslaught, the magic field was impotent, insignificant.

He was no longer aware of Azár at his side.

He struggled to his feet, panting, drowning, writhing in wondrous, frantic ecstasy. Above, the wall of billowing dust shuddered backward, collapsing in upon itself as if repulsed by the infernal assault that was being delivered.

Lightning flared and thunder clashed. Hail pelted the ground with vicious abandon, the roar of it almost deafening.

"What is that? *What are you doing?*"

Darien opened his eyes and peered at Azár in dazzled confusion. Submerged in the violent bliss of the Onslaught, he had a hard time even recognizing her. It took him a long, bleary moment to focus on her face. She was considering him, studying his features. Then something in her expression subtly changed. Inside, something clicked. Somehow, she understood what was happening.

Azár's eyes widened with excitement. She threw her head back with a whoop of elation.

"*Ishil'zeri!*" she exclaimed through her laughter. "You are magnificent! You are *my* Sentinel, now!"

Darien shot her a look of gaping dismay.

Above, the heavens flared as the clouds slammed back together, showering zigzag trails of sparks across the sky. Darien trained his attention upwards, focusing his mind on the approaching storm. The billowing wall of dust crumbled backward as if repulsed, collapsing. The wind reversed in direction, driven back the other way.

Darien could feel the moment when Azár added her own strength to the battle that raged above them in the sky. With delicate skill, she tamed the unruly currents of air, pacifying what was left of the storm's resistance.

A thick blanket of calm settled in around them, the wind stilling to a quiet breeze. Sand rained straight down from the sky, the failing updrafts no longer capable of sustaining it.

Azár was only second tier. But she was far more skilled than Darien in the ways of light and air and sky. Together, hand in hand, they quelled the storm's fury. The breeze ebbed, disappearing entirely. Eventually, the roar of thunder became a fragile, half-remembered whisper on the wind.

In the stark calm that settled, Darien finally relaxed enough to release the Hellpower and let it drain out of him. He fell to his knees, overcome by a jarring wash of dizziness. He felt suddenly, desperately weak. Azár's grip on his hand steadied him enough so that he didn't fall over on his face. Propping himself upright with a hand thrust down into the sand, he struggled to catch his breath, panting, his pulse echoing in his ears.

Azár ripped the scarf away from her face, revealing cheeks flushed pink with excitement. "I've made my choice," she announced proudly into the darkness. "I choose you."

Darien peered up at her, shoulders heaving as he gasped for breath through a ball of dust that choked his throat. "How can you say that?" he whispered in a gravelly voice, gagging a bit on the words. "What's changed?"

She cracked a grin, reaching out to brush away the sand that still clung to his face.

"Everything has changed," she assured him. "The Prime Warden said to trust you. I did not believe him, but now I do."

"Why?" Darien demanded, frowning in exasperation. "What changed your mind?"

"Because I have seen the power that Xerys has placed within you. It is pure. It is beautiful! There can be no going back for you. I understand that, now. You are His Eternal Servant, and I am your Lightweaver. I will follow wherever it is you lead, for you will deliver my people from the darkness just as you promised."

Darien gazed at her, mouth slack. He shook his head, patently confused.

That night, they camped by the side of the river. There were no tents; tents were too bulky and heavy to be transported across the wastes. Instead, Haleem's people camped under the clouds, building fires of coal bricks.

Darien ate alone off to the side, well away from the smoke of the cookfires and the constant stares of the people in the camp. He sat leaning back against a boulder, cupping a bowl in both hands. The thin stew was heavily spiced. He took his time about eating it, savoring the blend of flavors in his mouth, the heat of the stew warming his belly.

He glanced up at the sound of approaching footsteps. It was Haleem, his wife at his side. Behind the two of them stretched a long line of people. Darien set the bowl down and rose awkwardly, dusting off his pants and shaking the dirt from his cloak. Haleem's expression was enigmatic; Darien couldn't guess the man's purpose.

The caravan master stopped in front of him as the others surrounded him, their bodies pressing in closely. Darien gazed from face to face, alarmed by their proximity. The presence of so many people seemed like an oppressive weight bearing down on him, making him feel like he couldn't get enough air to breathe. He brought his arm up, wiping his mouth with a sleeve.

Azár appeared, stepping out from the crowd of people to stand on Haleem's right. Her hair was freshly plaited, her skin washed. She appeared completely unaffected by her part in the struggle against the storm. There was no trace of fatigue in her eyes. She was wearing a new shawl wrapped around her shoulders, a rich ochre fabric, frayed at the edges.

Without speaking, Haleem raised his hands, offering out a folded garment.

Uncertainly, Darien accepted the offered parcel from Haleem. He held the fabric up in front of him, shaking out the folds. It was a rectangular piece of black woven cloth, heavily embroidered with gold thread in an interlaced design. Two gold cords with thick tassels hung from either end.

"My thanks," he told Haleem sincerely. He gazed down at the splendid garment, having never seen anything like it before. He couldn't figure out how it was meant to be worn. "It's beautiful. But it's not necessary."

Azár moved to stand beside him. "Haleem is very grateful to you for protecting both his people and his investment."

Darien shrugged. "He doesn't need to thank me."

Azár muttered a rapid burst of speech under her breath, translating Darien's words with more than a few additions of her own. Then she plucked the garment out of his hands and moved behind him, reaching around to wind the fabric around his hips.

"It is meant to be worn this way. The tassels should hang to the left. It can be worn either over pants or by itself. It is a very fine gift."

She tied the cords, tugging the knot twice to make certain it would hold. Then, with a curt toss of her head, she stepped back, appraising him.

Darien ran his hand over the fine embroidery, continuing the motion downward to finger one of the cords. "My thanks. *Sukrien,* Haleem. I'm honored."

Haleem nodded stiffly, apparently satisfied. He brought his hand up to his chest, bowing his head. Then he turned and walked back toward the camp. As he left, another man approached, muttering something and smiling as he laid one hand on Darien's shoulder, his other hand on Azár. Yet another man moved forward and repeated the gesture before turning to follow Haleem. As Darien stood still, every person in the caravan came forward and laid their hands on the two mages in an expression of gratitude before turning back toward the camp. Eventually, the last woman turned and limped away into the darkness.

Darien was left standing alone with Azár. He stood as if in a daze, gazing in wonder at the retreating backs of the people whose lives they had saved. He was thankful for their gratitude, but even more thankful to be left alone. The closeness of so many bodies wore on his nerves.

"Did that trouble you?" Azár asked, considering him.

Darien shook his head as he brushed his palm over the new wrap Haleem had given him. "No. I just wasn't expecting it."

Azár nodded. She gazed at him with a searching look. "May I stay and speak with you for a moment?"

"Of course."

She dropped to the ground, sitting cross-legged, and motioned with her hand for him to sit down at her side. Darien hesitated, not wanting to soil Haleem's gift. He dropped to a crouch.

Azár made a clicking sound with her tongue. "Sit," she admonished him. "It was made to be worn and used. What, are you never going to sit or sleep?"

Darien couldn't help the small, fragile grin that slipped to his lips. She had a point. Carefully, he settled all the way down into the dirt, leaning back against the boulder he'd claimed previously.

Azár nodded in approval. "Tomorrow, I'll take you to my village. I would like to talk to you about the people you will meet. They are a good people. A hard people, full of pride, full of stone. But I must warn you: they will not like you."

That came as no surprise. "Because of Black Solstice?" he assumed.

Azár shook her head. "It is much more than that. You are a Sentinel of Aerysius. The warriors of my clan once followed a man who called himself a Sentinel. We followed him to our deaths. He lied to us, betrayed us, and then he abandoned us. In all the history of the Khazahar, there has never been a man so reviled."

"You speak of Braden Reis," Darien guessed.

Azár lifted a finger. "That name is never to be spoken. We speak only of his treachery. Because of this man, the people of the clans will have no trust for you at all. In truth, some may even try to kill you on sight."

"Then they'll try," Darien shrugged dismissively, spreading his hands. "There's little I can do about it."

And, indeed, there wasn't. He could defend himself if he had to, even without resorting to magic. He had been trained by a Guild blademaster; the sword that rode at his back was just as lethal as his mind. But he hoped it wouldn't come to that. Any defense he could offer would only solidify their distrust in him.

Azár was staring at him sideways, surveying him critically, her gaze harsh and full of doubt. "How do you intend to save my people, Darien?"

He hadn't anticipated that question. He was caught completely off-guard. Darien raised his eyebrows, spreading his hands and shaking his head. "I've no idea," he admitted.

Azár tilted her head to the side, her eyes narrowing. "If there is no other option, are you willing to lead my people south to invade the Rhen?"

Darien bowed his head, breathing out a heavy chestful of air. He sat there for a long while, wrestling within himself for the answer to her question. It was not the first time he had weighed this option. He had struggled with it before, many times. Just as always, the very notion made him shudder in dread.

He knew very well it might have to come to that.

As always, he found himself arriving at the same, terrible conclusion: it was not an option he could rule out.

"I'm hoping I won't have to," he whispered, staring at the ground.

Azár scooted forward until she was sitting right next to him. She gazed up piercingly into his face.

"You would, wouldn't you?" she pressed. She peered deeply into his eyes without blinking.

Darien said nothing, troubled by her directness. And her proximity. Azár's stare hardened, her lips compressing.

Somehow, somewhere in his eyes, she found her answer.

"You would," she gasped. "How is that possible? You gave your life in defense of the Rhen. Now you are willing to lead Malikar's legions against it? What changed?"

Everything, Darien realized. Everything was different, everything had changed.

Nothing could ever be the same again.

Ever since he'd started looking at the world through the eyes of a dead man.

Darien groped for the right words, struggling to find a way to describe the conflict within himself. "I didn't know the whole truth back then," he fumbled, desperate to gain her understanding. "I didn't know anything about Malikar, what the conditions are like here. I didn't know there were so many of you in such terrible need. I was always taught to just think of you as the Enemy…as if you weren't even human. Maybe animals or savages. Demons, perhaps. We were told you were evil, that you sought only to conquer, to enslave. To destroy."

He swallowed, looking down, unable to meet her gaze. "But I know better, now. Your people are not conquerors, Azár. And you're certainly not demons—you're not even the Enemy. *We are.*"

Those last two words he spat with contempt. Without looking at her. His troubled eyes wandered to the side, regarding the severe darkscape before them in angry doubt. A shadow stirred within him, settling deep into his bones, chilling his brittle soul.

He knew he was a traitor. In heart, now, as well as deed. Azár had been right; he could never go back to what he was before.

That man was dead. The part that mattered, anyway.

He had been dead a long time.

"*I'm* the demon," he whispered, gazing off into the distance. "Not you."

Chapter Thirteen
The Conclave

Glen Farquist, The Rhen

Kyel felt like a quivering mass of abraded nerves. He paced
relentlessly up and down the floor of the vestibule, fingers
interlaced behind his back. When he reached the far end
of the chamber, he turned on heel and doubled back. He finally
drew up in front of Naia with an exasperated sigh.

"Are you sure I look all right?" he said as he tugged at his shirt
collar with a finger.

"Stop fretting. You look like a Sentinel."

He adjusted his posture, squaring his shoulders. "Do I look
official?"

"Very official." She paused, frowning. "Except for that."

She reached out and smoothed the collar of his shirt. "That's
better. Now you look official."

Kyel groaned and ran his hands through his hair. "This is
bloody killing me. Why can't they just get on with it?"

Naia plucked a bit of lint from his cloak. "Be patient. There's
certain protocol that must be followed. Think of it as a series of
steps. Each step must happen in a particular order with a great
deal of pomp and ritual. They certainly won't rush the process
simply because we're the first mages who've had the audacity to
grace their doorstep in five hundred years."

"Well, it's unnerving."

They had been left in the vestibule of the Chapel of Nimrue.
Naia's father had told them to remain there while he presented
their request to the Conclave. Then he'd withdrawn, the great
mahogany doors shut and locked from within, the tumblers

echoing as they fell into place.

That had been hours ago.

There was a ringing, metallic noise, and then one of the tall doors was thrust suddenly open.

Kyel sucked in a sharp breath, heady with panic. He wasn't ready for this; politics had never been his strong suit. And yet, somehow, he was supposed to convince the most ancient governing body in the world to act in a way completely contradictory to its charter.

"The Conclave is ready to receive you now," a servant in bright livery announced, beckoning them forward with a red-gloved hand.

Kyel shot a glance at Naia, hoping against hope that she'd take the initiative and enter ahead of him. Just as he'd feared, she merely looked at him expectantly.

"You're the Grand Master. Not me," she reminded him.

Kyel wanted to growl. Instead, he bit his lip and followed the guard through the chapel door. *Emulate me,* Darien had once told him long ago. But every time he tried to imitate his former master's confidence, he failed miserably; he simply didn't have it in him.

But it was the only model he had. So Kyel shifted his stride, aiming for the same arrogant grace Darien managed so naturally. He felt like a fool. He clamped his jaw and clutched his hands into fists, doing his best to keep the anxiety he felt from reaching his eyes.

He stopped in the center of the chapel under the vault of the dome, Naia at his side. A straight line of six wooden thrones occupied by the various leaders of the Holy Temples stretched before him. Behind the great thrones sat rows of assistants, both lay clergy and fully ordained priests and priestesses.

Naia's father, the High Priest of Death, rose from his throne. He wore pristine white vestments with a silken stole draped over his shoulders. He seemed older than Kyel remembered, but he still had the same fire in his eyes that Kyel recalled very well.

Luther Penthos raised his hand, indicating the two mages before him. "I present to this great body Grand Master Kyel

Archer of the Distinguished Order of Sentinels. And Master Naia Seleni of the Distinguished Order of Querers."

Kyel nodded, acknowledging the introduction, just as Naia had instructed him to do.

"Thank you, Your Eminence," he responded tightly. To the others, he said, "And thank you for receiving us. It is a great honor that you do us."

He glanced down the line of thrones, noting that the temple monarchs were studying him with looks of intense mistrust.

"Grand Master Kyel, Master Naia," Luther Penthos continued, "as you know, I am the Vicar of Isap, Goddess of Death. Beginning on my right, may I present to you the Vicar of Om, God of Wisdom."

Kyel issued a brief nod in the old man's direction; he was very familiar with the bronze-robed and silent cleric.

"The Vicar of Athera, Goddess of Magic."

Kyel glanced toward an elderly woman in a purple brocade gown. The priestess regarded him with arched eyebrows, her gaze critical.

"The Vicar of Enana, Goddess of the Hearth."

This was a stout woman who wore her hair in a tight bun at the crown of her head. The woman regarded Kyel with an expression of distaste as she nodded formally in his direction.

"The Vicar of Zephia, Goddess of the Winds."

Another man, younger, with a muscular frame. His long hair was gathered back from his face. He wore a dark beard and an even darker glower. He disregarded Kyel, looking away as if unaware of his own introduction.

"The Vicar of Alt, God of the Wilds."

This man was large and impressive, with a mass of tangled beard that fell almost to his waist. He wore a belted tunic of forest green. He gave a grunt, staring at Kyel without blinking.

"And, lastly, the Vicar of Dreia, Goddess of the Vine."

Kyel flinched at the assault of color that confronted him. The High Priestess of Dreia peered at him with a sullen look through a cascade of honey-colored hair that draped over one of her eyes. She was garbed in an alarming shade of red, reclining sideways on her throne, a glass of blood-red wine held aslant between her fingers.

There were six temples accounted for, Kyel realized. The Temples of Grief and Chaos had no representation at the Conclave, for which he was grateful. Suddenly uncertain, Kyel glanced sideways at Naia for reassurance. She nodded without looking at him, her face confident as she gazed ahead at the temple monarchs.

Kyel cleared his throat, summoning the last scraps of confidence he had left. "Greetings, Your Eminences. Thank you for allowing us to present our petition before this great council. It is my understanding that this is the first time in over five hundred years that a mage of Aerysius has been allowed to address this body. I take that as a sign that the temples appreciate the gravity of the threat we all face."

As his words trailed off, Kyel's gaze slid to Naia. To his relief, he found her looking at him with a mixture of pride and appreciation in her eyes. He took that for a good sign, feeling his self-confidence bolstered.

The Vicar of the Wind raised his eyes from his lap to glare at Kyel. "Believe me, this council has a very *deep* appreciation for the gravity of this situation, which has been—yet again—forced upon us by the mage class. Which is the only reason the two of you are even here, I should point out."

Mutters of agreement echoed from all around the chapel, accompanied by a general bobbing of heads. The Vicar of Dreia tossed back a sip of wine with a grimace. Kyel glanced again at Naia, who nodded.

"Your Eminence," Kyel said, addressing Naia's father. "We accept that our predecessors are responsible for the inception of the Well of Tears in the first place. For that, we have never sought to avoid accountability. But please also understand that the Masters of Aerysius have born singular responsibility for the containment of that evil. So much of our blood has been spilt toward that end that there are only three mages left in the entire world."

Cadmus, who served as the Voice of Wisdom, raised a finger.

"That is untrue."

Kyel hesitated with a frown. He was unsure whether he should feel more confused or more affronted. He felt both in equal portions.

Cadmus clarified, "His Eminence wishes me to remind you that there are yet seven darkmages walking abroad in the world. His Eminence would also like to inform you, if you are not aware already, that the Enemy has mages of their own. Mages who have never been constrained by the Oath of Harmony."

Kyel felt his heart sink at hearing that news. He hadn't considered such a possibility. Not for the first time, he wondered how the Temple of Wisdom came by their troves of knowledge.

"I was...unaware of that, Your Eminence," Kyel admitted. "That news is...deeply troubling."

"Members of the Council, if I may?"

Kyel glanced sideways at Naia. She had taken a step forward, her hands clasped in front of her.

"You may," her father allowed.

Naia's smile was all-encompassing. Even the Vicar of Winds looked up to gaze with interest.

"The Grand Master and I understand your reservations," she announced in sparkling clear tones, eyes bright with purpose. "However, you must realize that all of the points you just mentioned only serve to bolster our argument."

"And what, exactly, is the nature of the petition you bring before this Conclave?" demanded the Vicar of Magic.

Naia motioned for Kyel to continue. He moved forward to stand beside her.

"As you are all aware, the Well of Tears has been unsealed. We will strive to close it, but that can only be accomplished by the sacrifice of a Grand Master." Kyel lowered his eyes and drew a long, quavering breath, swallowing the dread that clenched his throat. "I volunteer."

There was a hollow silence in the chapel. Kyel kept his gaze trained on the floor, unable to meet their stares. He was aware of Naia looking at him in stunned horror.

The priestess in the blood-red dress chortled in his direction.

"A very noble gesture, Grand Master Kyel. I will be sure to offer a toast if you actually manage to work up the nerve to match your bravado. But what I don't understand is why your decision to commit suicide must be ratified by this council?"

Kyel felt a flush of anger at the insult. "It doesn't, obviously," he said. "We came here today to beg the temple leadership to help us bolster the defenses of the Rhen. The last time the Well was open, Darien Lauchlin broke Oath to turn back the invasion of the Enemy. As it turns out, that solution was only temporary."

"What solution?" demanded the feral-looking Vicar of the Wilds. "That was no solution at all—for now we have a demon of Darien Lauchlin's abilities to contend with!"

Naia raised her voice. "Which is exactly why we need the help of the temples so desperately! Kyel and I do not have the strength to defend the nations of the Rhen by ourselves. There are only two of us and, besides, we are both Bound by the Oath of Harmony. I know there is great might in the assets entrusted to the temples by our ancestors. They were placed into your keeping as a safeguard, as a balance against the mage class. To prevent the Assemblies from becoming too powerful and despotic. I say it's time that the temples use those assets for their intended purpose: to defeat Renquist's darkmages before they destroy everything in this world we hold dear."

Kyel took up her point, "We ask this of you, not for ourselves, but for the people of the Rhen. Without the might of the temples, our combined military strength will not suffice. Naia and I will be of little help. We can't defend against something like this."

Cadmus raised a finger. "Grand Master Kyel. His Eminence is wondering what you will do if you are ever confronted by your former master?"

Kyel considered the question. It almost felt like a kind of test. He had no idea how they wanted him to answer.

"I suppose I would try to negotiate with him," he managed.

"*Negotiate* with him?"

"What else would you have me do? I am Bound. And Darien is not." It was the plain truth, even if it wasn't what they wanted to hear.

"Darien Lauchlin has sworn his soul to Xerys," the Vicar of Magic grumbled. "Do you honestly believe such a demon would pause to chat before slaying you outright?"

Kyel could only bow his head. "I think he might. Surely, something of the man must still remain. I'd have to try—I can't kill him. Against a darkmage, my words are the only weapons I possess."

But Naia's father shook his head. "There, you are wrong. Your Oath prevents you from striking out against him. But nothing prevents us. Working together, we should be able to bring Lauchlin down. We can bring them all down, eventually, one by one."

All around the chapel, the other clerics and their assistants were nodding, the room filling with whispered conversation. Luther Penthos turned back to Kyel. "That *is* what you're asking, is it not? Our assistance in defeating these demons and their armies? We have the right to ask: would either of you feel conflicted by such a plan?"

Kyel did feel conflicted. But he knew better than to admit it. "That is indeed what we're asking, Your Eminence. And, no. I would feel no conflict."

"And what about you, Master Naia?"

Kyel glanced at the woman beside him. Naia was staring at the ground, her hands clasped in front of her.

"Of course I would feel conflicted," she said honestly, her eyes wandering upward. "How could I not? But I have to agree, it's the right thing to do."

"Do you truly believe that?" her father pressed.

"*Yes.* Darien would have rather died than raise a hand against the Rhen. It might be that he is nothing more than a mindless shell, completely unaware of his own actions. But I suspect that's not the case. Much more likely, he's being compelled to act against his nature. If that's the case, then I cannot imagine the depths of his torment. I would not wish for him to exist in such misery."

Her father nodded, his expression softening. "Very well. Please excuse us while we deliberate."

Naia nodded. "Thank you."

Kyel took her by the arm, maneuvering her back toward the chapel's entrance. The double doors slammed closed behind them, the ancient locks clicking into place, sealing the chamber tight from within. They were alone once again in the vestibule.

Kyel sagged, scrubbing his face with his hands. "That went bloody terrible!" he gasped. "I'm not cut out for this sort of thing."

Beside him, Naia appeared wilted. Her serene air of confidence had melted clean away. She looked pale, her eyes sorrowful and downcast.

"It could have gone better."

He could tell by the sound of her voice how dispirited she was. He grumbled, "I don't even know what I'm doing in there! Why can't you do more of the talking? You're the one who's good at this sort of thing!"

Naia finally looked up at him. "Because you outrank me," she reminded him. "You are a sixth-tier Sentinel. You must learn to speak from a position of authority."

Kyel threw up his hands, barking a bitter laugh. "What authority? I can hardly call myself a Sentinel—what a joke!"

Naia's jaw clenched in anger. "You are Grand Master Kyel Archer of the Distinguished Order of Sentinels, the most powerful mage left in the world who hasn't sold his soul to Xerys. That is the man you are. *And that is the man we need you to be.*"

Kyel shook his head. "I don't know if I can be that man. I honestly don't think I've got it in me."

"You do. You just need time. And experience." She narrowed her eyes at him. "What were you thinking, volunteering your life to seal the gateway?"

He'd forgotten all about that. Kyel paced away, rubbing the back of his neck. "Well, that should be obvious. There's no other choice, is there?"

"Why not Meiran?"

Kyel shot her an exasperated look. "How could I ask that of

her? She's already made that trip once."

Naia sagged, looking defeated. "I understand," she murmured softly, But her eyes said otherwise.

The lock on the chapel doors clicked, and the massive doors swayed inward. A liveried guard appeared, beckoning them within. Kyel closed his eyes, gathering his courage. He drew in a long breath. Then he opened his eyes and offered Naia his arm. Together, they entered the chapel and walked forward to stand before the awaiting members of the Conclave.

"Grand Master Kyel Archer. Master Naia Seleni. We appreciate your patience."

Kyel straightened his posture as he strove to project the most authority he could muster. Despite his best effort, the clerics on their thrones surveyed them both with acute indifference. Even Naia's own father appeared to be looking at them through a murky pool of contempt.

At last, Luther Penthos rose to his feet. His voice resonated off the polished walls. "It is the decision of this Conclave to grant your petition…with one provision."

"What provision?" Kyel asked.

The Vicar of Magic rose to stand beside Naia's father. She explained in a crackly voice, "We agree that it has become necessary to commit the might of the temples to the defense of the Rhen. However, such a decision breaks with our covenants and puts in jeopardy many of our traditions. To offset our risk, this council demands that you surrender the governing authority vested in the office of the Prime Warden. Going forward, you will submit to the decisions made by this body."

Kyel stiffened, feeling the warmth drain from his face. His vision swam, his flesh going numb. For a moment, he couldn't react, not even in anger. He stood there gaping, breath stuck in his throat.

"What kind of offer is that?" he finally managed to gasp, still reeling from the sting of the insult. "The temples were created to balance the mage class, not dismantle it!"

But Naia's father differed. "The mage class has already been effectively dismantled. You've admitted as much yourself."

Naia spread her hands, face pale and eyes wide. "How could you even suggest such a thing? I know your intent, Father. This is no way of going about it!"

Kyel turned to her. "What is their intent?"

Eyes only for her father, Naia explained, "The temples and Aerysius have a very long history of vying for political advantage. The Conclave is exploiting our desperation to secure a position of dominance."

Luther Penthos shook his head, eyes cold and detached. "There's more to it than that. This council has access to knowledge that has, since the time of the Great Schism, been withheld from the mages of Aerysius."

Kyel demanded, "What knowledge? And why was it withheld?"

"We can tell you nothing more than what you already know. But be assured that this is the only way we can feel comfortable enough to move forward."

The grandmotherly Vicar of Magic crossed her arms across her chest. "Please consider this our final offer, Grand Master Kyel. If you reject it, then you'll leave us no choice but to align the Rhen's kingdoms against you. Which won't take much convincing; Darien Lauchlin seeded fear and distrust everywhere he went. The entire kingdom of Chamsbrey wants nothing more to do with you. Even Emmery, your greatest ally, has only suffered your presence because of Meiran's unfaltering diplomacy."

Kyel closed his eyes, his anger drowning in desperation.

Naia said, "The office of the Prime Warden has existed intact for thousands of years. Kyel and I will not be the ones to concede its authority."

Her father gave a slight, dismissive shrug. "The office is already vacant and obsolete. You would be conceding nothing."

"He's right, Naia."

Kyel was startled by the sound of his own voice. He hadn't meant to say that out loud. But he had. And Naia had heard him. She turned to gape at him in shock.

"What are you saying?" she gasped.

Kyel explained, "Aerysius is gone; there's only just the two of us. By ourselves, we can accomplish nothing. We *are* obsolete."

It hurt to admit it. But there was no use denying it, either. Before Aerysius fell, the combined might of the Sentinels had mattered for something. Even if they couldn't inflict harm with their gift, they could still protect, and what they couldn't protect, they could heal.

But the Sentinels were gone. Now there was only him.

And Kyel felt certain that, on a field of battle, he would be far more of a liability than an asset.

A strange sense of calm unfurled within his chest. He turned back to Naia's father. "Neither of us has the authority to enter into negotiations that might result in limitations to the office of the Prime Warden."

The Vicar of Magic waved a liver-spotted hand. "Then produce Meiran Withersby so we can negotiate with her."

"We don't know where she is."

The woman sat gazing at him down the length of her nose as she tugged at the bottom of her shirt. "You two *children* may as well admit it: Meiran Withersby is lost. Name her as such and be done with it. Grand Master Kyel, Master Naia. The patience of this council is not without end. One of you must volunteer to act as Prime Warden in Meiran's place."

Naia shook her head. "We will not."

"I will." Kyel took a step forward.

Naia's hand shot up, catching him by the sleeve. "Don't do this."

"I'm sorry, Naia. I have to." Kyel felt saddened as he turned away from her. He knew what she had to be feeling. He felt it, too. To the Conclave, he announced, "I am willing to speak on the Prime Warden's behalf."

The Vicar of Magic nodded. She clasped her hands together, eyebrows raised in anticipation. "Very well. Then as acting Prime Warden, we formally ask that you surrender to this body all rights, powers, and authority vested in the office of the Prime Warden. In exchange, this council formally pledges its support in the theater of war in the defense of the Rhen. Do we have your agreement, Kyel Archer, Acting Prime Warden of Aerysius?"

"You have my agreement."

To Kyel, the words didn't sound like his own. He heard them as though from a distance. As if they were just words floating toward him on the air. Words without substance or meaning. They settled in on him gradually, bearing down slowly on his shoulders, until he felt almost crushed under the sheer weight of them.

It was getting very difficult to breathe.

"Thank you, Acting Prime Warden Kyel."

The voice seemed disembodied, echoing from very far away.

"Don't thank me," Kyel gasped, staggering under the enormity of his own defeat. "Just help the Rhen. Help our people."

There was no mistaking the gloating triumph in the voice of the High Priestess as she commanded them, "Leave. Your business here is done."

Chapter Fourteen
Sharaq

Qul, The Black Lands

Darien wrenched his eyes from the ground, recalling Renquist's admonition against lowering his gaze. He looked Haleem directly in the eye as he brought his hand up to his chest, bowing solemnly. Above them, stormclouds roiled. Fat, round drops of rain began streaking haphazardly toward the ground, hitting the soil in random patterns. The rain made little difference; Darien's hair was already wet, plastered against the sides of his face. The sand at his feet smelled like wet, muddied ash.

"You have my thanks," he told Haleem. Darien lowered his hand, fingering the golden tassels of the embroidered wrap the man had given him.

Haleem took him by the arm, drawing him into a brotherly embrace. Darien winced as he felt the man's face brush the skin of his cheek. He was unaccustomed to such intimacy. The people of Malikar were used to far less personal distance than he was comfortable surrendering. Their constant closeness made Darien feel besieged, setting his already-frayed nerves on edge.

Haleem drew back, folding his hands and turning away. Darien was left staring after the man, trembling ever so slightly. He turned to find himself confronted by Azár, who stood gazing at him with a look of concern. The glare he shot her made her stare even harder.

"You don't like people, do you?" she said.

"No. I don't."

The rain was letting up. They stood at the head of a trail that wandered around the perimeter of a rock escarpment. A knee-high stack of flattened rocks marked the trail's entrance.

Darien took up the handle of one of the two carts Haleem had left for them. It was filled with bags of provisions, mostly salt and bricks of coal. He started down the trail, pulling the cart behind him, the thanacryst jogging behind.

The trail led them around the escarpment into a narrow box canyon bordered by tall cliffs. Darien didn't like the feel of the magic field in this place; it made his skin crawl. He wondered if they weren't close to another vortex. The field's energies were stronger here, more charismatic. There was a certain *pull*, urging him toward the back of the canyon.

After a short distance, the narrow corridor opened up into a gaping bowl surrounded on all sides by a tumbling array of blackened cliffs. A village had been erected in the center of the basin, a haphazard collection of jagged buildings and high, crumbling walls. The light of many lanterns spilled toward them through the darkness, emanating from balconies and windows, glowing from gaps and recesses in the cliffs above. The sound of distant laughter drifted toward them on the air.

Darien paused, taking it all in, feeling apprehension settle deeply into his bones.

Azár drew up beside him with her cart. "This is Qul, my home. My village." There was an uncharacteristic softness to her expression. "It is the home of the Jenn Asyaadi. They are my people."

Darien's eyes scanned over the layers of buildings separated by narrow paths between them. A thin gap cut into the outer wall marked the village entrance. He started toward it, dragging the wagon behind him. The hound padded after, head and ears alert. Its eyes glowed a sinister green.

The smell of coal smoke was heavy on the air, but not nearly as thick as it had been in Bryn Calazar. And there were other odors, as well, some pleasant. As they passed through the arch into a narrow walkway, the aroma of cooking made Darien's mouth water. There was also the smell of fragrant incense lingering on the air.

A man stepped out from one of the houses into the shadows of the alley in front of them.

Darien spread his fingers, signaling the demon-hound.

The man noticed them as he turned. He stopped and stared, as if trying to make out features in the darkness. He stood there frozen, blocking their path.

Darien's hand drew slowly toward his sword's hilt.

"Fareen!" Azár called out.

Hearing her voice, the man strode forward. He was thick and burly, clothed in coarse linen covered by a padded overcoat. He had the same dark skin as Azár, his hair worn drawn back behind his head. He wore a pair of knives tucked into his belt, as well as a long, curving sword. His dark eyes were startled and concerned, raking over every inch of Azár.

When his gaze fell on the ebony-hilted dagger at her side, the man's eyes widened in recognition. He bent forward, taking Azár by the hand and pressing her fingers against his lips. He muttered something under his breath that Darien didn't catch.

Azár smiled. "This man is Fareen son of Mohsen. He is my cousin." To Fareen, she said, "This man is Darien Lauchlin of Amberlie. He is here at the command of Prime Warden Renquist."

The man recoiled, his face twisting in anger. His hand went to grip the hilt of his sword.

Azár reacted, positioning herself between Darien and Fareen. Her arm shot up, staying Fareen's hand. "Darien has submitted to the will of Xerys!"

The man turned his head and spat upon the ground. He jerked his chin up, glowering as he bared threatening inches of his blade.

"Then deliver him to Xerys! Why did you bring him here?" He spoke perfect, though accented, Rhenic. He reached out as if intending to force the small woman from his path.

But Azár danced away, springing back to Darien's side. "Darien Lauchlin has been named Overlord of the Khazahar! He is *nach'tier!*"

A broad smile grew on Fareen's face, genuine humor filling his eyes. He scoffed as he slid his blade back into its scabbard. Then his expression chilled to ice. "Your hands are stained with the blood of the clans," he said to Darien. "You may be *nach'tier*, but you are not welcome in our village."

Darien nodded his head back in the direction they'd just come from. "What about over there?"

Fareen squinted, frowning as if he didn't understand the question.

"Over there," Darien specified. "The cliffs across from the gate. Is that part of your village?"

Fareen's expression remained troubled. "No…"

"Then that's where I'll make my camp." He turned and strode back toward the gate. He left the wagonload of goods behind for Azár and the people of Qul; he had no need of them. Thanacryst at his side, he walked back out through the narrow gate and crossed the dirt path to a pile of large boulders.

There, in a wide crevice between two curving legs of tumbled rocks, he rifled through his pack, finding a few morsels of flatbread and a small sack of coal. He grabbed his waterskin, throwing his head back and taking large gulps of the brackish water it contained. Then he threw himself down in the sand and began to go about the business of setting up his campsite. He found a flat rock and used it to hollow out a fire pit in the ground, laying out his blanket next to it.

"What are you doing?"

Darien glanced up into Azár's bewildered face. "Avoiding problems," he responded.

She lowered herself down onto a rock across the fire pit from him. Her face was set in grim lines of frustration.

"This avoids nothing," she said, leaning forward over her knees. Her long braid swayed over her shoulder. "You want my advice? You must eat him for lunch before he eats you for dinner."

"Are you suggesting I should murder your cousin in cold blood? That doesn't sound very honorable."

Azár scoffed. "So now you decide to worry about honor? Don't. The wicked live longer."

"I know."

She was staring at him in consternation, the smile half-frozen on her lips. She rose to her feet, flipping her long shawl back over her shoulder. "I am going to my home," she informed him. "You are welcome to come with me. If you decide to stay here, take mind: Fareen and his kin will most likely come for you in the night. You have no guest-right in this place."

Darien tilted his head to the side, studying her profile. "Why are you telling me this, Azár? Isn't your first obligation to your kin?"

"Normally, yes. But you are Overlord of the Khazahar, and I am your Lightweaver. It is my duty to help protect your life." With that, she left, walking back toward her village.

Darien woke to the sound of footsteps approaching in the night. Quiet. Stalking. He rolled over to free up his sword arm, lying still for a moment and listening, hoping the noises would retreat.

Of course, they didn't. He was never that lucky.

"Go home, Fareen," he grumbled into the night. He was exhausted; all he wanted was sleep. But his ears told him that Fareen wasn't alone. Azár's cousin had brought company. Which was problematic; Darien didn't want to kill even one man. He certainly didn't want to kill four. He pried his body up off the ground with an elbow, peering into the darkness beyond the rocks.

"It's late. Go back to bed," he called at the approaching figures. The glint of light reflecting off a drawn blade commanded his attention.

"We'll sleep when you're dead."

Darien recognized Fareen's accented Rhenic. He sighed, reluctantly scooping his sword up in his hand as he rose to his feet. He didn't bare the blade. Instead, he held it down at his side, trying to appear as nonthreatening as possible. The shadows in front of him stopped, still paces away. He couldn't make out the men's faces in the darkness.

Darien reached out with his mind and tugged at the magic field.

161

He summoned a glowing pool of magelight at his feet, feeding it with a trickle of power until the groping mist grew and spread.

Calmly, he uttered, "You've heard what I did to Malikar's legions. What do you suppose I could do to the four of you?"

One of the shadows in front of him took a step backward. Another wavered, shifting uncertainly. Fareen's face was revealed in the blue glow of the magelight. He didn't look intimidated. If anything, Darien's display of power seemed to only solidify the man's resolve. He nodded once, lifting his chin.

"You won't use your magic on us," Fareen announced. "There is no *sharaq* in such killing."

Sharaq. An ancient word for honor, or honor code. Darien understood the concept; he'd learned about it in his training, though he had no idea how the system actually worked in practice. Besides, the knowledge Darien had was a thousand years outdated.

Much had changed.

But he knew enough to guess he'd have to gain *sharaq* of his own if he hoped to stand a chance with these people. He couldn't risk losing even a drop of it. Reluctantly, Darien released his hold on the magic field, letting the glowing mist dissipate around his feet. He felt a sensation of loss as the energies drained away, diffusing into the air. The shadows returned to settle in around him, seeming thicker now than they had moments before. Slowly, he drew the scabbard down the length of his blade and flung it aside. He kept the tip of his sword lowered, swept back.

He said, "There's four of you and only one of me. How much *sharaq's* in those odds?"

Fareen scoffed as he raised his own blade, a long scimitar. "You are a Sentinel of Aerysius. Whoever spills your blood will receive great reward."

Darien trailed the tip of his own blade forward across the ground. He left his guard lowered, presenting Fareen an enticing target. "All right, then. Here I am. Come get your reward."

Two of Fareen's men fanned out to either side. The third rushed in, sweeping his blade downward. Darien moved as if to parry, but allowed the blow to knock his blade aside. He twisted his sword, slicing his opponent in the neck.

The next man was already advancing.

Darien stepped back out of range, drawing his sword back with both hands. He blocked a diagonal slice, letting his blade slide down the length of the man's steel. He stepped forward, pinning the man's sword against his chest. Then he struck out with his foot, taking his opponent in the knee.

Darien sliced downward, gutting the man as he fell.

He jerked back, spinning just in time to parry a strike coming at him from behind. He twisted, catching the attacking blade on his cross-guard. Darien pivoted his sword under the other man's blade. His opponent fell with an agonized scream.

Darien whirled to confront Fareen. He swept his blade back over his shoulder in a two-handed grip, winding his arms.

The big clansman made no move to attack. He was frozen in a defensive posture with his sword raised straight out in front of him. His face had lost all trace of its former confidence.

Darien advanced, thrusting forward. Fareen recovered himself enough to block, catching Darien's sword on the flat of his blade. Darien tested the pressure of Fareen's steel. He fanned his sword to the right, disengaging.

Fareen stumbled backward, losing his footing. He brought his sword up, thrusting out in an attempt to keep Darien at a distance. Darien shoved the attacking blade aside and dove in close, trapping Fareen's sword against his arm. He brought the hilt of his own blade up, bashing the man's face with the pommel of his hilt. He smacked him again. And again, flaying back the skin of his cheek.

Fareen's sword fell from his grip as Darien swept out with his foot, kicking his legs out from under him. He caught him by the hair as the clansman fell, holding him upright over his knees with his sword against the man's exposed throat.

Looking up, Darien realized that they were no longer alone. At least half the village had turned out and stood arrayed before him, weapons brandished and ready to attack. Darien swallowed, realizing the gravity of his predicament. He couldn't fight them all off. Not without magic. Not and retain any amount of *sharaq*.

He froze with the honed edge of his blade poised against Fareen's larynx. His eyes wandered over the agitated crowd, searching, at last finding Azár. She was weaving through the press of bodies toward him. Seeing him, she met his gaze and drew her index finger across her own neck.

Darien took her meaning.

He closed his eyes, sucking at the magic field as if sucking in life. He pulled until the field saturated him, filling him to capacity, until gleaming blue ribbons of energy bled off his body in distorted waves. The crowd drew back away from him, aghast, brandishing their weapons defensively. Men cried out, some falling to their knees. Others turned and fled. Some just stood there, mouths agape. Women pulled their children in close.

Fareen struggled against Darien's hold, his neck straining away from the pressure of the blade. Darien tightened his grip. He raised his voice to address the crowd:

"Whether you like it or not, Zavier Renquist named me Overlord of this region." He swept his gaze across the gathered mob, glaring at each face in turn. "Tonight this man betrayed my authority and led three of my own warriors against me. I sentence Fareen son of Mohsen to death."

He didn't hesitate. He drew the honed edge of his blade across Fareen's exposed neck. He held the man back against his legs and watched him bleed out, observing Fareen's face go from defiant to slack in the span of heartbeats. Darien released him. The body slumped forward over its knees, bowing into the spreading pool of blood.

Darien lowered his sword back down to his side. His body was trembling in a mixture of rage, revulsion, and chaotic energies. He raised his voice, scolding the people of Qul with the fury of his wrath:

"The rest of you'd better get it through your heads: I was sent here by *Zavier Renquist himself,* who saw fit to place the welfare of the clans *in my hands!* You are all welcome to my food, my fires, and my protection. I'll do everything in my power to further the interests of the Asyaadi, as well as the other clans of the Khazahar. But the one thing I will not suffer is stupidity. And

I'll not waste my time crossing steel with the next man who seeks my blood. I'll just drop him where he stands."

He turned and bent over, scooping his sword's scabbard up in his hand. Then he stalked off into the night, leaving the villagers behind to deal with their dead.

Darien walked alone the rest of the night. He had no idea when morning finally arrived; in a land without sunlight, day and night had little meaning. His shadow confronted him at every turn, cast by the muddled light that emanated from deep within the clouds above. But there was no trace of dawn's awakening when it came.

Darien wandered toward the glow of Qul's lightfields, attracted by the radiance. He hadn't made a conscious decision to go there, but then again, he hadn't made a conscious decision not to. So he followed where his feet led him. He found himself strolling the edge of the lightfields, gazing out across the manicured landscape in wonder.

Ahead, row upon row, were tilled, orderly stripes of cropland that extended all the way to the jagged edge of a ridge of mountains to the north. An impressive system of irrigation ditches fed the farmland with water. There was vegetation of every sort, orchards and berries, date palms and greens. Golden trails of magelight ribboned the sky, as bright as he remembered the sun. For minutes, all he could do was stare. Then he stepped a foot across the thin boundary that separated shadow from light.

He stood there for a moment, spreading his left hand beneath the dappled texture of magelight, half his body basking in warm radiance, the other half still lingering in the chill darkness of the waste. He turned his head, gazing harder into the verdant distance. A butterfly fluttered by right in front of him, lofting in random dips and arcs above the fields. Bees ranged from flower to flower, the sound of their myriad wings creating a low and consistent hum.

Darien stood still, mouth open, reveling in the serene beauty of the fields. He wanted to wander further in, to trail his fingers over the wispy strands of grain. But something held him back.

He swallowed his desire, turning instead away from the light. He stepped back across the boundary, back into shadow. Immediately, he felt an alarming sense of loss. He bowed his head, gazing at the ground.

On the trail back to the village, he encountered Azár. He drew up, considering the woman in silence. He had killed her cousin; yet another member of Azár's family had died by his hand. Darien didn't know what to say.

"Nur a'yiid," Azár uttered. *Morning's grace.*

Darien nodded. *"Nur a'yiid,"* he responded. He shifted his weight over his feet, staring down at his hands. They were still stained with Fareen's blood, he realized. The thought hadn't occurred to him to wash it off.

"Why did you have me kill Fareen?" he asked without looking at her. "He was your kin. And he was disarmed. Why not show him mercy?"

The woman was gazing up at him with the strangest expression on her face. He couldn't place it. The look in her eyes ranged somewhere between doubt, care, and concern.

"Because mercy is a sign of weakness," Azár told him. "You cannot afford to be seen as weak."

Darien shrugged. "They'll resent me, now."

"Maybe some will resent you, but you have won their respect. You gained much *sharaq* last night."

Darien spread his hands. "Where is it? I don't see it."

Azár moved a step closer to him. She had plaited her hair since the last time he'd seen her. She was also wearing a new ochre vest. It suited her complexion.

"Has anyone else challenged you?" she asked.

"No."

"You see? Had you spared Fareen, every man of this village would be seeking your blood. And perhaps some of the women."

Darien had to admit she was probably right. Wanting to change the subject, he gestured back toward the lightfields. "I was just admiring your work. What can you tell me of it?"

Azár smiled. It was a beautiful smile that brightened her whole face just as much as her magelight brightened the darkness.

"I will come here every day to weave the light," she explained, taking Darien by the arm. She turned him back around to face the lightfields. With her hand still on him, she strolled forward, guiding him alongside her. "The light can last for a week, sometimes more, before it begins to fade. I must weave new light where the old light has gone out. It takes much concentration and effort. I can only do this for so long before I must rest. Right now, there is much catching up to do. While my master was gone, the Lightweaver from another clan came and tried to help. But we were gone for too long, and it was too much for her to light both Qul's fields and her own. Already, we have lost more than half the harvest."

Darien looked to Azár with concern. "So your village will be short on food?"

"Not just Qul. Many villages are served by these fields." Azár released his arm, nodding her chin. "Look there."

Darien allowed his eyes to follow in the direction she indicated. There, across the fields, was a large patch of darkness. Now that he saw it and knew what to look for, he realized there were many other such patches.

He asked, "What can I do to help you?"

She appeared grateful for his concern. But she shook her head sadly. "There is nothing you can do. Even with all the power of the Netherworld, you cannot weave the full spectrum of magelight."

There was a long span of silence between them as Darien stared at the ground. Without looking at her, he muttered, "I'm sorry I killed your cousin, Azár. And I'm sorry I killed your sister."

There was another long gap of silence. Finally, Azár responded, "I never liked Fareen. But I am sorry that my sister was fated to die by your hand. She would have liked you, I think."

The bodies had been removed by the time Darien returned to his makeshift camp. But not the blood. The blood remained, staining the ground. Darien threw himself down on the opposite side of the fire pit he'd shoveled out of the dirt. His pack and blanket were still there, he realized with relief. His possessions appeared untouched. He wondered at that.

But he didn't wonder long. A low growl reminded him why no one would dare ransack his things. He'd forgotten all about the thanacryst.

"Narghul," he whispered, patting the ground at his side.

The demon-dog trotted out from the rock it had been lurking behind, green eyes glowering in the darkness. The beast settled down at Darien's side, nuzzling its big head into his armpit. The creature purred.

Darien reached up, running his hand through the hound's thick and matted fur. He was rewarded by a slobbering lick on the cheek.

"That's enough," he scolded the thing, scrubbing the wetness off his face with his sleeve. He snapped his fingers and pointed, ordering the demon-hound away. The creature slinked away a few feet then turned back toward him.

"Go," Darien chided it.

The beast trotted away, disappearing into the darkness.

When it was gone, Darien rummaged deep in his pack, hoping to find some of the dried food stores he'd brought with him from Haleem's caravan. There wasn't much left; he hadn't anticipated living in a ditch upon his arrival in Qul. All his search produced was a single piece of hard and moldering flatbread. Darien held the bread up before his face and picked at the areas of discoloration, peeling off the mold and flicking it away. He turned the bread over, examining the other side. Tearing off a bite, he stuffed it in his mouth and started the arduous process of chewing.

He lived in the ditch between the rocks for over a week. Every dark morning Darien watched a steady stream of villagers filing out of Qul's gate, headed toward the lightfields. Every evening they returned, weary and shambling. After the first day, Darien decided to follow the group of laborers, hoping to lend a hand.

But Azár saw him and shook her head, gesturing him away. Darien took that as a sign his help was not wanted.

So he stayed away. He spent his time exploring the shadowed landscape around Qul. He took long walks: sometimes down to the river, sometimes into the hills above the lightfields. Mostly, he just lingered about his camp. The time passed slowly, a relentless cycle of darkness followed by night. Fortunately, Azár took enough pity on him to spare a loaf of bread and a few sacks of dried fruit.

Darien waited, hoping for a break. None came. Azár seemed to be avoiding him, either by design or by circumstance. The villagers ignored him, often pretending as if they didn't see him, as if he didn't exist. Like an unwanted ghost lingering on the frayed margins of their dark and threadbare world.

After finishing a meager breakfast, Darien fished the pipe Haleem had given him out of his *sufan*, holding it up in his hands. He turned it over, admiring the workmanship. He had never smoked a pipe before; it was just not something that was done. The pipe sparked Darien's curiosity. Rummaging deeper into the satchel, he found a small supply of tobacco. He withdrew a pinch of leaf, wadding it up and stuffing it into the bowl.

He lit the contents of the pipe and took a long draw off the stem. Immediately, his eyes filled with water and he wheezed, his lungs burning. He coughed, sputtering.

From far away came the sound of distant screams.

Darien lurched to his feet, dropping the pipe and scooping up his sword. Without a second thought, he sprinted down the path toward the lightfields. When the cliffs opened up, he stopped, trying to get a sense of the cause of the commotion. More screams drifted toward him from out of the darkness. The glow of the lightfields on the horizon was an ominous red-orange.

He ran down the dirt path toward the fields. By the time he got there, it was already too late. Darien staggered to a stop, taking in the scene of devastation that confronted him.

Everywhere he looked, the lightfields were ablaze. Fires seared the earth, consuming everything in their path. Flames leaped high into the sky, engulfing the dry orchards and rows of light-starved grain. Hot ashes rained down, drifting all around him.

Darien just stood there, groping through shock. It took him a moment to gather himself enough to react. He bared his blade and, heart pounding, tried to summon enough courage to confront the flames.

"Azár!"

He started toward the fire, but fear got the better of him. Darien stopped, grimacing, his blade sagging in his grip.

A barrage of unwanted images flooded his mind, one after another in relentless succession. A crackling pyre. An inferno of his own creation, swifter than the wind and hotter than the sun. The torments of the Netherworld, searing his flesh and scalding his soul.

Shaken, Darien closed his eyes, shuddering as he strove to master his emotions. He called upon the fury of the Onslaught, hoping the Hellpower's wrath might cauterize his fear. Calm instantly settled over him, soothing the rage of his brittle nerves.

When Darien opened his eyes, the images were gone. So was the fear. His fear of the flames had been replaced by a white-cold sense of purpose. Darien used the Onslaught to quell the heat of the blaze in front of him. Then he stepped across the boundary, transitioning from a world of shadow into a world of fire and smoldering ash. Sword in hand, he trudged forward under the lambent glow of licking flames, smothering the blaze before him as he went.

"Azár!"

He could hear the sound of shouts ahead of him. He sprinted forward, dousing the flames to either side. He swept his gaze across the field, extinguishing the hot spots. Steam rose from the charred mat of scorched vegetation on the ground.

Motion ahead caught his attention. Darien drew up, bringing his sword back up over his shoulder. A man was riding toward him on a horse, a moving silhouette against a writhing background of flames. Darien held his ground, waiting for the rider to approach.

It wasn't until horse and rider were almost on top of him that the man's features were revealed by the lambent glow of the inferno.

Nashir Arman pulled back on his stallion's reins. The horse snorted and crabstepped, eyes rolling as it fought for the bit. The darkmage smiled down at Darien, a cold and gloating smirk.

Darien drew harder on the Onslaught, numbed by its fury. Even the sight of Nashir wasn't enough to unsettle the liquid calm that dampened his emotions. Darien raised his voice, challenging him over the roar of the fire:

"What do you want, Nashir?"

The demon regarded him. "I want your tears. But I'll settle for your blood."

Darien's blade wavered in his hands. He'd forgotten all about Nashir's promise of vendetta for Arden's death.

He brought his blade down to level, daring the man with his eyes. "Then come get it."

The demon barked a laugh, giving the reins of his horse a sharp tug to settle the dancing stallion beneath him. "It's not that easy." Nashir nodded his head toward the smoldering fields. "You seem good at putting out fires. That's good. Where you're going, you'll have need of that skill."

With a cry, he kicked his horse to a gallop, racing away across the burning plain.

Chapter Fifteen
The Double-Edged Sword

The Khazahar Desert, The Black Lands

Meiran staggered down a gritty, brittle hill that kept giving way beneath her feet. Quin moved much more skillfully, half-sliding, half-jogging all the way to the bottom of the slope. Sheet lightning flared across the sky, creating a momentary illusion of sunlight that cast Meiran's shadow out ahead of her. For a split second, Meiran caught a glimpse of Quin's eyes under the brim of his hat as he glanced back in her direction.

They made camp for the night in the open. There was no fire; they didn't need one and, besides, there was no fuel to burn. The evening meal consisted of hard sweetbread and dried fruit, the same as every meal. After dinner, Meiran took a brush to her hair, starting at the ends and working upward. She watched Quin out of the corner of her eye as she moved the brush down the sable length of her hair.

The darkmage was sitting with his knees pulled up against his chest. He closed his eyes and summoned a pale green light that raked over the flesh of his face and roved, groping, over the fabric of his clothes. When he released the light, his skin was freshly-shaven, his clothing unsoiled. Even his hair looked clean.

"Why do you rely on the Hellpower?" Meiran asked, working her brush a little further up the lock of hair she was holding. "Wouldn't it be less dangerous to use the magic field?"

At the sound of her voice, Quin twitched his eyebrows. "It keeps me cold," he stated in his usual clipped and melodic drawl.

Meiran kept the brush moving through her hair. The tone of

her voice was conversational. "Why the need to feel cold?"

Quin looked at her. "Because I'm a demon. Can you imagine the nightmares that await me every time I close my eyes?"

Meiran lowered her hairbrush in her hand. Using her fingers, she smoothed the long strands down over her shoulders. She cast him a skeptical look. "So, that's how you live with yourself? You numb your emotions with the Onslaught?"

Quin frowned slightly. Then he gave a casual shrug. "I used to drink in order to tolerate my own existence. I had to give all that up. There simply isn't enough wine to sustain the enormity of delusion it takes to preserve my sanity."

Meiran chuckled. "I can imagine. So, instead of drowning your guilt in wine, you immerse yourself in evil. How, exactly, do you justify that?"

The darkmage stared at her flatly. He was leaning over his bent knees, arms draped around them. "When we're drowning, we all have the tendency to grasp at whatever desperate straws are available."

Meiran supposed that made sense. Not the kind of sense she was used to. Darkmage kind of sense. She was getting accustomed to Quinlan Reis. She even felt that she understood him a little bit, at least most of the time. The man was fueled entirely by guilt, grief and apathy. There was no pride left within him at all. Just a false sense of ego he wore like a bandage over his heart.

"I want to hear more about this sensitive you say you loved. What was her name? Amani?"

"Yes. Amani."

The texture of Quin's voice was coarse. Meiran could tell that she'd broached a subject he would much rather avoid.

"Tell me more about Amani."

Quin slouched back, propping his weight on his elbows. He glared at her sideways, focusing on her with one disgruntled eye. "What do you want to know? She was my brother's wife."

"Keep going," Meiran ran her fingers through her hair.

"Amani was the daughter of Prime Warden Renquist," he said.

Meiran's mouth formed a wide 'O'. She hadn't expected that.

She leaned forward, motioning for him to continue.

"My brother and I both pursued her. But I think Amani was always fonder of me. She said I made her laugh, if you can believe it." His lips flirted with a weak attempt at a smile that disappeared just as quickly as it came. "But Braden was like a son to Renquist. The son he'd never had. Everyone expected Braden to follow after him as Prime Warden. So, it really came as no shock when Amani was promised to my brother instead of me."

Meiran nodded, commiserating. "I'm sorry, Quinlan. I can't imagine how that would hurt."

Quin glowered. "I loved my brother very much. But I was also very jealous of him. Braden was the man I always wanted to be. I just didn't know how. He always did everything *right*, never anything halfway. I don't have that kind of patience. Never did."

He glanced down, hiding the emotion in his eyes under the brim of his hat. "Braden's marriage to Amani was just more fuel for my jealousy. That's when I really started hating him. Well, hate is a strong word. I *resented* Braden very much. And then, when I found out that he didn't love her, well…that made me *very* bitter."

Meiran frowned. There was something distorted about the portrait Quin was painting of his brother. It just didn't seem to match the descriptions she'd heard of First Sentinel Braden Reis. From what Meiran had learned—and from what she could glean from Quin—Braden had been almost a paragon of righteousness. A marriage of convenience to advance his career just didn't seem to fit.

"Why did Braden marry Amani if he didn't love her?" she wondered.

Quin shrugged. "Oh, everything went fine until the day Braden found out that Amani was a sensitive. And even then, I think he still would have treasured her with all his heart—if it hadn't been for her father. You see, Braden didn't exactly see eye to eye with the Prime Warden on every issue. Renquist can be an exceptionally callous man, as I'm sure you can believe. I don't know what my brother was plotting but, whatever it was, he didn't want Renquist finding out. He distanced himself from

Amani. I think he was afraid."

"Afraid of what?"

"Afraid that his loyalties might be questioned."

"Were they?"

"Perhaps. Amani's death might have actually saved Braden's life. Who knows? After that, Renquist sent him away to Aerysius as an ambassador. I think he suspected that Braden was a threat. I think Renquist wanted my brother very far away from him, yet still within reach."

His voice trailed off. "I'm tired. I'm going to get some sleep. If you want to hear more, you'll have to ask me about it again some other time. Goodnight, Meiran."

With that, he lay on his back, sliding his hat down over his eyes. Meiran sat there gazing across at him for a little while, reflecting on their conversation. Despite herself, she found Quinlan Reis fascinating. He was a darkmage, yes. A Servant of Xerys. But he just didn't seem very evil. Complex, yes. Flawed, most certainly. But evil? She just didn't see it.

Against her better judgement, Quinlan Reis gave her hope.

Perhaps not all demons were as awful as she'd feared.

The next morning didn't dawn. It *darkened*.

Meiran awoke to a world blanketed in thick gray mist that had settled all around like a still and imposing ocean. She could see nothing through that haze, not even Quin. The fog had the effect of dampening all of her senses, not just sight. The world was rendered silent and drab, as if all trace of vitality had been sucked right out of it. It didn't even feel like the world she knew. It reminded her of what the Netherworld had seemed like.

She could hear Quin, even if she couldn't see him. He was rummaging around in his pack. Tentatively, Meiran reached out and probed his feelings, taking the measure of his emotions. But Quinlan Reis had wrapped himself in the chill detachment of the Onslaught; she could sense nothing through the link.

They ate a tasteless, meager breakfast by the wan glow of Quin's magelight. He didn't speak; he hadn't said anything since settling down to sleep. Meiran didn't bother to press him; she could sense his gloom. It was as cold and murky as the fog that encased them. She knew better than to try to draw him out when he was like that. He could clam up tighter than an oyster in its shell, and all the prying in the world wouldn't make him open up until he was ready.

After breakfast, they collected their things and shouldered their packs. Meiran followed as Quin resumed his interminable trek ever northward. At least she assumed they were still on course; the fog was disorienting. For all she knew, they could have doubled back on their path.

It was hours before the haze began to lift. And even then, the mist continued to roam in thick, slow-moving patches. Quin's magelight was like a diffuse, red glow. The silence was explicit, isolating. Meiran walked forward, hugging herself for warmth. Each step she took filled her with a deepening sense of foreboding.

The fog opened up into a flat plain of crisp, cold darkness. In the distance, there was light. Meiran couldn't help herself. She hastened her pace toward the glow, drawn toward it as if by compulsion. She caught up to Quin, drawing past him.

His hand shot out, pulling her back.

"Something's not right."

Meiran frowned.

"Stay here," he commanded, adjusting his hat. He stared at her until she finally nodded, relenting.

Then he stalked off without her. Meiran stayed where she was, letting a wandering cloud of mist envelope her. She strained her ears after the crunching sound of his footsteps.

From the distance came the sound of frantic screams.

Meiran shivered as a wave of panic washed over her. She thought about going after him. Instead, she stayed where she was, dropping to her knees in the dirt. She used the fog to her advantage, trying to make herself as inconspicuous as possible.

The sound of screams grew louder, rising to a shrill, blood-curdling climax. Then there was silence. Followed by another noise: the sound of distant keening.

Whatever had happened, it was over. And it was terrible.

Trembling, Meiran knelt on the grainy black dirt, her senses groping through the fog in despair.

"I need your help."

Meiran flinched, jerking to her feet. Whirling, she found Quin standing right beside her. His face was pale.

She gasped, "What is it? What's happened?"

Quin licked his dry lips. His expression was slack.

"There's been a raid on a village up ahead. Evidently, there's a new warlord in the region making his presence felt. His soldiers came demanding tribute. But the good people of Deryah had nothing left to give. So instead of taking food, the warlord's soldiers took their share of blood. I need your help; you're better at healing than I am."

Meiran started after him, running just to keep up as Quin jogged back toward a patch of light. Lightfields. It wasn't long until Meiran saw the small group of villagers clustered together on the edge of the fields.

The ground was littered with scattered bodies.

Meiran gasped, her hand coming up to cover her mouth.

Many of the corpses had been savagely skinned. Ribs had been separated from the spinal column and pulled out, one by one, sticking up through the flesh, giving the appearance of flayed wings. Some of the victims were just children.

Meiran gagged at the sight, clutching her stomach as the taste of acid rose to her throat. All around, she could hear the sound of moaning and weeping along with tortured, anguished groans.

"They're still alive," she gasped with a sob.

"Some of them," Quin confirmed. "I can't do it all myself. There's too much damage."

Meiran was already in motion, throwing herself toward the first victim at her feet. Trembling, she placed her hands on the man's shoulders, the only place on his body not covered in blood and exposed tissue. She closed her eyes and grappled with the magic field in desperation. Tears leaked down her face; she could feel the man's suffering as if it were her own.

Meiran threw back her head, screaming in anguish as she

forced a torrent of healing energies into him. The bones moved, popping back under the skin. Muscle rewove over the ghastly wounds and exposed openings. Flesh squirmed back into place. The pain of the healing was almost incapacitating.

Meiran turned her head to the side and vomited. Then she vomited again. She stood up, wiping her mouth, and forced herself to stagger toward the next victim.

This one was beyond saving.

With a cry, Meiran flung herself toward the next grizzly, tortured soul.

It was a child.

Meiran wept as she laid her hands upon the girl, her fingers shaking so hard she could hardly cup the blood-splattered face. When the pain hit, it almost took her to the ground. Crying out, Meiran screamed until she was hoarse, furiously working to reweave flesh and bone back together. When she was done, she rolled over onto her side. She couldn't get up.

"That's enough!"

Sobbing, Meiran looked up into Quin's contorted face. The darkmage's eyes were moist and reddened.

"You're a sensitive!" he gasped. "Sensitives aren't meant to be healers! You feel everything they feel!"

"It's what I do," Meiran protested, shaking, fighting against the pressure of his hands. There were still many others left to care for. "I'm a Querer! *It's my job.*"

He shook his head, aghast. "Why would they train a sensitive as a Querer? It's inhuman!"

She brought her hand up to her face, scrubbing the tears from her eyes. As she did, her sleeve fell back.

Behind her, a woman screamed. Then everything happened at once.

Meiran whirled as Quin flinched back, his eyes widening in alarm. The woman was pointing at Meiran's arm, screaming at the top of her voice. Meiran looked down and saw the exposed chain on her wrist. She jerked her sleeve back down to cover it, too late.

The woman fell silent. Her eyes glassed over. She slumped

sideways and collapsed to the ground.

People surged toward them, shouting, shoving each other out of the way.

Suddenly, Meiran was being hauled to her feet. Quin jumped in front of her, inserting himself between Meiran and the small but enraged mob that confronted them. He started yelling at the top of his voice in his native tongue. The way he ran the words together, Meiran couldn't understand a single thing that he said.

But the villagers understood. They drew back, settling into a mournful, quiet mass. One by one, they turned away, moving back toward the flayed corpses of their loved ones. Meiran was left standing there trembling, alone with Quin. She took his hand and led him back in the direction they had come, shaking in rage and shame.

"You killed that woman," she accused him under her breath. *"Why would you do such a thing?"*

Quin stopped walking, turning to stare at her. His eyes were reddened and intense. "I didn't exactly have a choice, now did I? Unless you'd rather be put to the torch?"

Meiran's lips contorted into a grimace. "That woman did nothing wrong!" she cried out in despair.

Quin raised a finger in front of her face, leaning forward. "Make no mistake, Prime Warden: this was your fault. Now, pray, *never let it happen again."*

Meiran gaped at him as Quin turned his back on her. She stood there in the darkness, shaking her head, sobbing in muted grief. She could feel the cold rage of his anger through her link with him.

He was right. The woman's death was her fault. Quin had done exactly what his nature demanded: he had acted decisively to neutralize a threat.

Meiran whispered, "Promise me something, Quin."

He was still standing with his back to her, hands on his hips. His shoulders rose and fell with every sharp, ragged breath. *"What?"*

More firmly, Meiran told him, "Never kill for my sake ever again."

He turned to glare at her over his shoulder, gaze narrowed and contemptuous. "I beg your pardon?"

Meiran turned fully toward him, lifting her chin. "I mean it. I swore an Oath of Harmony. 'Always to heal and never to harm.'"

Quin's lips curled in disdain. "I think I've heard it."

Meiran swallowed, unable to tell if he was being sarcastic or serious. She took a tentative step toward him. "I mean it, Quin. If you kill another person because of me, it will be because I allowed you to. It would be the same as if I'd killed that person myself."

Quin gaped at her. He turned fully around to face her, his hand shooting up to sweep his hat off his head. "Please tell me you don't believe that drivel!"

"*I do,*" Meiran stated adamantly. "Never kill for me again. Even if it means my death."

Quin stared at her hard for a moment, saying nothing. At last, he replaced his hat squarely back atop his head. "Let's make certain I understand this," he said at last. "You want me to escort you through the most dangerous and inhospitable territory in the entire world, where every person you meet—every man, woman and child—is your sworn blood enemy…but you don't want me to lift a finger in your defense?"

"That's right."

He stared at her very long and very hard. "Very well, Madam." He tipped his hat in her direction. "I hope that both you and your swelled sense of righteousness enjoy a glorious death together."

With that, he turned and strode away.

Meiran couldn't believe it. Was he actually going to abandon her there?

"*What are you doing?*" she called after him, trotting forward.

"What does it look like I'm doing? I'm leaving." He didn't turn to look at her.

Meiran shook her head, throwing her hands up in frustration. "*Why?* I need you!"

Quin whirled around with a snarl. The wind kicked up, billowing his longcoat out away from his legs as he strode back toward her. "You don't need me, Prime Warden. What you need is someone stupid enough to dignify your martyrdom. Trust me, any audience will suffice. But it won't be me."

Meiran stared at him, her mouth open, limbs trembling. Her eyes pleaded with him to change his mind. She could feel him, feel the enormity of his anger. He was suffused with it, and with the chill fury of the Onslaught.

"Quin. You go too far."

"No, Prime Warden. *You* go too far," he growled. "If you want to bind your own hands behind your back with those chains on your wrists, then go right ahead. Feel free. But no one—and I do mean *no one*—is going to bind me! I was there when my brother devised that wretched Oath you flaunt so zealously. It was the last thing Braden ever said—*right before they killed him."*

Meiran gaped at Quin in startled confusion. She hadn't known that the Mage's Oath had been conceived of by his brother. It made sense. But it still didn't change anything.

Tightly, she stated, "Then it sounds like Braden died with a great deal of honor and dignity."

The flood of rage that washed from Quin into Meiran was so forceful that it made her gasp.

"My brother died screaming in agony!" Quin raged. He stalked away a few paces, fists balled at his sides. He kicked out at something on the ground.

At last he turned back to Meiran with a look of desperation in his eyes. He licked his lips, his face a mask of grief. "Don't you understand? The Oath doesn't protect you from becoming someone like me! Generations of mages existed before Braden ever came up with it! If you don't want to end up like me, then just *don't end up like me!* You don't need some irrational and aesthetic Oath to keep you from doing something that's entirely against your own nature to begin with!"

Meiran shook her head. Tears leaked unbidden from her eyes. She didn't believe him. Quinlan Reis was a darkmage. How could he possibly understand?

"You can't convince me that the Oath of Harmony is worthless," she said gruffly. "Darien is a perfect example. Look what happened to him!"

"Don't talk to me about Darien!" Quin snarled. "You weren't there. The truth is, you really don't know a damn thing about him."

Meiran was shocked. *"How can you say that?"*

"Darien swore the Oath," Quin reminded her. "It didn't help him."

His anger was contagious. It was infecting Meiran, now. She could feel it burning at her from within, scorching her heart. Quin was wrong; that's all there was to it. He was a darkmage, a Servant of Xerys. How could he understand? His life and death were lived in complete opposition to everything the Mage's Oath stood for.

"Darien forswore his Oath," Meiran reminded him in a voice suffused with anger. "That's why he became a darkmage."

Quin barked a bitter laugh. "Sorry, darling, but you're getting it backwards. Darien was already a darkmage. That's *why* he broke Oath."

His words stung like a slap because she knew he had to be right. Her anger dissolved into anguish.

"That's not true!"

Quin strode right up to her, planting his feet just inches from her own. The brim of his hat pressed against the flesh of her brow. "Tell me something, because I've been curious about it." He peered intently into her eyes. "Whatever possessed you to give your mage-lover a sword as a fare-thee-well gift? Why a weapon of all things, out of everything else in the entire world you could have possibly given him? Why not a nice warm cloak or a new pair of boots?"

Meiran's face twisted in grief. Tears filled her eyes, blurring her vision. She pulled back away from him, bringing her hands up to cover her face. "You have no idea how often I've regretted that decision," she whispered, her voice shaking. "It was such a stupid thing to do. I acted on impulse!"

"But why?"

How could she explain? She had been so young then, so foolish. In the thrall of a man whose child she carried in her womb. She hadn't had the courage to tell Darien she was pregnant, to send him off like that, possibly to his death. So she'd kept it a secret.

Instead of telling Darien that he was going to be a father, she had given him a sword, instead. Then she had kissed him and sent him off to war. That was the last she had ever seen of him, until the moment he had appeared before her in the gateway. The moment of his death.

"When I gave him that sword, Darien was only just an acolyte," Meiran said. "Weapons were not yet forbidden him. And he'd trained so hard for so many years. Darien always had a passion for the art of the blade…and he was going into battle. So many men we sent to the Front never came back. I chose the gift that I thought would have the most meaning. I didn't think what kind of meaning it would have. I didn't think it through."

Quin's gaze had been softening the whole while she spoke. He stared at her with conviction in his eyes. "You chose the gift that suited him best, Meiran. That's why you did it. Darien was born to be a Battlemage. I think, even then, you understood his nature."

"I've regretted it every day," she insisted. "Giving him that sword…I may as well have been giving him my blessing to strip those chains off his wrists."

Quin shook his head. "You acknowledged the warrior within him. I can think of no greater gift."

Meiran strangled back a sob. "I damned him, Quin. *I damned his soul.*"

"No. You didn't. Darien damned himself." He reached out, touching the marking of the chain on her wrist. "So…am I leaving? Or staying?"

"Stay." She bowed her head. "Please don't leave."

His hand lingered on her wrist. He rotated her arm just a bit, causing the silvery luster to gleam in the light of the clouds. He glanced back up at her, eyes solemn. "Don't ever use those chains to justify weakness, Meiran. I guarantee you, that's not what Braden intended. And, besides, you're the Prime Warden of Aerysius. There's too much riding on your strength."

Chapter Sixteen
Oathbreaker

Qul, The Black Lands

Darien scooped Azár up in his arms, her head lolling against his shoulder. Her eyes were closed. She looked like she might have been sleeping, except for the blood that drained from her scalp, staining the side of her face. Darien reached within, probing her with his mind. What he found was comforting. The head wound was only superficial. There would be no lasting damage.

He used his power to heal her, anyway, and removed all trace of blood and grime.

He carried her, unconscious, all the way back to the village. But he had no idea which house was hers. So he took her instead to his own camp, laying her out upon his blankets. He settled back against a rock, determined to watch over her while she slept.

Sometime during the night Darien fell asleep at her side, his body stretched out beside hers in the dirt. When he awoke the next morning, Azár was gone.

Another week went by. Every day, Darien wandered out into the lightfields to help the people of Qul with the replanting. This time, no one objected. He worked all day, every day, very hard. He rarely saw Azár. And when he did, she usually avoided him. He didn't understand why. It was almost as though her old resentment had returned.

The fields were tilled entirely by hand; there were no oxen or horses available to turn the soil. Just hand-ploughs. He tried a few ways to use magic to lessen the chore. But it turned out to be more taxing than just resorting to muscle. He finally gave up and put his back into the labor. All the while keeping an eye out for Nashir.

But the darkmage didn't return.

Every night, Darien retired exhausted to his makeshift camp, taking comfort in the thanacryst's company. Every morning, he found a hot meal awaiting him, arranged on mats set out around the fire pit. The people of Qul had not yet accepted him, but they had at least begun providing for his needs. The households took turns every day preparing him food. He was grateful; it was a step forward, at least.

That night, Darien cast his tired body down beside the bowls of food and tore into the meal with more urgency than usual. He used his fingers and pieces of griddled bread to scoop the soups and stews into his mouth. He dipped and chewed, hardly tasting the mixture of spices. He was weak, his unwashed fingers shaking as he ate. His body longed for meat, but there was none to be had. His bones ached, either from lack of flesh in his diet or sunlight on his skin. Perhaps a combination of both.

After dinner, Darien leaned back against the demon-hound and stared up into the hostile sky. For some reason, his mood was even more melancholy than usual. His hand scratched absently at the thanacryst's neck as his eyes scanned the flickering lights in the sky above. His mind sought for images in the clouds he could recognize. He found none. Instead, all he found was conflict.

A hand shaking him by the shoulder startled Darien awake. He flinched, reaching for his sword. His arm was captured in a firm grip before he could get his fingers around it.

Darien struggled, opening his eyes to gape up into the face of the last person in the world he expected to see. His breath caught, his heart lurching in his chest. He sat bolt upright. He could feel the blood draining out of his face.

"Is she...? *Did you bring her...?*"

Quin nodded once, eyes lost somewhere in the shadows beneath his hat. "Of course. I told you I would, didn't I?"

Darien sprang to his feet, shrugging his sword's leather baldric on over his shoulder. Beside him, the thanacryst snarled. The beast's hackles were raised, its fierce green eyes glaring at Quin. That surprised Darien; he'd never seen the demon-hound respond so aggressively to another Servant.

"Theanoch!" Darien ordered. The hound gave one last snarl and then sat back down on its haunches. It looked up, gazing intently into its master's face.

Darien was breathing in gasps, his heart floundering. Whether in anticipation or fear, he had no idea. Not that it mattered; Meiran was here, somewhere close by, almost within reach. He couldn't stand it. His entire body quivered with a mixture of anticipation and panic.

"Take me to her."

Quin raised his hand, a small, reassuring smile on his lips. "Relax. You're living proof that love is the elevation of the irrational over reason. We have time. Meiran's not going anywhere."

Darien paced away, scrubbing his hands back through his hair. He leaned forward, taking slow, deep breaths, trying to calm the relentless fury of his pulse. He couldn't relax. Every nerve in his body was raw and frayed.

"What's she like, Quin? Tell me she doesn't hate me."

Quinlan Reis raised his eyebrows. "Of course she doesn't hate you. You're the love of her life, the sad, unfortunate fool. I'm just not certain she's quite up to trusting you as yet. You've both been through a lot. She might need some time to adjust."

Darien just nodded, eyes sliding sideways as he groped to sort through his scattered feelings. He paced away, trying in vain to gather up his thoughts. His heart was still racing, tumbling along at a furious pace. His mind spun in circles.

"I need to see her. *Please.*"

Quin pursed his lips, shaking his head. "Not like that. I mean, look at you! You look like something I just dug out of the ground."

Vexed, Darien raked his fingers through his hair, ripping through the snarls. He dove into his pack, rummaging around, finally drawing out a leather cord. He gathered up his long hair, tying it back. Then he took a long gulp of water, swishing it around in his mouth before spitting it out again, sliding his tongue over his teeth. He spread his hands wide with an exaggerated, questioning motion.

Quin shook his head sadly. "It's not good. But I suppose it'll do; you're actually not too awful-looking for a dead man. Shall we, then? I'm actually rather anxious to see how all of this is going to play out."

He turned and strolled away toward the bottleneck canyon. Darien jogged after him, turning back and commanding the thanacryst to stay with a gesture of his hand. The last thing he needed was the demon-dog following after him; Meiran already had enough changes to get used to without the sight of that.

"Did you run into any trouble?" Darien asked, nervously worrying at the wrinkles in his shirt. He tried to smooth them out with his fingers, dusting off a smear of mud on his sleeve.

Quin pursed his lips. "Not any more than one would expect. All in all, I'd say the journey was rather unexceptional. How about yourself? You seem rather worse for wear. Or is there some reason why you're camped in a ditch rather than ruling the hinterlands?"

"You knew?" Darien was surprised. Quin had left long before Renquist had revealed many of his plans.

Quin smiled. "It wasn't hard to guess Renquist's intentions for you. The Khazahar was Braden's and my own ancestral home. As it was, Arden Hannah inherited Braden's lands and legacy. Upon Arden's death, as her successor, the Khazahar has fallen to you. Guard her well." He tipped his hat in Darien's direction.

The narrow path they were following took a sharp turn, switchbacking up into the rocky cliffs above the village. Darien's stomach was tying itself into knots. He could hardly manage to follow the winding trail. He kept glancing up fervently, hoping for a glimpse of Meiran.

"What lands were you promised?" he asked, though he really

didn't feel in the mood for conversation. His feet ached to go faster. He wished Quin would hurry and pick up the pace.

The darkmage chuckled. "You're not going to like it. If Renquist's plans ever come to fruition, then Rothscard will be my capital."

Darien gaped at Quin's back. "You were promised the Kingdom of Emmery? That's your territory?" He hadn't known they'd already carved up the Rhen to dispense with as they pleased. The thought brought with it a flare of outrage.

Quin nodded. Then he stopped, gesturing toward the cliff beside them. "She's in there."

Darien turned, noticing for the first time that what he'd thought was just a recess in the rock was actually the entrance to a cave. Suddenly, he felt very lightheaded. He brought his hand up to steady himself against the cliff face. He turned to Quin with a look of uncertainty.

"Go on in," the darkmage prompted. "Take your time. I'll be right here."

Darien nodded, swallowing. "My thanks," he whispered. His eyes sought Quin's face for reassurance. Then he turned and slipped inside the cave.

Darkness encased him. It was colder inside, and silent. Darien conjured a glowing blue mist that groped ahead of him, illuminating his path. The passage was longer than he'd expected, angling sharply back into the rock. It wasn't a man-carved passage, but rather seemed to have been eroded by running water. He pressed his hand against the rough, chill wall and frowned. The rock was light-colored sandstone. It was the first natural-looking stone he had seen since entering the Black Lands.

Darien followed along the low passage, having to walk slightly bent forward, stooping to avoid hitting his head. His magelight spilled ahead of him, leading him forward with an iridescent trail. The passage opened up a bit, allowing him to walk fully upright. Darien slowed his steps, pausing to calm his ragged breathing. His mouth and throat felt terribly dry.

The passage swung to the right. Then it opened up into a

room-sized chamber. Darien paused, one hand resting on the rock wall beside his face.

She was right there in front of him.

He couldn't move. He couldn't breathe. He stood there stunned, unable to even blink. His eyes raked over every inch of her, taking in the sable luster of her hair, the perfection of her face. Her gaze was a siren song, and he was helpless.

Darien moved toward her, catching Meiran in his arms as she buried her face against his chest. He held her close, rocking her gently back and forth. He inhaled deeply, breathing in the silken scent of her hair, relishing the familiar fit of her body against his.

Then his lips were on hers, desperate and insistent, making up for lost time. Meiran gasped, her hands sliding down his shoulders. In his arms, he could feel her body stiffen. He sensed the hesitation in her kiss.

His lips stopped moving. Darien drew slowly back, searching her face.

Meiran's skin was flushed, her eyes full of compassion and regret. Her lips quivered, her whole body trembling. Looking in her eyes, Darien felt a gut-twisting wrench of loss. He drew her closer and buried his face in her hair. Closing his eyes, he walled the world away and just held her there.

"Darien."

It was the same, sad voice that haunted his dreams.

He wasn't ready to let her go.

"Darien…I have something to tell you…"

He grimaced, knowing their one, fragile moment was over. He knew another would likely never come. Darien strangled back a curse, resenting the hell out of fate. He squeezed his eyes shut, unable to bring himself to look at her.

He turned his back and wiped away his sorrow on his shirtsleeve. Somehow, he managed to compose himself, collecting what was left of his strangled feelings. He stood there with his back to Meiran, unable to turn around. He didn't want her to see the raw emotion written on his face.

He felt her hand against his. Her fingers laced softly through his own.

He let her lead him by the hand toward a woven rug spread out in the center of the chamber. Stiffly, he lowered himself to sit beside her, his fingers still entwined with hers.

He tried not to stare, but he just couldn't help himself. It was impossible to look anywhere else.

"I'm sorry," he managed feebly. "It's just..." he shook his head, his voice trailing off.

Meiran placed her other hand on top of his, caressing him softly. Her fingers wandered up his arm, pushing back his sleeve. Revealing the scars hidden there.

Her hand froze.

"Why?"

There was so much hurt in that one, simple word.

Darien felt a surge of shame. He leaned forward, his eyes imploring. "Meiran. I need you to trust me."

Tears fell from her eyes. "I don't think I can," she whispered.

He had to find a way to make her believe him. There was so much riding on this moment. Far more than just his own blackened heart.

"Look at me," Darien insisted. He took her by the chin, directing her gaze upward and into his own. "I died for you, Meiran. And I'd do it all over again. Right now, in a heartbeat."

"Don't."

She struggled to pull away. Darien refused her. He moved his hand behind her head, leaning into her. He stroked his fingers softly through her hair. "I need you to hear me out."

She was crying, her arms wrapped tightly around herself. She sagged against him, her body shuddering with the force of her sobs. "Your words are poison," she moaned into his chest as he hugged her against him. *"Why did I come?"*

Darien pressed his cheek against her, closing his eyes. Gruffly, he whispered, "I've always believed in you, Meiran. Now I need you to believe in me. I know it's hard. Here. I'll make it easier for you."

He released her and drew away. She gazed up at him with wide, bewildered eyes as he staggered to his feet. Darien felt his courage start to slip as he took a step back away from her. He felt a sudden, tangible fear. He had visualized this moment, rehearsed it over and over in his head. He'd thought he had the strength to go through with it. But now that the moment was upon him, Darien wasn't sure that he could.

But there was really no choice. If he stood any chance of gaining her trust, he could hold absolutely nothing back.

Darien closed his eyes and opened his heart and mind to the Onslaught. He let it fill him, bathing his soul in euphoric filth and vile ecstasy. He could feel hell's energies violating him, exciting him. He let the Onslaught sear away the cloak of vitality that covered him, exposing the depths of corruption that consumed both his spirit and his flesh.

Darien raised his hands, spreading his fingers. The skin appeared grayed, sagging. Desiccated. He reached down and lifted his shirt, exposing first his stomach and then his chest. Before Meiran's eyes, he turned slowly around, revealing the full extent of his ruin. Every tortured scar of hell's abuse of him, the decayed corruption of the grave. Before the woman he loved, he bared both his body and his soul, drowning in black depths of shame.

Turning back to face her, Darien lowered his shirt and tore his eyes up off the ground. He released hell's spent energies, shuddering as the Onslaught slipped away from him. Slowly, the chill of death receded as warmth returned to flood his veins. Darien glanced down at his hands.

His flesh was whole again, unbroken. Remade.

His aching spirit yet faltered.

Meiran's face remained fixed. She gaped up at him, gagging slightly, trembling in revulsion. She staggered to her feet.

In a dismal voice, Darien said, "Now you've seen me for what I really am. I'm a demon. A monster."

"So all this,"—she gestured savagely—"is just *illusion?*"

He nodded sadly. "I'm dead, Meiran. I've been dead a long time."

She was crying again. Darien let her. He bowed his head, sagging, his shoulders trembling in shame.

"You're not real!" she raged at him. *"I felt you die!"*

"I'm sorry," he whispered, knowing exactly what he'd put her through.

He took a step toward her, holding her gaze with his own. When she didn't retreat, he took another hesitant step. "I still love you, Meiran. Death can't change that." He reached up and stroked the side of her face. "You've come all this way. Would you please listen to what I have to say?"

"I'll try," she whispered. Her hand rose, wiping her tears.

Darien nodded. He lowered himself back down to the rug that had been spread over the floor of the cave. He waited for her to join him. She sat, not as close as before, hands folded in her lap. Her face was yet very pale, her body still quivering. He felt terrible for her.

Darien said, "I'm going to tell you a story. One I don't think you've heard before."

"Is it about Quin?"

Darien nodded. "And his brother. And me…and even you."

She relented, nodding her permission. He took a deep breath before beginning.

"A thousand years ago, a mage of the Lyceum discovered that the magic field reverses in polarity from time to time. I gather it's just something that happens periodically, every once in a great while. It was due to happen again. Had the Reversal been allowed to proceed, everything ever crafted by magic, along with every mage, would have been destroyed.

"The two Prime Wardens, Cyrus Krane and Zavier Renquist, decided to set aside their differences and collaborate in an attempt to stop it from happening. They forged a secret alliance with the Priesthood of Xerys. They created the Well of Tears in order to gain access to the Onslaught. They needed a power source that could stabilize the magic field at the moment of collapse. Together, they made a covenant with the God of Chaos; that's how the union of the Eight Servants came to be."

"And now you're one of them," Meiran stated with a glare of reproach.

"Aye. And now I'm one of them." He drew in a deep breath to calm his nerves. "Please, Meiran. I need you to listen."

He waited. When she said nothing further, he continued, "Quin and his brother Braden tried to stop them. They believed that the destruction of all things magic would be better than living in a world where Xerys held sway. Quin and Braden failed. The magic field was stabilized, at least for the most part. The Rhen survived intact, while Caladorn was savaged by Quin's mishandling of the Onslaught. But the Well of Tears was sealed, which betrayed the Servants' part of the covenant. The reign of Xerys never came to be."

"Thank the gods," Meiran whispered.

"Don't thank the gods just yet," Darien warned ominously. "We've yet to deal with the full consequences of the fallout. The Servants' covenant was breached, and Xerys was not pleased. And I'm afraid it was all just a temporary fix, anyway. The magic field is ready to depolarize again. And this time, we don't have enough Circles of Convergence left to stabilize it."

Darien leaned forward, taking her hand. Remarkably, she didn't try to pull away.

"Meiran, in just a few months, every mage, including yourself, is going to die. Everything ever created by magic will be lost from this world. All of the works of the temples. The infrastructure of the kingdoms. All of our stores of amassed knowledge—it will all be gone. You, Kyel, Naia…" His voice trailed off. He closed his eyes, summoning the nerve to continue. "There's absolutely nothing we can do to stop it."

The expression on Meiran's face did not change. Very quietly, she whispered, "Then whatever will be, will be."

The courage and determination in Meiran's voice broke his heart. It reminded him again of all the reasons he'd fallen in love with her in the first place.

"I wish it were that simple, Meiran. It's not." His soul was very saddened, very weary. "The people of Malikar, what you know as the Black Lands, depend on magic for survival. I know you've seen it. Without magic, there can be no lightfields. They'll have no way of obtaining food. They'll all die unless you allow them passage into the Rhen."

Meiran wrenched back, snatching her hand out of his grasp.

She surged to her feet. *"You're asking me to open up our borders to the Enemy?"*

Darien rose after her. "I am, Meiran. They're not the Enemy. They've lived in a world of darkness for a thousand years. All they've ever wanted was escape into the light."

She backed away from him, circling the rug to put some distance between Darien and herself. She glared at him with the hurt of betrayal in her eyes. Everything about her body language branded him a traitor.

"That's not the whole truth, and you know it," Meiran accused, raising her voice. "They've never come as refugees! They've always come as conquerors, seeking blood and vengeance. Your own father was immolated in their fires! How can you stand there advocating for them? They're savages—brutal and uncivilized, hostile and despicable! Since I've been here, I've seen nothing to convince me otherwise!"

Darien clenched his jaw in anger and desperation. "If you don't let them in, you'll be sentencing them all to death."

"Then so be it," Meiran dismissed him with a wave of her hand. "I am the Prime Warden of Aerysius. My first duty is to the Rhen—not the Black Lands! You should know; you swore the same vows I did, *Darien Oathbreaker."*

He sucked in a sharp gasp, feeling slapped in the face by more than just the sting of the insult. "You can't be serious, Meiran. They're people! Many are just children!"

He could tell by the set of her jaw just how serious she was. Her face was utterly dispassionate, thoroughly resolved. She stood up straight, composing herself like a queen.

"I'll think on it, Darien. It's not that simple, as you said."

"No, it's not simple," he agreed softly. "But it is what's *right."*

"So now I have a darkmage lecturing me on my moral duty?" The sarcasm in her voice bit deep.

Darien glared at her in wounded outrage. "If it comes down to it, aye." He started to walk away. But he couldn't help turning back to her, eyes full of hurt. "So, is that all I am to you now? Just a darkmage? Nothing more?"

Meiran scowled, her face hardening. "You're a Servant of

Xerys, Darien. What did you expect?"

He nodded thoughtfully. What had he expected? Not this. He lowered his eyes, staring at the ground. His hand fingered the gold tassel that hung from his waist. "We're not all evil, Meiran. We're not despicable. We're just *desperate.*"

Meiran took a few steps away from him then paused, looking back. "I'm sorry, Darien. I need you to go, now." She raised her chin, brushing her hair back away from her face. "You've given me much to think about. Now give me time to consider your petition."

To his dismay, he realized she was no longer the woman he remembered. Before his eyes, Meiran had transformed into the image of the Prime Warden, armoring herself in grace and formality. It stood like a shield between them, shutting him out. There was nothing more he could do.

Darien drew himself up and offered a stiff and proper bow in her direction. "May I return on the morrow?"

"Yes."

He nodded and turned to leave. But something stopped him. He glanced back in her direction. "Please. Do me one favor before I go?"

Meiran considered a moment before nodding.

Darien clasped his hands in front of him, offering her a gesture of supplication. "Please, Meiran. I need to know what happened to our son."

The fortified composure she had managed to gather around herself collapsed like sand. Meiran's hand came up to her face as her mouth contorted into a grimace. She choked back a strangled sob.

"I didn't want to tell you!" she gasped, her eyes glistening. "You were leaving for Greystone Keep. You had enough to worry about!"

Darien moved forward until he was standing right in front of her. He reached out, placing a soothing hand on her arm. "I understand why you didn't tell me. But I do need to know what happened."

Meiran gazed up at him with large, moist eyes. "I had to hide the pregnancy from your mother. I gave birth in the Vale and gave the babe up to be fostered. It was the only recourse I had. I named him Gerald in honor of your father."

"Thank you for that," Darien whispered. His voice was very gruff.

"I visited from time to time. He was a very happy babe. He had your hair. And my eyes. He had the sweetest cheeks…" Her voice broke. She turned away, bringing her hands up to cover her face.

Darien swallowed against the pain. "What happened, Meiran?"

She shook her head, dropping her hands. "I didn't know what happened for a long time. Not until last year. I went looking for the family just as soon as I could. They were hard to find; there's no one left any longer in the Vale. After Aerysius fell, all the villagers fled. I finally caught up with the family in Auberdale."

Darien closed his eyes, dreading to hear what he knew was coming next. He steeled his heart against it.

"Go on."

"Our son died, Darien." Her voice broke. Fresh tears spilled down her cheeks. "He took ill…his lungs filled with water. Darien…I'm sorry…"

He blinked, feeling only cold, bleak emptiness. His vision blurred. He couldn't bring himself to look at her. He felt her soft touch on his shoulder. He took a step away, pulling back out of range.

Meiran pressed on, "The day Aerysius fell, Gerald's foster mother tried getting him up the mountain for help. She told me about an acolyte who aided her, a man with black hair who wore a sword at his back. It was you, Darien…wasn't it?"

He couldn't respond. The entire world had stopped.

"It must have been," Meiran insisted miserably. "It was the same day you returned home from Greystone Keep."

Darien's entire body was trembling. He couldn't see through the tears that collected in his eyes, tears he was too numb to shed. A hard knot pressed against his throat like a garrote, tightening, strangling him in grief.

"I held my son," he muttered raggedly.

He blinked, eyes finally shedding their heavy weight of tears. *"I held my son."*

He turned and strode away, bringing a hand up to his mouth. He could hear Meiran's voice behind him, calling out his name.

He ignored her and just kept walking.

Chapter Seventeen
The Demons We Love

Qul, The Black Lands

Quin lingered outside the cave long after Darien had stormed past him. One look at the man's face was enough to warn Quin against trying to go after him. He didn't feel in any particular need of self-abuse. Neither did he have a desire to go inside and confront Meiran; he could practically sense the wake of destruction Darien had left behind. There was probably little he could do to better the situation. Not without getting his head bit off, at any rate. So he sat down on the narrow path with his back up against the rough cliff face. He bided his time, picking up a small rock and tapping out a rhythm with it against another, larger, stone at his side.

Time crept slowly by. Below in the shadows, the village of Qul was beginning to awaken. There was movement in and about the dwellings as people stirred from their beds and went about their morning routines. Women stoked cook fires on the flat rooftops of the houses and began preparing the morning bread. Below, children swept out the courtyards and ran to haul water from the village well. The foul odor of coal soot soon permeated the air, comingling with the aroma of roasting dough and fragrant spices. There were few people out and about in the streets; it was still far too early.

From his vantage, Quin had a very good view of the small camp Darien had made for himself in a ditch at the bottom of the ridge opposite. The campsite was empty; Darien hadn't returned to it. Above, on the stony cliffs, he could see a brief flicker of light. Quin peered intently into the shadows, wondering what could have possibly caused it. It had been there for just a second then was gone, almost like the eyeshine of an animal. But there were very few animals in all of the Black Lands. The flicker was gone and didn't come back again. The cliffs across from him yielded no answers, only shadows.

"Oh, hell," Quin groaned finally, rubbing his tired neck. His legs were sore from sitting so long, confined to the narrow ledge. He stood up, stretching out the aching muscles of his thighs. He stamped his feet until the feeling returned to them. Then, with weary reluctance, he stooped and entered the cave.

"I'm coming in," he called out, figuring he'd better give Meiran some type of warning. In a much quieter voice, he added, "whether you want me here or not."

He walked forward stiffly, taking his time, letting his magelight wander ahead to chase the gloom of the passage away. He listened, hearing nothing. The cave was quiet and austere, infinitely still.

When he came to the room-like chamber, Quin drew up and lingered in the doorway, his magelight collected in a glowing pool directly beneath his feet. Meiran glanced up at him from where she sat on the rug, lit by sinuous strands of mist she'd gathered around herself like a glowing azure sigil. In that cold, wavering light, Meiran looked very pale and very fragile. He could tell she'd been crying.

Quin moved forward hesitantly, lowering himself beside her on the rug. Meiran said nothing, but the look in her eyes was one of unspoken reproach. Quin frowned, skewing his lips as his eyes surveyed the terrain of her face.

"I take it that didn't go so very well."

Meiran shook her head, eyebrows knitting together in a frown. "Why didn't you tell me?"

"Tell you what, my dear?" Quin reached up, removing his hat from his head and resting it upside down in his lap.

"That he'd be so *different.*"

"Is he?" Quin shrugged dismissively. "I really wouldn't know, now would I?"

He'd never known Darien Lauchlin in life. While Darien had

been busy immolating Malikar's legions at Orien's Finger, Renquist had stationed Quin deliberately far away. He'd spent the entire war mired in Bryn Calazar, tasked with the impossible goal of resurrecting the Lyceum's lost Circle of Convergence. Not once had he come face to face with the man he now considered his closest relative.

Quin had only met Darien for the first time in the dark reaches of the Netherworld. Not the best place to get to know someone but, then again, not the worst place, either, if you wanted to truly judge the colors of a soul.

What had struck Quin most about him was how much Darien reminded him of Braden. He was just a more turbulent version of the man. Despite the gap of generations that separated them, much of his brother's character and mannerisms had endured in his bloodline. Quin could see Braden in the way Darien carried himself, the way he moved. That look of dangerous intensity that came so naturally to his eyes. The decisive, cool logic he employed. Like his ancestor, Darien was born to be a warrior. What he lacked was Braden's sense of grace and serenity.

"In some ways, he hasn't changed at all," Meiran remarked. "That's the hardest part. But the words coming out of his mouth…" She shook her head. "Darien was always an idealist. It's like he's abandoned every principle he ever had. I don't understand what could have changed him so much."

Quin scratched at the unkempt whiskers on his cheek. "Is what he's asking really so unreasonable? I mean, it seems entirely within the scope of your Oath of Harmony. Or does 'Always to heal and never to harm' only apply to citizens of the Rhen?"

Meiran shot a contemptuous glare in his direction. "Spoken like a true darkmage, Quinlan. Is your tongue just as poisoned as Darien's?"

Quin couldn't help the flicker of smile that jumped instantly to his lips. "You have but to taste to find out."

"*Ugh,*" Meiran groaned, grimacing as if in pain. She raised a hand as if to fend him off. "You're just as tactless as you are wretched."

This time, Quin didn't try to suppress the grin he felt. "Why,

Prime Warden, you do bring out the best in me."

Darien didn't return to camp. Instead he wandered into the cold and dismal waste, the demon-dog trotting behind. He walked with his head thrown back, staring up at the hostile sky. Strobes of lightning flickered deep within the clouds' murky depths. The sky's unrest mirrored the turmoil in his heart. It was oddly comforting to know he wasn't alone.

Above, lightning flared in a shower of sparkling wrath, followed by a swell of thunder. Darien stopped walking, gazing up through the afterglow left behind in his vision. He shook his head, grimacing against his anger.

He fell to his knees, throwing his head back, and wept. His shoulders quaked. He clenched his fists until his nails bit the skin of his palms. But the pain didn't help. It was insignificant next to the ache of knowing how far he'd fallen. He blamed Meiran, hating her for rejecting him after all he'd done. He blamed fate, blamed the gods. Hated them all, hated everything. Most of all, he hated himself.

Somehow, it seemed vastly appropriate when rain began to fall. A needling rain, driven by an icy wind, relentless and without mercy. Darien didn't try to escape it. Instead, he spread his arms out at his sides. He tilted his head back, letting the rain wash over his face. A soothing comfort settled in, his grief overshadowed by purpose, despair replaced by a sense of trajectory.

He rose and walked back in the direction he had come, making his way back toward his camp as the downpour subsided. Once there, he dug down deep in his pack, finding the clean, dry robes Renquist had provided him. Darien withdrew the folded garments, holding them out reverently in his hands. For the first time, he fully appreciated the significance of the robes. They were far more than just a gift; they were a symbol. A symbol he could no longer afford to ignore.

He reached up and removed the brooch that held his cloak in place, letting the wet fabric fall off his shoulders. He shrugged out of his shirt, wadding it up and throwing it down in the dirt at his feet. Then he pulled the indigo robes on over his head. He trailed his fingertips over the delicate, embroidered star. So much like the emblem of dead Aerysius he had once worn at his back.

That had been a lifetime ago, a different life.

He wasn't that man anymore.

Darien returned the next day to the cave.

He didn't feel the same anxiety he'd felt before. Those feelings had been washed away, replaced by the calm clarity of resolve. He didn't hesitate as he ducked inside and followed the low passage toward the back. He paused at the entrance of the room-size chamber, collecting himself as he regarded Meiran in silence.

She was standing next to Quin, garbed in an azure pool of magelight. Darien recognized the color; it was his own legacy, passed down to Meiran through the Soulstone. Only, she had come by it legitimately. The magelight Darien wove was like a lingering reflex, only made possible by the Onslaught.

When Meiran noticed him, Darien dropped to his knees, bending forward in the formal gesture of obeisance demanded by the office of the Prime Warden. He maintained that position, forehead pressed against the floor, palms beside his face. His mind was focused, his heart free of tension. It beat a deliberate cadence in his chest.

"You may rise." Her voice was rich and clear.

Darien regained his feet with a blademaster's grace. He reached up and drew the strap of his baldric over his shoulder, setting sword and scabbard aside. Then he turned back to Meiran with a questioning look.

Her anxiety was visible on her face. It was obvious she could sense the change in him, and it was profound enough to give her pause. She glanced sideways at Quin before finally nodding wary permission.

Darien approached Meiran carefully, one hand behind his back, the other held clenched at his side. When he stood in front of her, he took her hand and brought it up to his lips, pressing a kiss against her fingers in the manner of the clans.

"Nur a'yiid," he said. *Morning's grace.* He released her hand, drawing himself up to his full height. "Thank you for receiving me."

Meiran gazed up at him with grave concern in her eyes. She swept her gaze over him, taking in the significance of his new garments. Her eyes lingered on the emblem on his chest. After long seconds, she asked him simply:

"Why?"

There were so many subtle layers of meaning woven into the various textures of that word. He didn't know which Meiran wanted addressed. Darien stood looking at her for a moment, allowing himself one last opportunity to enjoy the sight of her. Finally, he spread his hands. "These are the formal robes of the Lyceum of Bryn Calazar. They were presented to me by Prime Warden Zavier Renquist."

"I know what they are," Meiran snapped. "What I asked was, why?"

Darien nodded, now understanding her meaning. "I decided it was important that there be no misunderstandings between us. I want you to be absolutely certain of who I am and what I stand for. And why I'm asking what I am."

The look on Meiran's face didn't falter. "So, you've finally picked sides, is that what you're telling me? I take it by your choice of attire that you didn't pick my side. Yesterday I branded you an Oathbreaker. I suppose 'turncoat' would be more appropriate."

"Call me what you like," Darien shrugged. The barb of her insult failed to find purchase in his feelings. "Just so you're aware, Zavier Renquist proclaimed me overlord of this region. But I want to be perfectly honest with you, Meiran. I don't have Renquist's permission to treat with you. Any agreement we make, I'll take back to him with my full support and recommendation. But I can't guarantee anything. That's the best I can offer at this time."

Meiran nodded. "Then it will have to do. Please, have a seat. You'll have my response."

He followed her gracefully to the floor, Quin lowering himself to his knees at his side. Darien sat cross-legged with his elbows draped over his thighs, hands clasped together in front of him.

Meiran wore her hair up in a knot of elaborate braids. She looked every inch a Prime Warden, despite her ragged attire. Meiran, too, had armored herself for combat in her own subtle way.

She gazed into his eyes, her expression fortified by her calm inner strength. "I thought about what you said. Here is my decision: I can't assume the risk of opening up our borders to the Enemy and letting your hordes pour unchecked into the Rhen. For all I know, you could be lying. Your entire story might be just a ploy to slip your legions past our defenses."

"I speak the truth, Meiran. You of all people would know if I were lying."

"I know you *think* you're telling the truth," Meiran contradicted. "But what if you're the one who's been lied to? Have you even considered that possibility?"

Darien shook his head. "No one is lying, Meiran. Although you've no idea how much I wish we were. Look. There must be some compromise we can negotiate. What if we offer to disarm? Leave our armor and armaments behind? Then we would be entirely at your mercy. That should give you some reassurance."

Meiran shook her head. "No. You would still have seven Unbound mages to bolster your armies."

Darien nodded, understanding her reservations. He didn't know what he could offer that might alleviate the threat posed by even one Unbound darkmage. He took a moment, thinking. At last he offered warily:

"Quin and I could surrender to you. You could use our lives as assurance against the others."

But Meiran wasn't having it. "No. Renquist could just sacrifice the both of you to cut his losses."

Darien scowled in frustration. "If you won't compromise at all, you'll give us no choice but to invade."

"What if there's another way?"

Darien glanced at her sideways, eyes narrowed in suspicion. "What are you talking about?"

Meiran raised her chin. "What if there's a way to lift the curse over the Black Lands?"

Darien looked at Quin. The darkmage shrugged. Apparently he, too, had no idea what Meiran was talking about. Quin cleared his throat, sitting up a little straighter. "And how, my dear, do you propose going about doing that?"

"I don't know," Meiran admitted. "But I think it's worth looking into. Don't you?" she added, turning back to Darien.

He shifted his posture, uncertain what to think. It almost seemed like a false trail meant to deter him from his purpose. But that wasn't a tactic Meiran would use. He argued, "If there was a way to remove the curse, surely in a thousand years, someone would have come up with it already."

Beside him, Quin fidgeted. "Not necessarily…"

Darien's eyes probed him sharply. "What are your thoughts?"

"Well, my first question would be, what's causing the curse to begin with? I mean, it's obviously not a curse; there has to be some rational explanation for it. So, what kind of force is holding the cloudcover over Malikar and darkening the sun? It's not the Onslaught, because the clouds persist even when the Well of Tears is sealed."

He was right. Some other force was maintaining the cloud cover in place.

"Then what is it?"

Quin shrugged. "I don't know…it's almost as if the Onslaught enclosed Caladorn in some sort of bubble, trapping in the clouds and keeping out the light. I'm not saying that's what it is, but it's as good an analogy as any. So…what if we could pop that bubble?"

"How do you propose doing that?"

Quin rose to his feet. He paced away a few steps then started circling the rug as he spoke, gesturing with his hands. "The Arcanists of Aerysius were always a pathetic lot compared with those of the Lyceum. When Bryn Calazar was destroyed, many of the most powerful artifacts ever created were lost to humanity. But an even greater loss was the knowledge of how to create those artifacts in the first place. I don't mean to brag but, in my own time, I was considered the foremost talent of my order. If there's ever been a mage capable of challenging the curse over the Black Lands, well…that mage is me." He stopped pacing and spread his hands.

"All right," Darien allowed. "What would you need?"

"First, I'll need access to Athera's Crescent. And for that I'll need a living Harbinger or Querer."

Athera's Crescent. Darien had forgotten all about that ancient relic. Just the mention of it filled him with hope. Not only for Quin's purpose, but it was also possible they might find one or more living mages educated enough to help their cause. He was thrilled with the idea, except for one part.

"So, you'll be needing Meiran to go with you."

Quin glanced back at him and nodded.

Athera's Crescent was an artifact so significant and complex that an entire order of mages had been dedicated to its study: the Order of Harbingers. There were no Harbingers left alive in the entire world, at least none that he was aware of. The next best thing would be a Querer such as Meiran. It had always been the Order of Querers who roamed the land, making themselves available for Query, or petition, by the populace. Most Queries involved healing. But Querers had to be prepared for almost anything, which was why they studied bits and pieces of the lore of every order. Of their number, Meiran alone would have the most knowledge of Athera's Crescent.

Darien turned toward her. "It's up to you. Are you willing to support him?"

"I think it's the only option we have," she responded with calm certainty.

Darien drew in a long, slow breath. He took a moment to deliberate. At last, he said, "I can give you four months. But after that…we'll be coming. Whether we're invited or not."

Meiran rose from the ground. "Four months," she agreed. She didn't sound very happy about it.

Darien followed her to her feet.

Meiran said, "Quin, would you mind waiting outside? I'd like to speak with Darien alone."

Hearing that request, Darien felt his stomach tighten. The cloak of dispassion he'd adopted slipped just a fraction, like a crack in the armor of his soul. He knew what was coming; it was inevitable. He'd thought he was prepared to hear it. But he was not, he realized sadly.

"Of course," Quin muttered. He fumbled for his hat. Then he turned and slouched away into the shadows of the passage.

Darien found himself alone with Meiran. He glanced down, staring at his worn leather boots. "You don't have to say it."

"Yes, I do."

"Then make it quick." He glanced off to the side, focusing his stare behind her on the wall of the cave. He couldn't bring himself to look at her.

Meiran gazed up at him, her arms held crossed against her chest. Her eyes were full of sadness and resolve.

"You were once my greatest love and the father of my child. But that was before you betrayed everything we ever stood for. Now...you've gone somewhere I can't follow, Darien. I will always love the man that you were. But I can no longer love the man you've become."

"You mean the monster I've become."

He pivoted and stalked away, pausing only to snatch up his sword and scabbard. Then he left her, striding briskly out of the cave.

Meiran lingered alone in the chamber a long time after he was gone. She stood there, head bowed, heart heavy with sorrow. She didn't cry, which surprised her. Not only did she feel the full measure of her own guilt and grief, but she also felt Darien's, a heavy weight that pressed against her chest. Because of their link, she felt his pain just as tangibly as she felt her own. She barely noticed when Quin slipped silently back into the room. He held his hat in his hands, eyes downcast.

"I'm terribly sorry," he offered awkwardly, moving toward her across the floor. "It's always hardest to cast aside those demons we love." He paused, looking patently uncomfortable. "Which leads me to wonder…are you still coming with me? Or have you decided to forgo the pleasure of my own disreputable company?"

Meiran regarded him silently, probing his intentions with her mind. Quinlan Reis did not seem to be hiding anything. His emotions were straightforward and reasonable.

Meiran reached down and scooped up her pack, striding toward the entrance to the cave. "Where exactly are we going?"

"Back to Ishara to use the transfer portal there," Quin answered as he shouldered his own pack. "Hopefully, we can transfer directly to the Isle of Titherry. If not, gods help us, we'll have to find another way. Which will probably involve a ship."

Meiran peered at him. "Don't tell me you're afraid of water?"

"Water? Of course not." Quin shook his head. "But I do become atrociously seasick."

Meiran cast a blue swath of gleaming magelight across the floor, making her way out of the cave. Once outside, she found the world encased by mist. Thick, billowing fog roved slowly over the ground, shutting out the rest of the world.

"How convenient," Quin muttered. "Maybe he didn't want a long goodbye."

Meiran glanced at him. It was possible the mist had been conjured, but unlikely. Darien simply wasn't the type to cower beneath a fogbank. She let her magelight wander forward, illuminating their path down the face of the cliff. "Goodbyes have already been spoken."

Quin followed behind her down the path, complaining, "Well, *I* didn't get a chance to say goodbye."

"Stop brooding."

"I hate to say this, but I'm having a hard time being silent."

"Then speak your mind," Meiran snapped.

The darkmage gestured with his hands as he talked and walked. "Now, I'm usually not one to judge, but looking at your situation from my lowly and contemptuous perspective, it just seems…well…"

"Well, what?"

"Well, it just seems to me as though you're being rather

hypocritical."

"Hypocritical?" she echoed, turning back to him with a look of amazement. "How so?"

"Well, by all appearances, you just set aside a man who loves you more than anything just because his soul is damned. A situation, I'd like to point out, he got himself into because of you."

Meiran stopped walking, feeling a sudden heat of anger flush her cheeks. She turned back to glare her resentment at him. "That's not fair. I never asked Darien to do what he did. Committing his soul to Chaos was his decision, not mine. I would have never asked that of him."

Quin spread his hands. "That's all very well, but that doesn't change the fact that he did it for you. How does it feel, Prime Warden, to break the heart of the same man who damned his own soul to rescue yours?"

His words were like a slap in the face. She reeled from the sting of the insult. "That's a disgusting oversimplification, and you know it."

"But it's the truth. If you find it either simple or disgusting, then I'm sorry. The truth is often exactly what we don't want to hear."

Meiran ran her eyes over him with a contemptuous look. "You really are his creature, aren't you?"

"Actually, Prime Warden, right now I'm doing *you* the favor."

"How so?"

Quin set his hat back on his head. He adjusted the brim carefully until his eyes were half-hidden beneath it. "I'm trying to talk you out of a decision that you'll likely regret for the rest of your life. However short that life may be. Why, just think of—"

There was a loud *crack* followed by a thick splatter of blood. Quin's eyes rolled back in his head as he collapsed to the ground. Before Meiran could react, his body slipped sideways, falling over the side of the embankment.

Meiran threw herself down against the trail, bringing her hands up to ward her head even as she summoned a glowing shield around her body. Her eyes groped through the murky darkness, but the fog was like an insulating curtain, cutting her off from the rest of the world.

"Quin!" she screamed into the shadowy ravine where his body had disappeared.

Two dark forms emerged from out of the mist directly in front of her. Meiran scrambled away from them, surrounding herself in a protective aura of blue energies. Terror chilled her heart. There was very little she could do to protect herself. She was no Sentinel, trained in the subtle gradations somewhere between attack and defense.

A large, bearded man reached out to catch her by the arm. She whirled away from him—into a third man standing right behind her. The grisly warrior surged forward, wrapping his arms around her and pulling her tight against him. She could smell the rank odor of his armor.

Immediately, Meiran lashed out with the force of her mind, shoving him off her with a whiplash draft of air. At the same time, she threw up a shield, blocking the strike of the other man's blade. She shoved him forcefully away, hurling him back against the rocks. The man with the sword lost his footing, teetering on the edge of the cliff as he groped desperately for balance.

Meiran gasped, feeling a sudden rush of panic. She couldn't let him go over. She couldn't let her magic be the cause of any man's death.

Meiran reached out and caught her attacker by the hand, wrenching him toward her and away from the cliff's edge. She fell backwards onto the path, the man she had saved falling on top of her with the full weight of his body. She struggled, trying to wriggle herself out from under him.

The man raised the hilt of his sword and brought it down hard, driving the pommel with force into her temple. The world flared briefly, brilliantly red.

Then everything went black.

Chapter Eighteen
Parting the Veil

Glen Farquist, The Rhen

Kyel gazed up into the face of the Goddess of the Eternal Requiem. The marble statue seemed to be condemning him with its sightless gaze. Her arm was outstretched toward him, perfect in every detail, every ripple of muscle and fabric. The hand was open, inviting.

Kyel considered the gesture. He brought his own hand up and caressed the cold stone fingers. "I can't imagine what it was like for him."

Naia's face darkened. *"It was awful."*

Kyel nodded, looking down. He had figured as much. The Oath of Harmony had meant everything to Darien. He glanced back up at the statue, finding its empty gaze terrifying. All of the atrocities Darien had committed had been set into motion in this room, with the knowledge and blessing of this very goddess. Perhaps that's where the blame should rightfully be laid: at the feet of this cold, inhuman effigy.

"Are you sure you want to go ahead with this?"

Naia's voice interrupted his thoughts. He forced his attention back to her. "What choice do we have left?" That was the point; they didn't have any. Especially after their meeting with the Conclave had so thoroughly tied his hands. "What are we going to do if she strikes out against us?"

"We can retreat through that portal." Naia pointed in the direction of the far corner, to a slender arch that appeared to open into a curtain of shadow.

Kyel didn't like the looks of that passage. He took a step toward it. "What's in there? Where does it lead?"

"It leads to the Hall of the Masters," Naia informed him. "It's warded. The spirit of one so damned as Sareen could never survive more than a few steps beyond the portal's entrance. Her soul would begin to unravel the moment she walked in."

"I suppose it's as good a plan as any." Kyel brought a hand up to scratch his beard. "The Conclave certainly hasn't left us too many options. Without Meiran, we're little more than their puppets. So when do we start?"

Naia glanced sideways at him. "In just a few minutes. I want to conduct a test first."

"Test? What kind of test?"

She was moving toward a ledge filled with small votive candles. A few were already glowing with soft, wavering flames. "I want to make certain we're not wasting our time."

She stooped down, lifting a small candle. With her other hand, she grasped a metal striker. She closed her eyes, her lips moving in silent prayer. Then she paused, hesitating for just a moment before depressing the striker.

The candle's wick flared instantly to life with a warm, vivacious flame. Naia smiled as she gazed down at the fragile light in her hand. Shielding it from the air, she bent forward and placed the glowing candle beside the others on the shrine. Then she moved to select another.

Naia lifted the next votive candle up in front of her. Once again, she closed her eyes as she prayed, then depressed the striker. The wick caught instantly. Another warm glow erupted in the cup of Naia's hand.

But then something altogether different happened. A shadow passed over the candle's flame. The dance of light sputtered, glooming. It changed, turning a putrid shade of green. Naia's eyes shot up, fixing on Kyel.

"Sareen's soul is still in the keeping of her master." Naia clenched her fist, crushing both candle and flame. She worked her fingers together, crumbling the tallow. She opened her hand and spilled out the remains.

"What are you doing, Naia?"

Kyel spun toward the shrine's entrance, his heart lurching at the sound of Luther Penthos' voice. He found the old man standing at the top of the steps, one hand on the shrine's great oaken door. His face was pinched into a frown of concern.

"Father," Naia gasped, sweeping toward him.

The High Priest of Death lingered in the doorway. He was staring back and forth between Kyel and Naia with cold conjecture in his eyes.

Naia moved up the stairs, her black cloak billowing out behind her. When she reached her father, she drew up and embraced him. The old man made no attempt to return the gesture.

"I'm lighting votive candles, Father," Naia explained, releasing him. She glanced back at Kyel.

"Votive candles? For whom?" Naia's father looked profoundly skeptical.

Naia shrugged, retreating down the stairs. She walked with her hands clasped in front of her, a tranquil smile on her lips. She appeared unbothered by her father's abrupt appearance.

"The first is for Mother." She stood before the shrine, indicating the first glowing candle on the ledge. It still gleamed with a wavering dance of light.

"The second is for Sareen Qadir. To make certain that her soul is yet confined to the Netherworld."

She dropped her hand, pointing downward at the scattered tallow on the floor. She nudged at a cake of it with her foot.

Her father nodded slightly. "That is wise, I suppose. What of the third?"

"The third," Naia echoed. Reaching down, she took an unlit votive candle into her hand and grasped a metal striker. "The third candle is for Meiran Withersby. To make certain she's still alive."

"And does she live?"

Holding the candle up before her, Naia muttered another brief, unspoken prayer and depressed the striker's mechanism. Another spark flared into being, wafting directly toward the candle's wick. The spark missed, arcing downward to the floor.

Naia repeated the motion, producing another spark. This, too, had no effect.

"I conclude that the Prime Warden is most likely still alive." She set the items in her hands down upon the ledge of the shrine.

Luther Penthos seemed accepting of the news. A thin smile spread on his lips. A proud smile. There was still a trace of sadness in his eyes, though, enough for Kyel to detect. No matter how impressed the priest might be with his daughter, he still regretted losing her.

"That's good news." Naia's father leaned forward, pressing a kiss against her forehead. "Continue with your prayers, my dear. Just please keep me informed of any changes."

"I will, Father."

Nodding, the High Priest of Death released his daughter and turned back toward the stairs. As soon as his foot reached the first step, he stopped and turned toward Kyel.

"And are you here to offer prayers, as well, Grand Master Kyel?"

Kyel shook his head. "No, Your Eminence. I'm not."

"Please remember that the Conclave is awaiting your answer. Are you still considering their request?"

"I am," Kyel answered stiffly.

Naia shot Kyel a questioning look as her father took his leave. She waited until the old man was well out the door before striding across the shrine.

"What is this about the Conclave?"

"It's nothing," Kyel grumbled. He wished Naia hadn't been made privy to that particular exchange. He intentionally hadn't told her; Naia was upset with him enough already.

"Don't be evasive," she admonished. Her eyes glimmered with impatience. "Out with it. What's going on?"

Kyel sighed, outmatched by her stubbornness. He ran a hand through his beard. "The Conclave wishes to address my training as a Sentinel. They feel that I haven't progressed as far as they think I should have."

"You can't be serious! The audacity—!"

Kyel cut her off. "We're beholden to the Conclave now, Naia, not the other way around. At any rate, I have a feeling they're going to want me to make a change. I'm not sure what kind. I suppose I'll be finding out."

Naia raised a finger, eyes gleaming with outrage. "Don't let them control you, Kyel. You may have yielded some authority to them, but that doesn't change the fact that you're still your own man."

"Not anymore," Kyel said. "Not unless we can get Meiran back. The truth is, I'm inclined to agree with them. I learned more in the few months I spent with Darien than I have over the past two years."

Naia looked troubled by his statement. "We both know Darien was much too hard on you."

Kyel hadn't shared his feelings with Naia on the matter. At least, not recently. Not since his feelings had changed. "Darien knew exactly how much time he'd have with me. And he also knew it wouldn't be enough."

Naia's frown deepened, but she nodded anyway. She gazed up at Kyel with turbulent eyes. "So, you've forgiven him?"

Kyel had to think a moment before answering that question. Like everything else, it was complicated. "For the way he treated me? Aye." Kyel's gaze hardened, his jaw tightening. "But not for what he did to you." He looked down. "For that, I'll never forgive him."

Naia reached up and patted his arm with a valiant attempt at a smile. "It's getting late. We need to start."

She turned away, striding across the floor toward the entrance to Death's Passage. "Bar the door."

Kyel followed her directive, moving quickly up the stairs and bringing the wooden beam down across the doorway, preventing anyone from accessing the chamber while they worked. He joined Naia at the base of the steps.

"Do you still remember the Stricture?"

Kyel nodded. "No talking to the dead."

"No *interacting* with the dead," she corrected him. She reached up, physically turning his face toward hers until he was looking into her eyes. "Not in any way."

Kyel nodded. He understood. She smiled, patting his cheek. Naia took his hand, guiding him forward. As they moved across the portal's threshold into Death's Passage, the world flickered. Kyel stumbled, feeling suddenly unstable on his feet. He could feel the small hairs on the back of his neck standing upright. No matter how many times he entered, he never grew accustomed to the Catacombs.

The light was different, surreal. Low-lying fog swirled around their feet, retreating from their footsteps. The air seemed different: thin, stretched. There was a distinctive odor to the place, like the smell of an old tomb.

The wheeled bier they had lain Sareen upon was still resting where they'd left it, pushed back into a dark recess of the passage. They hadn't moved her since arriving in Glen Farquist. The corpse lay draped with its thin shroud, features only visible in silhouette.

Naia moved to the handle of the cart, motioning Kyel toward the rear.

He gave a good push, putting his back into it. At first the wheels didn't want to give. With another shove, the cart lurched forward, Naia tugging at the long wooden handle. The wheels creaked, the cart shuddering. Kyel pushed as, together, they escorted Sareen's bier out of the Catacombs and back to the shrine.

Reality shivered as they crossed back over the threshold into the world of life. This time, Kyel was ready for the transition. He pushed on the cart, keeping his feet moving until they were on the other side of the room. He was grateful for the return of the shrine's golden light and for the scent of uncorrupted air.

Naia set the cart's handle down on the floor and moved to Sareen's side. She peered down at the corpse's shrouded form, her expression soft and reflective. Kyel took up position on the other side of the bier, watching as Naia lifted the edge of the fabric and folded it back, turning it down to expose the face beneath.

The corpse still looked fresh.

Kyel was mildly shocked. Sareen had been dead for almost a

month, and nothing had been done to preserve her body. Nevertheless, the corpse looked as though only hours had passed since the heart had stopped beating. Thus was the nature of the Catacombs: beyond the Veil of Death, time and distance had little meaning. But it was one thing to acknowledge such power, quite another to actually experience its effects.

"She's beautiful," he commented in wonder.

Naia raised her eyebrows. "She's dangerous," she corrected him.

Kyel nodded. He had no trouble remembering Arden Hannah and the evils that woman was capable of despite her feral allure. He tore his eyes away from Sareen's perfect face.

"How do we do this?"

Naia crossed her arms in front of her, suddenly pragmatic. "We need to heal her body. Give her spirit a place to return to."

Kyel frowned. "How do you heal death?"

"Death cannot be healed. All we can do is try to heal the flesh itself. I can't part the Veil of Death. Only the goddess can do that...or Xerys, if he is so inclined."

That did bother Kyel. The lines of his forehead creased. "So, now we're aiding Xerys?"

"We are *not* aiding Xerys," Naia insisted with a toss of her head. "We are simply helping Xerys help us."

Kyel didn't like the sound of that. He took a moment, muddling her logic in his mind. "There's a distinction?"

Somehow, he doubted that there was.

"We have to begin before my father returns," Naia changed the subject. She offered one hand out to Kyel. The other, she placed on Sareen's chest. "I'm going to probe her. Come. I want you to feel her through me."

Kyel reached over the corpse, accepting Naia's offered hand. He closed his eyes, opening himself up to the magic field. Immediately, he felt the warmth of the currents moving through him, through Naia, penetrating Sareen's lifeless body. The image that was returned painted a dismal picture of the cadaver's state. The body was lifeless, breathless, its fluids clotted and pooled, collected in the depths of the cavities. Every muscle was lax, devoid of tension. Deep within, there was only a constant, echoing stillness. There was nothing at all that spoke of life or vitality.

Worse, the body had deteriorated more than he'd expected, far more than it appeared on the surface. Through Naia's probe, Kyel could feel the breakdown of tissues, the collapse of capillaries, the destruction of nerves and fibers and connections.

Kyel looked up, feeling the retreat of hope.

"Did you get a sense of what we're dealing with?" Naia asked.

Kyel gazed down at the corpse. "I think so. There's nothing to be done, is there?"

To his surprise, Naia shook her head. She was animated, vibrant. It took Kyel a moment of disorientation to realize that she was very much in her element. This was death itself they faced, and to Naia, death was no adversary. Far from it; it was her area of specialty.

"There are two types of damage we'll be working through," Naia lectured, pacing away. "There's the wound that was the cause of death. Then there's the natural changes that occur as soon as the heart stops beating. Both types of damage will need to be overcome."

"I'll heal the wound," Kyel offered. Out of everything he had sensed through Naia's probe, that seemed by far the simplest task they would be performing. "You're more familiar with the other...things. The changes."

Naia smiled, pacing back toward the bier. She reached out her hand and caressed a lock of hair back from Sareen's face. "It's not going to be that straightforward. We'll need to go about this systematically if we're going to have any chance at all." She turned, pacing away again. "First, we must reverse any decomposition that's already begun. Then we can start worrying about other things: stability of the veins, fluid distribution, things like that. We'll save the biggest challenges for last."

"Which are...?" To Kyel, it all sounded quite impossible.

"Healing the brain enough to carry out basic functions. Maintaining body temperature, pulse, respiration. We'll have to watch her closely for a while to make certain the organs function properly."

Kyel shook his head, staggered by the enormity of the task ahead of them. "I wouldn't have thought of any of that. Are you certain this is even possible?"

"I'm not," Naia admitted, almost physically deflating. "As far as I'm aware, this has never been attempted before. At least, not for centuries."

She squeezed his hand. Kyel cast a doubtful look her way.

"The wound itself is going to be one of the last things we worry about," Naia continued. She placed her hand over Sareen's chest, where the ghastly rent had been sewn together and bandaged.

"And then...what?" Kyel demanded, gesturing with his hands. "Do we just wait and see if she wakes up?"

"That's all we can really do," Naia confirmed with a shrug. She was gazing down into Sareen's face with a whimsical expression. She fussed with another wayward curl, smoothing it back.

"Are you ready?" she asked softly.

Kyel knew he was not. Nowhere near ready, not for any of this. For anything *like* this. The vicars of the temples were right: he needed to intensify his studies. Quickly, while there was still yet time.

"Let's get started."

Naia nodded, gripping his hand in reassurance. She positioned herself over the corpse, a look of determination in her eyes. "This is what we'll do: I'll initiate the healing. The more I heal, the more other things are going to start falling apart. Your job is going to be more about damage control than anything else."

"I don't understand."

"You will. Right now the system is in balance," Naia indicated the body. "The moment I start healing, things are going to go out of balance very quickly. I'll make the changes. You stabilize."

Kyel swallowed, for the first time feeling tangible fear. He wasn't sure why; they couldn't make this corpse any more dead than it was already.

"Very well. Here I go." Naia placed her hand on Sareen's forehead, closing her eyes.

He wasn't ready. But Naia started anyway.

Kyel could feel her tug powerfully on the magic field, sending waves of healing out away from her fingers, spreading throughout the cadaver. He could feel it almost personally, as if he were doing the work himself. He could visualize exactly what Naia was attempting very clearly in his mind. Through the link they shared, he watched the slow changes she was making unfold.

She started with the tissues, reversing the process of decomposition, adding structure where structure had already broken down. She moved on next to the capillaries, restoring collapsed and disintegrated vessels, driving fluids back into the system.

Almost immediately, Kyel felt things starting to go wrong, just as she'd warned. Freshly repaired tissues, reawakening, screamed for blood, gasping for air. Sareen's body seemed to be dying again just as quickly as Naia was resurrecting it. Kyel scrambled, doing what he could, which amounted to frenetic scurrying, a continuous propping up of what was already falling back apart. Sweat broke out on his forehead as he concentrated, forcing himself to work faster, trying to keep up with the momentum of the healing. He strove to anticipate what was going to go wrong next, to get ahead of it.

Naia moved on to the congealed blood, thinning the clots, redistributing the fluids throughout the tissues. Saturating it with air. Kyel couldn't keep track of all she was attempting—it was too much, all at once. He could hardly keep up with his own struggle. It was all he could do to prioritize, react, and contain.

Gradually, he realized something was happening. What Naia was doing was having some type of effect. He paused just long enough to probe the corpse.

And was shocked by what he found.

The body was no longer still, silent and cold. Organs were stirring, reawakening. Heat bloomed in the depths of the body's core. Within her chest, Sareen's heart quivered for the first time in weeks, eager in its desire to start beating.

"Now, Kyel. The wound!"

Kyel reacted, mending the torn tissues, repairing damaged

membranes, shoring up the rent walls of organs. Beneath his fingers, Sareen's body shuddered. Her heart spasmed, lurching back to life. Blood, long stalled, rushed to fill waiting ventricles, coursing through long-emptied veins.

With a gasp, Sareen's lungs filled with their first breath of air since death.

Kyel looked up, startled, his eyes wide, mouth hanging aghast. His stare met Naia's, equally alarmed, equally frightened. Through his hands, he felt the body draw another, shuddering breath.

"What do we do now?" Kyel whispered, feeling a sharp pang of excitement mingled with a terrible sense of foreboding.

Naia looked down at Sareen's face, her eyes set in grim determination.

"Now, we wait. The rest is up to Xerys."

Chapter Nineteen
Transgressions

Qul, The Black Lands

Darien flinched at the sound of a distant, startled scream. An icy sweat broke out all over his body, prickling his flesh. He gazed out into the roving fog, eyes scouring the shadows. A shiver traced down his spine, caressing the small of his back like the lightest brush of fingertips. He ran forward two brisk strides then stopped.

He brought his hand up and whistled, a piercing sound that cleaved right through the mist.

Then he waited, the speed of his thoughts far outpacing the speed of his pulse. He stared with dread into the murky haze, disoriented, unsure which direction he was even facing. After moments, he heard a swift, pattering sound. A moving shadow burst through the blanket of fog, careening toward him and hurling into his legs, almost knocking him over. The demon-dog yipped as it pressed its muzzle into Darien's hand, tail thrumming against his thigh. A slobbering wet tongue slicked the palm of his hand. The smell of the beast was like mold and old decay.

"Find Meiran," he commanded the thing.

He didn't expect the beast to understand or obey. It was more an act of desperation than anything else. But the thanacryst shot immediately away, sprinting off again into the tumbling mist. Then it stopped, glancing back toward him, green eyes beckoning from out of the darkness. Darien followed after as the creature ranged forward, nose to the earth, intent on its purpose. It covered the dark ground in a broad searching pattern. Every so often it would turn and sprint back to Darien's side then turn and bound away.

This continued for minutes. Then, suddenly, the demon-hound abruptly froze in its tracks. Its tail went stiff, swept back straight as a stick, one forepaw lifted slightly off the ground. Then it darted off across the plain, following a straight trajectory across the rugged terrain.

Darien lost sight of the beast quickly in the fog. He did his best to run after it, hoping the hound didn't veer very much from its course. He eventually slowed to a walk and then finally stopped. There was no sign of the creature. He almost turned back. But then a distant baying sound urged him forward.

He jogged toward the noise. He found the thanacryst by following the sound of its guttural growls. The beast appeared to be worrying at something on the ground, making frantic, slobbering noises. Darien drew up, alarmed by the sight of the hound gnawing on a man's outstretched arm.

"Theanoch!" Darien gasped, using his fists to batter the creature away.

The demon-dog yelped and scampered off before turning back to him with a snarl, feet planted wide in the dirt. Its teeth barred, the beast lowered its head and glared at Darien with menacing eyes.

Darien ignored the thing, throwing himself down beside where Quin lay face-down in the dirt. Blood welled from puncture marks all along his arm and from a wound in the back of his head. Darien closed his eyes and drew quickly on the magic field, probing the man's condition. Satisfied that he had a good sense of his injuries, he turned Quin over, cradling him in his arms.

Darien squeezed his eyes tightly shut and set his mind about the task of repairing the damage Quin had sustained. He worked quickly, almost automatically. The magic field was by now like a treasured old friend, familiar and comfortable. Darien heard a low groan as Quin's body flinched. The darkmage relaxed, fully surrendering to the peaceful bliss of healing sleep. Darien waited until the sound of Quin's breathing was even and deep before squirming out from underneath him. He lay the sleeping form down gently in the dirt, slowly backing away.

Only then did he notice that the thanacryst had disappeared into the night.

Darien glanced around, frowning, wondering where the demon-dog had disappeared to. He hadn't liked the way the thing had growled at him. At the very least, it was enough to give him pause.

The fog was starting to break up. The sky had returned to its usual, sinister cloudscape. Thunder echoed as lightning forked in the distance. Drops of rain started falling erratically to the dirt. Darien paced away, whistling. But the beast did not return. His loathsome companion had abandoned him, it seemed.

And Meiran was gone, as well.

Another flicker of lightning sliced across the sky. Darien frowned, wrestling with indecision. He couldn't leave Quin lying prone in the dirt with a storm breaking over him. The slight depression where he lay could easily flood if enough water drained off the hillside.

But there was no trace of Meiran. She, too, could be lying injured in the storm.

Darien turned and glanced back toward the village. The town of Qul lay sprawled behind him, its dark walls lit by oil lamps and coal-fed fires. If he could carry Quin into the town, the people there might take care of him.

Or they might kill him, just the same.

Movement in the darkness caught his attention. Villagers were beginning to emerge, men and women moving through the shadows down the path that led away from the town toward the lightfields. The sight fed Darien with hope. He sprinted toward the road, eyes scanning desperately over the faces of the people emerging from the town's gate. The people of Qul paid him little mind, just strode past him with gazes lowered respectfully, keeping their distance. A few looked startled at the sight of the blue robes he wore, a look of wonder filling their face before they lowered their eyes.

Apparently, some people still recognized what those ancient robes once signified.

"Ranu kadreesh, nach'tier," one man muttered as he passed by, right hand pressed against his chest. Darien brought his own hand up reflexively, returning the greeting. He frowned in puzzlement.

But then he saw Azár's face coming toward him through the crowd. She looked up, eyes widening at the sight of him. She forged a path toward him through the press of people.

"What are you doing here?" Azár hissed, her face seeming to pale at the sight of him. Her eyes scoured the robes he wore, obviously troubled. "Have you decided to claim our village as your own?"

Darien frowned at her for a moment, at first not taking her meaning. He shook his head in confusion. "No. No, it's not that…"

He rubbed his eyes, shivering as he desperately tried to collect his thoughts enough to communicate his need. "I have a friend. Another Servant. He's been injured. I need you to watch over him for me."

A look of confusion pinched Azár's face. She pursed her lips, brow crinkling. "I didn't know you had any friends among the Servants. Except for Myria Anassis." Her tone sounded almost accusing.

Darien scowled. "It's not Myria. It's Quinlan Reis."

The rain was coming down harder. Fat droplets wet his face, drizzled down his cheeks.

Azár canted her head, staring up at him. "Quinlan Reis was not with us in Bryn Calazar. His name is…*malaaq.*" Darien had never heard that word before. But its meaning wasn't too hard to figure out. Like Malikar: blackened. Cursed.

Darien reached up to rub the back of his neck. He shifted his weight over his feet. "I knew him from before. From somewhere else."

"You met this man in hell," Azár concluded dourly. "What sort of friendship can be spawned in the Netherworld, Darien Lauchlin? It can't be very good."

"You'd be surprised." Darien stared past her to avoid her eyes. "Look, there's someone else who's gone missing. I need you to watch over Quin. Get him some help from the village. Don't leave his side, not for a moment."

Azár stared up at him, mutely searching his face. At last she nodded, seeming a bit saddened by what she saw. "This person you seek must be very important to you," she said at last. "Go, then. I'll watch your friend."

The Khazahar Desert, The Black Lands

The road was long. And dark.

Darkness fell like cloth torn from the long drape of sky. It bled like running dye trailing downward to the ground, seeping into the depths of rock and soil. Meiran regarded the ink-black sky through the tattered fabric of the scarf she wore tied over her face. The scarf kept away the scouring dust flung at her by the wind. The fabric was a kindness, one of the only two she'd been allotted on the journey. In her right hand she clutched the other: a thin string from which dangled a small sack of water. They had not allowed her any food. Meiran understood why. She was not a guest of the soldiers who accompanied her; she was their captive. Her life was not by any means guaranteed.

Meiran glanced sideways at the man who walked beside her. He was tall and heavily-muscled, with dark bronze skin and a meticulously groomed beard. Like the other soldiers in the column, he was dressed in a long blue tunic. He wore a curved sword and dagger tucked into the gold sash that encircled his waist.

The soldiers marched with the practiced silence that comes only with years of hard-earned discipline. The man leading Meiran with a hand on her arm kept her moving at a merciless pace. There was no slowing between halts, no matter how much her lungs and legs burned. If she stumbled, they dragged her forward until she got her feet beneath her again. The stone-faced warrior never glanced her way, never offered any words of assurance. His vision remained fixed on the back of the man ahead of him, one hand on her arm, the other on the hilt of his weapon.

There was nothing she could do to resist; they had taken her into a vortex. She had been forced to seal her mind off from the magic field, protecting herself from the surging currents that surrounded her.

Meiran loosened the scarf over her face and brought the water sack up to her lips. She tilted her head back and tried to shake the last few drops free from the sides of the container. There was barely enough to wet her tongue. She glanced at the silent man striding next to her, but he refused to look at her. Meiran drew the scarf back into place, letting her arm fall to her side.

She stumbled ahead, icy gusts of wind pushing at her from behind, rippling the skirt of her dress about her legs. Her mouth was horribly dry, her whole body weak and faltering. Meiran staggered, the iron-forged grip of her guard the only thing keeping her upright, keeping her in line.

They walked for hours through the darkness, through the cold and brutal wind. A mountain range grew upward from the ground in the distance, cutting like jagged teeth from the flat desert. The summits were encased with snow that shimmered with an eerie phosphorescence. The peaks rose before them, higher and higher, until they seemed to loom overhead, spiking upward to stab the clouds.

The road they travelled took a turn at the edge of a lake that lapped against the foothills. Here, there was no wind. The water of the lake was black and smooth, like polished obsidian glass. Meiran gazed down into the inky water, not liking the look of it.

Her escort led her across a stone bridge built over a narrow arm of the lake, to the walls of an imposing fortress carved into the mountainside. Conical towers and jagged fortifications marked where the walls of the mountain gave way before the labors of men. Narrow windows winked from random heights among the towers, lights flickering like a sky full of stars.

The entrance to the fortress was a high, vaulted arch guarded by an enormous raised portcullis. Meiran staggered forward through the opening, compelled by her guardian's iron grip. Once inside the outer gate, the soldiers assembled silently into two ranks, arrayed out to either side. Meiran sagged over her feet, lightheaded and shaking. She was grateful they had arrived *somewhere*. The long march across the desert was finally at an end.

But she was still within the raging torrent of the vortex. She knew better than to lift her hopes too high.

The air around them was cold.

The dark fortress was enormous and daunting in every dreadful way. The courtyard bustled with silent efficiency. Meiran's hand snatched the shawl from off her head and wound it instead about her arms and shoulders for warmth. Her exhausted trembling became shivering, her muscles reacting violently to the chill. All around the edge of the courtyard, flaming braziers provided light and heat for stationed sentries. But the warmth of the flames didn't travel very far.

A group of officers approached from the other side of the courtyard, plumed helms carried at their sides. Their uniforms were much more elaborate the than men Meiran had travelled with. The soldiers on either side of her remained standing stiff and straight, not twitching so much as a muscle. Their absolute stillness was both impressive and frightening.

The officers stopped in a line in front of her not an arm's length away. Meiran kept her gaze focused on the man positioned right in front of her. Like most of the other soldiers, this man wore a short beard expertly groomed to accentuate the angle of his jaw. His eyebrows were thick, his eyes black and penetrating. He stared at her with a face devoid of expression. After a moment, he issued a slight nod.

The two soldiers to either side of Meiran caught her up by the arms and dragged her forward, staggering, around the line of officers. She tried to keep up with their long strides, but her legs wouldn't work fast enough. She was too tired, too weak, too exhausted. They half-dragged, half-carried her toward a portal on the other side of the courtyard. At first, she struggled. But struggling took more energy than she had. Meiran collapsed, only to be scooped up in a rock-iron embrace.

Darien gazed up pensively at the sky. Then he lowered his eyes back down to the ground, at the gray-flecked sand beneath his boots. His eyes darted back upward before he swung his body around, heading back in the direction he'd just come from. His skin itched, crawling with the feel of infestation produced by the vortex that surrounded him. He'd walled his mind away from it going in, and had kept that barrier in place for half a day as his boots crunched on brittle clots of sand, every step harder to bear than the last. He had gone as far into the vortex as he could stand. He couldn't bring himself to take another step.

Gusts of wind drove clouds racing toward him. The same wind whipped at his face, fed his eyes with dust. He walked stooped forward into the wind, letting it beat against his brow and ripple his robes out behind him.

His eyes found the tracks he had followed into the vortex.

They had passed this way. A group of twelve men who marched in disciplined formation. Darien's eyes flicked across the ground, retracing the prints back again in the direction of Qul. The signs of Meiran's passage in their midst were obvious. Every so often she'd taken a lurching step to the side, breaking the even tracks of the files. She was alive, at least. That was some comfort. Darien trudged forward into the hellish wind, eyes narrowed against the chaffing dust.

You've gone somewhere I can't follow.

Meiran's words seemed to linger, tormenting him on the wind. They dripped with the bitter poison of irony. Meiran had gone somewhere Darien couldn't follow. He couldn't bring himself to, not without more assurance than just the sword at his back.

He trudged on, shoulders sagging and back bent under a heavy burden of guilt. He walked for hours until, at last, he staggered into the rock-strewn ravine by the village. The wind had died down; the night was still. The town of Qul was aglow with the light of dozens of lanterns and cook fires.

Azár and Quin were gone. Instead, in their place, lingered a tattered old man with leathery skin and a toothless grin, face pitted by years and disease. He sat leaning against a large rock, his skeletal hands encircling the protruding burls of his knees. His beard was like a thick mass of cobwebs that engulfed his neck, hanging low over his chest.

"Darien Nach'tier. Azár ni Suam asked me to wait here for you. I will show you to her home."

Darien drew up, considering the unlikely fellow before him with a mixture of gratitude and confusion. There was something peculiar about this stranger who stared blatantly past him. It took Darien a moment to realize that the fellow must be blind. He moved forward, helping him gain his feet.

He took the old man by the arm. The fabric of his tunic was coarse, no better than a shredded, brittle rag. The man reached up and laid a wrinkled hand on Darien's face. The hand roved slowly over his cheeks, exploring his nose and the angle of his jaw, the corners of his mouth. The stubble of his chin.

"Lead me into town." The man waved in the vague direction of the gate.

Darien couldn't help but stare into the man's face as he walked. He wondered who this new companion was. Was he a relation of Azár's? Or just someone convenient she had found to keep watch?

They entered the town through the thin opening in the wall. Darien allowed his guide to lead him down a slender path between the town wall and a mud-brick dwelling two stories high. The blind fellow seemed to know exactly where he was going, leading him forward with sure, unfaltering steps. He didn't seem to need much help to find his way; it was almost as though his feet had the path before him memorized.

"You are married?" the old fellow inquired. He spoke Rhenic very well. Darien wondered where he'd learned it.

He shook his head, glancing into the opening of an alley. "No. I never had the chance."

The old man patted his arm. "The chance will find you. It is better to be married."

Darien arched an eyebrow, the thought occurring to him that maybe his new companion wasn't aware of who he was. Didn't he know he walked beside a dead man clothed in borrowed flesh?

What woman would let herself be shackled to such a monster?

Not Meiran. The one person in the world he thought might understand had rejected him utterly.

Darien scowled, the expression looking more like a grimace. "Love is for the living. The dead can only regret."

The old man nodded, but it wasn't a nod of agreement. He was bobbing his head as he ruminated on the words.

"You can do better than regret," the blind man said at last. "You can atone."

Darien realized the old man was probably right. He had been given a rare and precious gift, an opportunity to put to right some of the wrongs he had committed in life. Not often was a soul given such a second chance. He had absolutely no idea what to do with it, or where to even begin.

Darien felt a tug on his arm and realized he'd stopped walking. He allowed the blind old man to guide him forward again, deeper into the shadowy heart of Qul. A thick blanket of darkness cloaked the village, the stench of coal soot heavy in the air. The unpaved path beneath his feet was wet and oozing with wastewater from the dwellings. He saw no trace of litter anywhere on the ground, no sign of insects or vermin. The streets were narrow and murky, oddly canted in places. They smelled of damp soil and mildew.

There were very few people about, mostly older women and young children who wandered the streets in small groups, thick robes swaying from their slight frames, fringed shawls draped from their shoulders. Some bore earthenware pots on their heads, others carried baskets in their arms. They took note of Darien with darting glances filled with curiosity and dismay.

The old man patted his shoulder, steering him through an opening in the wall. They entered an alley, so narrow that he could reach out and trail both hands along the walls of the houses to either side. The smell of mold was pervasive, the walls slimy to the touch. Darien hesitated.

"This way." The blind man urged him onward.

His companion guided him to the entrance of a dwelling halfway down the alley. There was no door. Strings of dark beads and threaded scraps of pottery hung like a curtain across the entrance. The old man swept a hand out, parting the odd drape with a tinkling clatter. He motioned Darien within.

He started inside, but paused, turning back around as he realized that his companion wasn't following.

"Aren't you coming?"

The old man grinned and pressed a hand against his breast. Still grinning, he turned and ambled off down the path, trailing a hand along the bricks. Darien frowned and turned away, letting the curtain of trinkets fall closed behind him. He walked forward into a shadowy courtyard. Ahead, he could hear the faint trickle of water. A fountain, perhaps. No one was about; the courtyard stood empty. His eyes scanned ahead, noting the openings of rooms to either side. Grilled windows looked down from the second story, some lit, some not.

Darien walked toward a gentle wash of light coming from the nearest doorway, his hand sweeping back a thick drape of cloth. He paused, looking in. His hand lingered by his side, holding the cotton drape at bay as he stood there motionless in the room's entrance.

Azár's face glanced up at him from where she was seated on a thin ledge that ran the length of the far wall. At her feet, Quin lay sleeping in a bed of padded matting covered by a thin blanket. His mouth was open, snoring lightly. Azár regarded Darien with a questioning stare before rising to greet him.

Seeing his face, she said, "I'm very sorry, Darien."

He nodded his head in gratitude. "I couldn't find her," he admitted gruffly. "It's my fault. I should have seen this coming."

Azar regained her seat, motioning her hand to the mats laid over the ledge at her side. "Sit. Rest."

He moved toward her, casting his tired body down next to her. He leaned back against the wall, stretching his muscles with a sigh. Glancing miserably around the room, he took in the barren chamber. There were no decorations, no furniture. Diverse pottery was scattered on the floor along the fringes of the room: various jugs and jars, plates and bowls. A few bunches of herbs hung upside-down from the ceiling, ostensibly to dry. A bronze lantern pierced through with hundreds of holes cast the room in an eerie, dappled light.

"How's Quin?" he asked, looking down at the slumbering figure.

Azár spread her fingers in a vague gesture. "He sleeps the healing sleep. He has not yet awakened. I'm thinking, though, soon. He has slept a long time."

Darien nodded, staring down at Quin's peaceful form. Odd, to think he was gazing into the face of the very man responsible for all this tragedy in the first place. Once, Darien had found it expedient to hate Quin. That hadn't lasted long. Despite his tarnished past and unfaltering penchant for misfortune, Quinlan Reis meant well. He was every inch an idealist, just a failed and broken one.

Azár lifted a pitcher from a tray on the ledge and poured Darien a cup of water. He accepted the cup from her hand, considering her face silently. Azár seemed older, somehow. She no longer had the look of a wild and furious child. Her rough edges had softened somewhat; her eyes had lost much of their accusation.

She said, "Tell me what happened."

He threw his head back and drained all the water in one swallow, his throat dry and aching from grit and thirst. He held the cup up for her as Azár refilled it, her eyes locked on his own.

Darien broke away from her stare, fidgeting and uncomfortable. He raised the cup to his mouth and took another drink. Lowering his hand, he looked down into the shadows of the cup.

"When I died, I used an artifact to preserve the legacy that was inside me. So that it wouldn't be lost from the world. It was too much power for me; too much for any one person. It was slowly driving me mad."

He drained the rest of the water, wiping his face on his arm. He leaned forward, setting the empty cup down on the mat by his side. His eyes wandered away, gazing off into the shadows of the room. Not at her.

"The legacy in the artifact was split between two people. Both were women I had loved. At different times. For different reasons. One of them, Meiran, became Prime Warden after me. When you brought us back from the Netherworld, Renquist took an interest in her. He sent Quin to bring Meiran to Bryn Calazar."

Darien indicated the slumbering darkmage with a nod. "Renquist intended to leverage Meiran the way he'd leveraged me. He can be very...persuasive." Darien scowled, swallowing his anger. "And very cruel. I wasn't about to stand for that. Quin owed me a favor, so I had him bring Meiran to me, instead."

Azár's eyes widened. Her posture stiffened, her hand dropping to her side. "You defied the Prime Warden?"

Darien sucked in a cheek. "Not explicitly."

Azár glanced sideways in thought. Even in the dim lighting of the room, the look of alarm on her face was easy to discern.

"This is very serious, Darien Lauchlin. What you have done...it could be considered treason."

"Perhaps." Darien dismissed her concern with a shrug. "But right now I'm not worried about Renquist. He's not responsible for any of this. But I know who is: Nashir Arman, the same man who put your lightfields to the torch. All of this is his own personal vendetta. He has a grudge against me."

Azár frowned, twin creases etching the skin between her eyebrows. "Why? What did you do to earn this man's wrath?"

Darien stared down at his hands in his lap. One of the sleeves of his robe had slid back, revealing the puckered red scar on his wrist. He answered Azár without looking at her, his voice gravelly and barren.

"I seduced Nashir's woman...and then I killed her."

He sat there for a long moment staring down at the awful scar. The lingering silence that filled the room was almost like a third participant in the conversation, its very presence obvious and awkward. It was a long time before he heard Azár's guarded whisper:

"You have very cold nerves, Darien Lauchlin."

He looked up at her, eyes full of spite. "I acted out of desperation, Azár, but that's beside the point. Nashir wants blood for blood, and now he's taken Meiran. I tracked his men as far as I dared into the vortex to the north. I couldn't risk going further in."

She threw her hands up. "Then there's nothing to be done. The only thing in that direction is Tokashi Palace. If this man Nashir has assumed control of the fortress, then he'll have legions of Tanisars under his command. I am sorry, Darien, but this woman you seek is already lost."

"Meiran's not lost," he insisted, rising from the ledge and moving over to kneel at Quin's side. He lay a hand on his chest, probing the man's condition. The sense of health that was returned to him eased his mind.

He stood back up and turned to Azár. "I'll get her back," he said.

Azár rose from her seat, moving to stand right in front of him. The top of her head came no higher than his chest; she had to look up to glare him in the eye. "You said there were two women that you loved. What became of the other?"

Darien frowned, realizing that since Meiran had returned, he had not even once given thought to Naia. Guilt seeped into him, cold and bitter. Of all the sins he'd committed in life, his transgressions against Naia were the ones that shamed him most. No amount of apology could ever suffice. He'd used Naia terribly and then cast her aside. He had robbed her of all she was. For him, she had abandoned her vocation, her identity, all of her aspirations. And then he'd taken his own life, leaving her selfishly behind.

Darien shook his head, staring emphatically into Azár's dark eyes. "It'd be better for Naia if she thought I was still in hell."

Azár seemed to accept his response. She backed away with a saddened expression on her face. "I've been here too long. I must go tend the lightfields."

He nodded, gazing down at his boots.

Azár reached up, draping her shawl over her head like the cowl of a cloak. "Stay here, Darien Lauchlin. Don't go north to Tokashi. Only death awaits you there."

Darien grinned mirthlessly. "Death and I have an

understanding." More seriously, he added, "I won't abandon Meiran."

Azár paused. "Do what you will, then. What will be is already written." She frowned, her eyes dropping to his side. "That knife you carry...may I have it?"

The question took him by surprise. Darien fished the knife Haleem had given him out of the satchel he wore at his side. Frowning in consternation, he extended it hilt-first toward Azár, searching her face as she plucked the weapon from his hand.

"I thought you already had a blade."

Azár shrugged, holding Darien's knife up before her face as she slid the hilt from its sheath. She rotated it slightly, admiring her new possession before tucking it back away. "I can always use another. It's a good blade and, besides, you won't be needing it any longer. The shroud has no pockets."

She turned and left.

Chapter Twenty
Tokashi Palace

Tokashi Palace, The Black Lands

When Meiran woke, she was lying on her back in a cold, lightless room. The stone beneath her was frigid, and the chill penetrated deep into her body, making her bones ache. She groaned, rolling onto her side before sitting up and wrapping her arms around herself for warmth.

She stared at the iron grate that served as the door. It was old, covered in rust. In the cold and silence, her mind began to drift. Would she die in this room? Perhaps. She had no idea whether Quin was still alive, or if Darien even knew she was missing. She shivered harder as cold and despair seeped further into her bones.

From somewhere outside came a loud, metallic *clang*. She heard the sound of footsteps. Someone was coming. Meiran hugged her knees against her chest, gaping through the bars of the iron grate. There was only darkness on the other side. The sound of footsteps stopped. She let her gaze wander upward.

A man appeared on the other side of the grate.

Meiran scrambled back against the far wall. The man stood still, staring at her with an impassive gaze. He was beardless and rippled with muscle, garbed in a long white tunic and formal coat. His face betrayed no hint of his intentions.

The man unlocked the grate, letting it swing open. He took a step into the room and paused. Crossing his arms over his chest, he stood motionless, black eyes considering her in silence. He said nothing, just stared, as cold seconds crept by.

He prompted her forward with a sideways jerk of his head.

Trembling, Meiran got up from the ground. She walked three lurching steps toward him, her legs shaky and weak. The dark man grabbed her by the arm, guiding her firmly out into the corridor. Meiran went along without struggle. They were well within the vortex, and the chiseled muscles of her guard brooked no argument.

She followed him into a wide corridor lit by the melancholy glow of hanging lanterns. The man guided her through an open doorway. There, her feet transitioned onto marble tiles. Meiran stumbled, her eyes drawn upward to the walls. Her mouth hung slack.

The hallway they entered was tiled from floor to ceiling in elegant, changing patterns. The designs scrolled around the walls, sometimes blue, sometimes red. Elaborate gilt metalwork wove in and out through the figures. Gold inlay wrapped around the columns that supported the vaulted roof, more gold than Meiran had ever seen in any one place.

Whoever controlled this fortress commanded enormous wealth.

And enormous power.

They passed other people in the hallway, mostly servants carrying trays and pitchers. Kitchen or serving staff, perhaps. Meiran had no idea where her escort was leading her, but it became apparent that they were heading deep within the living quarters of the fortress.

Her silent companion stopped in front of a large, gilded door. He paused there, seeming to take a moment to collect himself, straightening his posture, adjusting the collar of his tunic. Then he opened the door and guided Meiran inside.

A room-length wooden table was the focal point of a long chamber lined with dazzling wall tiles. The ceiling was painted blue, sprinkled with golden stars. Liveried servants stood like human statues, stationed at intervals along the walls. The table was empty, the chairs unoccupied.

A jerk on her arm pulled Meiran to a halt. She turned to glance up at him and found the man staring straight ahead at a golden screen at the far end of the chamber. She followed his gaze, her eyes drawn toward a motion on the other side.

A voice proclaimed, "Nashir Arman, Overlord of the Khazahar, Xerys' Shadow on Earth."

The screen slid back, admitting a man into the chamber. He was tall and dark of complexion, his eyes full of malice and shadow. Just the sight of Nashir Arman made Meiran's stomach spasm. She took an involuntary step back against her captor's chest.

Nashir fixed his gaze on Meiran as he took his place at the table's center, his eyes moving slowly over her. His angular face was rigid, devoid of all emotion. For just a moment, their gaze met. Meiran felt her stomach lurch; there was no trace of a soul left in Nashir's shadowed eyes. If there had ever been any humanity there at all, it had long since eroded.

Nashir Arman was far more demon than man.

Meiran swallowed, rocked by waves of revulsion that made her feel physically ill. Servants swept forward, helping Nashir settle in at the table, removing his overcoat and arranging his fine robes. A boy brought a silver bowl of water, placing it down on the table before him. Nashir dipped both hands into the bowl and brought them up to wipe over his face.

Movement on the other side of the table attracted Meiran's attention. She gazed in interest as a woman entered the room through the screen. Nashir's lips drew immediately into a smile at the sight of this newest arrival.

He raised his hand, beckoning the woman to join him at his side. She strolled into the room with a casual grace, her eyes flicking upward to alight on Meiran's face before shying away. She wore a brilliant green gown encrusted with jewels, the fabric swirling gracefully as she claimed a seat beside Nashir.

The demon made a gesture with his hand, inviting Meiran to take the chair opposite him. As she took a seat at the great table, none of the servants came forward to attend her, remaining at their stations along the walls. She stared down at the dinner service set out in front of her. The plate was jade-green celadon worked with a honeycomb motif. It was empty.

Nashir Arman smiled cordially. "Welcome to Tokashi Palace,

Meiran Withersby."

A line of servants filed into the room, carrying an assortment of trays and bowls, which they arranged in an elegant spread in front of Nashir and his guest. Meanwhile, other servants came forward to wordlessly remove Meiran's utensils and plate. The hospitality of a meal, then, would not be extended. Meiran felt a little of her courage slip, afraid of what that might signify.

She watched as Nashir and his lady helped themselves to the steaming platters of food. It was a sumptuous variety: breads and pickles, vegetables and grains. As Meiran sat there looking on, Nashir tore off a piece of bread, which he used to dip into a bowl. He talked as he chewed, staring down into his plate.

"The last I remember of you, you were kneeling at the feet of my Master's throne. I see that both your life and gift have been restored to you." His eyes rose to meet hers. "I am wondering...how was this accomplished?"

Meiran glared into Nashir's soulless eyes, watching him take another bite. He gazed at her expectantly, chewing slowly as he awaited her response. The woman at his side cast Meiran a condescending smile as she bit into a plump grape.

"I inherited Darien's legacy through the Soulstone," Meiran said. It was hardly a secret, and there was nothing to be gained by holding that information back.

Nashir's thick eyebrows flicked upward in curiosity. "Impressive. All eight tiers?"

Meiran didn't respond. She dropped her gaze to the table.

Nashir's smile faltered. "Not all eight, then. The legacy was split." He shared a glance with his woman as he scooped a morsel of eggplant into his mouth. "Who did you share this legacy with, I wonder?"

Meiran ignored the question, still staring down at the wood of the table before her. Her stomach growled. The smell of the food made her mouth water.

The woman leaned close to Nashir and whispered something in his ear. An affectionate smile flitted across his lips as he patted her hand. It was evident that he genuinely cared for her.

Nashir smiled proudly as he took his lady by the hand and said with a gracious smile, "I would like to introduce to you my newest apprentice, Katarya Safiye. Katarya has the potential. Alas, she lacks a living master to Transfer the gift into her. Perhaps Katarya can receive the legacy that gleams so brightly within you?" He reached up to stroke the woman's chin, smiling deeply into her eyes.

Katarya flashed Meiran a grin full of mischief.

Nashir plunged his hands into the fingerbowl beside his plate, wiping his skin dry on a cloth. He stood and moved behind his lady's chair, placing both hands upon her shoulders. He gazed across the table at Meiran. In a voice colored by a rich, melodic accent, he explained:

"I am the sovereign of a hungry, naked, and wretched people. It is my desire to deliver them from this state. With Katarya at my side, I intend to lead the people of Malikar out of these cold, forsaken wastes. Together, we will conquer the nations of the Rhen. We will force your monarchs to bow their heads and bend knee before us. We will show them that we are the iron race, and they will know what it is to hunger and despair."

Meiran raised her eyebrows, directing her gaze at Nashir. "Your own Prime Warden declared Darien Lauchlin overlord of this region. You are not the sovereign of these lands you pretend to hold."

The demon glowered, drawing himself up and placing a hand on the sheath of a bone knife he wore tucked into the sash at his waist. "I was born a thousand years ago on these very slopes, the son of a warlord who was the son of an overlord. My mother's grandfather was Khoresh Kateem, the most glorious and ruthless conqueror in all of history. Kateem's empire stretched from sunrise to sunset, from ocean to ocean. I was born to rule these lands. The Khazahar is mine by birthright."

Meiran chose to ignore the danger in his eyes. She stared at him unblinking. "And, yet, your Prime Warden saw fit to invest another with these lands. That must be so humiliating."

She had meant to bait him into a rage, forcing him to lose composure and face. Her words, however, had exactly the opposite effect. Instead of exploding in fury, Nashir Arman said nothing. He regained his seat, taking Katarya by the hand. To Meiran, Nashir's self-possession was even more frightening than his outright anger would have been. This, she decided, was a very dangerous man.

"A ghost cannot rule," he said finally, sitting back and taking a large goblet into his hand. "I will drink Lauchlin's blood from his skull and feed my fires with his flesh." He brought the goblet to his lips and took a swallow of its contents.

Meiran stared at him flatly. She knew how unwise it would be to provoke him further. But she also understood how unwise it would be not to.

"And how do you intend to do that?" she taunted with a toss of her chin. "Darien Lauchlin is far more powerful than you will ever be."

Her words somehow brought a smile to Nashir's face. He chuckled, a hand going to caress Katarya's cheek. "Did you hear that, my shining moon?"

He turned back to Meiran with a look of contempt. "I was trained by the greatest masters of the most ancient school of magic this world has ever known during the most enlightened period of human history. What is a fallen Sentinel of a shattered race compared to me? In this vortex, I alone have the advantage."

"Darien isn't fool enough to be lured into a vortex." Her words carried little conviction. Even as she spoke, Meiran knew she was probably wrong.

Nashir made a dismissive gesture with his hand. "He was lured into damnation for you, Meiran. My guess is Darien will chance a mere vortex."

"He won't," Meiran maintained. She spared a glance at Katarya. More softly, she added, "I am nothing to him any longer."

Nashir Arman appeared to contemplate her words. He stared deeply into Meiran's face as he raised the goblet to his lips.

"My eyes and intuition tell me otherwise," he said at last. He set the goblet down on the table. He extended his hand out toward Meiran, palm upward, across the table.

"Remove your necklace."

"No." Meiran's hand went possessively to the silver pendant at her neck. Not once had she ever taken it off.

Nashir's eyes flicked to the servant behind her. Before Meiran could react, an iron-clad arm slipped around her chest, bracing her back against the chair. She gasped as the silver chain was ripped away. She glared hatred at Nashir as the burly guardsman released her, necklace in hand.

"Have that delivered to Darien Lauchlin in Qul," Nashir commanded.

The guard bowed gracefully, stepping back. He handed the necklace to a page, who fled out of the room.

Meiran stared across the table at Nashir, appalled, her mind filled with confusion and resentment. "Why would you risk the wrath of your own Prime Warden to murder another Servant?" It was irrational; it made no sense.

"Zavier Renquist doesn't care what we do, just as long as there are Eight of us ready when the time comes. It makes no difference to him who those Eight are. My Katarya will make a fine Servant once she inherits the legacy of power trapped within you. I will enjoy watching you die," he added with a cold smile. The woman beside him leaned forward, planting a kiss on his cheek.

For the first time since entering the fortress, Meiran felt truly afraid. Her fear wasn't for herself. She reached down, pushing back her sleeves and baring the sparkling dual chains that were there. "Then here it is," she taunted, her eyes daring Nashir to act. "Let her come take it."

The darkmage cracked an amused half-grin. "Patience, little warrior. It is not yet time. For the death I have imagined for you, we require the proper setting. And the proper audience."

Chapter Twenty-One
Tangled Eternity

Qul, The Black Lands

D arien awoke, blinking his eyes to gaze upward at a ceiling steeped in shadow. It was dismally cold in the mud-brick room. There was only one source of light: a clay oil lamp perched on a shelf that cast a pale, wavering glow with its miniscule flame. It did little to drive back the darkness.

He lay on his back on a thin mat covered by his cloak, still wearing the robes Renquist had given him. His body was shivering despite the thick layers of fabric. The cold in the floor seeped upward through the mat, leeching into his skin. In a land that had long ago forgotten the warmth of the sun, ice and darkness ruled the seasons.

A movement on his right caught his attention. Darien rolled over, surprised to find Quin already awake. He brought his hands up to his face, rubbing his eyes. He rose to a sitting position and squinted at Quin, his vision blurry.

The darkmage was sitting with his back against a wall, eyes hidden by the brim of his hat. His attempt at a smile was a wan and mirthless endeavor.

"You're here and Meiran's not," Quin observed. "Does this mean I've fallen pathetically short of heroism yet again?"

Darien shook his head. "You were ambushed. You didn't have a chance."

"I'm sorry," Quin muttered, staring down at his arm as he tugged at a shirtsleeve. "Some people are just unfit to be heroes; they either try too hard or lack the necessary skillset. I fall into the latter category."

"There's nothing you could have done." Darien threw off his cloak and rose to his feet, stretching out his legs. His muscles were stiff and aching from the cold and the damp. He limped across the room to a tall water jug with a narrow neck, kneeling down beside it. He poured some water into a bowl, which he raised in both hands to his lips, drinking thirstily. When he'd had his fill, he cupped his hands and splashed chill water over his face.

"So, do I get to find out what happened?" Quin prodded, peering at Darien. He'd pushed his hat back so that it lay across his forehead at a slant. Quin's extreme age was apparent in his eyes. He had a defeated look about him, as if his soul were weary of the years. Darien understood. It was indeed possible for a soul to outlive its allotment of joy. His own tolerance for life had deteriorated well before his death.

He set the bowl down, moving back across the room. "Nashir must have found out about Meiran. He's figured out a way to get the revenge he's always threatened. He's established himself in a fortress to the north of here. That's where they took her."

Quin arched an eyebrow, sucking in a cheek. "So, if I may ask…what are you still doing here?"

"Nashir's fortress is protected by a vortex. I didn't dare go too far in."

Quin sat up straight, his face going tight with concern. "He's taken over Tokashi Palace? That was meant to be your stronghold, you know."

Darien shrugged. "No, I didn't know. Renquist never mentioned it. In truth, he never mentioned a lot of things."

Quin leaned his head back against the wall, gaze angled upward at the ceiling. "Tokashi Palace has been the bastion of power in the Khazahar for over four hundred years. I'm sure Renquist intended you to claim Tokashi as your base. But if Nashir got there first…he must be greatly emboldened to move against you so overtly. It's not like him, to take such a risk." He chuckled, sneering wryly. "I've got to hand it to you, Darien. More than any other person I've ever met, you really do know how to piss someone off."

Darien closed his eyes, shaking his head at Quin's graceless quip. He was right, of course, which didn't help.

"This is one honey of a pickle," Quin remarked.

"Aye, I guess it is." Darien brought a hand up to rub his temple. "I suppose I can't just walk in there and rescue her, can I?"

"No." All trace of humor fled Quin's face. "No, you cannot." The weariness came back to shadow his eyes. "There's really not much you can do. Not if Nashir's already established himself."

"It's a vortex," Darien grumbled. "That means there's a Circle of Convergence in there somewhere. Is there a chance I can reach it without being discovered?"

Quin shook his head. "I destroyed it."

Darien gaped at him. *"How?"*

Quin scooped his hat off his head, tossing it down in his lap. He ran a hand back through his hair, sighing heavily. "Tokashi Palace is built over the remains of an ancient fortress called Vintgar. Vintgar was…" His voice trailed off. He shook his head. "I don't know that I have the words to describe it."

He seemed to be struggling to gather his thoughts. "The ice caverns of Vintgar were the source of the River Nym. Vintgar's Circle of Convergence was tucked away deep in the bottom of the caverns, far below where Tokashi Palace exists today. That was my circle to protect. I was assigned to guard it on the night of the Reversal." He paused then, letting a long gap of silence stretch between them.

In the two years Darien had known him, through all of hell's tribulations, Quin had never once broached the subject of what had happened that night, so long ago. How it had all gone so terribly wrong. Except in fleeting moments of self-deprecation, Quin refused to talk about it.

"What happened?" Darien urged softly.

Quin took a deep breath. "I stabilized the magic field. But then I dropped the circle before tying it off. Braden…" His voice cracked. He brought a hand up to cradle his brow. "I thought that if I left right then, maybe I could get back before they executed my brother. I thought there still might be a chance I could save him." He shook his head. "I was wrong. Braden was already dead by the time I got there. And, in my folly, I left the vortex exposed to the Onslaught. Everything got out of hand before anyone realized what was happening.

"The air itself caught fire, the ground beneath seared to ash. The inferno swept across Caladorn, destroying everything in its path. It was as though all the fires of hell had risen up to consume the very earth." Quin spread his hands helplessly before dropping them back down again to his sides. He sat there, biting his lip, slowly shaking his head.

Darien stared at the ground with no words to offer into the heavy silence that followed.

Quinlan Reis looked up at him, fixing him with an ancient, desolate stare. "Vintgar was reduced to rubble. The River Nym jumped its course and flooded the ice caverns. The Circle of Convergence lies now lost somewhere beneath the waters of the lake that formed. It won't be of any use to you."

Darien nodded. He had heard of Caladorn's lost Circles of Convergence. He had read about the destruction of the Lyceum's Greater Circle, but he had never known where the other had been located or what had become of it. That Quin had a part in the circle's destruction did not surprise him in the least. Disaster seemed to follow Quin like a second shadow.

"Darien Lauchlin Nach'tier."

He glanced up at the sound of his name. Two men he didn't recognize stood in the open doorway. He rose immediately to his feet as Quin did the same.

"I'm Darien Lauchlin," he acknowledged warily, stepping forward.

One of the men had the appearance of a villager. The other did not. That one was a uniformed soldier, probably an officer, spectacularly arrayed in a blue and gold waistcoat. A long sash was tied about his hips, to which was affixed an array of various knives and implements.

The soldier nodded curtly. He was carrying a plumed hat tucked in the crook of his arm. Very formally, he effected a perfect bow, folding forward at the waist. Then he strode forward with measured stride, halting before Darien. He fell immediately to his knees, then bent forward until his face touched the cold bricks of the floor.

Darien stood frowning down at the prostrated man, his eyes flicking back to the villager still standing in the doorway.

"Rise," he muttered.

The man obeyed, bringing himself to his knees, but not to his feet. Keeping his gaze fixed on the ground between Darien's boots, he held a small silver box up before his face, proffering it with both hands.

"I, the Chamberlain of Armorers, Sayeed son of Alborz, have been sent on behalf of the Madashar Overlord Nashir Arman, Xerys' Shadow on Earth, to present to you this token."

Darien glared at the offered parcel, distrusting it. Very slowly, he extended his hand. But, instead of accepting the silver box, he curled his fingers into a fist and retracted his hand.

"Open it," he commanded.

Still with eyes lowered to the ground, the officer obeyed. He removed the lid from the small box and offered its small treasure up toward Darien in the palm of his hand.

Darien's face did not change. His expression didn't reflect the blunt thrust of anger that tore up through his middle, stabbing him first in the chest and then again in the stomach. He accepted the thin silver chain with an air of reverence, holding it laced between the fingers of his hand. Unable to breathe through the suffocating dread that filled his chest, he raised the pendant up before his eyes.

He didn't look again at the soldier on the ground. His eyes remained fixed on the pendant that hung swaying from his hand, turning, white globs of light running like quicksilver across its interlaced design.

The shadows in the room thickened visibly. The chill in the air crystallized as the chamber darkened.

Darien continued staring at the pendant as if mesmerized, his eyes tracking its motion. At his feet, the soldier began rocking back and forth, moaning, face contorted in a rictus of pain. The floor around him turned dark with spreading ice.

"Go."

Somehow, the trembling soldier managed to regain his feet with some semblance of grace. Cloaked by the dignity vested by years of discipline, he bowed stiffly and backed away. He turned and hurried out of the room. He was followed closely by the villager, who glanced back once with a look of horror in his eyes.

When they were gone, Quin shook his head and whistled softly.

"You really are a devil," he commented, striding forward from his position against the wall. "I suppose you've never heard the phrase, 'spare the messenger?'"

"I spared him."

Darien lowered the pendant, caressing it with the pad of his thumb.

"Narrowly," Quin scoffed. "For a moment there, it could have gone either way." Then, more gently, he asked, "What are you going to do?"

Darien's eyes locked with Quin's. "What are my options?"

"I don't know that you have any options. Nashir might be hellspawn, but he's wicked-cunning."

"It's a vortex," Darien argued. "He'll be at just as much of a disadvantage as I. What assets does he have?"

Quin quirked his face into a withered grimace. "He'll have warriors at his disposal. Tanisars: highly trained infantry. They've been preparing for hundreds of years, waiting for the day a Battlemage will return to lead them forth into glorious conquest. I'm sure Renquist meant them to be yours."

"And now they're Nashir's," Darien observed. The trap had a failsafe.

He frowned, slipping Meiran's pendant into a pocket.

"You can't win this," Quin assured him with a look of regret. "You have to let her go. I'm sorry, but there's no other choice you can make."

Darien sighed, gazing dismally down at the floor. Contemplating his options. His heart felt heavy, like a thick iron weight. He'd made a commitment to Azár and to the people of Qul to help them. He couldn't honor that commitment if he threw his second chance at life away. All for a woman who didn't love him back.

"There's always a choice," he said. "Some choices are just harder to make than others."

"You're starting to sound just like my brother," Quin grumbled, clearly irritated. "Don't. Don't fool yourself, Darien. You're no hero."

Darien flashed him a resentful look. "I never claimed to be."

His eyes fell on the sword at Quin's side. A thought occurred to him, jolting him right out of his melancholy. "Your sword—it's an artifact. Do you have any others? Something that might work within a vortex?"

Quin frowned, his face going quite serious. "Nothing that'll do you much good," he said thoughtfully. But he walked over to where his pack lay against the wall of the room and bent over. Scooping it up in his hand, he began rifling through the contents. Eventually, he withdrew a small copper cube, held it up before his face, then grimly shook his head. Replacing it back in the pack, he withdrew another item, what looked like some sort of scepter that ended in a carved wolf's head. This, too, disappeared back into the bag. With a sigh, he lowered the pack, setting it back down on the floor.

His eyes suddenly froze. Slowly, his hand moved to his side, coming to rest on the hilt of his sword. Quin's frown became deeper, much more serious. He stood there, one hand on the hilt of his ancient blade, staring at the wall in front of him.

"What?" Darien finally prompted him.

Quin turned toward him, a mischievous glint in his eyes. "My sword's a dampener."

Darien just stared at him, perplexed. "What good's that? Nashir can't use the magic field in a vortex."

Quin flashed him a wry, crooked grin. "It's not for Nashir. I'm going to use it on you."

Darien froze, at last understanding. Dampened, his mind would be protected from the fury of the vortex. But he'd still have access to the Onslaught. His mind reeled, filling with a euphoric sense of optimism.

"Have you ever used the Hellpower?" Quin asked. He was gazing down at his fingers, worrying at a hangnail.

"Aye."

"Then you know what it's like."

"A bit. Not much," Darien admitted. "For me, it's mostly just a way of reaching through to the magic field. I've used it, but...I really don't know much about how it works."

Quin brought his finger up to his mouth, biting off the torn nail. "There are some things you're going to need to know, then." He motioned with his hand toward the mats set out on the floor. He waited for Darien to settle cross-legged on one before following him down to the ground.

He flicked the shard of nail across the room, his eyes following its trajectory. "You can't use the Onslaught the same way you use the magic field. It has different rules. It's a bending of Natural Order, but it's tricky. Every use increases Chaos, increases disorder."

"So healing's out," Darien surmised.

Quin nodded. "By definition, healing is the restoration of order to a body that's injured or out of balance. Directly in conflict with the nature of the Onslaught. And then there's the issue of habituation."

Darien glanced up at him. "What's habituation?"

"The more you work with the Hellpower, the more you come to rely on it. Cyrus Krane's a perfect example of someone who didn't back off in time." Quin shrugged dismissively. "Just be careful. Don't ever let yourself get to the point where you feel like you *have* to use it. Don't become enslaved by it."

Darien nodded, fully appreciating the danger. Toward the end, he'd come to rely too much on the magic field. He had used it as a tourniquet to bind his pain. Thinking back, he realized what a mistake that had been. Immersing his mind in the field had distanced him too much from his feelings.

"Your best chance is to try to win the Tanisars over to your cause," Quin said. "It may be possible. By now, they must surely have some inkling that Nashir isn't the overlord that was promised. If you can appeal to the Zakai, their senior officers, you might be able to convince them to help you overthrow Nashir."

Darien doubted that. "Why would the Tanisars follow me?"

Quin cast him a withering scowl. "Darien, your reputation precedes you; your notoriety is just as legendary as your arrogance. You've already proven yourself a formidable adversary. Now, you just need to prove yourself a worthy ally. The Zakai won't just follow you out of the kindness of their hearts; you'll need to persuade them. Offer them something Nashir can never give them."

Darien spread his hands wide, shrugging hopelessly. "What could I possibly offer them that they don't have already?"

There was a heartbeat's moment of silence.

"Hope."

"Hope?" Darien echoed dubiously.

"Yes. Hope."

Quin lowered his chin until the brim of his hat overshadowed his eyes.

Chapter Twenty-Two
The Lion's Maw

Tokashi Palace, The Black Lands

Quin tipped his hat down further on his head as he gazed out across a hellish scene. Overhead, dark clouds raced across the sky. Below, the black waters of a lake stretched silently away from the hillside where he stood. The ground was white with recent snow, save only for the serpentine line of the road that followed the edge of the shoreline, meandering toward a narrow bridge that spanned the calm waters.

In this very place, a thousand years ago, the Black Lands had arisen from the ashes of dying Caladorn. Right here, where the headwaters of the Nym had sprung from caves of ice. This vale, once overshadowed by the hallowed gates of ancient Vintgar, now covered by the still, black waters below.

The lake was as old as Malikar itself. Its obsidian-flat surface obscured more than just Vintgar's fabled gates. The lake's deep, dark waters obscured the past. They buried secrets. They drowned the truth in their quagmire depths. Somewhere deep inside, Vintgar's Circle of Convergence yet slumbered. Quiescent, but aware. Lurking beneath. It was down there, somewhere.

Right where Quin had abandoned it a thousand years before.

He heard a crunching noise. He raised his head to note that Darien had come up to stand alongside him. The mage was still dressed in the indigo robes of the Lyceum, the same style Quin's brother had once been so fond of. Quin frowned, not liking it. The robes didn't suit Darien at all. They fit him well enough, but there was something about the look that seemed unsettling, even misleading. It took Quin a moment to put a finger on it.

Darien just wasn't Braden. No matter how much he wanted him to be.

Quin sighed, returning his attention back to the lake below. "Are you certain you don't want me coming with you?"

"I'm going alone."

Quin licked his lips, considering. "Then I'll wait for you back in Qul."

A ball of lightning flared briefly across the sky.

"Don't wait too long."

Quin nodded slowly. He turned to consider Darien's face. The man looked haggard. Drawn. Quin could hardly blame him.

"Are you ready, then?"

"Aye."

Darien reached down, hiking up his robe. He drew the fabric up, exposing his chest, shrugging the garment off over his head. He held it in a ball at his side, clothed only in the trousers he'd had on underneath.

Quin let his eyes trail over Darien's bare torso, observing every mark on him. The grotesque scars on his wrists, the etched white lines that striped his chest. Two small, V-shaped depressions where blades had pierced his skin. Quin considered the flesh before him critically, eventually deciding on a spot. The right arm; that would do best.

Darien was left-handed, just as Braden had been.

Decisively, Quin drew Zanikar from its scabbard. He raised the blade, setting the honed cutting edge against the meat of Darien's upper arm and, without hesitation, drew the sword swiftly down.

Darien didn't flinch. He stood with his eyes trained on the lake. Blood welled from the slice, running in thin red lines down his arm to his hand, thick droplets pitter-pattering to the ground. The warm blood made a random pattern in the snow at his feet.

Quin reached down and drew a rag from his warbelt, using the cloth to wipe Zanikar's blade clean. He sheathed the sword, then turned to consider Darien's new injury.

"I'll bandage that," he offered.

Darien stood still, allowing Quin to tie the cloth around his arm like a tourniquet. "Keep it clean," Quin advised.

Darien reached up, groping at his brow with his fingers. He looked suddenly upset. "Are you certain it worked? Is there any way to tell?"

Quin shrugged. "It just needs a healthy taste of blood. The binding does the rest. You've been dampened before; you know how it works."

"I suppose I'll just have to trust it." He grimaced as he drew the robes back on over his head.

Quin felt offended at the remark. Zanikar was his own creation, a masterwork exceeding every other artifact he'd ever fashioned. It was the only dampening sword in existence. To have its reliability questioned was downright insulting.

"You really do go to pieces in a vortex," Quin grumbled. "Are you sure you can hold yourself together? I'd hate to think what would happen if you started coming apart in front of Nashir."

"I'll manage," Darien muttered. He extended his hand across the space between them.

Quin considered the offered hand. He'd already forgiven Darien, but that forgiveness came at the price of other emotions. The plan they'd devised was by no means foolproof. Quin understood that this could very well be their last handshake.

He clasped Darien's arm with both hands, pulling him in close. It was a brotherly gesture, one from a different time, a different place.

"Darius dreoch," he whispered on impulse. The ancient, formal greeting of the clans. *May you offer protection,* was the loose translation. Quin used the phrase out of context on purpose; he did it to avoid saying goodbye.

He gazed with respect at the man before him with matted black hair and a hide full of scars. Darien had a wild, unkempt look about him, like the men of the horse clans Quin had been born to. Darien was not Braden; he never would be. But, then again, he didn't have to be.

"All right, then," Quin muttered.

Darien waited until he'd gained the road before turning back for one last glimpse of Quin. But the darkmage was already gone, obscured somewhere in the shadows of the desert. Darien wasn't surprised. He wouldn't have lingered, either. Not if he had a choice.

He turned his stare back to the still waters of the lake, setting his feet down the muddy path. The lake was black, devoid of life. There was no algae encrusting the rocks along the shoreline, no rippling movement of fish beneath the quiet surface. The lake was cold and still as death. The water wasn't murky, but crystalline-black.

He strode down the silent length of road, lost in troubled thought. His eyes stared with lazy focus at the sharp mountain peaks ahead and the looming fortress at their base. From this distance, Tokashi Palace seemed oppressive and sinister, like an upthrust shield made entirely of sharpened spikes. Dozens of conical turrets of varying heights were carved as if in bas-relief from the mountainside, like an enormous palisade. The tallest were quite spectacular, looming hundreds of feet above the valley and the lake. An enormous, gaping arch formed the river's channel where it emerged from beneath the mountain, tall and broad enough to maneuver a ship through under full sail.

Darien reached the bridge that spanned a narrowing of the lake. The bridge itself was a testimony to the industry of the people who dwelt in this place. It was made from enormous blocks of hewn basalt, jigsawed together without mortar or gaps. Gods only knew how deep the bridge's piers extended, deep down into the lake's gloomy depths.

He glanced back at the fortifications above, feeling a stab of trepidation. He was surprised they'd let him come this far, alone on the road. He'd marked their sentries a long time ago. He knew they were watching. They were waiting, staying their hand. They wanted him to come to them, not the other way around.

A bank of fog rolled in from across the lake, encasing the bridge in a murky haze. A queer, eerie silence settled in with the fog.

And cold. A frigid chill stung his cheeks and clawed beneath the cloth layers of his robes. Darien didn't like it. He didn't trust the fog, any more than he trusted the cold.

And the silence; that was the most unnerving of all. It was as though, one by one, all his senses were being purposefully deprived.

A shiver of foreboding crept across his flesh, followed by an urgent stab of panic. Darien's mind screamed for the comfort of the magic field. But there was nothing to reach for. That sense, too, had been stripped away.

Darien gained the other side of the bridge and stopped as his feet encountered soil.

Ahead, a line of soldiers barred his path. All wore uniforms of royal blue with long sashes of gold. One of the men stepped forward ahead of the others, striding toward him. Darien recognized the soldier; it was the same man who had brought him Meiran's necklace. The same man he'd almost killed.

Darien held his ground as the officer stopped in front of him. This time, the soldier did not fall to the ground in a gesture of deference. Instead, his hand rested on the hilt of his sword. He stared at Darien for a long time without expression. At last, he remarked:

"He said you would come. I did not believe him. I told him no man would ever be so foolish."

He made a sharp gesture with his hand. The men waiting behind him jogged forward, surrounding Darien with their bodies. He didn't struggle as they restrained his hands behind his back, searching him roughly for weapons. Finding none, two men took Darien by the arms, the rest fanning out around him. The officer moved forward until his face was uncomfortably close.

Darien gazed into the soldier's hardened stare, taking the man's measure. This was an officer who was comfortable with his command, steady and well-disciplined. There was no trace of fear in his eyes.

Calmly, the man asked, "I must know. Why did you come?"

Darien allowed himself a slight, wistful grin. "Because of a woman," he responded in all honesty.

The man in front of him raised his eyebrows. "Well, then. That does explain it." With a troubled frown, he wondered, "You are Aerysius' Last Sentinel. How is it that you are also *nach'tier?*"

"I'm no longer a Sentinel," Darien corrected him.

"It has been said that the Prime Warden himself chose you to rule the Khazahar."

"Aye. He did."

The man gazed at him, eyes narrowing. "Then why is it you enter Tokashi Palace in chains?"

Darien shrugged. "Because chains have never defined me."

He spoke figuratively, doubting the officer would be informed enough to take his meaning. To his surprise, the man nodded as if he understood the reference perfectly well.

"I am Sayeed son of Alborz, in case you've forgotten," the soldier said. He motioned to another man who stood slightly behind him. "And this is Iskender, first son of my brother."

Darien nodded a curt greeting. To Sayeed, he asked, "If you know Nashir is not the overlord that was promised, why do the Tanisars follow him?"

"Nashir Arman is the first Battlemage to ever walk the halls of Tokashi Palace. From birth until death, the Tanisars are sworn to follow whatever Battlemage is brought forth to lead us. It is our greatest honor, our most sacred duty."

"Wouldn't it be a greater honor to serve a commander who's actually ever won a battle?"

Sayeed son of Alborz fixed Darien with a flat stare. In a voice as cold as the surrounding air, he stated, "Your achievements are well-known to us, Darien Nach'tier. It is unfortunate that you chose to champion the wrong cause."

There was no disguising the resentment held barely in check beneath his disciplined composure. Darien sighed, realizing that Quin had been wrong about these men. There would be no winning over the Zakai. The officers that led the Tanisar corps had a very good idea of who he was. And they knew very well the enormity of atrocities he was capable of committing. They wanted nothing to do with him. Darien sighed, his hopes quietly shattering.

"I was a Sentinel of Aerysius before I ever swore allegiance to Xerys," he informed Sayeed. "I served my duty to the Rhen. I served it as best I could, even unto death. Through the will of Xerys, my soul has been remade. I serve a higher purpose, now. Your duty and mine no longer conflict."

Sayeed regarded him without a trace of compassion in his eyes. At last, he nodded curtly.

"Come. Let us enter your palace, Darien Nach'tier, last of the fallen Sentinels."

The men to either side prodded Darien roughly forward. He stumbled, staggering in their embrace.

They guided him under the high archway where the lake was born from the mountainside, down into a warren of passageways lit by flickering torchlight. It was dark and frigid, every corridor unadorned and monotonous. What was most remarkable about the fortress, Darien discovered, was the startling absence of sound. Many soldiers strode the long passageways, lined the walls of the hallways and courtyards. Not one word was ever spoken. The posted sentries stood as immobile as chiseled stone. The deeper they walked into the gaping quiet, the more conspicuous the silence loomed.

His guards guided Darien down into the depths of the fortress, to levels far below, where the cold, moist air was even more oppressive. The silence followed them even there. They stopped outside an iron door and waited while one of the men flipped through a ring full of keys, finally finding the one to throw the lock. The door shivered open on its hinges.

Darien flinched at the wall of ice-chill air that gushed out at them from the other side of the doorway. Goosebumps rose instantly to prickle his flesh. His guards forced him forward, his feet slipping on ice. It took him a moment to realize that the entire corridor was carved from the body of an enormous glacier. Darien gaped at the sight even as he shivered from the intensity of the cold. He had never seen the like. The walls of the glacier were black and sleek and transparent. An odd blue light shimmered down through its crystalline depths. The air was appallingly crisp, sucking the warmth right out of him. Even the thick robes he wore did little to contain his body heat.

His guards stopped beside another iron door, this one recessed into the wall of ice. Another man came forward to unlock it, throwing the door open. Darien gazed with dread into the narrow opening that was revealed. All he could see on the other side was darkness.

They shoved him toward the doorway.

"Wait."

He was jerked roughly back.

Sayeed stepped forward and grabbed him by the hair. He glared into his face. Then he shoved him head-first into the wall with all his strength. Darien reeled, slumping to the floor even as the soldiers hauled him back to his feet. They held him there against the wall as other men accosted him, slapping his face, shredding the blue fabric of his robes.

When they had him mostly naked and bloodied, Sayeed at last relented. He gripped Darien by the throat, pressing him back against the wall. The strength of his grip made it impossible to breathe. Darien's throat worked against the man's rigid fingers, to no avail.

"Tell me one last thing," Sayeed Zakai demanded in a patient voice. "If you did take rule of the Khazahar, what could you offer us that Nashir Arman cannot?"

Darien returned Sayeed's stare with a glare of his own. The man released his grip enough to let him speak.

"If you follow me, I'll give you back the sun," Darien said roughly.

Sayeed scoffed. An amused smile spread on his lips. He released his hold on Darien's neck and backed away. He turned, nodding in the direction of the doorway.

The men hauled Darien into the cell, throwing him to the floor. He scrambled, slipping on the ice. He managed to rise to his knees. A man came forward and doused him over the head with a bucket of frigid water.

Darien cried out and lurched back from the chill shock of it.

The water soaked his hair, running down his naked torso.

He fell to the hard ice as his body shook in terrible spasms of chill. The soldiers took turns dousing him with more water, soaking his trousers and his legs. Another pail was upended directly over his face.

At last, the sounds of the guards finally retreated. The hinges of the door shrieked closed. But the door's motion was interrupted. Into the darkness, Darien heard Sayeed's voice echo calmly:

"I hope you find the sun, Darien Nach'tier. Before you freeze to death."

The iron door was pulled the rest of the way closed, encasing him in shadow. Only the wan blue light of the glacier filtered down through the ice.

Darien curled up in a ball, shivering violently, alone with only his anger and his misery to keep him company. Reflexively, he reached out with his mind for the comfort of the magic field.

But the magic field wasn't there; its song was just a faded memory.

Desperate, Darien groped instead for the Onslaught.

Like a fickle lover, the Hellpower fled from his touch.

A terrible fear clenched his gut. Too late, Darien realized the folly of his mistake. In surrendering himself to Nashir, he had placed his own desires and concerns above the interests of his Master. And that was something Xerys would never tolerate.

Despair settled deeply into his bones along with the throbbing ache of chill. Both the Zakai and the Onslaught had rejected him. He'd been wrong to put so much faith in Quin.

Darien lay alone in the darkness, sprawled across the ice, shivering from the cold and shuddering with despair.

Azár had been right. He should never have come.

Meiran's stomach growled. She stared across the table at the elegant platters of food arranged before the beautiful Katarya, Nashir's new apprentice. The smell of the various dishes was enough to make Meiran's mouth water. They'd given her nothing to eat. Just water. Nothing more.

She watched Katarya eat, noting how well-mannered and elegant the woman was. Katarya plucked at her food daintily, taking small, delicate bites. She tore off tiny pieces of bread and took her time about chewing. Everything she did, every motion she made, seemed artfully practiced and executed. She was clothed in the finest silks and draped with gold and jewels. Her hair was curled and meticulously arranged. Her lips had just the faintest dash of color. Everything about Katarya was an elaborate pretense designed to both allure and obscure at the same time.

Katarya noticed Meiran's stare and smiled gently in her direction.

"The *bostalek* is scrumptious," she announced conversationally, indicating a particularly strong-scented dish. "The *mustaq* could have simmered longer, I'm afraid."

Meiran stared at her woodenly.

The woman's smile deepened. "What types of dishes do they prepare in the Rhen? Tell me, what are your favorites? I've always wondered what Southern food tastes like."

Meiran continued to gaze at the woman, lips pressed firmly together. She refused to be baited. She could sense the waves of amusement emanating from Katarya, and it galled her. She refused to be this woman's plaything.

A uniformed officer swept into the room, holding open the door. He was followed closely by Nashir. Katarya immediately rose to her feet and lowered her head to her chest, clasping her hands together in front of her. Her eyes glanced up beneath her long lashes, casting a hostile glare at Meiran, who made no attempt to rise.

Nashir approached the table and extended his hand, waiting as Katarya pressed a kiss against his fingers. A fond smile grew on his lips at the sight of her.

"My rose," he greeted Katarya as he seated himself at her side. "How is our guest?"

"Quiet," Katarya scoffed, fixing Meiran with a glare of disdain. "I try to make conversation, but she will not speak. She thinks she resists."

Nashir chuckled mildly. His hand went to clasp his apprentice's fingers, his thumb caressing Katarya's olive skin. He gifted Meiran with an indulgent smile. "So, our little warrior stages a protest?"

Meiran turned away from him in disgust. She fixed her eyes on the door opposite.

"It doesn't matter," Nashir assured her. "In the end, we will all get what we desire."

"What exactly do you think I desire?" Meiran spat, turning to glare her disdain at him. Nashir was demon to the core. It was his nature; there was something broken inside him. No matter how hard she tried, she couldn't get a sense of his emotions. It was as if they simply didn't exist. She was beginning to think he didn't have any.

Very patiently, Nashir explained, "Soon, you will long for death. You will wish for it more than anything you have ever wished for in your life."

His promise, spoken with such sinister assurance, sent a shiver of dread through Meiran's body. Somehow, she understood that his words were much more than mere threat. They had the ominous ring of prophecy.

"Why would I wish for death?" she asked softly.

Nashir was no longer smiling. He still held Katarya's hand in his own, stroking her skin gently. Gazing into Meiran's eyes, he explained, "Because with death comes the slow peace of the grave. It is a kindness, a gentle mercy. One that I will surely never know."

Meiran felt a hard knot of anger balling up inside. "You speak as though you're immortal. Are you?"

"No," Nashir corrected her firmly. "Xerys does not grant eternal life; what He grants instead is eternal servitude. In return, my Master demands unfaltering allegiance."

Meiran raised her eyebrows, surprised by his candid admission. "Do you regret your pledge to Xerys, then?"

"Not at all. I have no reason to regret my decision. Not yet. A thousand years in hell is a long time. However, it is but an eyeblink when compared to the wide span of eternity. You are very fortunate, little warrior. Your fight is almost over. Mine is only beginning."

Meiran lowered her gaze to the table's surface as she contemplated his words. So, Nashir Arman was not entirely happy with his circumstance. Which might explain why he had the temerity to defy Renquist's commands.

"What about Oblivion?" she found herself wondering.

"Ah, sweet Oblivion. The last refuge of the soul." Nashir smiled. His fingers froze, no longer caressing Katarya's hand.

Meiran pressed, "Wouldn't Oblivion be preferable to an eternity spent in hell?"

Nashir shook his head. He raised Katarya's hand to his lips, favoring it with a tender kiss.

"I am not yet so very desperate," he confided, gazing overtly into Katarya's eyes. "It is said that when a soul enters Oblivion, the spirit unravels like a thread pulled from a woven shirt. Oblivion is the negation of existence, the cessation of eternity. There is nothing after that."

He let go of Katarya's hand and reached for a bowl of crushed salt. He scooped up a large pinch into his hand, rubbing his fingers together to dispense the salt in a line across the table before him. "Everything that a person is, all that they ever were...all erased in a heartbeat." He leaned forward and blew across the line of salt, scattering the tiny crystals across the table's surface. "Like dust flung by the wind."

A gracious smile returned to his lips. "May your soul never be scattered by Oblivion. It is a gentle peace that you go to, little warrior. In the Atrament, you will know the companionship of all you have ever loved. You will never be alone or sad or afraid."

"That's not true," Meiran insisted, goading him on purpose. "Darien won't be there."

"No," Nashir agreed. "Darien will never be there. Like myself, the Atrament is denied him. But before you die, you can do your lover one last kindness."

"What is that?" Meiran shivered with an acute sense of foreboding.

"You can offer Darien the mercy of Oblivion."

"Why would I do that?" Meiran whispered.

"Because if Darien Lauchlin can be convinced to deny our Master, then his soul will be unmade. He will be spared an eternity of hell's torments."

Meiran's eyes widened in dismay. So that was Nashir's intention. He meant to use her as his weapon against Darien. Anger suffused her at the very notion; she could feel the heat of it scald her cheeks.

"I won't do it," she told him firmly. "I won't break my Oath of Harmony."

Nashir raised an eyebrow. "Would it truly betray your Oath to lead a damned spirit out of hell? Surely, it would not. Think of the favor you would be doing the man who gave up his life to deliver your own soul from such torment. And there is also this: there would be one less demon for your armies to face when the time comes for battle."

Meiran gaped at him, growing more horrified with every word. A chill panic suffused her, starting in her cheeks and descending to her core. Her emotions screamed in anger and outrage, appalled by the very notion of what he was suggesting.

And yet, the rational part of Meiran's brain was still groping to find fault in Nashir's logic.

Try as she might, Meiran could find no argument to refute him.

Because, appallingly, he was right.

Meiran's mouth went dry as she realized Nashir had left her no moral recourse.

She was still gaping down at the table when Nashir pushed his chair back and rose to his feet. He motioned with his hand toward the door. "Come. I have something to show you."

Thoroughly numb, Meiran made no attempt to refuse him. She followed in a daze, around the end of the table and out of the room, into a wide, torch-lit hallway. Nashir strolled at her side, one arm draped across her shoulders, compelling her forward. She had no choice but to go along with him. She was too weakened by hunger, too shackled by fear. Too appalled by her own sense of helplessness.

The walk was long and unremarkable, broken only by the

occasional flight of stairs. Nashir spoke not a word, but strode silently at her side. They were trailed by a small group of Zakai, Nashir's personal escort, though Meiran scarcely noticed them. Her thoughts were focused inward on her own mind. Exploring paths of possibility, differing avenues of choice. Until all possibilities eventually fused into none.

She drew up, realizing that Nashir had stopped walking.

Meiran gazed around, blinking and confused, finding herself in a dark corridor made entirely of ice. Nashir stood at her side. His hand squeezed her shoulder, drawing her close against him.

It was horrifically cold.

Nashir made a motion to one of his officers. The man came forward and immediately offered up his own overcoat. Nashir draped it himself about Meiran's shoulders, delicately adjusting the fabric. When he was satisfied, he gave a stiff nod.

"Come, see what I have found."

Two soldiers sprang forward and unlocked an iron door recessed into the wall of the passage. Meiran held her breath, dreading what she might find on the other side. The door shivered open. Frigid air poured forth from the gaping opening.

Meiran gazed ahead into the darkness within, seeing nothing.

Nashir reached out, grasping a torch from the opposite wall. He held it up in front of him and thrust it forward through the doorway.

Meiran gasped in dismay.

Darien lay on the floor of a cell made completely of ice. He was drenched with water, his flesh pale. He was curled into a ball on the ice.

"He presented himself to us just as I said he would," Nashir stated. His tone was smug.

Meiran felt the warmth of tears gathering in her eyes. "What have you done to him?"

"No more than he deserves." Nashir's hand wrapped once more about her shoulders. He guided Meiran forward into the cell of ice. "I'm not fool enough to destroy another Servant by my own hands. But I can make him suffer. And so I have."

Meiran gazed down into Darien's pale face. She whispered,

"What exactly do you want from me?"

"Convince him. Convince him to deny our Master and embrace Oblivion. It would be better for you. And better for him. You don't really think Aerysius' Last Sentinel ever wished to spend his afterlife fighting to destroy everything he ever loved? Of course not. Darien just needs to be made aware of his options. And he needs to exercise them."

Meiran looked up at Nashir in despair, marveling at the man's sadistic cunning.

"How does one become so evil?" she whispered, horrified.

"I am not evil," he disagreed. "I am merely a Servant of a cruel but effective god. All I desire is salvation for my own people, just as you desire salvation for your lover. Do as I suggest, and all of our interests will be served."

Nashir knelt to the floor. He placed a hand on Darien's forehead. Frowning, he rose and strode out of the cell. Once outside, he turned to face two of his Zakai.

"Fools. My order was to keep him alive and suffering. Instead, I find him near death and almost beyond the reach of pain. You failed entirely at your task. Go. Both of you. Provide blankets to the prisoners then present yourselves to the headsman."

Meiran flinched at the audacity of such a command. She whirled around just in time to see both condemned officers bow deeply in acknowledgement, just before the door swung closed with a jarring *clank*, eclipsing them in darkness. The only light was a wan blue glow shimmering through the surrounding ice.

Meiran squeezed her eyes shut, blinking back tears. She brought her hands up to cover her face. She wanted to be strong, but it was too hard. She felt so helpless.

She didn't want to become the instrument of a monster.

Meiran lowered herself down to the frigid ground, wrapping her arms around Darien's body. His skin felt horribly cold, his hair crusted with ice. She wormed her arms beneath his torso and heaved him up into her lap, hugging him tight.

The cell door creaked open just a crack.

A growing sliver of light revealed the silhouette of a man. One of the officers had actually troubled himself to find blankets on his way to the headsman's block. Meiran peered up, distraught, into the condemned man's bearded face. He handed her the blankets in silence, bowed low, then departed with grace.

Cold blue darkness returned at the *thud* of the closing door.

Meiran lay down alongside Darien and drew the blankets around them both, pulling him close to share her body heat. She closed her eyes and wrapped her arms around the man she had once loved, contenting herself with the feel of him. She was determined not to cry, so she didn't. She held him tight, wishing that the little time they had left together could last a bit longer. But she was too exhausted, the cold too depleting.

Far sooner than she'd intended, Meiran fell asleep.

Chapter Twenty-Three
Death's Doorstep

Glen Farquist, The Rhen

Naia awoke to an eerie, unsettling feeling that brushed down her back like the soft blur of spider's legs scurrying over her skin. She blinked her eyes, opening them just a crack. White, diffuse light filtered down from holes set high above in the ceiling, giving the marble statue above her the glowing appearance of warmth. The vacant eyes of the goddess stared down at her.

A shadowy motion on the other side of the shrine captured Naia's attention. She lay still, closing her eyes, pretending to be asleep. She slowed her breath, willing her fingers to relax. She focused on the slow, shallow rhythm of her breath as the sound of soft footsteps approached across the tiles. Fear wrapped around her spine, groped with chill tendrils through the pit of her stomach.

The rustle of fabric, soft, against the floor beside her. The brush of a finger, tracing her cheek.

Naia fought the urge to scream. She breathed in…then out. In. Out.

A hand, resting with gentle pressure against the fabric of her bodice. Fingers softly circling her stomach.

The touch sent shivers throughout her body, charged, like an electrical storm.

The rustle of fabric stirred again. The sound of soft, slippered feet moved cautiously away.

A gush of profound relief flooded Naia's mind, paralyzing. Her breath hitched in her chest. The sound of the footsteps paused.

Then they continued, retreating across the chamber.

Naia cracked one eye open, just a sliver, and gazed across the shrine in the direction of the bier. The wooden cart was empty. The shroud had slipped to the floor, where it lay in a sprawled rumple of fabric.

Naia turned her head ever so slightly, glancing over to where Kyel lay sleeping. A woman was bending over him. A woman in a dark robe, chestnut hair spilling down her back.

Sareen.

Naia clamped her mouth shut against a scream, both eyes opening wide. She squeezed them shut again quickly before the woman glanced her way. She fought to relax the tense muscles of her face.

In. Out.

She peered out from beneath the long lashes of her eyes. She could see Sareen's graceful form, a golden silhouette against the warm wash of light, settling down beside Kyel on the floor. He lay curled on his side, head resting on his hand, his cloak enveloping him like a blanket. Sareen set a hand lightly on his back. She tilted her head, tracing her fingers over the soft embroidery of the star on Kyel's cloak. She continued the motion, sliding her hand down the length of his arm, caressing his hand.

Kyel flinched awake.

As Naia watched through cracked lids, he scrambled back away. The woman before him stayed her ground, raising her hand in a gesture of reassurance.

"There's no need to be afraid," she whispered. "I suspect I owe you both a great deal of gratitude for returning my life to me."

Naia blinked at the sound of Sareen's voice, elegant and tender-soft, with an accent that was at once both exotic and sophisticated. She watched as the darkmage bent forward, laying a comforting hand on Kyel's arm. The expression on her face spoke of wonder and exhilaration.

Kyel gaped up at her, aghast, muscles flexed as if ready to bolt. His face was a medley of dismay, fear, and fascination.

"It was Naia that healed you," he finally managed.

Naia winced internally, hearing that. She didn't trust the enticing darkmage, who seemed to be trapping Kyel under the spell of her allure. He looked utterly baffled, captivated.

Sareen smiled down at him. Reaching out, she stroked her fingers over Kyel's bearded cheek. "But you helped, didn't you?"

"I did," Kyel admitted, gazing wide-eyed up into her face.

Sareen's smile broadened, her eyes sparkling. Leaning forward, she pressed a tender kiss against Kyel's brow. "Thank you so much. I owe you my life."

Naia felt an appalling chill slither over her body. Things were getting quickly out of hand. She didn't know what to do. Sareen's placid voice drifted toward her across the chamber:

"So…why?"

"Why what?" Kyel whispered, licking his lips. He struggled to sit up, resting his weight on his elbows. He gazed up into Sareen's eyes as if transfixed by what he saw there. Naia clenched her fists in consternation.

"Why did the two of you conspire to return the breath of life to one such as I?" Sareen traced her fingers down the sides of his face, first one cheek, then the other. She smiled, a tender, caring expression.

"We need your help," Kyel croaked, wriggling away from her.

"Truly?" Sareen scooted after him.

This had gone on long enough. Naia could no longer pretend to feign sleep. She sat bolt upright.

"Be very careful, Kyel," she warned.

"Kyel?" Sareen glanced back over her shoulder at Naia, flashing her a smile of gratitude. Then she turned back to the subject of her attentions. "That's an intriguing name." She reached out, taking his hand. She brought it up to her lips, kissing it.

Then she rose gracefully to her feet. Her body swayed as she paced across the shrine, dropping to her knees in front of Naia. She canted her head to the side, smiling coyly.

"So, here's the gentle beauty who woke me from my grave." There was a hungering desire in Sareen's voice that also simmered in her eyes. More for herself, Naia realized, then for

Kyel. "I owe a special thanks to you." Sareen's smile seemed genuine, as did her admiration. "That took quite a bit of talent; I've never heard of anyone healing through death before in all of history. What order are you trained to, dear?"

"You owe me nothing." Naia edged back away from her. Her eyes shot a stabbing glare at Kyel: a warning.

"Your name is Naia?"

There was no denying the interest of attraction in that voice. Sareen maintained her beguiling smile, her face smooth as butter cream.

Naia knew better than to answer. The woman was already armed with too much information about them already. She gazed defiantly at Sareen.

The darkmage smiled. "It's just a name. A very beautiful name. Nothing to be afraid of." She leaned forward, her lips brushing against Naia's ear. "Do you know my name?"

Naia shivered. Unbidden, the words slipped past her lips. "Sareen Qadir."

The woman's smile brightened. She straightened, taking a step back away. She moved to the center of the room, where she could stand and consider both Naia and Kyel together without turning.

"Now, tell me. What do the two of you need so desperately that you're willing to wake the dead?"

Naia glanced to Kyel, her eyes capturing his gaze and holding it. Fear needled her spine. Gathering her courage, Naia rose to her feet and stood facing the alluring darkmage. Kyel followed suit, edging closer to her until he was standing at her side.

"We want to know where Quinlan Reis took Meiran Withersby," Naia announced. She gazed at Sareen expectantly, hoping that her fear didn't show outright on her face.

Sareen spread her hands. "Well, that's a difficult question for me to answer. Being that Quinlan Reis was responsible for my own particular…condition."

"Why would another Servant try to murder you?" Naia asked.

"I have no idea. I could only speculate."

Naia narrowed her eyes. "Then speculate."

Sareen turned away to face the Goddess of the Eternal Requiem. She stared up into the statue's cold face. With her back still to them, she said softly:

"I imagine he was probably trying to avenge his brother's death."

Naia frowned. "You killed his brother?"

"Not directly, no." Sareen glanced back over her shoulder. "But I was involved."

Naia considered the explanation. It was possible Sareen was telling the truth; she most likely was. Only, Naia doubted it was the only explanation, or even the correct one.

"Where would Quinlan Reis have taken Meiran?" she pressed.

The woman turned back toward her, clasping her hands. "I honestly don't know. If he has turned completely away from Xerys, then his soul is forfeit. Perhaps he took your Prime Warden ahead to Bryn Calazar to give the appearance that he's still doing the work of our Master even as he plotted against me."

Naia clenched her jaw in frustration. This was going nowhere. This woman did not have the knowledge they sought. Either that or she was a subtle and convincing liar. The truth probably lay somewhere in between.

Naia asked, "What does Renquist want with Meiran?"

"Control," Sareen responded immediately.

Naia blanched, feeling her stomach sink. "What do you mean?"

The woman's smile returned, this time almost gloating. She strode forward until she was standing right in front of Naia, gazing down into her eyes. "I'm sorry, darling, but I do believe it's my turn." She trailed a finger down Naia's cheek. "If you want me to keep speaking, you must answer a question or two of mine."

Naia stared resentfully into Sareen's face, shuddering from the touch even as she fought the impulse to blurt out an affirmative. She regretted healing Sareen. She had vastly underestimated this demon's sophistication. Sareen was working on her mind, seducing Naia's will and intentions. Bending them subtly in the directions she wanted. Naia could feel Sareen's power working, helpless to do anything about it.

"I will answer two questions," Naia allowed. It was the most resistance she could manage. She swallowed, unable to break eye contact.

Sareen asked, "Where did you learn to heal as you did? To turn back the clock on death? The most talented healers of my own time couldn't have managed it. How is it possible that you were able to accomplish what has never before been achieved?"

Naia felt a sharp pang of fear. This, she knew, was very dangerous territory. But before she could stop herself, she was already answering.

"Before I became a mage, I was a priestess of Death."

Sareen's eyes widened with a look of astonishment. "That explains a great deal," she said, pacing away. "In my time, neither the Lyceum nor the temples would have ever countenanced such a dangerous union of knowledge. Yet, what a wonderful resource!"

Sareen paused, blinking.

She whirled back around, fixing her stare on Kyel. "And do you have any such special talents?"

Kyel immediately shook his head. "No."

"None at all?"

"Nothing," Kyel admitted with a shrug.

Sareen frowned, her eyes darkening. "That's too bad. I'm really very sorry, Kyel."

Her eyes filled with sincere regret.

"No!" Naia screamed, throwing herself forward. A strong slap of air brushed her easily aside, throwing her to the ground.

Kyel dropped to his knees, eyes bulging, mouth agape as he struggled for breath. His hands groped frantically at his chest.

"Kyel! By the goddess! No!"

Sareen turned to Naia with an expression of genuine remorse. "I'm sorry, little one." Her voice was full of sympathy. "He's just not valuable like you."

Kyel fell forward to the ground, limbs flailing helplessly. His chest seized, lurching for air.

With a scream of rage, Naia closed her eyes and lashed out at

Sareen. It wasn't planned, wasn't thought out. She used the knowledge gleaned from years of working with the dying and the dead. She didn't think of the consequences. She just acted.

Naia reached deep into Sareen's body and silenced the beating heart she had so recently brought back to life.

There was no gasping, no struggle. Sareen's expression went slack. She crumbled face-first to the floor, her hair shrouding her face.

Sobbing, Naia threw herself down on the floor beside Kyel. He was breathing again, his eyes watering as he gasped for air. Naia hugged him fiercely. She brought her right hand up to wipe away her tears—

—and saw the hideous red scar that twisted around her wrist in the place where the chain-like marking had been just seconds before.

Naia screamed. She scrambled backward, staggering to her feet. She grasped her wrist with her other hand, clutching it against her chest. She screamed again and kept screaming, over and over. Her panicked shrieks filled the room, echoing off the walls of the shrine. She collapsed to her knees as her wails faded into violent, wracking sobs.

A thunderous clatter echoed through the shrine. The great oaken door jolted as it was assaulted with force from the other side. Naia couldn't move. She hugged her arm against her chest, sobbing wretchedly. On her knees, she wobbled over next to Kyel. He was unconscious, but mercifully still breathing.

An echoing *crash* resounded through the shrine as the door gave way. Priests in white vestments rushed forward into the room, spilling down the stairs. Striding through their midst was Luther Penthos, rushing through them toward his daughter.

He swept Naia up into his arms, hugging her close against him. Then he pulled back, cupping her tear-stained face in his hands. His frightened gaze probed her eyes. He must have seen something there. His jaw fell slack as he stared at Naia's wrist.

His face collapsed in despair.

And then he reacted. Clutching her by the arm, Naia's father dragged her forward across the room. Before she could protest, he forced her across the threshold of the portal into the otherness of the Catacombs. The light shivered, shifted. His grip on her wrist was violent and painful.

Naia fought for her hand back, wrenching her arm free of her father's grasp.

He swung toward her, looming in his anger, more formidable than Naia had ever seen him. No longer was Luther Penthos a fragile old man. He was the Vicar of Death, the incarnation of his office, in all its fearsome majesty.

"Use the Catacombs to flee the Rhen!" Naia's father ordered her. "Flee the Rhen and never come back! Do you understand? Don't tell me where you're going. *I don't ever want to know.*"

Naia stared at him through tear-filled eyes, grimacing through her terror. *"What? Why?"*

Luther Penthos raised a hand as if to strike her across the face. But he clenched his fist, instead, eyes turbulent with sorrow and wrath.

"You broke Oath, Naia! By rule of law, your life is now forfeit!"

"Father, *I didn't mean to—!*"

He shook his head, eyes chilling in their fury. *"It doesn't matter!* The only thing that matters now is time. You must hurry! They'll be looking for you. Don't leave a trail for them to follow."

Tears streamed down her face as Naia shook her head in protest. *"No, Father!"*

He wrapped his arms around her, forcing her against his chest in a last, violent embrace. "I can't protect you, Naia. But neither will I be party to my own daughter's execution. *Now, go!*"

She walked away a few steps, burying her face in her hands, sobbing wretchedly. She stopped and turned back. *"Father, no! Please!"*

Luther Penthos waved her away, his glare terrible and uncompromising.

"Go, Naia. Go now and never come back. *Never.*"

Sobbing, Naia stumbled forward into the Catacombs, clutching her ruined wrist against her chest.

Chapter Twenty-Four
Chaos

Tokashi Palace, The Black Lands

M eiran felt warm, secure. Shrouded in comfort. As if everything wrong in the world had been suddenly made right. For the first time in years, she awoke to feelings of security and contentment. No longer was there that aching, throbbing place inside. That emptiness was now full. It abounded with warmth, gratitude, and compassion. They were not her own feelings.

They were Darien's.

Once, Meiran had awakened each morning saturated with the comfort of Darien's presence in her mind. She could feel him throughout the day, always there, always with her. She had never been alone. It was almost as if she wore him around with her, deep within her heart. She always knew what he was feeling, whether he was excited or melancholy, frustrated or confused, angry or desperate. Even after he'd left Aerysius for Greystone Keep. The connection between them had grown so strong she could still sense it, despite the distance. Though weak, the link between them had comforted her quietly from afar.

When Darien died, Meiran had felt that link shatter. One moment he was there with her. The next, he was gone. She was left with only a hollow, empty ache.

But now, somehow, he was back with her again. Filling her mind with feelings of warmth and a sense of solace. She could feel the heat of his body pressed up against hers, the peaceful rhythm of his heart. His fingers stroked her hair back away from her face, his touch soothing.

Meiran opened her eyes even though she didn't want to.

Darien was lying beside her. Propped on one elbow, gazing down into her face with a soft expression in his eyes. His skin was flushed from the warmth of the blankets.

"Are you all right?" His voice was low and hoarse.

Meiran nodded, feeling the urgency of his concern for her.

"I'm fine," she whispered. "Are you?"

"Better," he answered. He was smiling at her wistfully, fingers still absently stroking her hair.

"What?"

"I was just thinking of the day I fell in love with you."

She raised her eyebrows. "You can actually remember which day that was?"

Darien nodded. "It was the day of your Raising."

"Why that day?"

"It was supposed to be *my* Raising. Remember?"

She did remember. The legacy she'd inherited had come from Neria Terrant, Grand Master of the Sixth Tier, one of the most powerful mages in the history of Aerysius. The Sentinels had put forth Darien as their candidate to receive Neria's legacy. Since he had the backing of the Sentinels, Darien was an easy selection. But Grand Master Neria overrode the decision. She reconvened the Assembly, staunchly and publicly refusing Darien as her successor.

The result was a political skirmish between orders as both Sentinels and Querers set themselves at each other's throats. In the end, Meiran was chosen to be the recipient of Aerysius' most powerful magical lineage. Darien left the Assembly humiliated, still years away from another chance.

"They were awful to you," Meiran whispered. "Especially Grand Master Neria."

Darien's fingers continued their slow stroking of her hair. His eyes grew distant, a quiet smile forming on his lips. "I remember. She called me a 'cavalier delinquent.' She told me my greatest attribute was that I probably wouldn't survive long enough to do much damage."

"At least you proved her wrong."

Darien's smile turned devilish. "I did. She grossly underestimated the amount of damage I was capable of."

Meiran was taken aback by Darien's self-deprecating wit. It was so utterly out of character. It was something the old Darien would have said. The man who'd gone away to Greystone Keep, never to return.

He continued, "At any rate, that's why I fell in love with you. You were there for me when no one else was. And you didn't have to be; you really didn't know me well at all. But you went out of your way to walk me back to the Acolyte's Residence. Along the way, you told me something I'll never forget."

"What was that?"

"You said I needed to start ignoring everyone else's expectations and start living up to my own. It's the best advice anyone's ever given me." More softly, he added, "I just wish I'd have followed it."

Meiran stared up into Darien's face. His expression was pensive, his gaze remote. His eyes were focused somewhere far away, perhaps at the shadows, perhaps somewhere in the past. There was a quiet serenity to his features she hadn't seen in years.

"You were more deserving of that legacy than I was," he said. "You're a remarkable woman, Meiran. You've always had my admiration. And my heart. You still do."

His fingers caressed her brow, smoothing the strands of hair back away from her face.

Hearing his words, feeling the warmth of emotion that flooded into her through the link, Meiran felt a drowning ache of sorrow. She pulled away from him, sitting up in the cold darkness of the cell. Darien looked at her with eyes full of anxious uncertainty. The link didn't work both ways; he couldn't sense the layers of guilt and dread she was feeling. But he could see them implied on her face.

Meiran explained as levelly as she could, "Nashir intends my gift for his lover, a woman named Katarya. He wants me to convince you to deny Xerys and follow me to the grave."

Darien sat up. His eyes widened slightly, but his expression never changed. He looked her directly in the eye, his stare unfaltering. "I'll follow you anywhere you ask, Meiran. But you're not going to the grave just yet. I won't let that happen."

Meiran lowered her eyes. She took a deep breath. "What if there's nothing you can do about it?"

"I'll find a way." There was absolutely no trace of doubt in his voice.

"Darien...what if you can't?" Meiran insisted. She peered into his face, her voice firm. "If you don't, if something happens to me...then I want you to abandon Xerys."

A troubled sadness filled his eyes. He set his jaw, stubbornly shaking his head. "You've no idea what you're asking."

"I *do,*" Meiran said, leaning forward. "I know you, Darien. And I know that this...*existence*...it's not what you ever would have wanted. It goes against everything you always stood for, everything you love and believe in."

"It doesn't, though. That's what you have to understand."

"Then *help me understand!*" Meiran insisted, waves of frustration bleeding into her voice. "Because, right now, I don't."

Darien nodded. Meiran could sense the tension in him as he struggled to gather his thoughts. She could feel how exasperated he was, how desperate to gain her understanding.

He explained, "When I was a Sentinel, I was sworn to defend the Rhen. Now...I'm pledged to a higher purpose. I serve Chaos. The entire magic field is born of Chaos. That's what I protect. That's what I serve. It's bigger than the Rhen. Bigger than Malikar. Bigger than us all.

"It's my duty to bring the people of Malikar out of darkness. They've endured here too long, and for no good reason other than our own inability to find fault within ourselves. And, after that, I've another obligation: I have to make damn certain that something like this can never happen again. *That* is my duty. That's why I'm here."

Softly, he added, "I'm sorry, Meiran. This isn't my life to live any longer. I gave that up." He lowered his chin, staring up at her through tousled strands of hair.

"How would you define Chaos?" His words were little more than a whisper.

Meiran shrugged, not knowing how to respond. Frowning, she uttered the first words that came to mind. "Disorder, mayhem...evil."

Darien nodded. "That's why you're confused. You can't simply chalk everything up to disorder and mayhem. Good and evil. Those notions are entirely too simplistic."

Defiant, she lifted her chin. "What's *your* definition, then?"

He looked away. His expression was remote. "It's not what you'd think," he said. "It's hard to explain. I don't know that I can."

"Try."

Darien scowled as if daunted by the task. He took a moment before speaking, as if carefully framing his answer.

"Things happen the way they do because they're set in motion by our actions. And then, from there, they tend to follow a certain trajectory. Every decision we make has consequences. Tremendous consequences, so many that we have no way of foreseeing them all or anticipating what direction they'll take us in. Everything that happens, happens as a result of our own actions, our own decisions.

"That's what Chaos is," he said, leaning forward. "It's the sum of the consequences of every decision we've ever made coming back to haunt us in the end."

Meiran stared at Darien with profound sadness in her eyes, her heart quietly breaking.

They'd remade so much more than just his flesh. They'd reimagined everything about him that had once defined who he was. They had harnessed Darien's boundless passion for duty, turned it against him, corrupting it to their cause. Transmuted his guilt into a collar to constrain him. They had taken the pureness of his soul and worn it down into a soiled, gritty thing that justified ends with means.

She understood him better, now.

She also understood she couldn't leave him like this.

This was the man who had saved her when her soul had been past any hope of salvaging. Meiran took a deep breath, closing her eyes against remorse. She took his hands in hers.

"This is not your responsibility, Darien," she said, gazing into the shadows of his face. "It's not your fight any longer. That's what death is for. It releases us from our obligations, relieves us of the burdens life places on us. Only in death are we truly free." She added in a whisper, "If you deny Xerys, you can have that kind of freedom, Darien."

"You want me dead," he said dully, eyes flat and leaden.

"You're already dead." It was such a cruel thing to say. Nevertheless, it had to be spoken. "Now…I just want you safe. I want you someplace they can't hurt you anymore."

He turned away. "In my entire life, there's been only one person capable of hurting me. Thank you for the pain." The cold way he said it, combined with the raw depth of hurt flooding into her through the link, acted on her like a kick in the gut.

She couldn't hold back the tears. They spilled down her cheeks like rain. She brought her hands up and wept silently into her palms, face hot with scalding shame. Her shoulders shook with the quiet force of her guilt. All the while she could feel the heat of Darien's anger condensing, cooling, as the link between them faltered. To her dismay, she realized he was walling his emotions away, shutting her out.

The cell door creaked. Then it shuddered open.

"No!" Meiran shrieked, panicking at the sight of the thin strip of light that suddenly appeared, widening into the span of a doorway. She scooted back away from it until her back was pressed up against the chill wall of the cell. Her fingers clawed at the ice for traction.

At the sight of the first guard that entered, Meiran shouted, *"No! Please! I need more time—!"*

A group of men streamed into the chamber, surrounding them. They went for Darien first. They threw him down onto his stomach as one man knelt on top of him with a knee pressed into his back. They bound his arms behind him with a set of iron manacles. Then they grappled him to his feet, maneuvering him out of the cell.

The remaining guards spun Meiran around against the wall, holding her pinioned against the ice. One man forced her arm up over her head, holding her wrist with a crushing grip as he brought the other arm up, as well. They lashed her wrists together over her head, tugging fiercely on the rope. They shoved her backward. Hands grabbed her, forcing her through the doorway and down to the ground of the passage outside.

She fell to her knees beside Darien, who was crouching with his arms shackled behind his back. In front of him stood a man Meiran instantly recognized.

It was one of the Zakai officers Nashir had ordered to the headsman. Apparently, the man had chosen to ignore the command. He leaned forward, stooping down until he was almost at eye level with Darien. His brow was broken out in beads of perspiration despite the icy chill of the air. His expression was rigid, intense. His dark eyes simmered with brutality.

"You said you can give us back the sun. Tell me how."

Darien glared up at the man through wet strands of hair. She could feel the scorch of his anger even through the faltering link. Meiran heard every breath he sucked into his chest, the sounds sharpened by the intensity of his wrath.

"There's two options," Darien said through gritted teeth, looking up at him with an unwavering gaze. "First, I'll try to break the curse over the Black Lands. If that fails, then I'll escort your people southward into the Rhen. With the strength of my power and my knowledge of their command structure, their armies won't stand a chance."

Meiran gaped at Darien, her eyes widening in disbelief. Horror seeped into every crevice of her being, her stomach clenching into a hard burl of knots. Even after everything Darien had said back in the cell, the way he'd argued so passionately about Chaos, Meiran was still shocked. She would have never believed him capable of embracing such treachery.

He never even looked at her.

He crouched on the floor, gazing up into the bearded face of the Enemy officer, calmly awaiting a response. No emotions came back to her through the link. No remorse, no regret, no anger, no shame. Nothing. He was completely empty.

More men spilled into the corridor around them. One leaned forward and whispered something into the officer's ear. The bearded man nodded, righting himself. He glared imperiously down at Darien, hands on his hips.

"He sends for you," the officer announced, stepping back. "If you can defeat Nashir Arman, then you will have the support of the Tanisars." He turned and strode briskly away down the corridor.

Hands gripped Meiran by the arms, hauling her onto her feet. She resisted, thrashing frantically, struggling to break free.

"Don't!" she screamed back at Darien as they dragged her brutally down the corridor away from him. *"Don't give them what they want! Please! Don't do it! Don't let them destroy you!"*

Chapter Twenty-Five
Blood for Blood

Tokashi Palace, The Black Lands

He could still hear the shrill sounds of Meiran's screams echoing down the passage: frantic, pleading, hysterical. There was a sharp, scuffling commotion. Then silence. An eerie calm descended on the passage, clinging to the walls.

Darien knelt with his knees drawn up against his chest, wrists crossed behind his back, restrained there by cold iron manacles. He was naked from the waist up, his body trembling more from horror than from cold. He stared down in misery at the blue-ice floor of the cave beneath his feet as waves of shock, revulsion and despair broke over his body in rapid succession, one after another. He clenched his jaw until it shook, biting his lip against the despair trying to claw its way up from his insides.

They were going to kill Meiran.

Meiran, the woman he loved. The woman who wanted him dead.

That thought bore down on him like a cruel iron weight, crushing and brutal. He swayed over his feet, the muscles of his calves burning from the stress position they had him in. Someone slipped an arm around his neck, restraining him. Another guard shoved a filthy rag into his mouth, feeding it in all the way back past his teeth. He gagged and struggled, retching against the rough, dry taste of the rag.

They shoved a woven sack over his head, tying it with a cord around his neck. Not enough to choke him. Just enough to hold it in place.

With the rag in his mouth, the sack over his face, Darien

labored just to breathe.

Panic seized him. He flailed against the unyielding grip of the guards. They threw him down hard against the ice, restraining him there with the weight of their bodies as he fought and squirmed, bucking and kicking. At last he went limp for lack of air and will to fight. Darien slumped against the ice, struggling just to draw breath, gasping at stale air and rotten fabric.

"Are you done?" someone above him growled. The sound of the voice was muffled by the sack.

He couldn't respond.

They lifted his dead weight, hauling him forward. His heart surged, the sound of his pulse a careening thunder in his ears. He couldn't walk, so he let them drag him down the corridor. He felt consciousness slowly leaking out of him.

The sounds around him were muffled, distant, disorienting. He could see only darkness. His mind groped through a haze, desperately fumbling to cope with his situation. There was nothing he could cling to; his senses were deprived, the magic field just a memory. The fickle Hellpower had betrayed him, fleeing from his touch. There was nothing for his mind to latch onto. They had rendered him utterly helpless.

The guards halted, propping him upright with the force of their bodies. There was the sound of chains. Someone jerked his arms upward behind his back until his shoulders screamed in anguish. They held him there, securing his wrists above his head. Darien clenched his teeth against the pain, feeling the tendons of his shoulders starting to give. Behind, he could hear a sharp, metallic *clank*. Then another, much more ghastly sound.

The noise of gears going *click, click, click...*

His body began to stretch as his weight was lifted off his feet. Pain like molten fire seared down his arms and into his shoulders, radiating across his chest. He could feel the joints of his shoulders starting to give. There was a dull popping sound.

Darien howled against the rag.

He could still touch the ground with the tips of his toes. They left him there, dangling, twisting at the end of the chains, the tissues of his shoulders slowly separating. Darien groaned, gasping through clenched teeth, biting on the wadded fabric stuffed in his mouth. It didn't help. The pain was acute, relentless. It worsened by the second.

He could see nothing. Hear nothing except the sound of his own muffled groans and the sharp hiss of breath wheezing through his nostrils.

A disembodied hand rested softly against the skin of his back. It caressed him, the way a rider strokes the muscles of a horse. The sensation raised goosebumps on his flesh. A sense of appalling dread clenched his throat, terrorizing him from the inside.

He fought for every strangled breath, his consciousness reeling.

A deep, familiar voice addressed him from the darkness:

"I told you I'd have my revenge. 'Flesh for flesh. Blood for blood.' That's been the unwritten law of the Khazahar for thousands of years. It's still the law today."

The hand on his back moved, stroking downward across his naked flesh. Darien shuddered against the awful feel of it. That deep, emotionless voice resonated in the stifling darkness:

"Your greatest mistake was taking Arden away from me. Your last mistake was thinking that you might actually get away with it. What hubris you must have."

The hand lifted, moving away. There was a shudder in the chains restraining him.

Click…click…click…

Darien screamed into the rag as both of his feet lifted completely off the floor. The hand was back, this time resting against the back of his head. It clenched the material of the sack in a fist, drawing the suffocating fabric tight against his face.

Instead of sucking in air, his nostrils sucked only dust-filled cloth. His lungs spasmed, burning.

Darien thrashed, making the pain even worse. His arms were going numb, but his shoulders seared with fire. Spent, his body went limp. He sagged in his chains as the world faded little by little. Nashir's voice murmured something in his ear. Darien didn't have enough presence of mind left to make out the words.

The hand released its tension on the fabric. He drew in a desperate gasp of air through his nostrils. Head throbbing, he labored for breath, sucking fabric against his face.

"Does that hurt?" Nashir's voice echoed through the darkness of his horror. "Trust me. This is nothing compared to what I'm about to do to your Meiran."

Darien growled. He groped for the Onslaught like a drowning man scrambling for a length of rope. But the Hellpower was like a sadistic taunt, dangling just within reach before jerking back away.

From across the room came a frantic, muffled sound.

Meiran.

She was in there with him. Somewhere in the chamber. Panic seized him. Reflexively, Darien fumbled again for the Onslaught. Of course, it wasn't there. His body spasmed, shaking all over, his muscles quivering in terror and agony.

"Quiet, now," Nashir's voice whispered. "Listen. Can you hear it? More softly. Yes. There it is."

Darien listened, even though he didn't want to. Inside, he was silently sobbing. He couldn't hear anything. The sack muffled most of the noise in the room. All he could hear was the shuddering sounds of his own ragged breath.

From across the chamber, there came the softest whimpering sound. Then a startled, muffled shriek.

They were torturing her.

Darien howled and twisted, writhing against the manacles that held him up. The pain was ghastly. His shoulders were coming apart, the iron shackles sawing at the flesh of his hands. He bucked, fighting against them.

Another gruesome shriek filled his ears.

Darien collapsed in his traces, feeling the warm wetness of blood running down his arms, dripping to the floor. His mind groped in vain for the Onslaught.

"Katarya is very skilled with a knife," observed Nashir's patient voice.

Meiran screamed again, the sound curdling Darien's nerves. The sack prevented him from seeing what they were doing to her. All he could do was listen and imagine.

His imagination was a powerful thing. A powerful, toxic, vindictive thing.

"You do have a choice, of course," Nashir whispered, his voice very low. "Deny our Master and cast your soul into Oblivion. If you do this, I promise you, she will feel no further pain."

The offer brought some small shred of hope. Darien's thoughts went sadly to Azár. He'd promised Azár he would help her people. He'd had every intention of following through with that promise. But not at this price. This price was far too high.

Meiran screamed again, a horrifying shriek that trailed off into wracking sobs. Darien couldn't stand it any longer. Beneath the sack, he could only envision what they were doing to her. In his mind, he saw the strips of flesh being peeled away from her body, curling like apple rind. The exposed, bloody tissues revealed beneath.

Nashir's voice uttered softly, "I wonder how many days it will take to break you? How many screams? You *will* break…the only question is how much you will let her suffer before you do."

Darien drew in a gasping breath, letting it out again in a long, shuddering sob. His entire body shook in violent spasms. Nashir was right. Better to let go now, before Meiran suffered any further. Much better than to wait.

Maybe, in Oblivion, his soul would finally know peace.

Isn't that what Meiran had promised?

Only in death are we truly free. That's what she'd told him.

Anger suffused him at the thought. Anger at Meiran. Meiran, who'd rejected him, despite all he'd suffered to get her back. His death alone hadn't been good enough for her. Now she wanted his very soul torn to ash.

He would give her what she wanted. It would be the last damned thing he ever gave her.

One last time, Darien groped for the Onslaught. This time, the Hellpower responded. It rushed into him, filling him. It gushed through him with the violence of a flood, the fury of a maelstrom. It was as terrible as it was beguiling. It entranced him, bewitched him. Bewildered and comforted him. Darien shivered, not in pain, but with the violent throes of brutal ecstasy.

He turned his wrath on the iron shackles that held him up. A strange sensation gripped his wrists, like focused rays of sunlight. He could feel a warm wetness slick his skin as the iron melted and ran like searing, molten wax down the length of his arms.

Darien dropped to the ground, falling forward on his face. He tried to push himself up, but his arms didn't work. He thrashed on the floor, somehow managing to squirm his head out of the sack. Vision assaulted him, confronting him with a macabre and gruesome scene.

Nashir's face, pale, gaped down at him full of horror. Stunned guards ringed the walls of the chamber, a room made all out of jagged rocks, twisted hooks and dangling, rusted chains. Across the room lay Meiran, sprawled, strapped down by thick ropes. Her left arm was stripped of its tissues, completely denuded. He couldn't see her face.

Beside her stood a woman wielding a long and gruesome knife. She stood frozen, gaping at Darien as if staring into the face of death, eyes full of revulsion and dismay.

The room was aglow with a terrible green light. Darien couldn't tell where the light was coming from. It seemed to be seeping from every crevice all at once, shining through the mortars of the bricks, leaking from the shadows.

He surged to his feet, glancing desperately to Meiran. Then he looked back to Nashir. Hatred filled his eyes to boiling. He lifted his hands up, forcing his unwilling arms to move just enough to embrace the darkmage like a brother.

"Impossib—"

Nashir drew in a sharp, pitiful gasp. Then he blinked. A single drop of blood leaked from the corner of his eye, ran dribbling down his cheek. Blood trickled from his nose, foamed at the corner of his mouth. He staggered backward as strangled, frothing noises rasped deep within his chest.

Darien stood still, locked in place, watching the grisly scene unfold with acute dispassion. Before him, Nashir lurched, moving awkwardly like a wooden puppet. He collapsed to his knees, bloody froth gurgling from his nostrils.

Darien knelt beside him, placing his hands on the dying man's face. There was an awful, crackling noise. Then a smell like grilling meat. Nashir Arman moaned hoarsely, inhumanly. The sound didn't come from his ruined lungs; it came from the depths of his blackened soul.

The sound faded out into an airy, whispering hiss that sizzled with misery.

Satisfied, Darien rose from the ground and turned away.

He glanced back. There was no corpse. Only a dark stain on the floor where Nashir had fallen, as if his flesh had been seared into the stone. But it was more than that. It wasn't a stain; it was a shadow. A living shadow that coalesced and rose, solidifying as it drew upward from the ground. A shadow that took on a distinctive man-like shape, one that Darien immediately recognized.

It was a necrator.

His very first.

The woman behind him issued a hysterical, horrified scream. She launched herself at Darien with the knife. He reacted without thinking, trying to bring his hands up to ward her off. But his arms didn't work fast enough. He dodged back, a second too late. The blade took him in the gut, sinking deep under his ribs all the way to the hilt.

The guards swept suddenly into motion. They descended from the walls, weapons drawn. One caught Darien, hauling him back away. Another confronted the girl, dispatching her with a sword thrust through the throat.

Darien gazed down at the woman's body in shocked dismay, clutching his middle as the guard lowered him to the floor. He dropped the knife and glanced down at his hand, seeing the dark stain that coated it.

He looked to the necrator that seemed to be floating in the exact center of the chamber, a sinister observer rooted in silence and shadow. Awaiting his command.

Darien was too shocked to command anything. He could only gaze down at his hand, at the amount of blood, and speculate. One of the soldiers knelt beside him and began tending to his injury, using his own garments to bind and bandage the wound.

Darien stared up into the man's face, addled with confusion.

He nodded at Meiran.

"Help her first," he whispered gruffly. He didn't know how the men would react, whether they would listen to him or not. To his gratitude, they did. Two rose immediately and strode around the periphery of the room toward Meiran, covering her with their own coats as they worked to undo the bonds that held her in place.

He turned to the guardsman who still lingered over him. "I have to get out of the vortex. Where's Sayeed?"

The man shook his head without reply, as if he didn't understand.

"Get him," Darien commanded.

The soldier nodded once and rose without a word.

Chapter Twenty-Six
Never to Harm

Tokashi Palace, The Black Lands

Meiran trembled as she struggled into a warm kaftan held out for her by one of the soldiers. The man stood with eyes lowered respectfully to the floor, waiting for her to robe. Her fingers shook so violently that she could hardly work the coat's fastenings. Her arm blazed with fire from where the flesh had been peeled away. The guard had bandaged up her wounds with his own sash, which helped ease the pain just a little. But the damage was severe; Katarya had managed to strip off every inch of flesh from the underside of Meiran's forearm, all the way up to the mark of the chain on her wrist.

She let her eyes roam across the floor, over to where a living shadow hovered in the exact center of the chamber. Just the presence of the necrator filled Meiran with a harrowing sense of dread. She had once been touched by one of hell's dark minions; she knew the horrors they could inflict. This one seemed even more sinister, somehow. This shade had not been raised from the flesh of innocents. If necrators had souls, this one's was hopelessly damned.

Meiran backed away from it as far as she could go, pressing her back up against the rough wall of the chamber. She edged around the periphery, never taking her eyes off the ghastly thing. To her horror, the necrator responded to her movement. It rotated slowly, tracking her motion. An appalling sense of dread chilled Meiran's blood.

She used her fingers to grope along the wall, at last dropping down to her hands and knees. Keeping her eyes on the necrator, she scooted the rest of the way across the floor, clutching her bandaged arm against her chest.

She knelt at Darien's side, shaking, trembling with revulsion and dread. The evil shade hovered above them just an arm's length away, blacker than the deepest abyss, smooth like glass and utterly featureless. It had no eyes, but she didn't doubt it could sense. She could feel its hunger, its lust for life. Its soulless, yearning desire for her death.

She gazed down at Darien helplessly. He lay on the floor, a strip of cloth binding his middle. Blood had already begun seeping through the bandages. The wound's drainage was dark, almost black. Seeing that, Meiran felt numb.

She could do nothing for him in the vortex.

She bowed her head, trying hard not to grieve, even though she knew it was better this way. One glance back at the necrator confirmed what she already knew: Darien was far too dangerous to live.

Sounds in the corridor made her turn. Two Enemy officers staggered forward into the room. They stopped in the doorway, gazing around the chamber with wide and startled eyes, taking in the sight of the necrator and the scene of carnage that confronted them. To their credit, it took the men only seconds to recover.

One soldier dropped to Meiran's side, while the other moved off to check on the dead woman. She recognized the man beside her: it was the officer who'd been ordered to the headsman. She didn't know his name, but he seemed like someone in a position of authority. The man knelt over Darien, shaking him gently.

"Can you walk?"

To Meiran's astonishment, Darien nodded. "I think so."

With the man's aid, Darien rose unstably to his feet. The soldiers moved forward and helped support his weight. Darien clutched his middle with one hand, taking a step forward. He winced in pain.

"What's the quickest way out of here?"

The bearded officer frowned, considering. "We should make use of the boats."

"The boats?" Meiran echoed, surprised. She hadn't seen any boats, not since arriving in the Black Lands.

The Zakai officer nodded. "Yes. The river is the fastest way."

"What's your name?" Meiran demanded.

The officer glanced back her way. "I am Sayeed."

"Thank you, Sayeed."

They left the chamber, the two soldiers supporting Darien between them. Meiran followed after them, glancing back one last time down the passage. The necrator was not following, she realized with a profound sense of relief. She walked behind, watching with a grim sense of inevitability as Darien limped ahead of her. She took note of the dark trail of blood that marked his passage.

The soldiers might get Darien to the boats, Meiran decided, but they weren't doing him any kindness. Not with that injury. The best thing they could do would be to find a quiet place where he could rest.

"Don't press so hard," Sayeed admonished. "You'll just bleed more."

Darien nodded, grimacing. The pain was getting worse. Meiran could feel it through the link. Darien limped forward, sweat dribbling down his brow, wetting his hair despite the cold. Only force of will and the strength of the officers kept him on his feet.

Meiran walked with her eyes lowered, focused on the pitter-patter trail of blood she followed along the ground. She was beginning to grow more and more uncomfortable with what they were doing. It was just as futile as it was cruel.

As they turned a corner, the bearded officer announced, "We're almost there."

Meiran sighed regretfully. She didn't want Darien on a boat. She wanted him here, where she had some control.

The corridor opened up into a natural cavern formed by the passage of water. Meiran breathed in the humidity of the air, staring in wonder at the dark waters that stretched out before them. Lashed to their moors, small wooden boats bobbed up and down on the current.

The two soldiers helped Darien toward the nearest vessel.

Sayeed jumped onto the boat first, steadying it as they helped Darien climb in. They laid him out on the bottom of the boat then turned and beckoned for Meiran.

Hesitant, she accepted Sayeed's offered hand, the other man steadying her as her legs spanned the gap between the dock and the bobbing vessel. She dropped immediately down to the boards, trying to position herself as close as she could to the craft's center of gravity. The small boat rocked treacherously, threatening to spill them over.

Sayeed seated himself on a cross plank and took up the oars, signaling the other man to cast them off.

His companion stooped over, unwound the coils, then threw the rope back into the boat. As they drifted out into the river, Sayeed slid the oars into the rowlocks and dipped the blades into the water. He leaned back and, with deep and graceful strokes, began rowing.

Meiran shivered in the chill breeze that gusted out of the depths of the ice caverns. She scooted herself around, repositioning her body against the gunwale. Darien lay curled on his side on the floor of the boat, arms hugging his middle. He was shivering. Looking down at him, Meiran felt a knot of sadness in her throat. She reached down and felt his skin with her fingers. It was cold and damp, like the flesh of a cadaver.

"Give me your jacket," she said. The officer obeyed immediately, releasing the oars and struggling out of his coat. Meiran used it like a blanket to cover Darien, tucking it in around him as much as she could.

She glanced upward as they emerged from the cavern, noticing great stalactites that spiked down from the ceiling. They gave the cave's mouth the appearance of a monster grimacing with sharpened teeth. Sayeed put his back into the oars, propelling their little craft across the glass surface of the lake. The waters parted before them easily, their vessel making good headway.

Meiran's hand moved to Darien's head, stroking his hair. She took his hand in hers.

"How long until we're out of the vortex?" she asked.

Sayeed answered without faltering at the oars. "Difficult to say.

An hour, maybe two."

Meiran didn't think Darien had an hour left in him. She smoothed back a lock of hair from his face. He was resting comfortably, at least. Not as cold anymore. The wound didn't throb so very badly.

He mumbled something she couldn't make out.

She bent down to hear him better.

"Water."

Through the link, she could feel his terrible thirst. Even if she had water, Meiran knew better than to give him any. She felt saddened by her decision to withhold such a simple comfort. Saddened, but resolute.

"I can't, Darien. I'm sorry."

He didn't ask again. He closed his eyes and faded into restless sleep.

She held his hand as the lake narrowed into a river around them. Here, the waters didn't seem quite as black. The wind wasn't as chill. Overhead, churning clouds clogged the vast expanse of sky.

They rowed with a strong current that swept them speedily along, racing the angry clouds above. Sayeed's face was streaked with sweat, his body glistening with perspiration. In the muted light of the clouds, his features seemed jagged, almost surreal.

They followed the river for minutes, perhaps an hour. Black cliffs rose around them, forming a steep gorge. The night was silent, save for the constant drone of the river.

"Are we out yet?"

It took Meiran a moment to comprehend Darien's words; they were mumbled under his breath. And his breath was very weak. It took another moment to realize what he was trying to ask.

"No, Darien. Not yet." She caressed his hand tenderly.

With her mind walled away, she had no way of actually sensing the presence of the vortex. But she knew it was still there, still mercilessly compressing the currents of the magic field around them. She didn't dare open her mind to it; the backlash would kill her in a heartbeat.

And it really didn't matter. She had no intention of healing him, anyway.

Meiran stared down at her wrist, at the emblem of the chain that shimmered coldly in the cloud light. *Never to harm.*

She couldn't end Darien's life. But there was nothing in the Oath of Harmony that obligated her to preserve it. Meiran searched deeply within herself, realizing she had the strength to let him go.

She caressed his hand, running her fingers over his skin. He responded to her touch, his fingers trailing once over hers.

He was quiet after that. So was the river. It wound like a graceful ribbon down through the center of the gorge. The only sound in the darkness was the constant creak of the oars, the gentle lapping of water against the hull of the boat. Sayeed had fallen into a steady pattern with his rowing. The boat rocked them gently.

Minutes passed. Another hour, perhaps. The whole while, Darien was very still. Meiran was starting to wonder if he hadn't already slipped away, left her behind without her knowing.

With cold apprehension, she lifted the coat.

His bandages were soaked in blood. There was so much of it. The blood dripped thickly, pooling on the boards on the bottom of the boat. Meiran lowered the coat, tucking it back into place. She gazed up at the sky, studying the clouds.

More minutes passed. The oars creaked. The river rocked them in its arms.

Meiran frowned, recognizing one of the hills across the river. They must not be too far away from Qul. She hadn't realized they'd come so far so quickly.

"Are we out yet?"

The sound of Darien's voice unsettled her. Meiran flinched. She didn't want to answer. Yet, she couldn't bring herself to lie to him.

"Yes," she whispered. "We're out."

His eyelids fluttered open. He gazed up at her with the same gold-green eyes she'd fallen in love with. His face was haggard, pale. Exhausted.

"Will you...release the damper on me?"

His lips barely moved. He was gazing up into her face.

Meiran ran her fingers through his hair. "No, Darien. I'm not going to do that." Her voice broke. She hadn't wanted it to come to this. She'd prayed he'd be gone by now.

Darien frowned. A look of vague confusion clouded his face. "Heal me…please?"

Meiran shook her head. She clenched her jaw against the sorrow that wrenched her heart. "No."

His eyes widened with understanding. Then they darkened with hurt. He turned his face away, closing his eyes. For just a moment she could feel the depths of his pain, so intense that it almost made her retch. Right before he walled her out completely.

Meiran looked up and found herself staring into Sayeed's outraged glare. His expression was treacherous.

"If he dies, I'll kill you."

It was plain, simple fact. Not even a threat.

Meiran nodded. She could accept that; it was a price she was willing to pay. She looked back down at Darien. With her hand, she caressed the side of his face.

He didn't respond. He was unconscious again.

Meiran lowered herself down and curled up on the boards at his side. She pulled him close, weeping quietly into his hair. His flesh was pale. Moist. Already cold.

Qul, The Black Lands

"Madam, I cannot!" Quin insisted, waving his hands feverishly in the air. "I couldn't possibly take another bite of food from your family's plate!"

Across the low table from him, his hostess smiled graciously and gestured again at the platter she'd set down in front of him.

"You must eat! I insist!"

Quin chuckled, smiling around at the group of young women seated around him on pillows, all gathered around Uma Abada's table. They'd come under the pretenses of helping Uma prepare dinner for a special guest. But, curiously enough, not a single one of Uma's young visitors had lifted a finger or lent a hand to assist the hostess. They had piled into Uma's house, showering Quin with questions and responding to his answers with choruses of giggles.

Quin spread his hands helplessly. "I really can't eat another morsel. See? I'm stuffed!" He pointed at his stomach which, of course, didn't help prove his point at all. His frame was just as thin now as before he'd started the meal.

A fresh eruption of laughter chorused all around the room, followed by a sibilant flurry of whispers.

This was too much for Uma Abada. She threw her hands up in the air, exclaiming, "You must not like the food!" She began reaching for the platter to take it away.

"No!" Quin gasped, catching her arm. "The food is delicious! Truly! I've never tasted anything so exquisite! Please, I'd be grateful to have another plate?"

To Uma's never-ending gratitude, Quin scooped himself another serving, quickly shoving a large bite into his mouth.

"Scrumptious!" he announced around the mouthful.

The women that surrounded him burst into rippling laughter. Quin grinned despite himself. It had been a very long time since he'd been the center of anyone's attention.

A tinkling clatter of beads signaled someone's entry into the dwelling. Quin glanced up just as the girls' laughter extinguished like a doused candle flame. He took one look at Azár's face and swallowed his food whole. It went down hard.

"Quinlan Nach'tier!" Azár cried, her voice fraught with panic. "Please, come quickly!"

"Sorry!" Quin gulped at Uma and the girls as he sprang to his feet, in his rush knocking over the wash water that was offered. He dashed after Azár, but the woman was already gone, disappearing through the doorway. He paused only long enough to retrieve his shoes.

Quin ran after her into the darkness, onto the narrow streets of Qul. He staggered forward five or six steps and then pulled up short, realizing he had no idea which direction the girl had even gone.

"Quinlan!"

She was standing a block away, beckoning him furiously. Holding his hat, Quin sprinted after her. He followed her out of town and out into the open night, down the path that led away from the village. She didn't pause to let him catch up. Azár ran ahead at full speed, gradually outdistancing him.

Down by the bank of the river, she finally turned back, gesturing for him to hurry. Quin sprinted forward, at last seeing the cause for her concern.

A man lay on the beach by the river, another man stooped over him. Azár threw herself down beside them both, motioning frantically for Quin.

"He's near death!" she cried. "Can you heal? For I cannot!"

Quin gasped when he realized who it was that Azár wanted him to heal. He knelt down on his knees beside Darien, fear taking him in the chest like a sword thrust.

"Damn."

Closing his eyes, he placed a hand on Darien to gain a better sense of the extent of his injuries. His fear immediately collapsed into panic. He didn't dare wait another second.

Bracing himself, Quin reached within and pulled at the magic field as if grasping for life, drawing it in with all the force of his mind, focusing with every fiber of his concentration. He threw everything he had into Darien, all of his training, all of his skill, all of his effort and experience, uncertain if all he had would even be enough.

With a gasp, Quin shrank back, blood draining from his face. He reeled, almost passing out. He steadied himself with a hand thrust in the dirt, his other hand clasped against his forehead. He sat there, rocking himself, slowly shaking his head. It took him a long time to finally pull himself back together.

Leaning forward, he probed Darien one more time. He was sleeping deeply, mercifully still alive.

Quin closed his eyes, sighing in relief. He opened them just in time to see the other man fall to his knees, prostrating himself fully prone in the dirt.

Still a little dizzy, Quin had to use both arms to wrench his body up off the ground. He gazed down at the prostrated figure, absently chewing his lip.

"Get up," he chided the man. "Who are you? Can you tell me what happened?"

The bearded man regained his feet in one elegant, fluid motion. He effected a perfect bow, one hand pressed against his heart. "I am Sayeed son of Alborz, Chamberlain of Armorers," he stated proudly. Indicating Darien, he said, "This man was gravely injured. I brought him out of the vortex to you."

Quin chewed on that information, wishing the soldier would elaborate just a tad. It was only then that he recognized him: the officer from Tokashi who'd delivered Meiran's necklace. The man was Zakai to the core: direct, succinct, and thoroughly uninformative. "Where's Meiran?" he demanded. "Is she with you?"

"The woman is still in the boat," Sayeed gestured toward the craft. "She would not help. He asked, but she refused."

Quin's eyebrows shot up. "Refused?" he echoed, exchanging a wide-eyed look with Azár.

The soldier nodded. "Yes. She refused to help him even though he begged."

At that news, Quin hung his head, heaving out a long, exasperated sigh. If Meiran had refused to help Darien despite the ghastly nature of his injuries, it spoke volumes of her character. She had committed herself to his death, despite the depth of her feelings for him. It was a deplorable act, both selfish and selfless at the same time. In all his life, Quin had only known one other person capable of making such a decision.

Sagging, he removed his hat from his head and turned to Sayeed with a weary expression on his face. "Can the two of you get him back to the village?"

"Will he live?" the officer seemed surprised.

"Yes, but...he'll be sleeping for a couple of days." Quin bounced his hat against his thigh a few times, absently collecting his thoughts. Meiran was his responsibility, even more than Darien. He needed to make sure she would be all right.

The officer appeared to be considering. "I will take him back to Tokashi," Sayeed decided finally. "He will be protected there. It is where he belongs."

Quin frowned. "He has the support of the Tanisars, then?"

Sayeed solemnly spread his hands. "Darien Lauchlin is the overlord that was promised. He has the full support of the Tanisar corps."

Quin nodded, reserving judgement. He glanced to Azár, who was likewise staring at Sayeed with a shocked expression on her face.

"And do you have the authority to speak for all the Zakai?" Quin pressed. He needed to know Sayeed's claim was legitimate, and not some rogue faction of the Tanisars throwing their support behind Darien in an attempt at a coup.

The soldier bowed low. "I, Sayeed son of Alborz, have the authority to speak for all the Zakai and the whole of the Tanisar corps."

That was good enough for Quin. He turned immediately to Azár. The look of shock on her face only supported his decision. "Go with them," he directed her. "I'll take Meiran back to Qul."

Azár stared up at him with a mixture of disbelief and outright fear. "I'm a Lightweaver!" she gasped. "I can't just abandon my lightfields!"

Quin waved his hand in a dismissive gesture. Replacing the hat on his head, he reminded her, "Tokashi Palace must have Lightweavers aplenty. Send one of them back here to replace you."

Azár licked her lips, indecision knitting her brow. She glanced back up at Quin. "I do not have that kind of authority."

Quin shrugged, casually pointing a finger down at Darien. "He does."

Azár looked lost. Her brow furrowed even more. She seemed to be grappling with some enormous internal struggle. At last, something seemed to yield inside her. Nodding, she clenched her hands into balls at her sides. "I will go to Tokashi Palace," she said at last.

Sayeed nodded with a look somewhere split between gratitude, respect, and downright doubt. Quin wasn't quite sure how it was possible for one human face to manage so many emotions all at once. The soldier could convey in one look what it would take a scribe a page or more to fill.

"Let's get Meiran," Quin grumbled.

He left Darien lying on the shoreline and walked to the boat to check on the Prime Warden. He found her fast asleep, curled up in the bowels of the vessel, cuddled up in a kaftan stained dark with blood. Gore streaked her face, her hands, her skin. The bottom of the boat was coated with sticky filth. Quin felt an instant pang of fear. All that blood couldn't be Darien's.

Then he saw the bandage on Meiran's arm.

He reached out and probed her with his mind, getting a sense of her condition. She wasn't good. She had been starved for days on top of the torture she'd obviously been subjected to. Her skin was hot to the touch; the wound on her arm had already started to fester.

Quin mended her just as he'd mended Darien, then gathered her sleeping body up into his arms. He rested her head against his shoulder, staring down at Meiran's peaceful face. He tried to feel angry with her, but realized that he couldn't do it. He didn't agree with Meiran's actions. But he understood her, all the same. He understood her all too well.

"What are you going to do with her?" Azár asked, wandering over to gaze at Meiran as if she were something of a curiosity.

"I'll take her back to Qul. She's my responsibility. From there..." he shrugged. "Who knows?"

"I could run my sword through her," suggested Sayeed.

Quin barked a laugh, casting the man a sideways smirk. "Trust me, I've been tempted. Unfortunately, that wouldn't go over very well with your new overlord."

He knelt down, laying Meiran out on the black sand of the riverbank. Then he went to help Sayeed and Azár load Darien into the boat. When they had him in, Sayeed immediately sat down and took up the oars as Quin waded out into the water, pushing the boat and casting them off. He gave a good, hard shove that sent the little craft floating quickly away. Quin gazed at Azár, watching the distance between them slowly widen, standing in water up to his hips. He remained there as Sayeed dipped the oars into the river, pushing back, turning the boat into the current.

"Keep him safe," Quin called after them.

The little craft pulled slowly away even as a cloud of fog rolled in around them, cloaking them in mist. Quin turned and waded back toward the shoreline. But before he could gain the bank, a sudden splash made him turn.

His mouth dropped open. Darien's hound had thrown itself into the river and was paddling dutifully after its master. He watched the beast overtake the boat, bobbing furiously and pawing at the side of the craft. Sayeed stopped rowing, clearly perplexed.

Between the soldier and Azár, they somehow managed to get the demon-dog over the side and into the boat. The beast shook the water from its fur and, circling several times, finally positioned itself at the bow of the craft as if determined to keep watch. It's hellish-green eyes gleamed from out of the darkness.

"Now, that's quite a sight," Quin muttered, shaking his head.

Chapter Twenty-Seven
Hard Choices

Qul, The Black Lands

Meiran awakened to a pale amber glow. The flickering light of a lantern cast murky shadows on the walls, bizarre patterns of dappled light mixed with shadow. She was warm and comfortable. She stretched languidly, feeling the stiffness leech slowly from her bones. She felt content.

A sudden pang of emptiness jarred her fully awake. Meiran sat up, blinking as she gazed in surprise around a room that was altogether unfamiliar.

Quin's skeletal face was the first thing she saw. He was sitting, leaning against the far wall of the room with one leg drawn up against his chest, the other stretched out in front of him. He regarded her with a hard, callous stare. He was chewing on something that hung dangling from his mouth. Some type of root, it looked like.

"Where's Darien?" Meiran asked, her stomach in knots.

Quin's stare was like cold, unfeeling lead. "Alive. No thanks to you."

Meiran swallowed, feeling the grief inside tighten into a ball at the base of her throat. That was not the news she'd been expecting to hear. Not good news at all. She lifted her eyes reluctantly back to Quin. Yet another darkmage who was too dangerous to live.

"You healed him."

Quin plucked the root he was gnawing out of his mouth, gesturing with it in the air. "Well, I wasn't going to just sit back and watch him die. Like you were planning to do."

"I did everything I could to save him," Meiran said defensively. She *had* been trying to save Darien. In her own way. The only way she could.

Quinlan Reis sneered at her in mocking contempt. "What exactly were you trying to save him from? *Life?*"

Meiran grimaced, utterly resenting his cruel sarcasm. "I was trying to save Darien from hell," she informed him, not expecting him to understand.

"Darling, you bring new meaning to the phrase 'damned if you do, damned if you don't.'"

Meiran glared at him. "It's nothing to joke about, Quin. The man I loved has become a demon. A *true* demon. One who channels the powers of hell, raises necrators from the dead, and wants to rally the legions of Chaos against his own homeland. *My* homeland."

Quin sneered, gesturing in the air with the half-chewed root. "That's because the 'legions of Chaos' are going to starve to death if they stay here too much longer. Are you really so coldblooded that you'd condemn an entire nation to death? Honestly, Meiran, you're the one who's starting to sound more demonic."

The look on his face was haughty and insolent. He was a contemptible creature, just as wretched as Darien. Perhaps more so.

"There's hard choices to be made," Meiran said. "On *both* sides. I'm not denying it. Compromises will have to be made. But Darien's way—your way—it's not the answer. The Rhen will never submit to the rule of Xerys."

Quin popped the root back into his mouth and sprang instantly to his feet. Dusting off his long, black coat with the palms of his hands, he strode toward the door, making a sweeping gesture toward it.

"Well, then," he announced. "We'd better get started. Shall we?"

Meiran gawked up at him. "Started?"

Quin cracked a broad grin. "Titherry, remember? To find Athera's Crescent? Ending the curse over the Black Lands sounds like it just might be the only recourse we have left. If you're still willing to make the journey with me, that is."

Meiran glared at him suspiciously. So, the darkmage still wanted to go through with it. She'd thought he'd forgotten all about the bargain they'd struck with Darien. Well, she'd since had a change of heart. She'd had enough.

"I'm not going anywhere with you," Meiran told him coldly. "In fact, I'm going home."

Quin gazed at her levelly. Reaching up, he plucked the root out from between his teeth and flicked it away. She couldn't see his eyes under the shadow of his hat. But she could see the set of his jawline. He stuffed his hands into the pockets of his coat, facing her with feet spread apart.

"I wouldn't advise that, Prime Warden. If we don't find an end to the curse, you'll leave Renquist no choice but to invade."

Meiran glared up at him, her face set in anger. "I don't care. I've seen enough. You're just like Darien. They've manipulated you, Quin. They've manipulated your mind. I didn't know you in life, so I can't look at you the way I can look at Darien. I can't tell you exactly how much you've changed and how corrupt you've become. But I do know this: at one time, you were the brother of Braden Reis. You must have had some sense of honor. Just look at how far you've fallen. I'm sorry, Quin. I can't trust you."

With that, she stood up. Looking down at her arm, she rotated it to confirm it was indeed very well mended. Not even a scar remained. She was grateful for that. But not grateful enough to stay.

"I'm going home," she said. "I'll find my own way from here. Please don't follow me."

She started to turn away, but Quin's voice stopped her.

"Wait."

Meiran turned back around. She looked at him sadly. Somewhere deep inside that emaciated husk of a body there was a soul, a soul that once might have been worthwhile. Perhaps Quin was irredeemable. Perhaps not. It didn't matter; he wasn't her problem any longer.

Quinlan Reis moved toward her, pausing right in front of her. He gazed down plaintively into her face. The silence between them was long, echoing. The lantern on the floor revealed his eyes, no longer hidden beneath the shadow of his hat. His expression was full of regret.

Meiran tilted her head back, peering up silently into his face, exploring every coarse feature. With effort, she could almost visualize the man he used to be. The man he was no longer.

Quin brought his hand up from out of his pocket and pressed something against her palm, closing her fingers around it. His dark eyes never left her own. He didn't say a word. He squeezed her hand once, almost tenderly, then let go. With a sigh, he stepped back away.

Meiran looked down, opening her fist. Her throat constricted when she saw what it was that Quin had placed in her hand: the necklace given to her by Darien. The sight of it dredged up far more emotions than Meiran felt capable of dealing with at the moment. She swallowed most of them, deciding to nurse the anger for just a bit longer.

Glancing back at Quin, she held his gaze as she turned her open palm upside down, letting the silver necklace spill from her hand, falling to the floor at her feet. She didn't look down. She stood holding Quin's gaze with a steadfast glare of defiant resolve.

She turned and left.

With a tinkling clatter of beads, Meiran walked out into the crisp, cold darkness of night. She closed her eyes, breathing in the foul stench of coal smoke and ash. Overhead, turbulent clouds raced across the vast expanse of sky, lights flickering deep within their depths.

This was the Black Lands.

Not her lands.

She owed these people nothing.

To Be Continued....

Preview of

Darkrise

The
Rhenwars Saga

Chapter One
Darkening Dawn

Aerysius, The Rhen

There's a kind of promise the dark makes. Kyel Archer thought he remembered it well enough.

He stared up at the ink-black slopes of the Shadowspears, at the ghostly lights that flickered in the rushing clouds. Kyel's memories of this place were vivid with shadow. The darkness whispered at him from the gullies and ridges, echoed off the high mountain passes. Unfurled before him in the storm-tossed sky. Its vast emptiness raked dread into his heart, feeding his soul with trepidation.

The dark that encased the Shadowspears promised only a legacy of sorrow. After a thousand years of conflict, that's all it had to give.

Kyel glanced at the gray-cloaked sentries warding the long stair ahead. It was not the same stair he remembered, just as Greystone Keep wasn't the same fortress. It had evolved. The Pass of Lor-Gamorth had changed a great deal in the past two years.

Below, he could make out the ruins of the old keep, now just a shattered and scorched foundation. The new stronghold lay farther up the ridge, perched high on the cliff. The new keep made better use of the natural defenses of the slopes, half-built and half-carved out of the mountainside itself.

The stairs to the keep were narrow, zig-zagging up the ridge. Kyel felt short of breath before their party was even halfway up; he wasn't used to the elevation. Or the exercise. At his side, a weary Cadmus panted and gasped, grappling his considerable weight up the treacherous stair. Kyel felt sorry for the layman. Cadmus hadn't journeyed a step outside the Valley of the Gods in decades.

It took their party long minutes and hundreds of steps to gain the entrance of the fortress: a narrow arch formed from hewn granite that opened up into darkness. A tunnel leading straight back into the heart of the mountain itself.

Kyel stopped to catch his breath, craning his neck back to glance up. Far overhead, a high curtain wall skirted the summit of the ridge. There were no stairs that could be seen; the keep's entrance must be buried somewhere deep within the rock. Kyel was impressed. Whoever had designed this new stronghold had intended it to be impregnable.

He moved forward with Cadmus at his side, a small group of uniformed soldiers treading silently behind them. The Conclave had seen fit to provide him with five Guild blademasters to form his personal retinue. As deadly an honor guard as a man could wish. Unfortunately, the swordsmen were a necessity.

Kyel was, after all, the last surviving mage left in all the Rhen.

He'd sworn a vow to serve his land and his people. He'd sworn another vow never to inflict harm upon a living thing. Those two Oaths, each contradictory, nagged at Kyel every moment of every day. He could feel the oppression of their conflicting doctrine dragging him down, like iron counterweights dangling from his wrists.

Within the tunnel, the dark descended with its promise of sorrow.

The roof was vaulted, the walls curving to meet the floor. Vibrant torchlight labored in vain to constrain the shadows, forming orange pools of flickering light. Kyel moved forward in the space between pools. The flames did little more than light the path beneath his feet. He walked with his head bowed, hands clasped in front of him.

The tunnel ended at a portcullis. Kyel and the others waited as soldiers labored to raise the iron grate, heaving on long chains suspended from a mechanism overhead. On the other side, a stairway veered upward, angling steeply.

"Avoid the wood. Walk only on stone," cautioned a Greystone sentry.

Kyel nodded his understanding. Behind them, the portcullis lowered with the clattering whirl of chains racing through systems of pulleys. The stairs were made of steps arranged in alternating patterns of wood and stone. Kyel obeyed the sentry's instructions, moving carefully to avoid stepping on the boards. He didn't know for certain what would happen if he missed a step, but it wasn't difficult to imagine. Kyel had no wish to plummet to his death.

The stairs ended at a wide courtyard surrounded by crenelated towers and soaring palisades. The keep itself loomed before them, its dark, imposing stone ending abruptly in a jagged array of blocks. The main fortress was left unfinished, Kyel realized with dismay.

"Bloody hell," he muttered under his breath, his gaze scanning the structure. It reminded him too much of the old Greystone Keep, with its crumbling rear wall and caved-in roof. The sight of the incomplete stronghold made his stomach clench in apprehension.

"Great Master."

He turned to face the soldier who was acting as his guide. The young man carried a hornbow slung across his back, a quiver strapped against his leg. Probably a conscript, Kyel presumed.

"This way."

He motioned the young soldier forward, falling in behind. His gray-cloaked escort led them across the bailey to the castle's upper ward. From there, they proceeded through a series of hallways to a rather unremarkable door on the second floor of the tower. The young soldier he followed knocked twice.

The door opened immediately.

"Your men will need to wait outside."

Kyel nodded, signaling his guards. Then, gathering his courage, he stepped forward into the room.

The first thing he saw was Traver's narrow face, now covered by a wiry growth of whiskers. No longer lanky, Traver had the hardened body of an infantryman. Kyel's mouth dropped open;

he almost didn't recognize his old friend. Before he knew what was happening, Traver crossed the room in two large strides and scooped Kyel up in his arms, hefting him off his feet.

"You damnable fool!" Traver exclaimed, giving Kyel one last squeeze before finally setting him down again. "You've no idea how worried I've been!" He grinned wryly, a shaggy lock of auburn hair falling forward into his face. He flipped it back with a toss of his head.

"I'm fine, Traver. Really." Kyel made a half-hearted attempt at a smile. It was difficult. He was dearly glad to see his old friend. But the sight of Traver was accompanied by a pang of sadness. He felt suddenly homesick. "How've you been?"

"Well enough." Traver grinned and raised his left hand, wiggling the three fingers he had left. "Except for this. But I rather think I'm better with half a hand than most men are with a whole one. Forces me to use my head."

The other man in the room shifted his weight conspicuously over his feet. Kyel turned toward the imposing form of Devlin Craig. Craig's straw-gold hair was pulled back from his face, which was covered in what looked like a week's growth of stubble. He wore a quilted gambeson that hung to his knees, an enormous sword strapped across his back. Kyel extended his hand, smiling at his former commanding officer.

"Force Commander Craig."

"Archer." Craig nodded curtly. His gaze travelled quickly over Kyel, lingering for a moment on the black cloak that fell from his shoulders. His face conveyed a look of profound skepticism. He took a step forward and accepted Kyel's handshake with a firm, double-fisted clasp.

"Thanks for coming. We've got a problem." His voice was low and gruff. Kyel could see the tension in his eyes.

"I know."

Craig shook his head. "No. I don't think you do."

Kyel frowned, uncertain what the soldier was alluding to.

"Come with me." Craig tossed his head, already moving past him.

Kyel fell in behind, following Craig's burly form as the man strode out through the doorway, moving directly toward a flight of stairs. Kyel mounted the steps after him, having to jog to keep up. He followed the commander up a long, spiraling staircase that ascended into the reaches of the unfinished tower.

He trailed his hand along the wall as he climbed, at once taken back in time to the old Greystone Keep of his memory. The old fortress had a very similar stair that had led to Garret Proctor's quarters at the top. This new tower preserved much of the same character, down to the arrow slits that followed the rising curve of the stair. Only, this tower ended halfway up. Kyel gasped as he realized that he was standing on the last stair with one leg already lifted off. One more step would send him over.

Kyel flailed his arms, groping to catch himself on the unfinished wall at his side. Craig's hand shot out and caught him by the scruff of his cloak, clenching a fistful of fabric. He jerked him roughly backward. Kyel dropped to his knees as the world surged beneath him.

"Watch your step."

He nodded, trembling in panic. He rose, trying to catch his balance and his breath. He gazed up at Craig with startled eyes. Then, leaning over, he looked down over the unfinished portion of the wall.

The view below was harrowing.

Kyel's vision swam as his stomach dropped right out of him. His palms broke immediately into a sweat, toes curling in his boots. His eyes traced down the length of the tower, past the curtain wall and parapets, all the way down the side of the mountain. Before him rolled the sprawling black peaks of the Shadowspears stabbing out of a murky bank of fog. If it wasn't for the fog, he might have been able to see all the way down to the bottom of the pass. Perhaps all the way out into the Black Lands themselves.

"Look."

Craig raised his arm, pointing out across the foggy sea below. Kyel tried to make out what the commander was trying to indicate, but there was nothing to see. Just thick, blanketing mist that extended like an ocean to the distant horizon.

But then the mist parted.

Kyel's mouth fell open as he saw what the fog had been obscuring. Black sinister forms arranged in geometric patterns extended across the dark plain ahead, no natural design. Fires glowed in the distance: thousands, perhaps tens of thousands. So many. Strangest of all, a set of dark, parallel lines, curving away toward the north.

"Mother of the Gods," Kyel whispered, feeling his heart seize in his chest. "What is all that?"

"That," Craig responded, lowering his hand, "is the Sixth Invasion."

To Be Continued...

Glossary

acolyte: apprentice mage who has passed the Trial of Consideration and sworn the Acolyte's Oath.

Acolyte's Oath: first vow taken by every acolyte of Aerysius to serve the land and its people, symbolized by a chain-like marking on the left wrist.

Aerysius: ancient city where the Masters of Aerysius once dwelt. Destroyed when Aiden Lauchlin unsealed the Well of Tears.

Alt: God of the Wilds.

Amani: daughter of Zavier Renquist and wife of Braden Reis who was executed for treason against the Assembly of the Lyceum. *(deceased)*

Amberlie: town in the Vale below Aerysius.

Anassis, Myria: ancient Querer of the Lyceum, now a Servant of Xerys.

Archer, Gilroy: son of Kyel and Amelia Archer.

Archer, Kyel: sixth tier grand master of the Order of Sentinels.

Arman, Nashir: ancient Battlemage and Servant of Xerys.

Arms Guild: institution for the study of blademastery. Also called the School of Arms.

artifact: heirloom of power that has been imbued with magical characters or properties.

Asyaadi Clan: group of kinsfolk who live in the village of Qul in the Black Lands.

Athera: Goddess of Magic.

Athera's Crescent: Mysterious and ancient artifact on the Isle of Titherry.

Atrament: the realm of Death, ruled by the goddess Isap.

Auberdale: capital city of Chamsbrey.

Azár ni Suam: Lightweaver of the Asyaadi Clan.

Battle of Meridan: infamous battle in which the Enemy was turned back in large part due to the efforts of the Sentinels.

Battlemage: ancient order of mages who accompanied armies into battle before the Oath of Harmony.

Black Lands: what was once Caladorn, now the desecrated home of the Enemy.

blademaster: title awarded to graduates of the School of Arms, or Arms Guild.

Black Solstice: The battle that ended the Fifth Invasion, when Darien Lauchlin destroyed the legions of the Enemy.

Bloodquest: ancient rite of vengeance condoned by the goddess Isap for righteous causes.

Bluecloaks: slang for the Rothscard City Guard.

Book of the Dead: ancient text wherein the Strictures of Death are inscribed.

Bound: describes a mage who has sworn the Oath of Harmony.

Bryn Calazar: ancient capital of Caladorn.

Cadmus: Voice of the High Priest of Wisdom.

Caladorn: fallen nation to the north, now known as the Black Lands.

caravansary: in the Black Lands, a large courtyard with attached rooms built for the purposes of accommodating caravans resting overnight.

Catacombs: place of burial that exists partly in the Atrament.

Cerulian Plains: large grassland region in the North of the Rhen.

Chamsbrey: Northern kingdom ruled by Godfrey Faukravar.

Chapel of Nimrue: A temple in Glen Farquist where the Conclave of Temples meets.

Circles of Convergence: ancient foci of magic designed to draw on the vast power of a vortex.

clan: in the Black Lands, a kin-based group of close, interrelated families.

Clemley, Sephana: ancient Prime Warden of Aerysius and lover of Braden Reis. *(deceased)*

Conclave: Council formed by the vicars of the Holy Temples that decides religious policy.

Connel, Byron: ancient Battlemage of the Lyceum, now a

Servant of Xerys.

Craghorns: mountains that border the Vale of Amberlie.

Craig, Devlin: Force Commander of Greystone Keep.

Curse, the: term used to describe the darkening of the skies and earth of the Black Lands, as well as for the unusual weather patterns and electrical storms experienced in the region.

dampen: to shield a mage from sensing the magic field.

damper: an object that has the ability to dampen a mage from sensing the magic field.

darkmage: a mage who has abandoned moral principles.

Death's Passage: *see* **Catacombs**.

Desecration, the: the apocalyptic event that destroyed Caladorn by blackening the skies and the earth.

Deshari: Goddess of Grief.

Desmond, Carol: priest of Death.

Dreia: Goddess of the Vine.

Eight, the: the Eight Servants of Xerys.

Emmery: Northern kingdom of the Rhen.

Emmery Palace: the Queen's palace in Rothscard.

Enana: Goddess of the Hearth.

Enemy, the: collective name for the inhabitants of the Black Lands.

Esvir: wife of Haleem.

eye: area at the heart of a vortex where the lines of the magic field run almost parallel.

Fareen son of Mohsen: man of the village of Qul, cousin of Azár.

Faukravar, Godfrey: King of Chamsbrey.

field lines: currents of the magic field.

First Sentinel, the: *see* **Braden Reis**.

Front, the: area bordering the Black Lands.

gateway: portal to the Netherworld.

Ghost Waste, the: desert in the Black Lands where the Spirits of the Wild are said to roam. Formerly known as the Dhural Uplands.

Glen Farquist: holy city in the Valley of the Gods.

Goddess of the Eternal Requiem: statue of an aspect of the Goddess of Death; her face of Righteous Vengeance.

Grand Master: any Master of the forth tier or higher.

Great Schism: separation between the Assemblies of mages and the ruling bodies of the temples.

Greystone Keep: legendary fortress in the Pass of Lor-Gamorth that fell during the Fifth Invasion.

Haleem: caravan master in the Black Lands.

Hall of the Watchers: Fallen stronghold of the mages of Aerysius, where existed Aerysius' Circle of Convergence.

Hannah, Arden: ancient Querer and former Servant of Xerys. *(deceased)*

Hellpower: *see* **Onslaught.**

High Priest: title of the religious leader of one of the ten Holy Temples.

Ironguard Pass: passage from the Black Lands into the Rhen created by Aiden Lauchlin.

Ibri: port village on the River Nym in the Black Lands.

Isap: Goddess of Death.

Ishara: border town in the Black Lands, in the region once known as Skara.

Jenn: nomadic people of the Cerulian Plains, remnants of an ancient Caladornian horse culture.

Kateem, Khoresh: infamous Emperor who united all of Caladorn under a singular rule before the Desecration.

Khazahar Desert: arid region in the Black Lands that was once an expansive grassland.

Krane, Cyrus: ancient Prime Warden of Aerysius, now a Servant of Xerys.

Lauchlin, Aidan: firstborn son of Gerald and Emelda Lauchlin who unsealed the Well of Tears. Brother of Darien Lauchlin. *(deceased)*

Lauchlin, Darien: former eighth-tier Sentinel and Prime Warden of Aerysius, now a Servant of Xerys.

Lauchlin, Emelda: former Prime Warden of Aerysius. *(deceased)*

Lauchlin, Gerald: father of Aidan and Darien Lauchlin, forth tier Grand Master of the Order of Sentinels. Executed by ritual immolation during the Battle of Meridan. *(deceased)*

lightfields: in the Black Lands, places where food is grown using light produced by mages called Lightweavers.

Lightweaver: in the Black Lands, mages who have the ability to produce a color of magelight that mimics the full spectrum of the sun.

Lyceum: ancient stronghold of the Masters of Bryn Calazar.

Mage's Oath: *see* Oath of Harmony.

magelight: magical illumination that can be summoned by a mage that takes on the signature color of the mage's magical legacy.

magic field: source of magical energy that runs in lines of power over the earth.

Maidenclaw: one of the two mountains that mark the entrance to the Black Lands.

Malikar: modern name of the nation that was once Caladorn.

Master: any mage; more specifically, a mage of the first through third tiers.

Meridan: *see* **Battle of Meridan**.

nach'tier: Venthic word for darkmage.

Natural Law: law that governs the workings of the universe that can be strained by the application of magic, but never broken.

necrator: demonic creature that renders a mage powerless in its presence.

Netherworld: realm of Xerys, God of Chaos.

node: place where the lines of the magic field come together in parallel direction but opposite in energy and cancel out.

Norengail, Romana: Queen of Emmery.

North, the: the Northern kingdoms of the Rhen, including Emmery, Chamsbrey and Lynnley.

Nym: ancient river in the Black Lands once considered sacred.

Oath of Harmony: oath taken by every Master of Aerysius to do no harm, symbolized by a chain-like marking on the right wrist.

Oblivion: outcome for a soul who is denied entry into both the Atrament and the Netherworld, which results in the complete destruction of that soul and the denial of eternity.

Om: God of Wisdom.

Onslaught: the corrupt power of the Netherworld, also known as the Hellfire.

orders: different schools of magic among the Masters of Aerysius and the Lyceum of Bryn Calazar.

Orguleth: one of the two mountains that mark the entrance to the Black Lands. Also called the Spire of Orguleth.

Orien Oathbreaker: infamous Grand Master who used the Circle of Convergence on Orien's Finger to turn back the Third Invasion almost single-handedly.

Orien's Finger: crag on the edge of the Cerulian Plains where Orien Oathbreaker made his stand and where Darien Lauchlin turned back the Fifth Invasion. Formerly known as Xerys' Pedestal.

Pass of Lor-Gamorth: pass through the Shadowspear Mountains that guards the border of the Black Lands.

Penthos, Luther: High Priest of the Temple of Death.

potential: the ability in a person to sense the magic field.

Prime Warden: leaders of the Assembly of the Hall of either Aerysius or the Lyceum.

Proctor, Garret: legendary Force Commander of Greystone Keep *(deceased)*

Qadir, Sareen: ancient Querer and one the Eight Servants of Xerys.

Qul: village in the Khazahar Desert in the Black Lands, home of Azár.

Raising: Rite of Transference, during which an acolyte inherits the legacy of power from another mage.

Reis, Braden: ancient Caladornian Battlemage who was executed for treason against the Assembly of the Lyceum. Founder of the Oath of Harmony and the Order of Sentinels. *(deceased)*

Reis, Quinlan: ancient Arcanist and brother of Braden Reis. One of the Eight Servants of Xerys.

Renquist, Zavier: ancient Prime Warden of the Lyceum, now a Servant of Xerys.

Rhen: name of the collective kingdoms south of the Black Lands.

Rhenic: common language spoken throughout the kingdoms of the Rhen.

Rothscard: capital city of Emmery.

sakeem: lethal sandstorms that spawn in the deserts of the Black

Lands, fomented by the Curse.

School of Arms: *see* **Arms Guild**.

Safiye, Katarya: apprentice of Nashir Arman.

Sarik: grand vizier of Bryn Calazar.

Sayeed son of Alborz: Zakai of the Tanisar corps at Tokashi Palace, Chamberlain of Armorers.

Seleni, Naia: former priestess of Death, now a third-tier Master of the Order of Querers.

sensitive: ability in some people to detect the emotions of others. Not dependent on the magic field, and not limited to mages.

Sentinels: order of mages chartered with the defense of the Rhen.

Shadowspears: mountains that separate the Black Lands from the Rhen.

saturation: Battlemage tactic of overloading with magical power in anticipation of creating an enormous discharge of force.

sharaq: ancient system of honor code of the Black Lands.

Silver Star: symbol of the Masters of Aerysius and the Lyceum, indicative of the focus lines of the Circles of Convergence.

Soulstone: ancient artifact created by Quinlan Reis as a storage receptacle for a dying mage's legacy.

South, the: Southern kingdoms of the Rhen, including Creston, Gandrish, and Farley.

Strictures of Death: laws of Death.

sufan: a type of small satchel or bag common among the clans of Malikar.

Swain, Nigel: prince consort of Emmery, husband of Queen Romana and Guild blademaster.

Tanisar corps: legions of highly disciplined elite infantry units of the Khazahar.

temples: various sects of worship. Each temple is devoted to a particular deity of the pantheon.

thanacryst: demonic creature that feeds off a mage's legacy.

Thar'gon: magical talisman carried by Byron Connel that is the symbol of the Warden of Battlemages of the Lyceum.

thar'tier: word for Battlemage in Venthic, the language of the Enemy.

tier: additive progression of levels of power among Masters. The higher a Master's tier, the greater that person's ability to strain the limits of Natural Law.

Tokashi Palace: fortress in the north of the Black Lands.

transfer portal: ancient system of artifacts capable of transferring a person to various locations.

Transference: process by which an acolyte inherits the legacy of power from another mage, resulting in the death of the Master who gives up his or her ability.

Unbinding: the act of forswearing the Oath of Harmony.

Vale of Amberlie: long, narrow valley in the North of the Rhen.

Valley of the Gods: valley where exists the holy city of Glen Farquist.

Venthic: the language of the Enemy.

Vintgar: ancient ice fortress and source of the River Nym.

vortex: cyclone of power where the lines of the magic field superimpose and become vastly intense.

Well of Tears: well that unlocks the gateway to the Netherworld.

Withersby, Meiran: Prime Warden of Aerysius.

Wolden: town in the Kingdom of Emmery.

Xerys: God of Chaos and Lord of the Netherworld.

Zamir: Lightweaver of the Asyaadi.

Zakai: officers of the Tanisar corps that formed their own distinctive social class.

Zanikar: magical sword and artifact created by Quinlan Reis.

Zephia: Goddess of the Winds.

The Eight Orders of Mages

Order of Arcanists: order of mages chartered with the study and creation of artifacts and heirlooms of power.

Order of Architects: order of mages chartered with the construction of magical infrastructure.

Order of Chancellors: order of mages chartered with the governance of the Assembly.

Order of Empiricists: order of mages chartered with the theoretical study of the magic field, its laws and principles.

Order of Harbingers: order of mages chartered with maintaining watch over Athera's Crescent.

Order of Naturalists: order of mages chartered with the study of Natural Law.

Order of Querers: order of mages chartered with practical applications of the magic field.

Order of Sentinels: order of mages chartered with watching over and protecting the Rhen in a manner consistent with the Oath of Harmony.

Acknowledgements

I would like to thank Kyra Halland, Andrew McVittie, and Daniel Crabbe for being terrific beta readers. I would also like to thank Morgan Smith for her excellent editorial advice. And special thanks to my family for putting up with me.

Connect
MLSpencerFiction.com
Facebook.com/MLSpencerAuthor
Twitter.com/MLSpencer1

Made in the USA
Middletown, DE
19 July 2022

69720748R00198